Aetna Adrift

Erik Wecks

Other Works by Erik Wecks

Fiction:

Brody
A Kindle Pax Imperium novella

The Device
A Kindle short story

Non Fiction:

How to Manage Your Money
When You Don't Have Any

Getting Beyond Paint Chips:
A guide to managing your HOA or condo in a
professional manner
(Coming 2013)

1
Pulling Strings

"Jack, what am I going to do with you?"

The rotund man with a pencil mustache led Jack from the small foyer into his well-apportioned offices on the 20th floor penthouse of the tallest building on Aetna.

"Well, Lewis, you could demote me." Lanky and tall with a slightly receding hairline, time had been kind to the forty-three year old Jack Halloway. He retained his strong frame and his alert brown eyes. If his eyelids had recently begun to droop like those of a hound, then all it added to Jack was a tinge of mystery, making him all the more intriguing to those around him. Jack showed every sign of entering late youth, as the 40s were called, as that rare specimen whose physical appeal got better with age. He sat down in a chair in Lewis' office as straight as always, attentive to the details of his environment, his face passive, inscrutable.

"You'd like that, wouldn't you, Jack?"

Jack shivered slightly from the residual cold as he took off his thick company issued parka.

Lewis noticed. "There's a blanket in the warmer if you need one."

"Thanks," Jack said. He gratefully went to the warmer, grabbed a synthetic wool blanket, and wrapped it around his shoulders. It had been cold on Aetna when Jack had arrived from the orbital which was his home, -40 C at least.

By rights, Aetna, a mid-sized moon in the Sicily system, should have been a modest rock with a deep solidified methane crust and little to no atmosphere.

However, fate, chance, or whatever it was that controlled these things put what would have been a frozen world in just the right orbit around Catania, its gas giant parent, to create salty water and with it an unlikely diversity of life, which teemed in the warm waters far below its thin icy crust.

Jack always thought of Aetna as a bit of a Mama's boy. It orbited very close to its mother, Catania. Moving fast, Aetna completed an orbit around Catania once every 72.36 hours. Living that close to a planet 1000 times larger than old Earth had consequences for even a large moon like Aetna. Catania exerted a huge gravitational pull on its nearest offspring. As the inside moon closest to Catania, Aetna often got caught between the gravitational pull of its mother and the 14 other moons which also orbited Catania.

The tug and pull of all these busy bodies trying to have a say in Aetna's orbit stretched and pulled on Aetna's rocky core until it warmed and melted, much like pulling on taffy makes it soft and pliable. Aetna was home to the largest number of active volcanoes in the Sicily system.

In a galaxy with planetoid bodies of every shape, size, and ranking on the Zhào habitability index, what made Aetna much more unusual was the composition of its atmosphere. Eons before, its volcanism melted the frozen methane and other ices which covered Aetna's surface, creating salt-water oceans buried beneath a relatively thin icy surface. These oceans became progressively warmer the closer you got to the writhing surface of the core. The volcanism combined with the water and melted methane eventually gave Aetna a reasonably thick atmosphere of oxygen, nitrogen, and carbon-dioxide.

The surface temperature on Aetna was one hundred and fifty odd degrees Celsius warmer than it should have been for a mid-sized planetoid placed well outside Sicily's Goldilocks zone. On a good day, citizens of Aetna might even notice a bead or two of water running on their windows. All of these favorable moments of chance made life on Aetna possible.

These grand and fortuitous happenstances were far from the provincial concerns which occupied Lewis Lutnear as he sat in his office. The mind wrapped inside his pink head with its whisps of blondish hair and occasional moles was too focused on the mundane activities of daily living to think about such things.

Lewis interrupted Jack's thoughts. "But where would you go? There isn't anywhere else in the Unity which would put up with the likes of you. But why are you here? That is the real question." Lewis squinted at Jack as he sat down in the high-backed executive chair at his desk. The chair squatted slightly under his weight. "A man of your considerable skills could go anywhere he wished."

Jack answered quickly with detached irony. "Well, Lewis, I guess I'm just too lazy to apply my talents like you."

Lewis sighed ostentatiously, "Yes. I guess that's it. You just don't have the work ethic for climbing the ladder, do you? Now take today for instance, what will you be doing this evening?"

"I was planning on buying drinks for my staff if we get done fast enough for me to get back on the 1 PM shuttle." Jack needled his boss by making a show of looking at the time on the wallet strapped to his wrist.

Lewis either chose not to respond or didn't notice. "Yes, that's just it," he said with sudden animation. "That's exactly what I'm talking about. Tonight I will spend my evening supervising a move of this whole city far to the north, while you are having drinks with your staff. If you would just apply yourself more I am sure you could get appointed to a post like mine."

Jack smirked. He had no desire to have a post like Lewis' but it was more amusing to him to recognize that the volcanism which allowed Lewis to breath oxygen while he pontificated also forced him to work late on many an evening. On an all too frequent basis geysers of boiling water sent tsunamis racing across the landscape. Eventually they froze into tall mountain ranges of pack ice. The volatile waters caused Aetna to regenerate an area the size of its whole icy surface close to once every six years. In other places, consistent weaknesses in Aetna's crust warmed the waters above to such a level that open oceans appeared on its surface.

For the 120,000 or so people who made the surface of Aetna their permanent residence, life was a nomadic quest for stable ice. Half of those people lived in Utopia, the little burg which Lewis supervised directly and which held the rather modest building in which Jack sat.

The need for stable ice made tall construction on the surface of Aetna impossible. Twenty stories of building set on treads, using positioning satellites and gravitational stabilizers, was about all the feat of engineering this backwater little moon could muster. All buildings on Aetna used positioning satellites and treads to keep themselves on solid ice if possible, although they could float if push came to shove.

For the last week, the city of Utopia had been preparing to move. That had meant late nights for Lewis. Jack knew he was the last little piece of business on Lewis' agenda before he gave his full attention to the final preparations. He had hoped it would keep their meeting brief. Apparently, he'd been wrong.

Lewis shook his head with a kind of pretentious disgust. "What am I going to do with you?" he repeated mostly to himself as he reached for the last three black jelly beans in the cheap crystal dish on the corner of his desk. "Well, I guess there's nothing for it," said Lewis.

Not being one to miss out on a moment of pageantry, Lewis stood up and tugged the corners of his casual uniform straight. Executive level citizens all wore standard uniforms to work. As the orbital station manager, Jack remained several levels below executive level and as such blissfully free of the starched shirts and synthetic fibers his superiors wore.

Lewis began to pace. Jack didn't move, attentive as ever, his face deadpan. Lewis spoke in a formal voice. "Jack Halloway, on behalf of the Unity Corporation and the government of Unity-owned space, I am privileged today to offer you the post of Deputy Executive Director of Aetna."

Jack opened his mouth and started to answer, but Lewis held up his index finger and waved it at him as he continued speaking.

"Promotion to Deputy Executive Director in the Unity is a privilege offered to few. There are only 14 higher ranks available to citizens of the Unity. This offer comes with a considerable increase in your monthly stipend, a larger housing allowance, and all the privileges accorded to its rank. What say you?"

Ignoring the question, Jack looked at the ceiling and asked no one in particular, "Why do they insist on saying the Unity and the government? The Unity Corporation is the government."

Flustered at being put off his game, Lewis answered as a parent instructing a wayward child, while dismissing the question with a wave of his hand. "It's just simply a leftover from when the legislature was dissolved 200 years ago. It is the same as saying 'under God' when we pledge our allegiance to the Corporation."

Still pondering and apparently not paying attention to Lewis, Jack said aloud to the ceiling, "Well, I wonder if we ought to change that."

Lewis blushed. "Jack, I can't have you saying that in this office. That is dissention. It is a crime."

Appearing to suddenly return to the present, Jack said with the barest hint of irony, "No, Lewis. I was wondering if they should change the proposal for promotion to reflect the reality that the legislature was dissolved 200 years ago. What did you think I meant?"

Lewis sighed irritably. "Never mind." Then he repeated his question with more firmness. "Jack, what is your answer?"

"No."

Not wanting to let Jack derail him again, Lewis plunged forward. "While turning down such an offer will in no way hinder your career in the Unity, this is the eighth time you have turned down promotion to Deputy Executive Director, and as such, I must punish you by docking your pay."

"Lewis, I'm already on minimum stipend. You can't dock my pay."

Lewis began to lose his temper. "Jack, I know that, but it's what I am supposed to say. Now just let me finish so we can get on with this. As I was saying, I must punish you by docking your pay." Without saying another word, Lewis pulled out a piece of electronic paper from his desk which had already been filled out. "Now, if you will sign here, Jack. I will sign there."

Jack reached over and pressed his thumb to the paper. The paper registered his thumb print and matched it to the DNA it sampled from Jack. Lewis did the same and dropped his formal tone, walked around the front of his desk and leaned on it. Jack could smell some kind of sweet cologne.

"Jack, Julia and the kids were wondering when you were coming for dinner. Jo has been asking to see Uncle Jack."

Jack allowed a small smile to creep onto his face. "Tell Julia to get with Molly and put it on my calendar. I'll come."

Lewis smiled broadly. "Excellent. Now, I must be off to dedicate a new ice driller. If the volcanologists are right, we will need it soon enough. It's a busy day in Utopia."

As he talked, Lewis moved away from his desk and Jack stood up, gathering his parka and his not-so-regulation fur cap. Lewis kept up a stream of conversation all the way until they parted in the lobby of his building. He headed to the parking garage, where his driver and personal hover car lay hidden. Jack headed out the public entrance of the warm lobby into the much colder public vestibule. He shivered and buttoned his fur hat over his ears.

The Unity administration building on Aetna, like all buildings, had a heated lobby on its ground floor with entrances scattered on all sides. Beyond this warm interior was an attached transition zone between the building and the harsh conditions outside. These public vestibules ran around the perimeter of almost all buildings on Aetna, including private residences. They had several entrances which could be connected to other buildings when the city was stable and staying in one place. This allowed pedestrians to walk from one building to another without having to face the bitter winds and occasional snow.

Shapeless, metallic, and painted a standard gray, these vestibules always reminded Jack of the inside of shipping containers. Although attached to their buildings, they were considered public spaces, similar to the pedestrian malls under the flying traffic in larger cities.

On Aetna, where corporate discipline was relaxed, to say the least, these vestibules also acted as a kind of unregistered flea market. The local gendarmes did a good job keeping the most unsavory items in check, but a payment here and a freebie there allowed the legitimate business people to stay out of harm's way. Jack walked past the various stalls hawking everything from electronic components to hats almost identical to his own.

Jack took a particular pride in the flea market. Indirectly or directly, he had provided almost all the goods sold on Aetna. In one sense, this was his baby. These people depended upon him for the extra cash above their minimum salary from the company. Through selling illegally on the black market, they gained a better lifestyle and a chance to express their individuality in ways which the corporation did not provide. Jack didn't quite become wealthy from the smuggling he did here on Aetna, but he sure came close.

He stopped near one of the cold entrances to the wan brownish light outside and put a gloved hand on a screen with a large sign over it stating "Automated Taxi Stand." The screen lit and in green lettering announced: Thank you, Mr. Halloway. Your Taxi will be available in 4 minutes, 30 seconds. The numbers began to count down.

Jack kept an eye on the countdown and stepped up to the coffee stand nest to the queue. Jack ordered a coffee and a sandwich, and chatted genially. Just as he was finishing, he heard the electronic whine of the approaching taxi. He held up the wrist wallet he had used to call the taxi, transferred the necessary dollars and a tip to the man behind the counter, and then picked up his coffee and sandwich, both in containers insulated against the cold. He was about to walk away when Hank reached out and shook his hand, surreptitiously passing Jack a small slip of paper. Jack smiled and stepped out into the piercing cold of Aetna at dusk.

Recognizing its ride, the taxi aimed a warm jet of hot air in his direction. Jack took the few steps necessary in the 40 below temperatures and then hopped in the open door of the taxi. The door closed behind him, the car rose into the air, and an automated voice asked, "Destination?"

"Fishing dock B, entrance 8," Jack said as he undid his jacket and slipped Hank's note unread into an inside pocket.

"Thank you," came the reply. The pilotless car banked gently left and arced around the administration building as it made its way to the outskirts of town.

Jack zipped up his jacket against the cold and worked on his coffee and sandwich during his short flight. He glanced at the clock on the dash of the AI taxi. He had about two hours before he needed to be on the shuttle back topside. He had plenty of time. Jack relaxed for a minute, enjoying the salt and vinegar flavor of his cold fish sandwich. Oily fish of all sorts were a staple on Aetna.

Even as he flew, Jack could see the huge warehouses on the outskirts of the city which were his destination. His taxi landed eight minutes later. Jack took another bite of his fish and vinegar sandwich, threw the rest in the garbage, and stepped out from the vehicle, coffee in hand. Despite the warm jets of air from both the taxi and the vestibule entrance ahead of him, drips of Jack's coffee still froze before he made his way inside.

As he entered the door, Jack held his coffee up to the heater to make sure he didn't freeze his lip to the cup while trying to get at the warm liquid. This vestibule was very different from the one outside of the administration building. This one was an extension of the warehouse it surrounded. It smelled of salt, ocean life, and fish in all stages of freshness. Crates of fishing nets, lines, and other gear lay in heaps here and there. Giant traps for catching bottom dwellers stood in neat stacks, all painted with the name of the submersible that owned them.

Fishing the rich seas on top of which Jack presently stood was one of two major industries which propelled the economy of Aetna. From the point of view of Unity Corporation, it was by far the least important. But to the men and women who made Aetna their home, fishing by submarine was a way of life. Like all fisherman, they were fiercely proud of their work.

Jack stepped through a door to the main warehouse. Inside, the warehouse boomed with noise and activity. It was a moving day, Jack noted. There were at least 60 people on the docks trying to get ready. Even as he walked in, a 30 meter long submarine rose slowly out from the hole in the ice at the center of the warehouse. Jack stood and watched as the cylinder lifted itself out of the water below. The noise of its anti-grav units became deafening. Jack set down his coffee on a low metal walkway next to him and plugged his ears. He stood that way for about ten seconds before he noticed a pair of boots standing on the walkway. Looking up he saw his business contact Rick Carter above him.

Rick was a thick man with a wooly brown beard and arms that could have substituted for one of Jack's legs. He nodded in greeting and threw Jack a pair of bright yellow ear covers with a small heads-up display that fell down over one eye. Jack put them on and instantly the noise subsided. Rick didn't say anything. He and Jack stood and watched as the sub raised itself out of the ice and piloted itself into its cradle high up on the walls of the broad warehouse.

The heads-up display showed basic details of the ship, its name, the captain's name, and its speed and direction. Jack idly wondered what kind of fish they had caught. The built in intra-mind scanner on the ear protectors read Jack's brain activity, took it as a command, and placed the catch information from *The Behemoth* on his heads-up display. By the time the city began to move, this warehouse would be filled with 23 other vessels all in their cradles.

When *The Behemoth* finished docking, Rick nodded for Jack to follow him into his office. Once inside the sound proofed office, Rick took off his ear protection and sat in the chair behind his desk. Jack followed his lead.

"How's the fishing, Rick?"

Rick just rolled his eyes and pointed with his bucket sized arms to the chair across from him. "Shit, Jack, do you know how much a fisherman hates being asked that question?"

Jack's face broke into a grin, which deepened the perfectly placed crow's-feet now taking up residence at the corner of his eyes. "Yes, I do."

Rick let out a huge guffaw. "Of course, you do. That's why you ask me every time I see you. How the hell are you, Jack?"

"Good, Rick! I'm good, all things considered."

"Glad to hear it." Rick pulled the coaster out from under the cup of coffee on his desk, held it a few inches above the desk and let go. Instead of falling back, the device flew up into the air, hovering over both him and Jack.

Jack smirked and said with a hint of sarcasm, "You aren't afraid of Lewis listening in, are you? He wouldn't touch me. Who else would supply him with licorice jelly beans?"

Rick looked seriously at Jack for a moment. "Jack, you can't be too careful. Human Resources is no joke and a man in your position ought to know that."

Jack snorted with laughter and absent-mindedly picked at a loose thread on the fur cap he had taken off his head. "What do you think is going to happen, Rick? The Corporation doesn't even remember that Aetna exists. When was the last time you saw an actual human resource officer come through here? If they do think about us, then we're nothing more than a seedy fuel depot on the way to the gate out of Sicily. And I do believe that is the way most of us like it."

Rick just shrugged. "Yes, that is the way we like it, and I don't think we can be too careful in keeping it that way."

Jack decided to change the topic. "I turned down the Deputy Executive Director position for the eighth time today."

Rick laughed again. Jack always enjoyed hearing Rick laugh, something he did quite often. "Why does he do that? Lewis has to know what you'll say."

Jack grinned, "You know Lewis never misses a chance to look officious. He enjoys tweaking my nose once a year to remind me who pulls the strings around here."

"Uh huh, right."

"You sound skeptical. You think he has some dark hidden motive hiding behind that balding pate?"

"No, I just think the idea of Lewis pulling strings is a little bit ridiculous. We all know why this place keeps running."

Holding the hat in both hands, Jack looked at the floor and said with an "aw-shucks" tone, "Well, one does try." He then added with a grin, "If it pays."

After letting his words sit for just a beat, he looked at Rick. "So, what can I do for you today?"

"Just the usual list: gear, bait, rations for the crew." Rick took out an actual file folder from his desk and opened it. Inside there was an antique—a pen—and a sheaf of papers. He took out a hand pressed piece of low quality paper and slid it across the desk to Jack.

Jack figured that human beings in the Unity would have forgotten how to write long ago if it weren't for the black market. Electronic communication could be traced. Old fashioned written communication demanded that the spy had to be on site to see it, and you had to understand what you were looking at. The black market tended to develop a kind of short hand that only specific buyers and sellers could read.

Jack folded the piece of paper and put it in an inside pocket of his parka. "I'll get this to Molly when I get back topside, and we'll get the bids out. Should have something to you by the end of next week."

Rick smiled, "Thanks. Payment will be in the usual fashion. So, when are you going to go fishing with us? You keep saying you're going to come on a trip, but then you never do."

"Well, you know. Someone has to keep running the world."

Rick laughed.

2
Topside

Jack was the lone passenger on the afternoon shuttle back to Unity Standard Orbital 1358. Ernie, the pilot, was trustworthy, so Jack took a deep breath and removed from his pocket the eight scraps of paper he had been handed on his visit to Utopia.

The trick with running a successful black market was deciding what could and couldn't be done. Rule number one: keep a low profile. If you couldn't get it quietly and for a profit, you didn't do it. Most of his customers understood that. He had turned Rick down many times and he had never been upset by it. Rick always just shrugged his shoulders, said "you do what you can," and went on about his business. Jack knew that sometimes he had desperately needed the spare parts Jack couldn't provide. Rick got it.

Then there were the desperate ones, the business owners losing everything they had, the childless couples looking for exit visas to someplace which didn't mercilessly persecute partners without children. They didn't get it. Desperation bred stupidity and inflexibility.

Eight pieces of paper, six of which he knew he could fulfill without even thinking about it. Jack checked the list. Fishing gear for Rick wouldn't be any problem at all. There was a milk run between Sicily and Oceanus. He knew the captain on that run. He had a whole slew of contacts that would gladly transport a new coffee grinder for Hank.

He skipped through the list to the last two pieces of paper. Jack wasn't sure what to make of the first one. A desperate looking woman had stepped up to him just as he entered the vestibule of the shuttle port. She had a huge bruise on her cheek. He hadn't recognized her at the time, but without a word she had handed him a note. She wanted a gun. Jack hadn't run many guns into Aetna. Most residents couldn't pay the price it took to make it worth his while to stick his neck out that far. Besides, Jack always worried that someone somewhere might get hold of one and use it on him. One of the perks of the black market was a healthy list of unsatisfied customers. Jack didn't figure he would appreciate the irony of being capped by one of his own guns.

He read the note again. Well, this woman probably had the money. She wanted to meet the courier at the Red Carpet Club. That club was haunted by the wives of the élite, such as they were, on Aetna. No doubt, she was attached to somebody important.

This realization put the pieces together for Jack. The woman he had seen was Cora Hanson, the wife of the police commissioner on Aetna. Jack had seen her a few times at various functions. He didn't recognize her at first because she had been beaten so badly.

This was a problem. Jack had no doubt now how Cora had received her bruises. Her husband was in charge of security on Aetna and the station which Jack administered. If anyone but her husband Frank, or someone he assigned, had beaten Cora, then they would have already been detained, if not found dead from exposure or some other accident.

As a police commissioner, Frank Hanson was all right in Jack's book. He stayed out of the way of the black market, taking a "don't ask, don't tell approach." His officers let things slide as long as a bribe was paid and you didn't sell anything which damaged public safety.

But Frank was still HR. Technically, he still reported to Lewis, but HR had its ways of getting what it wanted. Before Lewis had come along, the previous Administrator on Aetna had tried to put his own woman in as commissioner. This was just before Jack had arrived, although he had heard the story from Lewis many times.

Apparently, HR felt like this little peon was getting uppity and decided to teach him a lesson. The compliance audits and random checks by HR officers were a nightmare. Within three months, HR had the central administration demote him for all his violations of company policy. Lewis was promoted to replace him and wisely changed course and picked whoever HR wanted for the office of commissioner. HR, which had demanded the highest of standards for Aetna, melted away as quickly as they had appeared. Since then, they had seen a compliance officer once every couple of years, and that was over fifteen years ago.

Jack never seriously considered Cora's request. There was no choice when it came to getting her a gun. The shooting of a police commissioner was bound to get someone's attention. The bureaucrats at HR would be smart enough to wonder how Cora had come by a gun and that would be a problem for Jack and all the people who depended on him. Jack calmly took out a small stub of pencil he kept deep in a pocket and wrote in his distinct hand "For Frank" at the bottom of the note. He re-folded it, and put it back in his pocket

The final note was from Dr. Tony Musgrave at the hospital. Jack appreciated Musgrave. Musgrave didn't fit within the existing order as Jack perceived it. That made him interesting in Jack's book.

When he had first arrived to take over the hospital, Jack hadn't given him much thought. Most doctors believed pretty strongly in the "stability" created by the Unity. They may not have believed in the system when they set out to become doctors, but by the time they were done with their ten years of schooling, most of them had succumbed to the indoctrination.

Somehow Musgrave survived with his sense of reality intact. A short six weeks after he arrived, he made a visit to Jack's office on the orbital. Since then, Musgrave had become a regular customer of Jack's. At first, his requests had made no sense to Jack, all of them related to cosmetic treatments and enhancements. The stuff he wanted Jack to get was pretty risky, so Jack always charged a premium. But he had yet to flinch when Jack got him a price.

It wasn't until Jack saw the first cynthy from Sicily 4 walk by his office and head for the shuttle to the surface that he began to understand Musgrave. Wealthy women in the Unity needed their beauty treatments, and they had the money to pay for them, rules be damned. Most of them were almost half lab grown by the time they hit 35. Regular people called them cynthys—a mutation of the word "synthetics."

Now, if you ran in the right circles in six different systems, the public hospital on Aetna was your destination for high quality, off-list synthetic treatments. If Dr. Musgrave used the profits from his little endeavors to better the treatment for the rest of Aetna's residents that was his business. Getting paid was Jack's business, and Musgrave paid Jack well.

It was while watching the immaculate body of the first cynthy to walk by his office on the orbital that something clicked for Jack. *I'll be damned*, he had thought. *Entrepreneurs are everywhere.*

The Unity didn't appreciate competition. In fact, owning your own business in the Unity without a permit was a crime. Last time he had checked, Unity had given out about 100 business licenses each year for the last three decades. The vast majority of these went to the sons of board members and other well connected politicos. For everyone else, the good of the Unity was to be the sole business of every citizen.

Until Musgrave had come along, Jack had seen people similar to himself as misfits who existed on the margins of society. Musgrave showed him that invention, creativity, and a business mind existed everywhere. It just needed a spark to light it.

Watching the bulbous, enlarged ass of the cynthy walk away from him, Jack suddenly understood why people like him were considered pariahs, why the Unity feared them. Independent thinking and competition threatened to undermine Unity control. Yet no matter how hard the Unity tried to stomp out human ingenuity, it remained.

Throughout the Unity, black market entrepreneurs tended to gather in out of the way places like Aetna. Asteroids and orbitals were full of them, and the Unity merchant marine wouldn't exist without the money the sailors made on the side.

Today, Musgrave wanted three tissue growing tanks. Jack wasn't sure how he would get them, but he had no doubt he would try. Creative entrepreneurs, like Musgrave, had a way of getting Jack to stick his neck out a little farther than he would for just about anyone else.

Jack arrived back in his office late in the orbital work day. Molly was still at her desk, Joe was in his office typing up end-of-the-day reports, and Robert was sitting in a chair in Jack's office waiting for him, thumbing through manifests on his tablet.

"What cha got, Robert?"

Robert Logan was Jack's senior cargo inspector. He was in his late 70s, with a rounded belly that made his inspector's coveralls pooch and a white beard trimmed long. He had one calloused hand in the strap of his company issued inspector's overalls as he sat in the chair in Jack's office.

Robert smirked. "Oh, nothing important, I just caught *The Leroy* trying to unload a container full of engineered salmonoids. They looked to me as if they were pretty well tailored for Aetna."

"No shit? Charlie?"

"Yep, I was surprised myself. He says that he recently hired a new cargo master. Some kid straight outta school looking to make extra on his first time out. Anyway, I had to turn it over to Frank's boys. Charlie should be OK as long as he didn't know anything about it."

Jack appeared puzzled for a moment. "Don't think we could have fenced them, do you? You know threatened them with the Gendarmes but then offered to make it all go away for a price?"

Robert was already shaking his head. "I looked. Nothing available to carry them to any place that would take 'em. That was one of the reasons I knew they had to be for here."

Jack nodded in agreement. "OK. You do realize they're going to give that ship a shakedown. There wasn't anything that could have been traced back here?"

Robert smiled. "Nothing that wasn't walked off the dock before I reported in to Frank. They had a good half an hour or more to clean things up before the Commissioner's agents arrived. We're fine."

Jack returned Robert's smile. "You're a real pro. You know that?"

"Damn straight, young pup! And don't you forget who taught you everything you know." Robert had been in the Administration and Inspection office of the Audit Division on the Aetna orbital for 45 years, three years longer than Jack had been alive. "I sat in your chair for 25 years."

Jack's office served both as the administrative department head for Aetna's only orbital and as an Audit Division inspection point for company vessels coming through the Aetna system. As the head of the office, Jack was both the administrator in charge of the orbital and the person who was supposed to make all ships entering the system adhere to Unity corporation regulations. "So why did you give it up?"

Robert folded his hands on his belly, "After a while it got a little boring. I had stashed away what I needed, and I was tired of taking the risk. When you came along as an eager beaver cargo man, it seemed like a good opportunity to pass the job along to someone else." It was Robert who first showed Jack that the office was the perfect place to organize the black market on Aetna.

Jack grinned, "You ever think about how weird it is that we are both cop and criminal on this station?"

Robert chuckled, "Once in a while. We're just corrupt bureaucrats like everyone else in The Unity."

Jack thought for a moment. Speaking mostly to himself he said, "I'm not sure anything would get done without corruption in this swamp." Turning to the matter at hand he continued, "Any idea on the buyer for those fish?"

"Not sure, I left that to Frank's people. Not that I'd want to be them. Mother Unity takes a bit of a dim view on unauthorized genetically-modified species."

Jack shook his head. "Isn't that the truth. What was it they did to that iceboxer over near Dignity who tried to sneak in the Manila clams?"

"Six months of re-education and then execution."

"Not a very forgiving mother, is she?"

"Cold and hard as the vacuum she came from."

Molly interrupted from the door. "Well, isn't this a cheerful conversation," she said crisply.

Jack smiled, which for Jack amounted to lifting the left corner of his closed lips ever so slightly. Molly Vargas' title was Assistant to the Administrator. However, neither Jack nor Robert had any illusions about who kept all of them out of re-education.

Molly was the real brains behind the black market. Her job was to provide legitimate destinations and electronic documentation for all the cargo headed out from Aetna. A separate set of paper books was kept on the actual goods which came and went through their office. In 8 years, Molly had only been spotted three times, and each time she had had a plausible back up story on why the manifest was wrong.

Molly wore a tight red knee-length dress, modest on the top, which complemented her curly auburn hair. Bright red lips and freckles went along with the outfit. Molly was about five years younger than Jack. He thought she was nice looking but nothing to write home about—kind of plain with no chest.

That didn't mean she didn't have her more soft spoken husband Todd eating out of her hand. He thought she was stunning. Molly was easy to get along with, humorous at times, with a ruthless mind when she needed it. She was interesting.

But, with no desire or need for a life partner, Jack was not the type to think about members of the feminine sex as anything more than a fine bottle of wine. When the bottle was empty, it was time to pull the cork on the next one and see what was in the new bottle.

It was for the same reasons which Todd appreciated having Molly as a partner that Jack enjoyed having her around the office. She was damned good at her job, and Jack respected talent wherever he found it. Jack figured Molly appreciated him because he treated her like a human being. From Jack's perspective, associating with talent got you places. If talent came with a vagina, that was fine by him.

Molly walked over to his desk and put down three pieces of electronic paper and one badly pressed piece of real paper. Jack thumbed his electronic signature onto all three pieces of official business and then read over the unofficial business. As he read, he enjoyed the hand crafted antique feel of the actual paper. He nodded to Molly. Once again, her work was efficient and clean. Jack pulled the eight slips of paper out of his pocket. He handed Molly six of them.

"I think we could get Michael on *The Titan* to help us with Musgrave's stuff. I know that one is going to be a pain in the ass, but I think we should try," he said, while holding out the seventh slip of paper.

Molly pursed her lips. "What does he want now?"

"Skin tanks."

"Seriously? We're going to try and smuggle skin tanks in here? What happened to not sticking your neck out?" She rolled her eyes.

Jack smiled wryly. "It's just business."

"Yeah, well, your business is going to get all of us strapped to a chair while we watch holis on the glory of the Unity. You do know that skin tanks are class 5 goods; genetically modified animals like those Manila clams are only class 4."

Jack looked at Molly. "Just do what you can. If we can't, we can't."

Molly still scowled but took the paper. "All right, but you understand we don't want to get caught with this."

"I understand."

"You're becoming a softie, you know that?"

Jack let the matter drop, and, without looking at it again, drew the eighth piece of paper out of his pocket and handed it to Molly. "Lewis is out of jelly beans, and would you see he gets this personally? I don't want Cathie to see it, and you don't want to read it. It would be a liability." Molly took the piece of paper by the corner, touching it as little as possible, as if it were toxic. Robert's eyes narrowed as they locked on the piece of paper.

Molly said, "I have a package of licorice beans ready to head down with our papers in the morning." Jack gave Molly a wide smile. It would have appeared very natural on anyone else. Few people in the world besides Molly and Robert would recognize that the eighth slip of paper made him nervous.

He decided to lighten the mood. "Good," he said. "Let's all get out of here. It's a Friday night, and I need a beer. First round is the boss' treat. We're celebrating."

Robert piped up from his chair, "What's the occasion?"

"My reprimand from Lewis for refusing promotion."

Robert smiled. "Eighth time's the charm. Maybe he'll quit asking."

Molly shook her head as she turned to go back to her desk. Over her shoulder, she said, "No, you watch, Robert. Lewis won't stop asking until he reaches ten. At eight, he has two fingers left."

That got everyone laughing.

Jack stood, grabbed his parka and hat, and followed. From the lobby, he yelled across the room to Joe, still busily typing in his office. "Come on, Joe. Quit trying to write a perfect report, and let's go get a beer. I'm buying."

"Right with you boss, almost done," came the reply.

"Forget about it. She'll still find something wrong with it when you turn it in. It can wait 'til Monday. That's an order."

Joe looked up shaking his head, and Molly let out a little snort behind her desk. Joe and Molly had a running bet that any time he turned in a report in which Molly couldn't correct his grammar, she would buy him lunch. In the 15 months since Joe had joined the team, it hadn't happened yet.

Jack headed out the door as Robert walked to his office to find his things. With the door open, Jack turned back to Molly. "Tell Todd to join us. His dinner is on me tonight. I think I still owe him one for our bet on the last ice runner races." With that, the glass door closed behind Jack, and he was out in the corridor of the station.

Jack enjoyed reading a bit of history in his spare time. As far as he could find, in every system in which one party controls economic production, the rights of citizens quickly become undervalued. This held true both for socialist forms of government, in which the government came to control production, and corporate monopolies, like the Unity. Jack found the truth that both corporatism and socialism led to tyranny comforting in some odd way, as if all was as it should be in the cosmos, even if it added a tinge of bitterness to every smile, laugh, and gesture from the citizens of the Unity he passed as he walked the corridors of the station he managed.

Corporate governments tended to believe choice and individual expression represented a lack of efficiency. Producing too many types of space stations meant extra labor wasted on questions of design and an inefficient system of production which had to be customized to suit different products. Thus, the Unity restricted its production of orbitals to six standard models of Unity orbital, each with their own distinct purpose.

From the perspective of the Unity, Aetna represented one thing—fuel. Ever since human beings first left old Earth on the first fusion drives, water represented much more than something necessary to maintain life in the void. It represented easily separated hydrogen—hydrogen which could be compressed until forced against its will to become helium. This fusion of hydrogen atoms into helium was the most energetic process in the known universe and the basis of all space-based transport within every civilization in the Empire.

Starships used fusion within solar systems. Transit between stars was a different matter. Unless governments and fleets wanted to deal with all the impossibilities of time dilation and relativity, travel between the stars required bending time and space in such a way that two points touched. That required giant gates which ships could pass through and messing with gravity in a way which just wasn't very safe inside the boundaries of a star system. Warping gravity over and over again tended to alter orbits and attract asteroids and comets to the gate. For this reason, gates were kept well outside the ort cloud in a stable position relative to the star they served. Most systems had two gates located on opposite sides of the system, one serving outgoing traffic and one serving incoming ships. Gates tended to alter their roles based on where sources of fuel were located.

Moons or planets with water far out in systems like Aetna were goldmines for the Unity. They allowed for much easier fuel calculations and acceleration curves when moving ships out to interstellar gates. For the Unity, snowballs like Aetna meant shorter transit times and profit.

To the minds that ran such things, Unity Orbital 1358 orbiting Aetna was nothing more than a greasy floating fuel depot, a place to top off on the way out of Sicily. To Jack and the 10,000 people who lived on the station, it was their home.

Jack walked the short distance around the station perimeter to one of two restaurants which served the station's inhabitants, Chuck's Place. There were very few ways in which individuals had a say in their lives in the Unity; running a government owned restaurant could be one of them. All profits still belonged to the corporation, but if a person could get a permit, they were free to serve whatever they wanted and decorate the restaurant however they could within their budget. This crack of freedom from scrutiny tended to make restaurant ownership a highly popular career choice.

Homes and restaurants were nearly the only places which didn't have prescribed decorative styles. This tended to make both of them quite garish. Chuck's was painted pink, with neon-orange booths around a polished steel bar that ran in a rectangle in the middle of the restaurant.

Jack walked in the door, waved at Chuck behind the bar, and began pulling bright yellow tables together. Leanne, one of Chuck's young bar maids, came to help. By the time they had the tables arranged, Robert and Molly walked in the door. Jack ordered a couple of pitchers of beer from Leanne. Joe followed, and Todd arrived shortly thereafter.

Jack spent a pleasant few hours drinking and eating with his staff, enjoying a Friday night ritual. The bar quickly filled with station personnel and crews from the various docked ships. Jack was happily buzzed by 11pm and just beginning to think about finding someone to go home with. He considered Leanne, but he would probably have to buy her a bunch of drinks. Besides, she didn't get off until late.

He put down his half empty glass, paid his tab, and was just standing from his chair when a little old man came wandering up to his table unsteadily. Earlier, Jack had noticed him at the bar taking in what now appeared to be liquid courage, a shot at a time. The old man came too close to Jack and put his hand on Jack's arm to steady himself.

Jack sat back down, guessing what was coming next, the alcohol not helping his mood.

"Somebody told me that you were the man to talk to about getting papers to Jersey Prime." Of course, he said it loudly enough that half the restaurant would have heard him. Jack didn't know where the man would have gotten the idea he could help. People smuggling was not on his resumé.

Jack's expression went cold. With a clear edge of irritation in his voice, he said with equal loudness, "You must be mistaken, old man." He turned around in his seat. All the expressions at the table matched his. Half the patrons in booths along the wall behind their table were now watching.

The old man bent down quietly and tried to whisper in Jack's ear. Again the effect was much louder than it should have been to be safe. "My wife is sick. They say she's unemployable. They're going to kill her."

Jack's answer equaled the old man's in volume as his anger rose to the surface. "What problem is that of mine, old man? I told you, I can't help you." He could already see Chuck coming out from behind the bar with another beefy barkeep.

This time the man tried pleading. His voice cracked with emotion. "Please. You have to help me. I can't be without my Emma. We have been married 80 years." Jack stayed facing away from him, his face unyielding. At this point, Chuck and the barkeep dragged the old man away, who broke down into sobs. "You have to help me."

As if nothing had happened, Jack prepared to leave again. "I'll see you all on Monday. I need a distraction." He was just about to leave the table when he saw someone come in the door who made him stop. Molly and Robert followed his gaze. "And unless I am mistaken, there comes my distraction now."

Molly just began shaking her head. "Jack, she is bad juju."

Jack picked up his half-empty glass of beer and finished it in one long drink.

"Seriously, Jack, go find yourself a nice wench down at the spacers club. Go anywhere. Go home alone. Hell, Leanne would go home with you if you ask nicely. Just don't go over there," Molly pleaded.

Without acknowledging Molly, Jack walked away from the table.

"Well, my week just went to hell."

Molly, your week would have gone to hell no matter what I did. Remember, we have to get skin tanks for Musgrave, Jack thought.

For the last three years, Anna Prindle had been a drug he couldn't put down. In Jack's world, in which sex was merely another form of consumption, Anna was something of an enigma. Here was a bottle which didn't ever seem to run dry.

She was a provisioner for Sicily 4, who specialized in protein. Provisioning officers were responsible for purchasing food for their given territories to be resold to the public in the company run stores. Anna came by Aetna every three or four weeks to pick up frozen and processed fish for the markets in New Amsterdam.

Eight years younger than Jack, Anna was a 175 centimeter brunette in her early thirties. Fit, she was all curves, olive skin, and green eyes. Tonight, she wore a neon green dress cut high on the legs and low on top. She matched the lack of subtlcty in Chuck's perfectly.

Jack walked up to the bar and sat down next to her. Anna didn't see him arrive because she was busy chatting up the crewman on her other side. He was big, handsome, and athletic, probably worked in cargo. He was also young. If Jack felt threatened, he didn't show it. To his knowledge, Anna had never been with anyone else while she was on his station.

Jack ordered a cognac neat, for himself, and a Brandy Alexander, nodding toward Anna when he ordered the brandy. He waited, listening to Anna's bubbly girl next door voice and watching her use her warm smile to great effect. When the drinks arrived, he took the cognac. Chuck set down the Brandy Alexander in front of Anna. Anna stared at Chuck with a question on her face. Chuck just smiled and tipped his head toward Jack.

Anna turned. "Oh, Jack," Anna squealed, the sparkle of her eyes matching the enthusiasm of her voice. She leaned over and kissed her greeting, lingering just a moment with her face next to his. She smiled, her nose wrinkling along with her freckles. Jack loved her eyes.

"Hey, kiddo. You didn't tell me you were coming through."

"I didn't know myself until this week. Then there was so much to do to get ready that I figured I would just surprise you."

Jack enjoyed the irritation on the face of the crewman behind her. Grabbing his drink brusquely off the bar, the crewman slopped a little of the brown liquid onto the polished steel. *Watch and learn, young one*, thought Jack as the crewman stalked off in search of other prey. To Anna, Jack said aloud, "Well, it's a lovely surprise."

Jack and Anna chitchatted for a few minutes while they finished up their drinks. Jack paid his second tab of the evening, and they stood to go. Anna reached over and took Jack's arm. As he stood, Jack could see Molly across the room just shake her head.

Outside the noise of Chuck's, the station was silent. The shops had closed for the evening, and most residents were either already tucked away in their apartments or out for the evening at either Chuck's or the more enthusiastic restaurant and club Pogo's.

As they walked, Jack absorbed the closeness of the girl at his side. He breathed deeply, enjoying the smell of her hair. She leaned into him. He walked slowly. He didn't walk slowly with most women he took home.

Jack asked Anna about business and what had happened since he had last seen her. Through long years of experience, Jack had found that the walk between Chuck's and home was best used discussing the mundane. The bird had been caged at Chuck's. Now was the time to compliment it and flatter it so that it would spread its wings when the door closed at home.

"You made quite an impression on that crewman tonight. He wasn't very happy when I stepped in."

Anna laughed. "Yes, I bet he wasn't. But I didn't let him buy me a drink."

"Why not? He was good looking and stacked."

Anna shook her head. "You think that's what I want?"

Jack lifted one shoulder in a kind of 'I don't know what you want' fashion. "Whatever it is you want, I just hope you keep finding it in this old bugger."

Anna put her arm around him and gave his lanky frame a squeeze. "Underneath your tough exterior, you're kind. You were kind to me the first time I met you. I don't think you know how rare it is to find kindness on a station."

Jack grinned. "A hard candy shell with a soft chewy center, eh?"

The wanton look in Anna's eye and the groping she gave his rear end furthered a process begun by the alcohol and the kiss back at Chuck's. "Something like that."

"Shush, that's our little secret," he said with a wink. Jack wasn't convinced he cared what Anna thought he was. If she thought there was some deep hidden layer inside Jack, that was fine by him. If she wanted him to play the gentleman, he would, as long as it kept her coming back for more.

A few minutes later, they arrived at Jack's neat and sparsely decorated apartment. Jack unlocked the door with a palm reader, opened it, and gestured for Anna to enter. Even before the door closed, Anna was reaching back to unzip her dress.

3
Free-fall

The night on which Jack met Anna had not been her best. Having had one too many, she found herself at the mercy of a scumbag named Larry Wilson. Wilson had been a dock worker on the station who didn't last very long. He arrived with a foul demeanor and a hair trigger to match. He had set Jack off from the moment he met him, but Larry hadn't been Jack's hire, so he hadn't done anything to get rid of him.

By the time Jack had arrived at Chuck's on the night in question, Anna was drunk, laughing at everything Larry said. Jack had never seen her before, and that meant she was likely a new arrival. Larry kept trying to put his hand underneath her yellow halter top. She was slapping his hand, but her body was responding to the attention.

It hadn't taken Anna's dilated pupils for Jack to put two and two together. The situation irritated Jack. Chuck, and for that matter the whole bar, looked nervous. Only Larry, with his three day stubble and greasy coveralls, seemed to be enjoying himself.

After watching Chuck towel dry the same glass for the third time, Jack decided he needed to do something. Setting down his drink with more energy than usual, he stood up. The movement and the noise got Chuck's attention. Jack stared hard at him. Chuck nodded imperceptibly and from under the bar flashed the stick taser which Jack had procured for him sometime before.

Larry remained oblivious, intent upon his goal. Jack walked up behind him and Anna. With one quick motion he grabbed Anna's hands and pulled her away so she wasn't touching Larry. At the same moment, Chuck reached over the bar and gave him a jolt that would have felled an elephant. Anna stopped mid-laugh. Larry went rigid and fell forward onto the bar. Jack picked up Anna and began to carry her to the door.

"Let me go!" Anna shouted, trying to kick and punch Jack. Jack kept walking.

"Chuck, you better call the Gendarme."

"Leanne's already on it."

"I'll get her out of here, but you better keep him down until they show up."

Chuck just nodded. "You know what bothers me most about this?" Chuck said grimly.

"What?"

"I'm going to have to clean his piss up off my floor."

Jack just nodded, continuing to carry Anna out the door. He took her to his apartment. By the time they got there, Anna was coming on to him, begging him to do her. Jack got her in the door and decided the easiest strategy was to play along. After he had gotten her to use the restroom, he told her to go lie on the bed and that he would follow shortly. She willingly complied, unbuttoning her pants.

While she was fumbling with her zipper, Jack grabbed a blanket from the hall closet, along with a spare pillow, and headed for the master bathroom. Telling her he would be right out, he locked the door behind him, used the can, brushed his teeth, spread the blanket and pillow on the floor, and decided to try to get some sleep.

Jack enjoyed sex as much as the next man, but he had standards, and taking a woman—even a hot one, like the girl on his bed—while she was hopped up on aphro-d was beneath them. As far as he knew, Anna never tried to come in. Several hours later, when the soreness became too much for him, he quietly crawled off the floor and peeked out in the dark.

Anna hadn't moved. She hadn't even taken her pants off. She had just passed out on his bed. Jack checked on her just to make sure she was still breathing. He went to the kitchen and got a glass of water, which he set next to the bed with an impossible to miss note saying, "DRINK THIS!"

In the morning, Jack woke up stiff and in pain on his too short couch. He rolled over and found Anna sitting in a chair watching him.

"I am sure that I owe you a huge thank you, but, to tell the truth, I don't know exactly what for. The last thing I remember, this grubby looking guy offered to buy me a drink."

Jack rubbed his eyes and sat up. "Well, it wasn't just a drink."

"The rest of it is pretty hazy, but that was my guess." She stood up. "I don't want to keep you from your day. Thank you." She walked briskly to the door. "And thanks for the water." She tried to smile as she palmed the latch, and then she was gone.

Two days later, Larry had an accident while doing an EVA on a freighter that had just come into port. Mysteriously, his suit sprung a leak in hard vacuum right in the small of his back and he died. Whether the other dock workers took care of it or if Frank's boys cleaned things up, Jack never found out. He didn't want to know. Knowing would have been a liability.

Jack didn't think any more of it, until later in the week when he was sitting at the bar in Chuck's finishing a beer and someone set down a Cognac in front of him. Jack looked sideways at Anna, who was wearing a little black dress, emphasis on little.

"I think I at least owe you a drink," she said, as she flashed her winning smile.

Saturday morning, Jack left his bed quietly and headed to his kitchen. He always had fun cooking for his overnight guests. He put on his heads-up display and checked his email while he cooked. The device appeared similar to the ear protection Rick had thrown at him in the submarine hanger but without the ear muffs. Jack's email was unusually empty. Typical Saturday mornings meant sorting through Lewis' forwards and attempts at humor. Grateful, Jack put the heads-up on the counter.

He put a couple of small dark red fish steaks in the pan along with some synthetic greens. Anna emerged from the bedroom wearing one of his button-down shirts and a pair of his boxers. She was toweling her hair just as Jack was putting the fish and cooked greens on plates. Jack took them to the table while Anna poured two glasses of Breakfast Juice—another Unity synthetic. This one was supposed to taste like oranges, whatever *they* were. Jack had never seen or tasted one, so he couldn't say.

After finishing, Anna picked up her plate. "What do you want to do today, Jack?"

"Oh, I don't know..." Jack ran his hand up Anna's thigh and under her shirt as she walked by.

Anna skittered away from him, shaking her head and giggling. "You know life does offer other pleasurable activities."

"None that match my time in bed with you."

Anna shook her head and rolled her eyes. This time her answer had a bit of a bite to it. "How many women have you said *that* to over the years? I'm serious. Let's go do something today."

Jack turned his chair away from the table. He shrugged his shoulders, "What do you want to do?"

"There's a new surrealist art exhibition at I-MAM."

Jack groaned. There were several reasons to avoid I-MAM if possible. First, when Anna said she wanted to go to I-MAM, she didn't mean the physical Imperial Modern Art Museum. That was located hundreds of light years away on Apollos. She meant visiting the museum via the intraspace.

Jack glanced over at the intraspace cap on a low shelf near his table. For Jack, putting on an intraspace cap was something quite different than its country cousin, the heads-up display. A heads-up display was a communications tool one used in the real world. It read your thoughts and turned them into commands and messages which you controlled.

On the other hand, intraspace caps, like the one Jack stared at on his shelf, caused the wearer to enter an altered state of consciousness in which the cap could project people, places, and activities into the mind that the subject experienced as authentic sensory input. It *showed* you things. It took over your mind.

Some fifty years before, this technology had been combined with what was known as the internet and intraspace was born. Deployment had slowly percolated across the galaxy. Always wary of foreign meddling, Unity Corporation had resisted intraspace. Caps had reached average Unity citizens late in the process.

Jack didn't enjoy entering intraspace. He picked up his cap and looked at it for the thousandth time. He decided again that intraspace was unnatural. It was bad enough that anything could read his thoughts. But to Jack, the cap crossed the line when it projected sensory experiences into his mind. He felt invaded.

Kids like Joe and Anna had grown up with intraspace and took this stuff for granted. Jack, on the other hand, had vague memories of a time before he was ten in which heads-up devices and caps were solely used to control a world safely outside of him on a screen. He still tended to transact all his business in that way, staying out of intraspace unless absolutely necessary.

Occasionally, he visited a virtual brothel when boredom and frustration overcame his control. But Jack didn't see the online world as a place for socializing. However, he was becoming increasingly isolated in that opinion. There were now couples who had never met in the real world. They spent their whole relationship in their heads.

Jack knew that part of the allure of I-MAM was the fact that it was one of the few intraspace destinations average Unity citizens could visit, not officially sanctioned by the Unity board of directors. The Unity was not the end-all and be-all of human expansion in the Milky Way.

Unity Corporation belonged, unwillingly, to a confederation of states headed by an emperor. The Pax

Imperium had been forced on the Unity nearly 300 years prior, when the Unity had been humiliated at the end of the last galactic war. The House of Athena and its allies had led the resistance to the Unity and its puppet states, eventually forcing an unconditional surrender from the Unity. The Department of Education still taught Unity school children about the Athenian atrocities of the Great War. While he had no proof, Jack instinctively understood that Unity history glossed over similar atrocities on their side.

Establishing the Pax was an attempt to keep the peace by creating a new federation of states without allowing a single state to dominate. Most of the time, the Pax Emperor was virtually powerless, and Jack still wasn't sure how thc Empire had managed to force I-MAM access on the Unity, but the rumor was that the Emperor himself had intervened.

No one had ever told Jack that it wasn't safe for Unity citizens to visit I-MAM. Jack didn't have to be told. When you lived under a suspicious and unforgiving government like Unity, you just knew certain things. Jack's whole mode of operating in Unity had been to hide, to keep his head down, and keep a low profile. Going to I-MAM had nothing to do with keeping a low profile.

Finally, there was the fact that the Imperial Modern Art Museum wasn't Jack's cup of tea. When young, Jack had let a date talk him into going to an art exhibition in intraspace—once. Apparently, while suiting up for the party, Jack had picked the wrong avatar—a purple dinosaur, which was only in the art gallery collection as an ironic joke. It was a joke he never understood, and no one bothered to explain it to him. That evening ended coldly. It was not a pleasant memory for Jack.

Anna came back from putting the dishes in the washer and sat on his lap facing him, putting her legs around him and the chair. She wrapped her arms around his head and smiled at him. She spoke quietly, playing with his hair. "Come on, Jack. Let's go have some fun. It's me. We'll go have a good laugh at the pretentiousness of it all."

"'Pretentiousness' is a rather large word, my dear. I'm not sure that I'm qualified to date someone who uses 'pretentiousness' in casual conversation." Jack moved his hands up under her shirt, feeling the skin around her waist.

"Pretentious, pretentious, pretentious." Anna whispered the word in Jack's ear, letting her lips brush him. Jack found the nape of her neck and began to kiss her as his hands began to roam. He was brought up short by pain in his ear lobe.

"Hey. Ouch!"

Through teeth clenched onto his lobe, Anna said, "Are we going to I-MAM?"

Jack was amused. Anna always knew how to make him laugh. He thought through the implications and decided that a little mild rebellion against the system might do him some good. "OK, we'll go see the art gallery," he said, while trying not to laugh too hard and pull on his ear.

Anna let go of his ear lobe. "Good," she said, as she went back to kissing him. "Don't stop now," she crooned. "That was feeling good."

Late in the morning, Jack picked up the cap and walked into his bedroom where Anna waited for him. Caps took the mind into a state that was very similar to REM sleep. So, while the body didn't thrash around, spending anything more than a few minutes to an hour in intraspace was best done lying down. Otherwise, one tended to come out stiff and sore.

Jack had heard that in other countries in the Pax, citizens could take intraspace trips lasting for days. Supposedly, these were done in special care centers where medical professionals monitored patient's health and kept them fed and hydrated intravenously. Jack doubted it. There were so many rumors flooding around about how life was better in the other countries that Jack didn't believe any of them. In Athena, everyone was supposed to have their own vehicle as well.

All Jack knew for sure was that regular Unity citizens didn't have access to these long trips. Of course, if there was such a thing as an intraspace care center, the Unity elites would have it. Even though Jack wasn't sure why one would ever want to spend that long in intraspace, the inequality still pissed him off.

Jack lay down on the bed and put the cap on his head. He closed his eyes. Anna reached out and held his hand. Jack took a deep breath, trying to let go of everything on his mind. On the exhale, his world changed.

He stood up from a desk which looked almost exactly the same as the desk in his office. He was in his transition room. Transition rooms allowed the mind a consistent frame of reference when it first entered intraspace. As a rule, transition rooms were highly personal, often safe places from childhood—places where the mind could relax. With nothing in his brutal upbringing worth remembering, and unmotivated to create something personal, Jack had chosen his office at work to stand in as his transition room.

He faced the large screen on the wall and, using his thoughts, brought up the I-MAM as his destination. He stepped out of the door of his office into a high marble hall, with an ornate ceiling inlaid with gold. *Well, if I didn't have a security file with HR previously, I do now*, he thought.

The lobby was busy with people from all over the galaxy coming and going. Behind him, doors opened and shut on a world which to him appeared blank, an off-white void. That world, the virtual world of the Imperial capital on Apollos, was not available to average citizens of the Unity. Those coming in the doors appeared out of the void.

Jack turned away and stepped up the four broad marble stairs into the cavernous entry hall. Anna waited for him at the top. Now that he had arrived, Jack felt exposed. His mantra had always been to keep his head down and avoid attention, and here he was heading into I-MAM. As he reached the top of the stairs, Anna took his hand. Jack swore that everyone was watching them.

"Nervous?" Anna asked.

Jack smiled. "Of course not. Let's go look at some art. Although, you're going to have to interpret it all for me."

"Have you ever been here before?" Anna regarded him with a questioning look in her eye.

"No. I usually don't do things which the authorities wouldn't like."

Anna giggled. "Oh, don't worry about that. They don't care. Why didn't you tell me? So we'll take it slow." Anna took his hand and led him toward the turnstiles at the other end of the hall.

Once they entered the gates, Anna took a few minutes to look over a map and then headed for their first exhibit. Anna stepped through the threshold of the room, spreading her arms wide as she did so. She disappeared into a bright white mist which filled the space beyond the door.

Jack followed and felt himself enter free-fall. Instinctively, he spread his arms. With the spread of his arms, he felt the change. He didn't seem to be falling so quickly, but his arms felt all wrong. They were placed back on his body as if they were far down his torso. His fingers felt splayed well apart. When he tried to move them, they seemed fused in place, as if there was webbing between them.

The mist parted below Jack, and he began to comprehend what had taken place when he entered the exhibition hall. The ground lay far below him. He was plummeting toward a coastline. Next to him, as if waiting for his arrival, a black bird with a very long neck began honking excitedly. He assumed it must be Anna. He turned his long neck to look at it, and it struck him that he was gliding instead of falling. He examined himself. His body had morphed into a similar black bird. From somewhere in the recesses of his mind, Jack pulled out the word 'swan.'

He flapped his arms, or rather wings, but no matter what he did, the ground continued to rise at him at an alarming rate. He wasn't worried about hurting himself. He assumed that was impossible in an art piece like this, but he just didn't want to embarrass himself. Anna seemed a natural, gliding where she wanted and gaining altitude with ease. Jack felt a long dormant sense of competition rise up in him. He didn't want to let his date beat him.

There were already several other black swans who seemed to have stranded themselves on the shoreline. The small piece of Jack's mind not devoted to trying to stay aloft was highly amused as one couple seemed to be fighting about it all, honking madly at each other and nipping at each other with their beaks.

He was very close to the rocky shoreline now. He flapped his arms madly and eventually gained some purchase. All the while, the swan next to him continued to honk at him. With a frantic effort he slowly gained altitude, and then he felt the lift from the nearby surf. He surged upward.

The next few minutes for Jack became a desperate struggle to hold altitude, but he found himself readily adapting to his new body. Once he seemed to have learned the basics, Anna honked at him and led him past the surf over open water. Jack was beginning to enjoy himself. They zoomed lower and lower, surfing the air currents just above the swell.

Without warning, Anna dived in. Giving in to an adventurous streak which he did not know existed, Jack followed without hesitation. This time he recognized the sensation as his body changed shape. His vision changed. He could see beside him and behind him and in front of him. He surfaced and instinctually drew a breath, but what a breath. He had vast lungs that took in huge volumes of air and his nose seemed to be located somewhere on his back. A creature of vast bulk swam by him and he recognized that its bulk equaled his own—Anna, he guessed. They were some kind of air breathing fish. Anna brushed up against him and then took off swimming with all her might. He watched as she lifted her bulk out of the surface of the water and crashed back again. Jack tried to imitate her and managed to pull his enormous body out of the water on the third try. He was huge, perhaps some 20 meters in length. On his fourth leap, Jack managed to get far enough out of the water that he once again reverted to the swan.

Anna followed and then led him on a short flight across open water to a grass covered plain. Upon landing, she morphed into some kind of cat type creature. It somewhat resembled a creature Jack knew as a New Samoan Camel, but it didn't have water sacks. Jack landed and found himself running on four paws, covered in golden hair, his head surrounded by a mass of auburn fur.

Jack and Anna spent the next couple of hours putting all sorts of fantastic animal life through their paces. When finished, they bounded through one of the many exit portals he had seen on their tour. Jack was laughing even before he had fully returned to his own body. He grabbed Anna and held her to his chest. He couldn't ever remember a time in his life in which he had given himself so fully to the pure joy of the moment as he had done in the last couple of hours. Anna leaned in and laughed with him, tears streaming down her face.

"What was that?"

"Old Earth."

"No! Seriously? It was amazing."

"The artist Nanami Komatsu had a strong environmental thread in all her work. In this piece, she wanted us to understand that humans have much more in common with the life on Earth than on other planets. Her argument is that we understand Earth life instinctually because we evolved with it. She thinks the instincts of the whale—that air breathing fish—the swan, and the lion—the cat—are buried in our DNA."

Jack listened but only a little. He was too drunk with the sound of Anna's voice and his enjoyment of the last two hours to listen carefully to what she was saying. He stopped and held Anna away from him by the shoulders. He gazed into her eyes. "Thank you."

She reached out and took Jack's hand, as she had done many times before. Precisely what made this instance so different, Jack couldn't have said, but when she took his hand, he understood that Anna meant that she enjoyed him, that he was part of her laughter. Jack was unnerved to discover that she meant the same to him. He hesitated.

Anna smiled. "There's more to see." She tugged him forward.

For the second time that day, Jack embraced discomfort for the sake of Anna. He allowed her to lead him down the corridor toward their next adventure.

After several more hours of all sorts of mind and reality bending exhibits, Jack was ready for a break. He suggested that they find something quieter, a place to sit for a while. He and Anna walked hand-in-hand into the Imperial Peace Garden which sat under glass in the center of I-MAM. Jack inhaled the damp aroma of growing things as if it were an elixir. As someone who had spent his adult life on space stations, barely habitable moons, and asteroids, the smell of living plants and fertile soil always smelled amazing to Jack.

After taking a break on a bench and then wandering the various paths surrounded by plants of every variety, Anna said, "There's one more thing I want you to see Jack, but it definitely isn't on the Unity approved list." Anna stood and reached out her hand for Jack to follow.

Instinctively, Jack recognized in the request both the danger and Anna's reason for coming to I-MAM. He sensed danger and hesitated. So far what they had done had been innocent enough but Jack was so used to keeping his head down. He looked at Anna's outstretched hand. *I've come this far it doesn't make sense to back out now*, he thought and he shrugged. Looking up at Anna's face he said, "It's been a day of bending rules. Why not?"

Anna led Jack to another corner of the peace garden. As they approached a bend in the path, Anna began to grin. "Watch out. They might try to glare us to death." She gripped his hand a little more firmly, straightened her back, and walked confidently forward.

Scanning the sparse crowd, Jack easily picked out two beefy Unity human resource officers eyeing everyone as they walked around the bend. They stood to the side, evidently powerless to interfere, dressed in the charcoal gray suits and purple ties of HR.

"They can't stop us from going in, but they definitely try and scare you."

Jack was already so far outside his comfort zone today, he decided to just go with it. *What could they do?* Jack straightened his back and confidently matched Anna's pace. As they approached, the HR thugs watched them the whole way, jaws clenched. Jack stared strictly forward, refusing eye contact. Once around the corner, Jack and Anna slowed their pace.

They walked a path between two highly ornamental gardens like none Jack had ever seen. On the one side, four foot trees clustered in places of artificial sunlight. Every couple of minutes or so, the sunlight would be moved to some other space in the exhibit and the trees would use stubby root-like feet to follow the light. Their leaves were long and triangular and trailed stiffly behind them as they 'walked.'

On the other side of the path were also trees of about four to six feet, but these did not move. Their stems appeared somewhat crystalline in appearance, but at the top, greenish blue leaves erupted for photosynthesis. Jack recognized these as the native trees from the Unity home world of Cyprus 4.

He looked back at the first side of the exhibit and something from his early studies came back to him. The home planet of the Unity's chief rival in the empire, Athena, had trees that moved. Without speaking, Jack and Anna stepped forward.

Mixed in with the trees on either side of the path were striking black and white holographic images from over 300 years prior. Each image, taken from an implant, a heads-up, or security camera, showed the moment at which horrific destruction rained down upon a planet during the Great War—the very instant at which that planet was made uninhabitable. Underneath each photograph was a simple plaque stating the name of the planet and the number of humans killed.

Every person raised in the Unity knew that twenty-four worlds belonging to the Unity and its allies had been made uninhabitable during the Great War. An estimated 110 billion Unity citizens died. Yet as Jack walked, something didn't make sense. There were two planets listed on the Athenian side before any were listed on the Unity side of the path, and from then forward there was a simple tit-for-tat trade—a back and forth—for several planets. Right at the end was there a long list of planets destroyed on the Unity side in quick succession. This destruction was the famous Catastrophe that every Unity school child learned about. What confused Jack was the similar list of planets on the Athenian side. Jack had never learned anything about that.

Jack felt betrayed, angry. While he may not have much affection for the Unity Corporation, he had always seen it as the victim of aggression in the Great War. Here was a narrative which showed something different. Unity had been the first to push an asteroid into a planet. In fact, they had done so twice before Athena responded in kind. By the time Jack reached the end of the path, he was sick to his stomach. There, at the feet of a statue honoring the first Emperor, the gardens merged. The walking trees of Athena moved among the crystalline trees of the Unity.

Jack sat heavily on a bench.

Anna wiped tears from her eyes. "It's a lot to take in the first time you see it, isn't it?"

"Yes, it is. It can't be true."

"Can't it, Jack? I don't think you believe that it's a lie. The HR thugs at the gate are the best proof. If this weren't true, they wouldn't be there."

"Typical HR behavior, isn't it? Make a problem more obvious by trying to keep it secret."

Anna just nodded as she wiped away tears. Then standing up, she turned to Jack. "Well, this isn't how I want our time at I-MAM to end. Let's go find something crazy and laugh ourselves silly."

Jack stood with her, and this time as they walked past the guards, he wasn't nervous; he was furious.

Sometime early on Monday morning Jack woke up, lifted his head off the pillow, and rested it on his hand, while he listened to Anna's slow breathing. He curled up behind her naked body, wrapping his free arm around her. He put his face close to the top of her head and kissed her gently. Anna grinned at his touch and, keeping her eyes shut, snuggled closer. She wrapped his arm tighter around her as she settled down to sleep again.

Ever since their visit to I-MAM on Saturday, Jack recognized that he needed to quit pretending his regular visits from Anna were about sex for him. Truth be told, he had known it for some time. At the beginning of the relationship, he told himself that it was just the relaxed, easy quality of the intercourse which kept him interested. With Anna, sex never felt like a performance, as it was with so many others, but, as he lay there in the dark, he wondered how long he had been fooling himself. He may tell himself that he didn't care about what Anna thought of him, but he did. He wanted her to come back.

A few hours from now, Anna would leave his bed and not return for another three or four weeks. Jack knew he would come home that evening and drink. Anna was too polite to talk about it, but Jack was no fool. He knew that Anna didn't spend their time apart pining for him. She simply moved on to the next station and found herself another warm bed. He knew, because Anna never tried to contact him between visits. He knew, because it was what he would have done at 32. Hell, most of the time when he was in his 20s he didn't always bother to stay the night.

Jack wasn't jealous. He liked to sample the wine, and living on a station gave him ample opportunity. There were always travelers coming through looking for a quick bit of companionship. Yet Jack had to admit to himself that something was different with Anna. This wasn't strictly sex any more. In the past, the answer had been easy. If things got intimate, he just moved on. For reasons he didn't understand, he hadn't moved on from Anna.

The idea of fidelity had never appealed to Jack. Limiting himself to sex with just one person just didn't seem sustainable to him. He figured boredom would set in at some point, and he'd wander.

Looking back, Jack figured that things had gone astray the first night Anna bought him a drink. That night in the bar, the attention of this thirty-something had flattered him. At the time he had just turned 39, and Jack knew that by most standards he was handsome, in a late youth kind of way. Yet, he found himself wondering what a younger woman in her prime like Anna saw in him.

Out of curiosity, Jack followed her lead. He wanted to see where *she* wanted to go. When they finally got back to his place, Anna had just cuddled with him for a while, soaking in the feeling of being in his arms. Of course later they had sex, but for Jack his memories always tended to linger on the simple enjoyment of holding her and their conversation. She seemed to feel safe with him. That simple moment had thrilled him in a way which none of his virtuoso erotic performances, or his conquests of perfectly formed cynthies, ever had. It still thrilled him every time he thought about it.

Anna opened her eyes, laughed, and reaching down behind her, said, "Well, good morning to you, too!" Then turning, she kissed him slowly. Jack felt his sense of strength grow. Anna rolled over onto her back and pulled him on top of her. Jack took control.

4
New Management

Jack entered the office promptly at eight AM, ready for a mundane day of paperwork. He and Anna had kissed their good-byes a couple of minutes before, as he left for the office. As usual, Jack didn't know when he would see her again. They both said they would stay in touch while they were apart. Neither of them meant it.

Jack refused to feel anything. It wouldn't do any good. Most importantly, he refused to give Molly or anyone else in the office any reason to discuss it with him. Molly, in particular, didn't approve of Anna. She had made it clear that she didn't think Anna was good for him. It always took him about a week to get back to top form after she left, and that tweaked Molly, because she had to pick up the pieces he dropped. Having her boss in a bit of a daze pissed her off, so poor Anna never had a fair shot at being Molly's favorite.

Molly was already at her desk. She didn't say anything to Jack as he walked by. Her silence communicated her position as effectively as a three page, single spaced memo. Jack walked into his office and shut his door.

Fifteen minutes later, he recognized that he had sat down at his desk and had yet to open the briefcase full of reports he was supposed to read over the weekend. Jack put on his heads-up. With his thoughts, Jack commanded the company server on the station to project his inbox onto the large screen which sat above his desk. In most business settings, workers avoided the full intraspace experience. Instead, they used heads-up displays or projected communications onto screens, leaving themselves available for interruptions and visitors.

Jack's email appeared on the screen only to be abruptly overridden by a direct message from Lewis. "Please take the 8:30 shuttle to the surface. There is a meeting for all department heads in my office at 1 PM standard time." The message startled Jack. He didn't even know there was an override which would let Lewis ping him that way.

At the same moment, Molly knocked on his door and entered without waiting. "Jack?" She was staring down at the tablet she had in her hand, sounding nervous. "Have you seen the docking manifests from this weekend?"

"No. Should I?"

"HR put two ships on the surface. Admin brought in three. I have another HR ship scheduled to dock here later this morning."

Jack felt an instant rush of adrenaline. "No shit?" He took the tablet out of Molly's hand, and his mind began to race. It could be a trick, but he doubted that. He kept his face carefully neutral as he thought.

When done, he smiled casually. "Well, Molly dearest, things are about to get interesting around here. I have a meeting in Lewis's office at one. "

Molly turned pale.

"Have a seat." Jack nodded to the chairs along the wall, as he reached into his desk for a bottle of scotch and two glasses. Now is not the time to panic." He heard the door in the lobby swing open. Jack lifted his eyebrows and asked Molly an unspoken question.

She shook her head. "They aren't due in until 11."

Jack reached back in his desk and got out a third glass. Joe would be at home today. He had finished up the weekend inspection and cargo duties early that morning. The door would be Robert.

Robert came in the door to Jack's office. Jack held out a glass of scotch and gestured to the seat next to Molly, then handed Molly a glass.

Robert smiled. "I don't usually drink before three. What's the occasion?"

Molly leaned forward, pulled the tablet off the desk, and handed it to Robert.

"Mother of God, protect us."

Jack just smiled. "Have you ever seen anything like it, Robert?"

Robert shook his head and answered, "No."

Jack took a gulp from his glass and looked at the wall clock. He had about ten minutes until he had to be in the shuttle with Ernie. He took a moment to throw a message to the shuttle pilot with his cap and ask him to hold the shuttle for him.

"All right, we have a plan in place for this. Now we have to work quickly," he said to his staff.

Jack stared out the window all the way down to the surface. He needed time to think. They were going to have to be cautious moving forward until they could get the lay of the land. It could all be some kind of inspection. They had gone through those before, nothing to worry about. They simply showed the inspectors the cooked books. HR, or whoever, glanced over them, and that was the end of it. It wasn't as if they could find anything by looking at the electronic records, not without digging deeply into them. One of the geniuses of heading the black market on Aetna from the inspection office was that the shipping records could be made to match from start to finish. Sometimes even the ship's captain didn't know that instead of carrying a load of bulk wheat he was bringing in supplies for the fishing fleet.

Even as he thought it over, he recognized that with this many 'troops on the ground' it was unlikely that all Unity had in mind was a typical inspection. Changes were coming to Aetna. That was all right by Jack. Jack had yet to meet a Unity official who couldn't be corrupted if you offered them the right thing. The trick was figuring out what they needed that they couldn't get. Offer the wrong item to the wrong official and that could be the end of everything. Jack would have to sit back until he could see all the angles.

Jack took a relaxed breath. HR would just have docked at the station. They would likely have made their way to his offices almost immediately. He breathed again. *Molly would be ready*, he thought. *She has never let you down. Trust your staff.*

The shuttle landed and Jack disembarked, chatting with Ernie as he exited. There was a taxi waiting at the stand when he approached. He got in and took the short ride to the Sub dock. Jack arrived just in time to see Rick come out of his office.

He appeared surprised. "Jack, what are you doing here?"

Jack gave him an easy smile and a shrug. "I was in the neighborhood, and thought that I would just drop by."

Rick nodded, and from the tightness of his smile, Jack knew that he suspected why he had dropped by.

"Come in." Rick gestured to his office door.

This time he didn't use his floating coaster before he said, "What's on your mind, Jack."

Jack glanced at his coffee cup.

Rick gave him the barest hint of shaking his head. Jack shrugged and began to talk. "Do you know what's coming our way?"

"Not really, but I guessed something was up when three or four ships landed late on Friday, and Lewis delayed our move until they were all tucked in."

"Two from HR and three from admin."

Rick looked surprised but answered with an almost exaggerated ease. "Well, I guess that means we're probably getting some new management."

"It might mean we won't be able to get your shipment in for a while. We've had to put everything on hold."

Rick turned a little pale but didn't miss a beat. "Naw, anything coming through regular channels should be fine." He stood up. "Thanks for coming by to tell me."

Taken a little aback, Jack stood as well. It was like Rick feared they were being watched. Jack was out the door before Rick spoke again. With an overly genuine smile and a pat on the back, Rick said, "Jack, if you ever get serious about taking that little fishing trip, just let me know. And don't try it by yourself. This moon has a lot of surprises up her sleeve that people from the orbital don't know anything about. A man could get lost out there."

Jack decided to play along. He chuckled and grinned. "I'll remember that. You have a great day, Rick. I better get to my meeting."

Jack got back in the waiting cab, a little confused. Rick was scared, more than usual scared, and suspicious. He no longer trusted that his office wasn't bugged. In fact, he was so concerned about it that he hadn't wanted to even reveal that he could undermine it with his talking coaster thing.

Yet, even though he was scared, Rick had made sure to offer Jack a way of escape if things got interesting. Jack wondered why he was willing to stick his neck out for him.

When Jack exited the cab at the admin building, he did the usual duck and run to get out of the cold into the comparatively warm vestibule. It was empty, not a vendor in site. Jack had anticipated that. He couldn't decide if this was good or not. Probably they all had been warned, but maybe not. Either way, he didn't figure the vendors would be showing up today. He put on his most passive look as he walked by two HR gendarmes he didn't recognize and entered the building.

He smiled his usual smile to whoever was running the lobby desk and proceeded to the elevator. He checked the time; he would be fine, a few minutes early in fact.

He calmed himself as he stepped out, walking naturally through the door. Reassuringly, Cathie was behind the desk where she should be. Jack had half expected to see someone from HR at the post. Jack smiled and said nonchalantly, "What's the scoop, Cathie?"

Cathie jumped as she looked up at Jack. There were tear stains on her cheeks and her eyes said her mind had been occupied elsewhere. "You'll just have to see for yourself," she replied evenly. Her tone lacked its usual warmth.

Jack entered the office, deciding to take a more subdued tack. He slipped in quietly and took the last seat available. Although about ten minutes early, he was the last to arrive. The twelve different heads who reported directly to Lewis were there. All were seated in a single row of conference chairs organized around the desk. None of them were talking to each other.

Seated at the desk was a man in a dark blue suit with a red striped tie and white shirt, the uniform of business executives for almost 1000 years. This year's model of tie had tiny blue pinstripes running up and at an angle to the right. The man was a perfect Unity executive. He had dark brown hair, cut short, with a perfect part on the right side. There was just enough salt showing through the pepper on the sides of his hair to give him that sexy, older man look. He had thick eyebrows, a strong chin, piercing blue eyes, and a square jaw line. Even as he read over the papers in front of him, he had the permanent smirk Jack associated with those in power.

Next to him, on his left, stood a security officer in the dark purple jumpsuit of the gendarmes. His hands behind the back of his lean muscular frame, he stood in perfect at-ease posture. He had a military buzz cut to go with his silver hair, and his eyes constantly scanned the row of individuals in front of him. Jack checked down the row to see if Frank was in the room. He sat on a chair at the end of the row with a grin on his face that made him look like a kid in a candy shop. As Jack glanced back down the row, he realized that most of the eyes in the room, particularly those of the women, were not watching GI Joe. They were elsewhere.

On the other side of the Suit stood Venus herself, perfect in every way: straight blond hair—highlighted—a face both innocent and capable, and a medium frame. She wore the strictly regulation blue skirt suit of a female HR officer. She had turned the collar of her perfectly white shirt up. Two sizes too small, the shirt had been unbuttoned to expose the swell of her tan breasts. There was not a freckle, wrinkle, or flaw of any kind to be found on her skin. She had a designer heads-up display over one eye, and she was concentrating on something, likely checking her email, Jack decided. He immediately pegged her as a cynthy, but this one had treatments far beyond what even most could afford.

From Jack's perspective, it was a lovely view. The women in the room were pissed. Red in the face, Bonnie Stuart, the head of Fuel Processing, looked as if she was about ready to launch herself across the desk and strangle the bitch as she smoothly took off her heads-up and folded it with a loud click.

Where was Lewis? The thought hit Jack like a freight train. He quickly surveyed the room and found him sitting in a chair off to the side, hands nervously folded on his belly. He wore a double-breasted blue suit which Jack had never seen him wear. Jack recognized it as an official executive's uniform which went out of style about twenty years ago. Lewis appeared uncomfortable. Every once in a while he would wipe the sweat off the top of his balding head with a white handkerchief. Then he would return to fidgeting in his chair.

Jack checked his watch. It clicked over to 1:00 PM. On the second, the Suit started talking. *The guy must be wired*, thought Jack. *All the better, maybe we can figure out a way to hack his brain.*

His manner of speaking was polished, too polished. He said exactly what should be said, smiled in all the right places, and paused just where he should, all without any of the warmth or good natured clumsiness that would have made it human. His eyes were anywhere else but in the present. The effect was off putting but helped Jack get a better picture of the man Jack suspected would be his new supervisor.

"Good afternoon, everyone. I am pleased to be here today. My name is Timothy Randall. I am an administrative vice-president with specialties in resource development and compliance. This past week, by an executive order, signed by CEO Cowhill himself, I was asked to replace Director Lutnear as the head of the administration here on Aetna." Here the suit smiled at Lewis. "Director Lutnear has agreed to stay on as the deputy director." The suit started clapping. GI Joe and Boobs immediately followed his lead. Most of the staff followed suit. Lewis started clapping with them; then, realizing it was for him, stopped and bobbed his moist pink head.

"We have important changes in our future, but, before we get to that, I would like to introduce the other members of my staff. On my left is Colonel Andrew Gunderson, our new head of security." Here he paused again for a round of polite clapping. Jack gave the new head of security two claps. "Frank Hanson will be taking over as head of security on the orbital."

"I am also delighted to introduce senior executive director Carla Savage, our new human resources officer. There are enormous advantages to having our own human resources staff here on Aetna." This time Jack clapped right along with the rest. Boobs smiled politely and, after looking around the room, made eye contact with Jack. She held his gaze as she smiled and absentmindedly ran one hand through her hair. Jack decided that he could see the benefits, and he agreed they were enormous. He also decided HR might not be such a bad department after all.

"In the Unity, we are one family, a unified team headed for the same goals. Right now, the Unity needs team Aetna to pitch in and carry a greater share of the load. We have a shortage of processed fusionable hydrogen. The Unity needs to produce more if we are going increase our rate of growth. I have been given a mandate to triple the production in the next two years here on Aetna. I know all of you will be as excited as I am to help accomplish the goals which the board of directors has set for us." Here he smiled and paused, waiting for a response from his audience. No one moved. The suit continued without giving any sign that he was surprised.

"In the coming days, I will be meeting with each of you individually to discuss how we can work together to accomplish the task set for us by the board. Cathie will be in touch shortly to let you know when you will be expected in my office. Thank you very much. Have a good day."

The suit stood, faced the Unity flag in the corner of the office and put his hand over his heart. Boobs and GI Joe did the same. Recognizing the ritual, Jack stood with the other staff. Suit started. They all followed. "I pledge allegiance to the flag of the Unity Corporation..."

Crossing the room at the end of the meeting, Jack walked directly up to Lewis. Jack smiled warmly, holding out his hand and said sardonically, "Lewis, congratulations on your demotion. I have an evening free on my calendar. I was wondering if tonight would work for that offer of dinner."

Shell-shocked, Lewis took Jack's hand and shook it. "Thank you," he said with a vacant stare. Jack waited, while his words penetrated a mind thickened by worry. He watched his words register as Lewis' eyes focused.

Lewis spoke clearly this time. "I would like that Jack, I really would. What do you say to this evening at six? You'll come by the house?" He was now shaking Jack's hand vigorously.

Jack pulled his hand away, surreptitiously wiping the sweat off before he put it in his pocket. "I'll see you at six." He projected confidence, trying to reassure Lewis. He needed to get it together.

As he finished talking to Lewis, Jack had the distinct impression that someone was now standing very close behind him. He turned to leave the room and found himself confronted by Boobs, who was standing a step and a half inside the perimeter of polite social distance. Jack looked her in the eye.

She put her hand into the small space between them. "You must be Jack Halloway." Without looking down, Jack took her hand and shook it. Carla held on a moment longer than was polite.

Jack's mind recognized the invitation. He didn't even make a conscious choice to follow. Years of habituation and practice made that choice for him. "So I am, and you are Ms. Savage, our new compliance officer."

She nodded slightly, holding his gaze and remaining within the perimeter of familiarity. She smiled. "You and I will be working closely together in the coming weeks."

"Then I will count that as one of the benefits of having our own HR staff on Aetna."

Boobs put her hand on his arm and leaned in, allowing her chest to brush into him ever so slightly. Jack leaned down to listen, this time looking down to enjoy the view. "I have a particular problem, which I believe of all the people in this room, you are the best qualified to handle." Her hand strayed to the buttons on Jack's shirt. "Would you meet me in my office in 30 minutes? I took one of the corner suites on the 18th floor. Go right from the elevators."

Jack savored the pleasant rush like a fine wine. For a connoisseur like himself, anticipation was as much a part of the fun as the actual joyride itself. "I would be happy to meet with you. Since we are going to be working so closely together, it makes sense that we get to know each other on a professional basis."

Carla laughed politely. "Well said. I'll see you in 30." She turned and walked away. In the crowded room, Jack chose not to observe the view. He could wait.

Instead, he surveyed the room and almost burst out laughing. Vice President Suit was standing and talking with Bonnie from Fuel Processing. She had her arms folded across her barrel-sized chest and didn't look happy.

Tall for a woman, Bonnie equaled Suit in height, but Jack guessed she had 40 pounds and 20 years on him, not that she was fat. Jack thought of her as thick, built square for heavy work. There was a rumor that she had earned her supervisor's job by reporting her senior for harassment. Jack didn't believe it. She wasn't handsome enough to harass. Jack figured she did it the old fashioned way, working twice as hard as her male counterparts.

Bonnie and he didn't see eye-to-eye on just about anything. They were barely on speaking terms. But they both respected what the other could provide. As the head of the largest industry on Aetna, Bonnie was a major customer of Jack's, but she usually let a male surrogate get orders to him.

Jack walked toward the pair. As he approached, he could hear Bonnie. "...I just don't see how it can be done without new workers. It seems dangerous to me."

Suit reached out and put a reassuring hand on her arm. *Big mistake*, thought Jack.

"Director Stuart, we can do this. I have tackled much more difficult projects in the past, and we succeeded every time. I am sure that we are going to make a great team." Suit saw Jack approaching and decided to shift the conversation. Looking away from Bonnie, he turned to Jack and gave him a smile with teeth unnaturally white.

Jack returned the smile and held out his hand. "Associate Director Jack Halloway, sir."

"Jack, I am glad you came to say hi." Suit returned his handshake warmly.

"I just wanted to say that I am looking forward to the challenge which is before us."

"I bet you are." The suit paused for half a beat and continued. "There is going to be so much work to be done on the orbital in the next few months. We are going to have to ramp up her capacity. In fact, why don't you stop by the desk and talk to Cathie. I think I have some time late in the day today. I would hate to see you have to come down again for another meeting."

"That would work well, sir. I'll look forward to hearing more about what you're thinking. For now, I just wanted to say if you need anything from me, don't hesitate to ask." Turning to look at Bonnie, he said with a smile, "That goes for you, too."

Already blotchy from anger, Bonnie's face turned scarlet.

Suit rescued Jack. "Well, thank you, Jack. I will be in touch, and I look forward to our meeting."

Jack smiled, said "thank you," and ducked away, enjoying the simmering wrath he had created in the shrew, Bonnie.

Jack left the room, quite a bit less worried than when he went in. He stopped off with Cathie and scheduled a meeting with The Suit. There was a spot open late that same afternoon. Jack glanced at the time. He had twenty minutes before he was to meet with Carla.

He grabbed a quick bite in the cafeteria and called up his email on his heads-up. Molly didn't say much but didn't use any of their code phrases for trouble either, so Jack assumed the inspection had gone well.

He knocked on the door to Carla's office just after his appointed time. Set to private, the window next to her office was a dark gray.

"Come in."

Jack opened the door and was greeted by much more of Boobs than he had seen at the meeting earlier. He shut the door behind him, giving his attention to enjoying the moment.

Twenty minutes later, as he finished tucking his light blue oxford shirt in and zipped his fly, Jack asked, "Was that all the business we had to discuss today?"

"Mainly," Carla said, with a mischievous grin. "Why? Wasn't that productive enough for you?"

"Oh, it was quite productive."

"I will need to schedule some time with you on the station after you meet with Timothy."

"That sounds lovely." He patted her ass as she bent down to put on her other shoe.

"Yes, it does, but at that time we will have Unity business to discuss and our professional relationship will have to take a back seat." Carla gently removed his hand.

"All right, I have my meeting with Vice President Randall this afternoon. If you throw a message to Molly, my assistant, she should be able to get you on my calendar, the day after tomorrow."

Straightening up, she looked at him as she leaned against her desk. "That should work well."

"I will see you then." This was always tricky. He offered his hand to Carla to shake. She took it and leaned in and kissed him hard. "That's so you don't forget me."

Jack used the time between his rendezvous with Boobs and his meeting with the Suit to visit some of his customer base on Aetna. It was about as bad as he expected. Half of them were panicked out of their minds. The other half of them still had their wits about them but were just about as scared. Jack spent a couple of hours repeatedly explaining to people like Hank the coffee guy and others why the new folks from admin and HR were here. Once they understood that it wasn't some sort of raid, most of them calmed down. Jack encouraged them to stay low for a little bit, work their regular jobs and take their company pay, while he and his staff got the lay of the land.

Jack arrived back at the executive suite just before his appointed meeting at 4 PM corporate standard time. After cooling his heels in the lobby for about five minutes, Cathie peered up at him and said he could go in. Jack noticed that she appeared calmer, more collected.

He opened the door and sat down in one of two chairs in front of the desk. Suit already had a set of crystal glasses sitting on his desk. Jack recognized them as contraband he had procured for Lewis through the black market. He was busy filling them from a bottle of Lewis' scotch, also contraband. Lewis' crystal dish with jelly beans was sitting in its usual place on his desk. Jack felt the hairs on the back of his neck stand.

"I hope you don't mind if we don't follow the rulebook exactly."

Jack smiled, maintaining a deliberate calm despite the adrenaline. "Not at all."

"Of course, you don't. After all, you provided these things for Lewis." Picking up the tray he said, "Have a jelly bean."

Jack was instantly alert to everything. He half expected to hear GI Joe come in behind him. He took two jelly beans from the proffered tray and put them in his mouth as a means of stalling to think. He could have just gotten this information from Lewis. Candy and alcohol were petty offenses, no big deal.

Jack decided there was no point in denying what Dick in a Suit already knew. "Do you know how hard it is to get these?" he said, plucking another from the dish. "We don't even make them here in Unity."

Dick in a Suit smiled, taking a handful of the jelly beans himself. "I like you, Jack."

Jack wondered if this is what a mouse felt like as the cat played with its dinner. There wasn't anything he could do but wait until he found out what Suit wanted. Jack took his drink off the tray on the desk and took a sip. He decided to be patient and not say anything.

Suit smiled for an appropriate length of time and then recognizing Jack's choice to wait, continued forward unperturbed. "Let's cut the crap, Jack. You're half the reason I decided to take the position here on Aetna."

This surprised Jack, but he didn't let it show. He continued to sit passively and let The Suit continue to speak.

Suit picked up a data pad from his desk and threw the image from the data pad onto the huge screen behind him. Jack recognized what appeared to be his HR file. Suit absentmindedly scrolled through a list of pilfered and smuggled items, all traced to him.

Early on in his career with the black market, Jack had learned to be cool under pressure. Often, the more tense he got, the more still he sat, the more deliberate his movements. Fight or flight had to be controlled. He waited, impassive.

They knew a lot. They knew most everything in fact, everything important anyway. It was enough for a dozen death sentences. As Jack scanned the list scrolling by, he noticed that his purchases for Musgrave were missing. That struck him as odd. He still didn't know what the suit wanted. He sipped his drink.

"You're a very talented man, Jack. I could use talent like yours on my team. Frankly, I've never seen anything like your little enterprise. It took a sophisticated understanding of how cargo flows through Unity space to pull it off."

In an instant, Jack knew what Suit wanted, and he knew he wasn't going to be arrested or killed, at least not yet. Internally, he relaxed. He still refused to say anything. He took another sip of his drink.

"Jack, the idea that the Unity is one consolidated corporation led by an undivided board is bullshit. It doesn't work that way at the top."

Jack raised an eyebrow. "I always figured that had to be the case."

Suit nodded and continued. "Anyone with two brain cells figures that out, and you have many more than two."

Recognizing the compliment, Jack raised his glass at Suit. Suit continued, "The boardroom is an everlasting combat between unrelenting enemies. There are alliances, backstabs, and turns of fate almost daily. I would guess there is a murder at least once a week based on the board infighting, all dolled up to look like an accident, of course. "

"So you want me to be part of your team?" Jack was always amused by how smart you could look by merely repeating what had already been said.

"I do."

"I am not much of a team player. You'll be disappointed."

"Oh, I doubt that. I can provide you with what you want. I like to keep my team happy."

"And what do I want?"

"From what I can see, not much—wine, women, and song, mostly. If there is anything else, just name it."

"Autonomy."

The Suit nodded and brought his hands together at his chest, leaning his elbows on the desk and intertwining his fingers. He put his two index fingers together and tapped them under his nose.

"Jack, let's get something straight. You have done well for yourself. You have built a little trade empire on the fringes of nowhere. You managed to stay under the radar until you started putting stuff together for Musgrave. Once the cynthies started making for this system, HR figured that somebody had to be supplying him with the equipment. That was your mistake. I had some of my people at HR do some research and I was impressed. Your little network is by far the biggest independent network I have ever seen in the Unity. But I have you dead to rights."

He tossed the tablet to Jack across the desk. Jack caught it with his free hand. The Suit continued, "So far my little research project is just that, mine. Anytime I choose, a simple little toss of that information to the right people and you will go down, hard. You don't have many choices here, do you?"

Dick in Suit looked at Jack with a deadpan expression. Jack recognized that he had done this before. He wondered what he had on Carla and GI Joe. Suit continued, "But it doesn't have to be that way. I have a lot to offer you. Here's the game. You take care of getting me what I need to get things done around here, and I don't pay you any more than your salary. I only pay the carriers and suppliers. But after that, I turn a blind eye to whatever it is that you bring in or trade elsewhere. Jack, I have networks you haven't even dreamed about. No more of that craft stuff. No more flea market kitsch and single bags of coffee. The need to keep your head down meant you had to stay local and keep it small enough not to make ripples. I can offer you the protection you need to take it across Unity and even international.

"If you're smart, you're already wondering why Musgrave's gene baths and tissue tanks don't show up on that when I know about them." He pointed at the tablet.

"The thought had crossed my mind. Let me guess, a nip here and a tuck there for the right people, and the right people look the other way."

"I knew I liked you." Suit again showed his unnaturally white teeth. "So what do you say?"

Jack was furious. He didn't want to play on someone's team, beholden to their good graces and subservient to their beck and call. There were always strings in a situation like that. Jack didn't do strings, but he knew there was no other option but to play along. "I don't have a choice, and I don't like being forced into things."

"Who does? But you're smart enough to know when I have you by the balls."

Jack took all the emotion out of his voice. "What do you need?"

5
Tagged

An hour later, Jack left the office with a folded piece of use-once electronic paper in his pocket, his first list of demands from his new boss. He had just enough time to get to his dinner with Lewis. His former boss' house was located not far from the admin building, but he hadn't been there since the city had moved. Once outside in the vestibule, he zipped up tight, grabbed his heads-up display, and threw it a request asking for directions. A green path now lit his way.

Jack followed, heedless of his surroundings. He decided that he had to respect Suit in a prey respects predator kind of way. He wasn't dumb. You didn't find many of that type of Admins out in the hinterlands. Suit had blocked all the exits and left one way out of the maze—his way.

Jack still had no sense of how the pieces were placed on the board or why they were placed on this little insignificant board way out in the middle of nowhere. For some reason yet to be seen, Aetna was now important to somebody, somebody big enough to drag Suit, GI Joe, and Boobs in his or her wake. Jack knew he couldn't maneuver until he could see those pieces. He had to know the board to know where the leverage lay. For now, he didn't have any options. He would do everything Suit asked, and he would wait.

Jack arrived at his destination before his mind had registered that he had left the admin building, a bright blue door inside a vestibule which had been painted a shade of pure, bright yellow. He touched the hand plate, identifying himself, and took off the heads-up, putting it in a pocket.

Julia answered the door, strained but smiling. "Come in, Jack."

Jack noticed a red and orange calico patterned jumper tucked behind one of Julia's legs, blonde curls sticking out from the sides of the long skirt which covered the warm pants Julia wore underneath. Someone was pulling down on the skirt. Julia was a rather round woman, matching the shape of her husband. To Jack's eyes, she was a typical mom, all curves and folds with little shape left. Plain of face, there was nothing pleasing to look at that Jack could see, but she was smart and quick witted, in contrast to the more plodding Lewis.

He took off his hat and coat and handed them to Julia who hung them on a coat rack. All the while, little Jo clung to her mother's skirt, and tried to stay hidden. Jack took little notice and walked past them into the living room where he found Lewis opening a bottle of wine Jack had provided him some time ago.

Without consulting, he poured three glasses of the dark red liquid, handed one to Jack and called, "Julia dear, wine." Coming in from the entry, Julia stepped down into the deep green carpet of the living room and grabbed the third glass from the tray.

Lewis held up his glass. "To the family we have been given and the family we create."

"Hear, hear, "echoed Julia.

Jack drank. He looked down to find blue eyes, blonde curls, and a calico jumper patting his leg. "Uncle Jack, you didn't say anything. You're supos' to say something when people are toasting."

Jack grinned at Jo and looked up. "Hear, hear," he said, holding up his glass to the room.

"Jo, don't correct our guests, please." Her father used a tough tone—a tone based on Lewis' day, not Jo's behavior. Jo scowled and stomped out of the room, dramatically pounding on the floor.

"You keep marching like that and some day they're going to make you a soldier, sweetie," Jack called after the retreating Jo.

Jo stopped stomping, turned to face the assembled adults, and announced, "I'm not going to be a soldier. I'm going to study comparative herpetology."

Jack almost choked on his wine. Jo stomped away, and Jack, Lewis, and Julia broke up laughing.

Jack gave Lewis a quizzical look, "What did she just say?"

"Comparative Herpetology is the study of animals that start out water breathing and end their lives breathing air."

"OK? Where did she hear about that?"

"Teddy," said Julia, standing up. "It's one of his interests. He's determined to get into the science academy. He says that if he got into the science academy, he could study what he wanted without being told what to do."

Jack thought for a second, took a sip of his wine, and said, "Well, we all have our little dreams of escape, don't we?"

"Yes, we do," said Julia with just a little too much emotion in her voice. "I have to get dinner finished." She abruptly left. Jack caught her wiping one of her eyes as she walked around the corner toward the kitchen.

Jack and Lewis chit chatted about nothing for a few minutes and were soon called to dinner. Dinner was a more somber affair than usual in the Lutnear household. Normally, one could hardly hear oneself think as several of the six Lutnears talked over each other. Lewis and Julia had four children. At 12, Teddy, the oldest, took after his father in many ways. He was thoroughly bookish, with an interest in all things natural. The eight-year-old twins Finn and Hugh were somewhat unruly. Jack tended to egg them on when possible, enjoying the chaos they created. Then there was four-year-old Josephine, all princess and completely spoiled. Tonight the kids seemed to understand not to press it. It made dinner a quieter experience than usual.

Afterward, the kids were hustled to their rooms, Princess to bed and the others left to their own devices. The three adults gathered back in the living room.

All three were silent for a couple of minutes. Lewis spoke first. "What do you make of it, Jack?"

Jack sipped the glass of wine Lewis had recently refilled. "You're asking me? I hoped you could fill me in."

Lewis distractedly played with the fringe on the throw pillow next to him in his overstuffed chair. "I'm not yet sure what to make of it. I might know more than you, but I want to hear what you think first."

"We're important," said Jack. "I don't yet know why, but for some reason, Godforsaken Aetna is important to someone."

Julia nodded her agreement.

Jack continued. "Have you ever heard of any ship having trouble getting H2 for fusion?"

"No, I haven't, Jack. This is just what I was saying to Julia. The whole thing doesn't make any sense. How could we have a processing shortage? Our plant has had idle workers for years because we were running at 50% of capacity. If we had a shortage, wouldn't we be putting them to work?" Agitated, Lewis gestured wildly with the glass of wine in his hand, threatening to spill the bright red liquid on the carpet. Any time Lewis talked, he gestured with his arms like he was conducting an orchestra.

"Jack, aren't you afraid you're going to be arrested?" Julia always asked the pointed question, shepherding the conversation toward more important matters.

"Suit, I mean Randall, scared the shit out of me this afternoon when he showed me the list of items they know I smuggled in and out of here. For several minutes I kept waiting for what's his name, GI Joe, to come bouncing into the room to take me away. He had enough on me for about twelve death sentences. Instead, he recruited me. I get him what he needs to increase production, and he'll look the other way, while I make some money on the side."

Julia looked pale. "They know?"

Jack nodded. "Almost everything. Just about every transaction."

"Do they know who you delivered to?"

Jack suddenly realized what Julia was worried about. "Probably not. They don't have access to the paper records, which we destroy as soon as the goods are delivered and payment made. Randall had recon work done on me through HR before he came here. I'm sure the best they could have done are the falsified electronic records. That would give him what came and went and nothing more. I think everyone is safe, but we all have to be careful right now until I know more."

"Jack, you're underestimating them," said Julia.

"Oh, Julia, don't go scaring him. This is difficult on all of us as it is," Lewis chided his wife.

Julia responded to her husband's patronizing words by raising her voice slightly. "Lewis, I am not scaring him. You're the one who isn't seeing what is happening."

"I know it's bad, Julia, but sometimes you just have to make life lemonade from life lemons."

Jack ignored Lewis' butchered metaphor and turned the conversation back. He smiled at Julia, keeping his tone even and calm. He thought of himself calming an over-emotional child. "What's happening, Julia?"

Julia turned to her husband, and spoke with calm intensity, like smoldering steel. "Lewis, you and I came here because we wanted to raise our children away from the pressure to perform for Unity. Almost every person here on Aetna has built a life on this Godforsaken snowball because they didn't want to be in the center of things when it came to Unity. We wanted to be in the hinterlands.

"Well, for whatever reason, we are no longer the hinterlands. We are in the middle of things, right in the thick of all the rigidity, corruption, and soulless inhumanity that is Unity Corporation. How do you think people on Aetna are going to deal with that?"

She turned on Jack. He got the distinct feeling that Julia felt that the world of men was conspiring against her and her family. The emotion behind her voice made Jack feel like he had a target on his chest. "You're no different, Jack. You don't want to play for a team, to calculate all the angles, to climb to the top of the heap. If you did, you could have done that long ago.

"Jack, you're happy running your own little business off in the corner, as long as it's yours. Guess what, Jack? It isn't yours any longer. You're at the beck and call of someone else who doesn't give a rat's ass what happens to you and needs you for only as long as you serve their purposes. All the looking the other way and sex with that HR slut won't change that central fact. Mark it down, Jack. From this day forward, you're somebody's pet, being trained to bark on command, to sit, and to roll over when they want you to."

Jack let the silence linger. This little tirade amused him. Julia was probably more right than he wanted to admit, but the personal attack didn't make it any easier for him to listen. He wasn't going to give her any ground at this point. "I don't know. The sex was pretty good."

"I told you!" Julia looked at Lewis with smug satisfaction. "I told you that no one would put a slut like that on their team without deploying her. Jack's an easy mark for that kind of thing."

"Julia! That was uncalled for!" Jack was surprised by the tone Lewis used with his wife.

"Lewis Lutnear, if you cannot think straight about what is happening around you, there is no hope for you. Lemonade from lemons is not going to cut it when they start imposing Unity discipline on our little community. Jack better have his head straight by then, or he will be in trouble just like the rest of us, but his problem is that his gonads do most of the thinking while his brain is just along for the ride."

Jack decided the conversation had gone far enough. He stood. "Thank you, Julia, for a wonderful dinner, and the advice. Lewis, I will see you around the office." He walked into the hall with Lewis in his wake.

As Jack was shrugging on his jacket, Lewis came to stand next to him. Speaking quietly, he said, "I'm sorry about Julia. This has really torn her up. I tried to talk with Director Savage about Cora Hanson, and she threatened to send me to reeducation for questioning HR personnel. I think she was trying to intimidate me, nothing to worry about. Cora is a good friend of Julia's."

Jack was relieved to understand Julia's attitude better. "Well, that makes sense of things." He took a moment to look Lewis in the eye. "Do be careful, Lewis. I don't know what to make of all of this yet."

Lewis nodded vigorously. "I'm already looking for a place to go. This isn't a safe place for our family any longer. There is a directorship open on an asteroid over near New Amsterdam which might work. I'm looking into it."

Jack put his hand on Lewis' shoulder and leaned in conspiratorially. "That's a good idea. I'll see what I can do with Carla."

"I would appreciate that, Jack. I really would."

Jack stepped out into the cold and headed to find some sleep in one of the guest rooms in the admin building.

Somewhere in the middle of his sleep cycle, his heads-up bleeped him—someone wanted to talk to him. It took a little for him to come to and make sense of the bleating machine on the night stand. He put it on. The sensation was like nothing he had ever felt. The border between reality and what the device demanded to show him blurred and then ripped itself to shreds. He lost control over his body. He couldn't move. He was invaded, his mind hacked. *This isn't supposed to happen with a heads-up*, thought Jack. He desperately sought some connection with his limbs, and, finding none, his adrenaline crystallized into vibrant, liquid rage. He waited, impotent, held to his bed against his will—only his eyes were allowed to move.

The door opened and Gunderson strode into the darkened room with a black bag in one hand. Dressed in black and gray fatigues and a black beret, he no longer wore the purple uniform of the Gendarme. He sat next to Jack on the bed.

He smiled. "Jack, you and I didn't get to meet this morning." His voice was gravelly and deep, hard edged, like someone familiar with barking orders and being respected.

He opened the black bag and took out a pair of nano-carbon surgical gloves and slowly put them on as he continued to speak. "I wanted to stop by tonight and welcome you to the team." Snap. On went one glove.

"Jack, on Team Randall, we all have one goal and that is to make sure Timothy Randall rises to the top." Snap—a second glove.

"For the next few months, Jack, you're going to be watched like a hawk." Gunderson opened the bag and began rifling inside. He glanced up at Jack. "We want to find out what you're made of, Jack. We want to know how you tick, and we want to make sure you're a good fit for our mission. Consider yourself on probation. If at any point in time we don't like what we see, we can and will hurt you in a time and place of our own choosing."

Gunderson held up a surgical laser cutter and flicked it on. Jack felt his adrenaline spike. Terror flooded him as his impotent mind desperately tried to move his limbs. He tried to speak but no sound came from his gaping mouth. It slapped open and closed like a fish seeking water.

"And if we ever find that you have betrayed us in any way, be certain, we will kill you." With that, Gunderson reached down, picked up Jack's left arm, and slowly cut off his hand with the laser cutter.

Pain erupted. Through a distant tunnel, Jack could hear himself screaming, although his mouth didn't make any noise.

When he had finished, Gunderson stood and put his gloves and cutter back in his bag. "See you around, Jack." He smiled. Numb with pain, Jack could hear himself whimper, but he couldn't hear right. His whimper sounded like it was coming through cotton. He stared at the dismembered hand lying next to the cauterized stump. The door closed.

The device held Jack for a moment longer, and then as if someone had snapped their fingers, it let him go. The cotton was gone, and Jack's whimper became loud in his ears. Jack grabbed at the stump, holding it against his chest. He closed his eyes against pain which no longer existed. He looked down, expecting to see a bloody and burned stump but instead saw a hand, healthy and complete, still attached to his arm. He tried to move his fingers, and they moved.

It took Jack a good minute of checking out his hand before his mind would believe that all the pain, the smell of burning flesh, and the severed hand on the bed had all been illusions from the mind hack.

As he relaxed, bile rose in his throat. Jack ripped the heads-up off his head and threw it across the room. He rolled over on the bed and vomited into the waste can. He stumbled from his bed, stripped off his underwear, turned on the shower in the bathroom, and stepped into the warm water. Jack took three or four deep breaths, getting control of his panic and rage. He focused.

An hour later, he walked, dazed, out into the cold and silent light of the Aetna day and hailed a cab. Jack tried to keep himself focused on the present. He had brought his overnight bag with him. He wouldn't ever be going back to that room.

Walking out the door, he had tucked the heads-up into his bag, silently grateful it wasn't broken. It had hit the wall hard, replacement was expensive, and at times could take weeks.

After hailing the cab, Jack took off his wrist wallet and added it to his overnight bag with the heads-up. He walked back into the admin building and handed the bag to the night watchman at the front desk, saying that he would be back to pick it up later. He then returned to wait for his cab.

Although it was light, the streets were deserted. His jacket felt warm. Jack was grateful. He took a careful survey of the skyline. He had hoped he might get lucky and see the hospital tower from the street, but he couldn't. The eight-story commercial building blocked the view in front of him, and the towering admin building blocked his view in the other direction.

The taxi arrived. He barely remembered hailing it. He lethargically walked to it, allowing the cold air to sting his cheeks. If this was going to work, he had to focus. He got in.

"Destination?"

"No destination. Slowly circle the administration building." Jack had decided what he was going to do while in the shower.

The car pulled into the air.

Jack didn't know where Musgrave lived, but one thing he knew, he wouldn't be putting his heads-up display on to find out. He also had no intentions of entering another building or public vestibule until he spoke to Musgrave. His entrance would automatically be noted, and if Gunderson hadn't been lying, the cameras would follow him.

The taxi circled. Jack wanted to speak to Musgrave without Team Randall knowing what he was doing. In order to do that, not only would he have to avoid being seen by the cameras, but he would also have to leave his wrist wallet and his heads-up behind, because they constantly interacted with the cloud and could be used to track his whereabouts.

Looking out the windows, Jack got the lay of the land in the new city. He had visited Musgrave's home once. He thought he could remember what it looked like if he could find it. It would likely be parked somewhere near the hospital. The hospital complex wasn't hard to spot—five rather flat and large buildings laid out in a cross with heated connections. Jack worked out his route through the connected vestibules and streets between them. After about five minutes, he was sure enough of his surroundings to have the taxi put down exactly where he had boarded it. They would know that he left the building, got in a cab, and got out again at the same spot. Jack figured they would know what he intended to do. He just hoped he could succeed.

Jack stepped out into the cold and started walking. It was close to minus 15, a relatively warm day on Aetna. He glanced at the time. It was 3:00 AM Unity standard time.

Musgrave would be in bed. Jack threaded his way down the icy street, trying to stay close to buildings in the shadows. He wasn't equipped to hike in the great outdoors. He was wearing flat soled dress shoes. He had to be careful. Luckily, he wasn't standing on sheet ice. This surface was uneven and had some fresh snow on it. Threading his way several buildings south of the admin building, he found the residential neighborhood he had spotted from the air. He ducked into its interconnected vestibules. Residential sections didn't tend to have cameras. If he was lucky, he had just disappeared from view.

It took Jack 45 minutes to find his way through empty streets, open spaces, and neighborhood vestibules to the residential neighborhood located next to the hospital. He was warm by the time he got there. He could have gotten there in 30 minutes if he hadn't felt the need to avoid public buildings and skirt widely around the hospital.

Jack's plan had been to walk up and down the vestibules until he found the home he remembered. Instead, he caught a lucky break. Hospitals always had people coming on and off shift. As he came around a corner, he nearly ran into an older woman wearing hospital scrubs and a white coat. She had her gray hair pulled up in a bun. As she passed, she gave him a funny look. He figured she must not have liked what she saw, because she grabbed his arm and said, "Can I help you?"

"I'm looking for Musgrave's home."

She furrowed her brow and said, "It's behind you. One street over about three houses down." She gestured as she talked. She followed up with, "You sure you can get there on your own?"

Jack just nodded and thanked her. Gratefully, she let him go on his way. Five minutes later, Jack stood outside the door.

Jack nearly pressed his hand to the palm reader when he realized that all the work he had done to get there undetected would be for nothing if the reader sent his location and identity to team Randall. Instead, he pounded on the door and waited. After a moment, he pounded again.

After another long pause, a tall bleary-eyed man in his sixties answered the door in a gray robe which perfectly matched the wavy gray hair which graced the head on the top of his towering lean frame.

"Jack? What are you doing here? You look like hell."

Jack maintained an impassive expression and a neutral voice. "May I come in?"

Musgrave nodded, took a look both directions down the vestibule and, seeing it empty, moved back out of Jack's way. Jack stepped out of the cold. Musgrave's living quarters couldn't have been more of a contrast to the Lutnear's. Lewis' chaotic home was full of well used and abused kitsch. Nothing seemed to match and there was certainly no theme carried throughout the space, unless one counted the wear and tear caused by children.

Musgrave's living space felt Spartan in contrast. As soon as he entered, he was reminded again of the first time he had been there. This was the home of a mind which thrived on order and deliberation. He got the feeling that every single object in the home, from the art to the furnishings and the décor, had been chosen with a purpose. Case in point, Jack noticed that the robe which Musgrave wore complemented the shade of sky blue on the wall, which matched the color of his eyes. With few furnishings and organized spaces, it was a very muted and sedate living space for the home of a Unity citizen.

Jack breathed and let the surrounding order calm him. He sat in a gel chair which automatically adjusted to his ergonomics and let his breath out.

Still standing by the door, Musgrave looked at Jack. "What brings you here, Jack?" Musgrave casually pointed some kind of weapon at him.

Jack didn't answer. Instead, he raised an eyebrow at the gun and waited for an explanation.

"It's a neuro-overload device. It fires a specific frequency of electromagnetic radiation which will shut down your nervous system. It can stun you or kill you. You won't know the difference—unless you wake up." At this point, Musgrave shrugged. "It appeals to me as a doctor."

Jack tried to break the tension. "I'm disappointed. You didn't get that from me." He pointed at the gun. Musgrave stood silently at the door, still pointing the gun at him. Jack continued. "Do you always greet your guests in this fashion?"

"No." He paused and waited for a beat, then repeated his question. "What brings you here, Jack?"

"I've had a bit of a scare tonight. I got mind jacked by the security troll Randall brought with him."

Musgrave stepped away from the door and let it close behind him. He came and sat in an identical chair facing Jack, still pointing the gun at him. "Sorry, Jack. I haven't had time yet to figure out what is going on around here. I've been working trauma shifts in the ER over the weekend. All I know is that Lewis is out and some VP from admin replaced him. You'll have to slow down and catch me up. Who is Randall?"

Jack related the events of the previous day to him, starting with arriving at his office on the orbital. He was vague about his meeting with Savage, figuring it wasn't germane to their discussion. Musgrave listened attentively. When Jack finished, Musgrave put down his gun on the end table next to him. Jack noted that he didn't put the safety on.

"Well, Jack, at least he had to use the heads-up to get to you. That is some comfort. It means they haven't yet figured out how to get the little buggers to broadcast loudly enough to avoid needing a device."

"Little buggers?"

"The nanites Gunderson used to take over your mind tonight. Admin and HR have been using them for awhile. My sources say that R&D is trying to get them to be able to broadcast loudly enough to project into the cloud. If that were to happen, they wouldn't need to use a heads-up device to take over your mind. They could just do so at any time."

"They put nanites in my brain? When?"

Musgrave grinned and chuckled a bit. "Jack, it isn't that hard. It's just like the emergency medical nanites we give you if you show up in the emergency room. We usually inject them, but you don't have to. They're microscopic. They could have been in the drink Randall gave you. The question isn't how they got in there; the question is, what are we going to do about them?"

Jack felt his pulse rise. The idea of intraspace repellent enough, but the notion that Randall had placed microscopic robots in his brain and could take over his mind almost at will made him feel trapped in a way which nothing else had. Jack answered Musgrave with more irritation than he would have liked to show. He was off his game. "What do you mean what are we going to do about them? We're going to get them out! That's what we're going to do."

Musgrave stayed calm. "Jack, it's a little more complicated than that. You live in a very quiet, out of the way part of the Unity, so you don't understand this, but observational nanites are a standard political recruiting tool. In the rough and tumble world of Unity corporation, team leaders want to be able to make sure that you're not planning to double-cross them in some way. Most team players have them." Seeing that this didn't comfort Jack in any way, Musgrave added hastily, "but we have options."

Jack felt his eyes stray to the gun on the table. Part of him wanted to run. "I'm listening. But what you say doesn't make sense, because they can't be activated without the heads-up or a cap. If I'm going to try to double cross Team Randall in some way, I am going to do it in the real world—in meat space."

"Yes, Jack, you would, but you're a bit of an anachronism in that way. You ran your black market in a very old fashioned way, on paper. I think that is a major reason you have been so successful.

"Most people are much more scared of a micro bug or camera than they are of the seeming anonymity of the intraspace. Most nefarious deals now take place in encrypted intraspace. The irony is that the Board spends very little time watching meat space any more. Nanites like those inside of you keep you from doing anything in the cloud which you wouldn't want them to know about. That little scene tonight was Gunderson's way of letting you know that Team Randall was watching."

Jack felt his thoughts bounce around in the nexus between sheer terror, anger, and an increasing paranoia about heads-up devices and intraspace caps. They tended to favor anger. Jack noticed his flat tone as he talked. "You said we had options. What are they?"

"Well, there are several things we can do. We can do as you suggest and make a clean break of it. A simple EMP will disable every nanite in your body and flush them from your system. Then we add back the ones needed for medical purposes, and you're on your way. But as soon as we do that, you are in a world of hurt. From then on, you're a marked man. People who flush their nanites—without a plan—usually end up dead.

"We could try to hack them. In the major cities, there are places where you can go, and they will hack your bots for you. Theoretically, this allows you to move freely in intraspace without being watched, but even that is tricky. If the logs of your activity deviate even an iota from what they are supposed to show, standard procedure would be for Team Randall will kill you, slowly, painfully.

"The third and, probably best option, is to try to stalemate them somehow. Team Randall can watch what you do in intraspace, and you can keep them from taking over when you don't want them to do so. They get what they want most—the ability to check up on you—and you get what you want—control of your own body. Team leaders usually accept this arrangement, but they aren't going to tell you that up front. They want you scared, so you have to make the call and hope they don't dispose of you for disloyalty."

Musgrave was silent for a second. Jack allowed the silence to linger, thinking through what he had just been told. Musgrave stood and left the room. When he came back, he was dressed in hospital scrubs, the iridescent antibacterial copper threads reflecting the late day glow from the skylight above them. Jack hadn't moved. He was still staring at the gun. Musgrave walked over to a small metal dry bar located in the corner of the room, poured a glass of something brown, and brought it back to Jack. "You look like hell."

"Thanks," said Jack. "I don't feel so good, either." He took the drink from Musgrave's outstretched arm, enjoying the astringent smells of the brown liquid before letting it warm his throat. Jack looked up from his drink. "What do we have to do to block the bots?"

6
In Deep

It was dark, just before 5:20 AM, when Jack climbed into a cab outside of the admin building. The sun had just set. He had ten minutes to make the shuttle at the airport. Unless he messaged the pilot, he wasn't likely to get there in time. As the cab lifted off the ground, Jack looked down at the device in his hands. He clenched his jaw. Jack recognized that no matter when he put that thing on, the first time was going to suck. He was determined not to let Team Randall win, and he needed to be on that shuttle.

Once he had made the decision to keep the bots but block their ability to take control, it had taken Musgrave a bit to get things set up at his home. As soon as he had agreed, Musgrave had made a quick trip to intraspace and contacted one of his nurses at the hospital. The nurse had arrived at his home around a half an hour later with an injection patch hooked up to a data pad and a bunch of different vials. After the nurse got the IV patch attached painlessly, Jack sat on the couch while the data pad and the nurse did all the work. The procedure took about 20 minutes.

Somewhere during this whole thing, Musgrave explained what was to happen. Blocking observation nanites followed a two pronged approach. The first line of defense was to upload software to the heads-up device which would keep the observers from being able to broadcast codes which could cause unwanted sensory experience—basically the kind of anti-venom, anti-virus, and anti-icebreaker software used to keep your email safe. Except this software targeted a different set of Trojans and cyber-grenades which most citizens of Unity didn't even know existed.

The second line of defense was the procedure Jack had done at Musgrave's. It deployed recon nanites to investigate the bots already in place. This was done by tricking them into giving themselves away by putting a simulated heads-up on Jack's head. Once recon was completed, the data pad identified the types of bots being used and tailored a set of counter bots which would attach themselves to the observation nanites and then block their ability to receive commands which would alter Jack's sensory perception or other brain functions. It wouldn't keep them from observing and reporting, but it would effectively keep them from exercising control.

Sitting in the cab as it rose and took off toward the shuttle terminal, Jack put on the heads-up. It didn't yet have corrective software, but he did have the defensive nanites in place, and he decided he wasn't going to let anyone scare him away from living his life. Besides, he decided he still needed to make it look like he was still on the team, at least for now.

Jack sent the message without a hitch and was soon trying to get some sleep as the shuttle blasted its way toward the orbital. As he shut his eyes, he felt his body begin to relax after the previous night's events. He felt back in control, but his mind had a new kind of alertness which had not been there before. He slept fitfully and awoke with a start as the shuttle gently bumped to a stop, nose into the orbital. Jack grabbed his overnight bag from the overhead and walked to the office.

He opened the door and stepped in just after 8:40, coat in one hand, bag in the other. He paced quickly through the foyer, past Molly's desk. She was in Joe's office discussing something with him. Jack wasn't ready for questions. He had to think through what he wanted to tell his staff. He threw his coat and bag on a chair next to his door, locked it, and sat down behind his desk.

From a drawer he pulled out a pair of form fitting, carbon surgical gloves. Only then did he go back to his coat and remove the use-once electronic paper which he had been given by Randall yesterday. Electronic paper, whether it was use-once or not, could easily record the fingerprints of who had touched it and time stamp them. If he could help it, no one from his office would leave any electronic traces on this stuff. Plausible deniability was their best defense. He put the paper on a piece of black felt which he also retrieved from the desk for this purpose.

Jack looked through the list, all of it regular office supplies which couldn't be accessed through requisitions for months but were needed soon. A few items were obviously for the new staff that Randall had brought with him—nothing extraordinary and nothing difficult to get. In it all, he saw the usual efficiency of Cathie, Lewis' former assistant.

Jack sat back and thought for a moment or two and decided what he wanted to say to his staff. He was about to put on his heads-up display when he decided against it. Defense bots or no, he would now be avoiding that thing for mundane uses like talking to Molly. He stood, walked over to the door, and poked his head out into the lobby. Hearing his door open, Molly looked up as he spoke. "Staff meeting in my office, in five."

Molly nodded, her eyes scanning him intently for any sign. "I cleared everyone's schedule yesterday. We obviously have things to talk about. You look like hell."

Jack managed a small laugh. "Thanks."

"You might fool the boys with a chuckle like that, but you aren't fooling me. How bad is it?"

"We're in deep. We'll talk about it in a minute."

Jack sat down at his desk to wait. He folded his hands and just stared at the cap and heads-up sitting on his desk. He wondered if he would ever feel comfortable using them again. He pulled a data pad over to him from across the desk and gave it verbal commands to bring up his email. He grabbed a protein bar from his desk and opened a sealed wrapper of dried fish he kept there in case he needed something to eat. He was just beginning to read his first message when his staff trooped in the door.

Molly picked up his things from the first chair and walked them to the coat rack in the corner of his office. Robert and Joe found seats. When Molly returned and had sat down, Jack started.

"Well, who wants to tell me what you know and how it went here yesterday?"

Molly began before the others could even put their thoughts together. "There isn't much to tell. We had a regular lax inspection from HR. The only difference was Inspector Cox told us he would be opening an office on the station. He asked for space 3G and quarters for three. He was young. Apparently, he's married and has a new little citizen on the way—a model Unity family."

Molly's bit of sarcasm about family would have brought a reprimand in many offices. One of the reasons she and Todd chose life on a far off station was their choice not to have children. The prejudice and persecution of childless married couples in most major cities was intense. Sexual liberty was never in question in the Unity—just don't get married. From the corporate perspective, marriage and fidelity were for children—intimacy and fulfillment be damned. If you felt you could be with the same person for 18 to 20 years, the Unity wanted you to make a baby. Yet another reason Jack avoided both marriage and fidelity.

Often, neither spouse in a childless professional couple could find work. Unless she was incredibly talented, there were few jobs available for married women. Most of society felt that a married woman who worked took a job from a man who needed it to support his family.

Normally, Jack would have let the comment pass. But today it sat in the air like a sour smell, and he was forced to decide what to do about it. "Molly, I couldn't care less about whether or not you have kids... Scratch that, I don't want you to have kids because then I'll lose my best employee; no offense guys."

Joe just smiled and shook his head. Robert pretended like Jack had shot him in the chest and then said, "None taken."

Jack continued. "But, things just changed around here pretty radically yesterday. Right now I can't afford to see you get yourself in trouble. So I can't have you saying things like that in the office anymore. Although you're free to think them all you'd like."

Molly blushed with anger. Jack could tell that he had pissed her off. She raised her eyebrows, and said with a smirk, "You're scared, Jack. I don't think I've ever seen you scared like this before."

Jack figured it was the lack of sleep and the events of the night before, but he was highly irritated by Molly today. Her habit of announcing all the little things she had "discovered" about Jack irked him right then. If she thought he was scared, that was her problem. Bringing it up in a staff meeting made it his problem.

Jack saw his anger color his response. "Molly, let me tell you about my day yesterday. Yesterday I had the distinct privilege of having a VP from admin show me every item we've shipped in the last five to six years. There was enough bad stuff there for 12 death sentences, if I counted correctly. Then under the penalty of death, I was recruited to join his team, to help him ascend through the glorious ranks of the Unity, which means all of you were recruited too, and we have to do everything in our power to keep our new corporate overlords happy. So we're in deep, Molly. If you want to end up with a long sentence to a work camp, reeducation, or worse, you go right ahead and shoot your mouth off any time you like. Right now, though, my advice would be to cool it until we can get the lay of the land, because none of this makes sense. Is that clear?"

For a couple of seconds, the room was absolutely silent. None of the four of them moved. Jack just looked Molly hard in the eye. She turned white as a sheet and answered, "Crystal clear."

Jack went over the previous day. He was rather vague regarding his appointment with Carla in the afternoon, saying he had "established a working relationship" with her. And mostly for Molly's benefit, but also for the others, Jack briefly explained what had happened to him last night. Jack wasn't sure which was more effective, his actual description of what happened or the cold, detached way in which he described it. When he was finished, Molly was shaking, and Joe looked like he was about ready to piss his pants. Only Robert looked like he wasn't surprised by any of it.

He spoke up. "So what's your plan, Jack?"

"At this point, I think that we play along. So far what they have requested isn't anything worth getting upset about. I think we see what happens."

Molly was shaking her head before he was even finished. "What's your end game, Jack? I don't want to become another company stooge, and I can't believe you want to do that either."

Jack answered calmly this time. "I won't ever be anyone's stooge, Molly. I don't have an end game at this point, because I don't understand all the pieces on the board. I don't even know what this is about. For now, I don't think we have much of a choice but to play along."

Molly nodded her agreement, "The problem is, Jack, they aren't going to show you the pieces. You're dealing with people and places way beyond your ability to control. If what you say is true, I don't think you'll be able to get control back. They will use you and spit you out when they're done. If we want to stay in control, then we need to find a way out, an exit."

As much as she occasionally got under his skin, Jack liked having Molly on his team just for moments like this, when she spoke his exact thoughts. "Molly, if you see one, let me know. In the meantime, in order to find an exit for all of us, I think we should do a little research on Randall and company. Start with the innocent stuff. Just run the regular queries you would run if you got a new boss, Molly. You know, the official news nets and maybe one or two of the less-radical black nets. Make a basic HR inquiry. All the stuff you would do if you were thrilled to have a new boss and wanted to suck up to him. Let's find out where this guy comes from. I don't want you to try and get anything more detailed. I will talk with someone down on the docks about getting it for us. For now, we are thrilled to be part of Team Randall."

He switched his focus to Robert. "Does this hydrogen shortage thing make any sense to you?"

Robert had sat through the whole meeting with his arms crossed on top of his modest potbelly. "No, it makes no sense at all. Prices on the wholesale level are rock bottom. If anything, I would say we have an oversupply. Hell, they've had Bonnie running at half speed for over three years now."

"So, why don't you spend some time down on the docks and see if you can get any leads on what is taking place here? Talk to Bob over on the *Goliath* or Ricky on the *Superman*. If anyone is going to know what this is about, it'll be the tanker captains."

Jack turned and looked at Joe. He had always looked young. He had an innocent face and wore his blond hair close-cropped. At the age of 28, he looked 16. He had a clean-cut look and, in general, his behavior followed. Jack had never seen him take home a girl from the bar, and only once had he seen him drink more than a pint in one sitting. Of course, Joe knew about the black market in the office, but Jack had never had him involved. Joe's job had been to keep the station running, while Jack did other things.

"Joe, for now I want it to be business as usual. I want you to keep your nose totally clean. In fact, I want you to become a perfect Unity choir boy. We are going to change our policies in this office a little. Everything will be done by the book on this station going forward. We'll get the word out gently in front of you so you don't have a riot on your hands when you go out for inspections, but I want everyone on this station to be toeing all the lines. We are going to make this place a model Unity station. So when you see something which isn't according to standard, put on that 'aw shucks' charm you have and then ticket them. Got it?"

Joe nodded, but looked a little confused.

"See if you can't get cozy with our new HR inspector along the way. Say you've hated the way I ran things and you're glad to finally have a free hand to make it right. You know everyone hates the audit division and HR. We're supposed to be on the same page about compliance. Let's see if we can live up to that reputation a little."

"Ok, but why?"

Jack looked him in the eye. "The honest truth is I don't know if we're going to be able to get everyone out of this. Being the good boy keeps another card in your hand. It may end up that you can stay here longer than the rest of us and just exit out through a transfer somewhere down the road. In the meantime, gaining someone's trust in HR can't hurt either. We might get information that we wouldn't have otherwise."

Joe thought about that for a second and then nodded his head. "So we're breaking up the band."

Smart boy, thought Jack. "Something like that," he said with a grin.

Jack and his staff took the next half hour to discuss basic safety precautions when dealing with Randall and his people. They decided they wouldn't be going out to eat with anyone from the team because of the danger of nanites. They also decided they weren't handling any paperwork without some kind of gloves from now on. Jack didn't want his staff leaving fingerprints on anything, and he supposed paper could be another way to deliver nanites. Jack asked everyone to keep calm, and, for now, their black market activities would be restricted to what they could do for Randall. Jack didn't want to give Randall and company any more reason to take them down than they already had.

Once the meeting broke up, the rest of the day went along as reasonably as could be expected under the circumstances. Nobody managed to get any serious work done. All four of them seemed to be distracted, and the mood was somber.

Late in the afternoon, Jack sent Molly out to talk with shopkeepers and other station personnel. He wanted to give them a couple of days' warning before Joe changed his ways, and to let them know that HR was now on station. Jack feared he could have a riot on his hands if things tightened up without warning. It was going to be hard enough on personnel who had known only one way of doing business their whole lives.

He had a headache. He was looking over the same inspection records for the third time without comprehending them when a name caught his attention, *The Clarion. Clarion* was captained by Gloria Soren, a woman Jack found helpful on occasion; although she tended to deal in items which Jack hadn't felt the need to have around until yesterday, like weapons. He flipped through the rest of the manifests, hurriedly signed his paperwork, and grabbed his things.

He dropped his overnight bag at home before heading down the stairs several levels to the docks. In order to make it look legitimate, he brought along some form or other which he had decided he needed Captain Soren to fill out. The glory of the Unity bureaucracy was there was always something which he could decide on a whim he needed filled out. Forms gave him and his staff legitimate excuses to interact with merchant marine crews.

The living quarters, offices, and commercial areas of the Aetna orbital in which the 10,000 residents made their home occupied a small fraction of its vast bulk. The great majority of the station was dedicated to docks for commercial vehicles, warehouses, and fuel storage. Jack had always thought that while Aetna orbital wasn't a dedicated commerce center, its location closer to one of the interstellar gates would have made it an ideal place to store goods brought out from the inner planets deeper in Sicily's gravity well. But that was too difficult for the Unity to comprehend in their top-down linear thinking. Aetna orbital remained by and large a hydrogen storage and refueling facility.

Jack stepped out onto the docks one level above the refueling stations. This was the level on which crews disembarked. It resembled a cheap small-town shuttle port, much like the one on the surface of Aetna. Except here, instead of adverts for the latest Unity consumer goods, Mother Unity saw fit to put up HR posters warning against the evils of STDs and drunkenness—and to extol the virtues of marriage and children. Jack walked past docking gates extended to hulking ships until he came to bay 13.

He put his hand on the palm reader on the outside of the airlock, pinging the bridge. Somewhere on the hulking beast of a ship, an officer's heads-up registered that Chief Inspector Halloway was at the airlock looking to board. Of all Jack's many titles, Chief Inspector was the one title which a ship docked at the Aetna orbital could not ignore. As an Inspector with the Unity Audit division, Jack had a right to enter a docked vessel 24 hours a day.

A moment later, the deck officer on the bridge of *The Clarion* replied on the com, "Shipman Jones will escort you to the captain's quarters, sir."

Jack waited at the door, arms crossed loosely, leaning against the bulkhead. A couple of minutes later, shipman Jones appeared at the door. Jones was short, red-haired, freckled, slightly paunchy, and male. His gender made him a bit of an oddity on *The Clarion*. Soren tended to keep an almost all female crew, but, like Jack, she respected talent where she saw it. Jones must be good at something.

"Right this way, sir," he said, while looking at his shoes. He turned without ever looking at Jack and tromped away, giving him the back of his red jumpsuit.

Jack quietly followed the reflective letters which spelled out *Clarion* on the back of the suit through the corridors of the ship until Jones stopped at a door. Without saying a word, he pressed the pad and waited until he heard Soren's voice from within, commanding them to enter.

Jones opened the door, finally looked Jack in the eye, and gestured for him to go in. He followed, stood stiffly, and waited until Soren said "Dismissed" without looking up from her data pad. Jack sat in one of two chairs facing her desk. She continued to work. "He's good at computers."

Jack raised one corner of his mouth in a grin. "I figured it had to be something like that."

"He's also good in bed."

Jack laughed. "That I doubt."

Gloria looked up from her work, smiling, ran a hand through her wavy dark hair and looked at Jack. "Never judge a book by its cover, Jack." She looked Jack over. A worried expression crossed her face.

Jack rolled his eyes. "You know I don't read books, Gloria. I like things to look at. The interesting part *is* the cover." Gloria just shook her head and smirked. Jack continued, "And before you say anything—yes, I know I look like hell. It's nothing a good night of sleep won't fix."

"So, what's so important that it brings you my way instead of heading off to your bunk?"

"Supplies and information."

Gloria put down her data pad and looked him over. She leaned back in her chair and put her arms behind her head. In a cautious tone, she asked "What's up?"

"I need a fletch gun, ammunition, anti-bot software to protect from a mind jack, and all the information you can get me on one Administrative Vice President Timothy Randall and his team."

Gloria was silent. Her face turned sober. "Jack, I should tell you to get the hell off my ship. You don't have to use that stuff out here in the provinces. That's why you're out here. What kind of trouble are you in?"

"Trouble which came to me. VP Randall is in charge down on the surface, and we have HR staff opening offices here. I got recruited yesterday. I'm trying to find an exit, but so far VP Dick in a Suit has blocked every path except the ones he wants me to take."

"Did you get tagged?"

"Tagged?"

Gloria smiled at Jack's lack of knowledge. "Botted, bagged—you know, little robots in your brain watching your every move in intraspace?"

Jack nodded. "They made contact last night. It wasn't pleasant."

"It never is. They intend to intimidate."

"Musgrave down on the surface did the defense bot work this morning. I just need good software for my heads-up."

"So why do you need the gun?"

"I don't trust any of them, and I don't want to end up dead."

Gloria folded her hands and put them on the desk. She leaned in a little. "Jack, I'll get you the gun, but you have to hear me on this first. I've delivered weapons to twelve people who have been tagged. Of those, ten of them ended up dead. The other two got reeducation. Your best bet right now is to play along. You're owned."

"Oh, I'm playing along, all right. I just don't intend to find myself strapped in a chair going through re-ed. I'd rather go down swinging. I promise, I won't use it until I don't have a choice."

"Suit yourself." Gloria shrugged. She was silent for a few seconds, looking absentmindedly down at the data pad on her desk while she thought. Without looking up, she spoke. "Why is a VP sitting out here in the middle of nowhere? Something isn't right about that."

Jack sat still, letting her think. After a pause he asked, "Got any thoughts about that?"

Gloria looked up. "A couple. Nothing concrete."

"They're probably better than mine. Can I hear them?"

"Well, there are only two explanations. Either Randall has been sent down for punishment, which is a distinct possibility, or Aetna suddenly matters to someone on the board of directors somehow. There can't be any other explanation. The question is, which is it? Did he say why he was here?"

"He said that Cowhill signed an order giving him the post because there was an H2 shortage which needed attention. He has a mandate to triple production in two years here on Aetna."

"It's not a very good cover story. The H2 shortage doesn't exist, that's for sure. In a funny way, that makes me think that he's following the company line. I would guess that someone smart enough to make VP could come up with a better cover story than this if it were punishment.

Plus, he seems directed toward a task, like he has something to accomplish while here."

"He did say that his specialty was in system development."

Gloria raised her eyebrows and nodded slowly at this. "Well, that settles it for me. Mother Unity wants more H2, and Aetna is going to provide it. Weird though, there isn't a shortage. I wonder what Cowhill is thinking?" The last sentence she said to herself, almost forgetting that Jack was in the room.

"Well, Gloria, that's what I want you to find out for me."

Remembering him, she looked at Jack again. "If you want the gun, it's going to cost you $110,000 for all three items and the information you want. Can you swing that?"

"90 is the best I can do."

Gloria sighed. "You know I hate haggling. Make it 105 and you have a deal."

"100."

Gloria smiled. "$102,000. I'll be back in about three weeks with what you need. I kind of like you, Jack. You make sure you're staying safe. Ok?"

"Always." Jack put a piece of electronic paper down on Captain Soren's desk as he stood. "Electronic short form environmental inspection. Get it filled out and back to me before you leave."

The captain nodded. Jack found his own way off the ship.

7
Team Player

When Jack woke the next morning, he felt better. He'd come straight home from his meeting with Gloria, walked in the door, gotten a REM pill from the auto pharmacy in his bathroom, downed it with a shot of whiskey, and fallen asleep a few minutes later on his bed. Nothing disturbed him until morning.

He savored the calm and tranquility of a clear mind as he woke up. He had a plan and was taking action. That felt good. The realization that Carla had blocked out a large chunk of his morning schedule threatened to undo it.

His eyes opened, and he sat up in bed. After thinking for a few minutes, he realized there wasn't much he could do but react to whatever came next. He didn't have enough information to plan. About the best he could do was act as if the night before last didn't happen. He was part of the team, and she wouldn't get to see him sweat.

Jack arrived at the office about an hour before he was due to meet with Carla. He put his mind to work, determined to keep himself busy. He had just finished digging through a mound of communications when Molly threw a message up on the wall screen. It chimed at him. "Director Savage has arrived."

Jack stood, straightened his shirt, and walked to the door. He put his hand over the palm reader and paused. He wasn't sure how this was going to turn out. The one thing he knew, he was determined to maintain control of his own body and mind. No matter what the cost, no one would own his mind or his body.

He opened the door and smiled warmly. From across the room, Carla smiled in return. Wary now and paying attention to more than her assets, which were again prominently on display, Jack recognized neither of them liked the other. *You can always tell by their eyes*, he thought. Carla's smile alluded to warmth, openness, confidence, and availability, but her eyes and something indistinct in her body language communicated loathing and hidden disgust.

Jack met Carla's gaze and instantly recognized an unspoken struggle for control. He had seen that before. Jack may have gained access to many women's bodies, but most often they kept their eyes to themselves. Not all of them had contained the same loathing he felt at the moment in Carla, but almost all of their eyes had been reserved, separated from the euphoria which overcame the rest of their flesh—Jack saw it as a preservation of the self from the intrusion of a stranger. At that moment, it struck him that Anna's eyes were different, open to him. She didn't hold herself away. Involuntarily, Jack flinched away from Carla's gaze. They shook hands in the middle of the room.

"Come on in." He gestured to his office.

"Thank you."

Jack turned his back on Carla and walked briskly to his desk. He sat comfortably behind it. Carla took a seat facing him. She crossed her legs, allowing her skirt to ride up. He waited.

After an awkward moment of silence, Carla spoke first. "Well, first off, I wanted to say congratulations on joining our little team."

Jack managed a semi-genuine smile. "Thanks." He waited again. He wanted to know why she was here.

Jack caught the corner of a grin cross Carla's face. He noticed it around her eyes, and it was there for much less than a second.

Her expression sobered. She leaned forward, maximizing the view. "Jack, I owe you an apology." She looked down at the desk and blushed a little. "I'm sorry about the other night. I hate tagging. I wish we didn't do it, but it's the way things are done."

She almost pulled it off. Jack almost believed her. Mostly, he found himself annoyed that he wanted to believe her. "It wasn't any fun. I didn't like it."

Carla nodded. "I don't blame you. Neither did I." She looked him in the eye. "Maybe I can make it up to you."

Jack didn't answer. For a moment, he kept his expression strictly neutral. He could still sense her underlying need to control him. *Fool me once*, thought Jack. He allowed his hard expression to break a little. "Maybe, down the road."

Carla nodded, and, again, the smile which didn't exist appeared and disappeared so quickly, Jack wasn't even sure he had seen it. Carla sat back in her chair, diminishing the effect of her cleavage. She straightened her skirt. Seeking to break the tension, Carla changed the topic. "I have your first real assignment."

"You do?" It wasn't really a question. Jack just spoke to draw out more information.

"We need two shaped plasma charges."

Jack furrowed his eyebrows but felt the adrenaline pumping again. He kept his voice level and calm. "What do you need them for?"

"Jack, over time you'll learn that it's best if you don't ask these questions."

He looked at her warily and smiled. It wasn't a warm smile. "I disagree. You're asking me to hand you the makings of a bomb, a bomb which could be used to depressurize the station I'm living on. It seems in my best interests to know what our team intends to do with said bomb."

Carla looked irritated. Jack enjoyed it. "Jack, you're part of the team now. We don't do that to our team members."

"Uh huh. Just like you don't cut off their hands if they disappoint you."

Carla remained silent for a minute, staring at Jack. When she next spoke, all hint of irritation was gone. Her eyes had a pleading look. She was Jack's friend wishing for him to just understand.

"Jack, the reason you aren't target practice for the army in a live fire simulation right now is that you're valuable to Randall. You don't get to ask questions." She paused, then smiled warmly, trying to loosen Jack up. "I can't tell you what is going to happen, and you don't really want to know. All you need to know is that it's politics, always politics. Play the game, and you stay alive."

Sensing that he wasn't going to get anywhere, Jack managed a shrug and decided to appear contrite. "I just want to make sure my own skin is safe," he said.

"You're safe as long as you play the game, Jack."

Jack nodded. Plasma charges were a type of shaped charge used in mining to bore into asteroids, allowing ore processing bots and machines to follow once the way had been paved. These wouldn't be hard to get since asteroid mining was both part of the commerce in Sicily and the surrounding systems, but Jack had never tried to fence explosives before. He had no idea who to ask to get such a thing.

"That's great, Carla, but I've never smuggled explosives before. I tried to avoid getting killed."

Carla pulled a folded piece of electronic paper out of one of the pockets of her jacket. "Timothy wondered about that. Here's a list of captains who frequent this station who might be able to help you. They all have contracts with the Mining Department." She held out the paper. Jack sat still. Eventually, Carla laid it on the desk.

"If I know anyone on the list, I should be able to get them for you in three weeks or less."

Carla smiled and looked him in the eye, just a little too long. "That should do nicely, Jack."

Jack irritated himself by smiling back.

"Jack, why don't you show me around the station? I would like to see what we are dealing with up here. Distribution is going to be a key part of our plan to increase hydrogen production on the surface. We need to know if you have the capacity up here to handle all the new ships and H2 that will be coming through."

The next couple of hours were taken up by walking Carla around and introducing her to section chiefs and staff on the station. Jack explained how he had Molly out letting everyone know to tighten things up.

Carla seemed sympathetic and nodded at this. "The transition is always the hardest, but people usually get into the swing of things pretty quickly." She chatted politely with everyone they met on the station, suggesting ways to make changes which would bring shopkeepers and staff into compliance. All the while, she criticized nothing.

While they walked, Carla stayed one step within polite social distance again. Her laugh was warm and inviting. Every so often, she put her hand on his arm. Jack began to relax, despite himself. He found himself fantasizing about the last time he had been with Carla. She was being reasonable. *Perhaps the worst was over*, he thought.

They were coming back up from the fuel loading docks when Jack decided to bring up the little business about Cora Hanson. He palmed the call button for the lift and waited. "Lewis told me that he discussed with you the note I received from Cora Hanson."

Carla's demeanor changed instantly. Her face colored with anger, although her voice was calm. "Yes, he did talk to me about it."

"I was just wondering what you were going to do. I mean, after all, I do get notes like that every once in a while."

Carla stepped back. Her voice was flat as she answered. "Jack, you are part of a team now. There is one goal—make sure your team rises to the top. If you get any requests which would damage that team, it is important that you bring them directly to me. How would it help the team to have the number two in the police commissioner's office caught in a scandal for abusing his wife?"

Instantly, Jack's guard went back up. He answered with an equally flat voice. "I see your point. So what do you plan to do about it?"

Carla shrugged. "Accidents have been known to happen."

Jack waited silently until the lift arrived and stepped aboard.

After the doors closed and they began moving, Carla commanded the elevator to hold. It stopped abruptly. Carla turned toward him, allowing her breast to brush against him. Jack stayed passive. This time her voice was soft and inviting. She was his counselor, his friend again. "Jack, if this is going to work out for you, you will have to get one thing straight. We don't do dead weight. You've got skills; you're useful. Lewis and everyone like him are just dead weight. It won't do you any good to support dead weight."

"I'm listening," said Jack more warmly than he liked.

Carla's hand wandered down to his crotch. "Good, because I do want this to work out for you." She teased him for just a second or two before stepping back and commanding the elevator to continue.

Jack took a deep breath. When the elevator opened, he turned and smiled stupidly. "Is there anything else I can do for you this morning, Carla?"

She looked amused. "Not at the moment. You have work to do, and I need to help eager beaver Anthony Cox get his office all arranged. I'll definitely catch you later."

Jack said his thanks and watched her walk away. He hated himself for watching. For the first time in his life he felt used. He forced himself to turn away and put Carla out of his mind.

Jack returned to his office and had a relatively productive day. He opened the electronic paper on his desk with gloves and found several names he could check out. One of them was already in dock. A quick run down just after lunch, and he had the explosives on the way. They would arrive in a couple of weeks.

Late in the day, Molly knocked on his door.

"Enter."

Jack noticed that Molly wasn't wearing her omni-present heads-up. "Feeling a little nervous?" He pointed to his own head.

Molly grimaced a little. "Yeah, I guess I am."

"Not á bad idea to keep off that thing right now. What's on your mind?"

"I have a copy of everything I could find through legitimate means on Randall." She handed him a single sheet of electronic paper.

Jack scanned through multiple pages of images and articles stored on the single sheet. Randall wasn't shy about publicity; that was for sure. Molly had organized them from oldest to newest. Deciding to look them over in detail later, Jack them a quick skim while Molly waited.

Randall had started out with a tour or two in the military. This was a typical start for ladder climbers. After his exit from the military, his rise through the ranks of Admin seemed relatively quick. He started with various department head assignments in various places. Then he disappeared for awhile, only to appear again about five years ago as the head of a small mining operation, which was later militarized and classified. Then for the last couple of years, he had taken a job overseeing a research facility on Cyprus 4, the homeworld for the corporation. The facility was running some kind of experiments in directing small-scale fusion reactions. This facility was also militarized shortly before Randall left.

Jack put down the file.

"Creepy, isn't it, Jack?"

"Yeah, it's creepy."

"He smells military, through and through, doesn't he?"

"And well-connected," answered Jack. "He has two years right at the heart of power. Two years in which he moves from a director's position to an executive VP."

"So why is he here?"

"Beats me, Molly. Soren thought that maybe he was being sent down for punishment. It would make sense. Or for some reason, we're important to somebody." Jack leaned back in his chair and looked at the ceiling. "I have Soren trying to get us the real dirt. She won't be back for three weeks. Hopefully we'll be able to make it all out by then."

"Jack, Todd put in for a transfer. He has a family friend running a Ranching colony over in the Delphinus system. He needed an IT guy. It's almost near the Jersey border. I may not be here very much longer."

Jack looked at Molly. "I don't blame you for running. Do you think you can disappear?"

"I was thinking of getting pregnant."

Jack recognized the desperation Molly felt to consider motherhood as a means of escape.

Molly continued. "Or at least not going back to work for a while. Basically, trying to get off grid. They haven't tried to come after me yet, so I figure I should be OK."

"Maybe, Molly, but right now you're needed because you work for me. If you leave, that won't be the case. That concerns me."

"Yes, Jack, but for how long? How long before we aren't necessary any longer, and this facility is militarized? Are you just going to keep doing Randall's bidding because he threatened you? If you do that, he'll just drag you further in. At some point, you will have to make a break for it."

Jack was silent for a moment. Molly didn't even know about the explosives. That made death sentence number 13. "You're probably right, Molly. If you go, make it quick. Just don't show up for work one day. Go fast and keep quiet for a while."

"I plan to, Jack." Molly stood and left his office.

At the end of the day, Jack headed home for a quiet evening. He wasn't in the mood for companionship. He wanted to slow down and study the material which Molly had dug up on Randall. After a quick dinner, he lounged on the couch with a glass of scotch in one hand, and the electronic paper Molly had given him in the other. He slowly read the articles he had skimmed earlier searching for clues. He was reaching to refill his glass when his door chimed.

Jack opened it.

Carla was there, still dressed in her HR uniform. "Can I come in?"

Oh shit, thought Jack. *I wonder if this is bitchy Carla or horny Carla.* He backed away from the door. "Of course."

Carla entered his apartment.

"Can I get you a glass of something?"

Seeing the scotch on the end table near Jack's chair, Carla answered. "That looks lovely."

Jack went to the small kitchen to grab a second glass. Carla sat down on the couch. From the kitchen, Jack asked, "So were you planning on heading back tonight?"

"Actually, I figured I would catch the early shuttle down to the surface. I don't have anything scheduled until the afternoon. I can do my paperwork for the day on my heads-up. One of the reasons I stopped by was to let you know that you'll be coming with me. Randall has called a meeting for department heads tomorrow afternoon."

Jack walked back into his living space, glass in hand. Carla's jacket, skirt, and shirt lay over the back of Jack's couch. He discovered that something sheer and lacy lay underneath.

"I hope you don't mind if I get comfortable."

Well I guess that decides it. Jack hesitated for a moment. The smile was warm, the body inviting, but the eyes still held a tinge of fury that worried him. He considered asking her to leave, but he didn't. His rising pulse won out. "Not at all."

Late in the evening, Jack shut the door and headed for a shower and sleep. Carla had emphatically refused his offer to share his bed for the night, saying she wasn't interested in "being someone's pet."

Jack stood in the hot water and thought over his evening. After their erotic interlude, Carla had put her clothing back on and sat on his couch, sipping scotch. Jack asked her about the meeting tomorrow, but she wouldn't say anything. All she would say was that it was a mandatory meeting for all department heads. She seemed a little jumpy about it, almost nervous. He would have to throw a message to Molly before he went to bed.

Jack turned off the wash cycle and began to dry himself off with a towel. He thought over the last couple of days. So far he hadn't done anything to help his cause. In fact, he had just finished screwing the enemy.

He wasn't sure if that was beneficial or not. The sex itself had been good, nearly technically perfect. Carla seemed to be in sync with his every move, like she was anticipating him. It seemed a bit odd, unnatural. Jack was beginning to suspect that the fucking was just one more part of Team Randall's recruitment plan. Yet, she seemed to enjoy herself. Jack could never tell for sure, but Carla had made all the right noises in the right places.

Then there was the question of where this was heading. So far it was just sex, but Jack wasn't used to the idea of repeated casual sex with his boss—or most of his partners, for that matter. He chose most of them from among the visitors to the station. There was less chance of a misunderstanding when they moved on and didn't come back.

But Carla wasn't going away. How possessive she would be of Jack he couldn't be sure. It was becoming clear to Jack that she didn't really enjoy his company. Unless she was underneath him squealing, Jack wasn't very fond of Carla either. To tell the truth, in the last few years he had been finding himself somewhat bored with sex. There wasn't much that he hadn't done. Fucking didn't seem to assuage the beast inside any longer, and looking back, Jack wondered if it ever had.

Sex with Anna was always so different. With that thought, Jack felt his stomach tie itself in a knot. He knew that something in his attitude toward her had changed last weekend. Jack still wasn't sure what he thought about Anna, but he found himself feeling a kind of loyalty to her which he had never felt for any woman. It disturbed him and made him feel uncomfortable with his encounters with Carla.

Jack looked in the mirror at himself, wishing for the sounds of another person in the apartment. Still naked, he picked up his heads up display. He thought about calling

Anna. Then he thought better of it. He didn't want to know what she was doing right then. A few minutes later he went to bed with a nagging sense that he should have refused tonight—once was saying "hello," twice was a problem.

8
Opening Moves

The hairs on the back of his neck stood up long before Jack walked off the shuttle with Carla. When he had boarded, he noticed that the shuttle was unusually busy for a work day. He found this a bit odd but didn't give it much thought. As they came in for a pass over the shuttle port, Jack noticed a military transport ship parked off to the side on the ice near the landing Tarmac. Once in a great while they came in to the orbital looking for fuel, but he had never seen one on the surface. He was willing to bet that this was the first ever to land in Utopia.

A small portable building had been set up next to it. Jack just had time to see military personnel setting up equipment before the shuttle banked away. He strained to get a better look but never saw them again. Jack turned to Carla and started to ask a question. Glancing around at the other passengers on the shuttle, she shook her head with a bemused smile, like a parent correcting a wayward child. He shut his mouth.

As they exited the shuttle port, a contingent of gendarmes had taken up positions on either side of the door inside the large covered pick up and drop off area. They stood behind portable barricades of the type Jack had once seen on a pirated clip of a riot on Sicily 4. Instead of their usual purple jump suits, they wore the same snow fatigues and black berets which Gunderson wore when he had invaded Jack's mind. Jack counted six of them, armed to the teeth with energy assault rifles and fletch grenade launchers. He didn't even know the local gendarmes had such equipment.

Jack felt his adrenaline kick in while walking by all the fire power. His flight or fight reflexes kept wondering if they were going to come after him. The passengers arriving on the shuttle from the orbital also reacted to the change. A few stared brazenly, but most seemed to feel the tension and kept their distance.

Carla turned away from the taxi queue and toward a pair of black hover vehicles. As they approached the vehicles, armed security guards stepped out into the chill air. Jack flinched and stopped walking.

"Relax, Jack. They're for your protection. You're part of the team, remember?" Carla's voice had just a hint of disdain.

Jack gave Carla a silent grin to cover his concern and walked warily forward, getting in the second vehicle beside her. When they were settled and moving, Jack spoke. "What's going on, Carla?" Jack chose a tone which showed no fear, only frustration at being left in the dark.

Carla didn't even bother to look at him. Instead, she continued looking out at the lights of the darkened sky on Aetna. "When you do development work, like we do, the opening moves are always the same. It only gets interesting after today. You'll see."

Ten minutes later, the cars landed at the municipal stadium, not at the administration building. Carla exited the vehicle. Jack followed.

Jack stepped out and involuntarily hesitated for just the slightest minute. The noise of a crowd filled his ears. Fatigues, barricades, two snow cats with crowd control microwave dishes aimed directly at the entrance to the stadium, and military troops greeted him. Instinctively, Jack put aside his rising panic and followed Carla. They were not the only people arriving. Crowds of workers, most of them from the H2 plants, were also streaming into the stadium. Along with them came school children and families.

The stadium seated over 30,000 people, just over half the city's population. It looked very much like Team Randall intended to fill it. Jack wondered what had been said to get all of them to the stadium on such short notice.

The message had to have gone out last night. With that thought, Jack knew exactly why Carla had kept him entertained last evening. Team Randall was afraid he would bolt, if he knew what was coming. That made him all the more nervous because he had no idea what was about to happen.

There was an atmosphere of celebration, although parents held children close and hushed them if they pointed at soldiers and equipment. At the door, each person was greeted by a smiling Admin staff member who handed every person a Unity flag to wave and had painting kits on electronic paper for each of the children. As he got close to the gates, Jack heard a staff member telling each child that there would be a painting contest during the patriotic assembly, and, afterward, the child who did the best work would be given an award by Vice President Randall.

Jack noticed Carla getting a few steps ahead. He worked his way through the crowd to catch up. Security surrounded them both.

An adjunct greeted Carla just inside the door. She was shorter than Carla but equally perfect in looks. Jack figured she was a protégé. Without saying anything more than "right this way," she turned and walked them through a side door into the back rooms of the stadium. Jack was familiar with these rooms from the few patriotic gatherings he had done with Lewis.

The adjunct led them into a room packed with around 75 people. Randall was discussing something with another suit when he looked up and saw Carla and Jack come in the door. He stopped what he was doing and said loudly above the hum of small talk in the room, "There are my other two staff members."

He walked over and gave Carla a greeting hug and a very appropriate peck on the cheek. He reached out to shake Jack's hand, then pulled him in, and put his arm around his shoulder. He turned to the assembled room which had gone almost silent as soon as Randall had greeted Carla.

"Ladies and gentlemen, I want to introduce the newest member of my immediate staff. Besides continuing his regular duties as the head of our orbital, Jack Halloway has agreed to add to his responsibilities and become my head of procurement, as well. Jack is a real go-getter, and I encourage you to speak to him any time you need something which will help the cause. As many of you know, Jack here is an expert at getting supply to cough up needed items. Now, if we could only get him to help our little moon to cough up some more H2." Dick in a Suit laughed at his own joke. His staff followed automatically, clapping for Jack.

Jack looked around the room and hoped he managed some sort of dignified smile. He wasn't happy with the attention. The responses from Randall's staff were all as well-groomed as the man himself—over-polished and machine smooth. The reactions from the local department heads and other local staff varied between suspicious and shocked. Bonnie looked pissed and didn't clap. From her perspective, Jack was on the wrong side of some divide.

"Jack here doesn't know it yet, but he has also been given a promotion to a full Directorship with a significant pay raise."

There wasn't anything Jack could do. He forced himself to look appropriately shocked and played along, looking at Randall who still had his arm around him and saying, "Thank You!" above the hoots and hollers of the crowd. As the applause quieted down, Randall released him.

Jack took the opportunity to step back and stand beside Carla. He noted that Colonel Gunderson stood on the other side of Randall near the Unity flag. The effect was to put the four of them plus a couple of uber-serious security guards located near the door at one end of the room and the rest of the staff at the other end of the room watching them. Randall stood one step in front of the other three of them while he addressed his troops.

I'm one of Randall's people now, whether I like it or not, thought Jack.

Randall sobered his demeanor before speaking again in well-rehearsed deep tones. "Members of my staff will recognize today as the *opening move.* For those of you local to Aetna, I want you to know this is not always an easy day." Randall paused.

"Change is always difficult and at times painful. But I want you to trust me when I say we are heading somewhere great, and this is a necessary step on that journey. If there is trouble today, I want you to stick close to the security staff. They will know what is best."

Here he paused again, changing gears. "For those of you who look back at their past and recognize that they have not been giving 100% for the good of the Unity, today is a chance for a fresh start, a break on the path, a chance to learn from the past and do something different in the future. Every one of you is in this room today because you have been valuable contributors to the Unity on Aetna. Today is a day to observe, to learn, and to redouble your efforts for the glory of mother Unity which clothes and protects us all."

Without allowing Jack or anyone else to ask questions or process what they had just heard, Randall turned and walked to the door. The two security guards dropped their heads-up displays over their eyes and walked out, one in front and one behind him. Carla followed. Jack stood still for a moment. Gunderson smiled at him and gestured for the door. The site of Gunderson smiling at him caused Jack to shudder on the inside. He involuntarily grabbed at his left hand, turned, and followed Carla.

Three steps across a hallway, out a door, and they entered the stadium to the cheers of the crowd. The stadium had been filled. School children lined the rails of the seats which sloped above them as they came out of the tunnel. Vice President Randall stopped to shake hands with some of them. Everywhere, Aetna citizens waved Unity flags.

The next thing Jack knew, he felt Gunderson's hand gently nudge him in the back, and he was following Carla's lead and shaking hands with school children as well, smiling. The citizens of Aetna had never in their life seen an Executive Vice President, let alone had one as their leader. They greeted Randall and his team like rock stars.

Above them, a towering 3D hologram of Randall was projected to the crowd. The projection cameras hovered near the ceiling. Jack was asked to autograph several pieces of electronic paper and the painting kits offered to the children as they came in. He held up his wrist wallet, adding a time and date stamp to the paper. Team Randall threaded its way across the stadium floor which had been decked with chairs, except for an area cleared out in front of the dais. Jack didn't recognize most of the people lining the aisles, but many of them reached out to shake his hand as he passed by.

Toward the front, Jack saw the mayors and municipal directors of the sparse towns and villages which dotted the landscape of Aetna. Rick was also seated, somewhere near the front, with other leaders from the local chapter of the Unity fishing guild. He clapped politely, but his tight expression said that he wasn't enjoying the scene.

Randall and his staff climbed the dais set at the far end of the stadium. Jack followed Carla to four chairs which had been set off to the side of the other seventy-five or so which filled in the background behind the podium. Jack noted with displeasure that the whole of Aetna now knew that he had joined Team Randall. When all of Randall's party was seated, local directors in front and Randall's administrative staff behind, Randall stepped up to the podium without any introduction.

"Good morning, my fellow Aetnans." Here a short applause interrupted Randall. He waved his hands for the crowd to calm down. "I know we all have busy lives, so we want to make today's patriotic celebration relatively short.

"I am Timothy Randall, Administrative Executive Vice President, and I have been appointed by CEO Cowhill to manage Aetna. We have some great things in store for Aetna in the coming years. We are going to get better schools for your children." Again a cheer. "Better drilling equipment, and if we can swing it, we will possibly be upgrading to a floating city for all Utopians, permanently located on water. No more losing your neighbors and community every time the city has to move." Here there was a tremendous cheer from the crowd.

Once the crowd quieted, Randall continued. "Now before you get all excited, Mother Unity is going to require something for all these changes. We are going to have to grow up a little around here, and we are going to have to make ourselves worthy of this attention from Cowhill and the Board of Directors." Randall paused here. The crowd waited.

"When I came here, CEO Cowhill gave me a mandate to triple H2 production in two years on Aetna." Again he paused. Jack could hear the intake of breath from the crowd. "I want you to know that I believe in every one of you. I believe in your potential and your ability to play a role in helping us achieve this incredibly high goal.

"Today, I want to introduce you to some of your fellow citizens who have agreed to help us make this goal a reality."

As Randall spoke the last words, troops—not gendarmes, but actual soldiers—marched out from the tunnel and lined both sides of the aisle to the podium. Jack also noticed that they appeared at various strategic points throughout the stadium. They positioned themselves along the balcony railing, as well as at the bottom of the first level. These troops didn't hold the traditional assault rifle; instead, they held a weapon which was about half as long as an assault rifle and reminded Jack of the weapon which Musgrave had pulled on him.

As soon as the troops lined the aisles, they positioned their weapons facing the ground and turned to face the crowd. At the same moment, a group of ordinary people walked out from the tunnel. Lewis Lutnear and his family appeared first. Lewis held his head high, but tears freely streamed down his face. Julia kept track of her four children. She looked ashen gray. Behind them was a group of about 50. Hank, the coffee guy, was among them.

Jack recognized many of them from his black market. In fact, the majority of them had been the most successful business people on the planet. They sold goods which made the lives of residents in Utopia easier. They were known to everyone. All of them looked either terrified or disheartened. Most of them looked at the ground as they walked. Once on the overhead projector, Jack thought he saw a bruise on a young woman's face who had sold hats in the flea market.

Lewis led them to the open space before the dais. As Jack scanned the small group of entrants, he felt the pair of eyes before he saw them. He made eye contact. Lewis looked at Randall, but Julia Lutnear stared at him, her eyes a mixture of pleading and judgment. Jack looked down at his feet, not knowing what was coming, ashamed to be on the dais as a member of Randall's staff.

"In interviews over the last few days, these citizens of our great moon have realized that they have been ill-suited to their current roles within our great Unity. They have come to see their need for retraining and a fresh start. It takes great courage to recognize that you are not suited to your current job. We should honor that courage." He began to clap. His staff on the dais followed. Jack clapped with them. Most of the local officials clapped as well. Bonnie steadfastly crossed her arms across her chest.

"Mother Unity rewards such integrity with fidelity and compassion. This is why I am excited to announce the opening of a new floating facility for retraining and education in the equatorial waters on Aetna." He paused. There was no applause from the crowd, only silence.

Everyone in the stadium knew what retraining meant. It was a codeword for starvation, abandonment, and brainwashing. Retraining centers were where the Unity threw away unwanted people. No one ever came back from retraining the same. Most never came back at all.

Somewhere into the silence someone began to scream "No!" The sound cut off so suddenly that Jack wouldn't have had time to see what had happened if he hadn't already been facing the majority of the crowd.

Low in the balcony to his left a young man had stood up and tried to begin shouting, but the soldiers were already moving before he had even had time to stand. Barrels lifted, and there was an audible "thwap" as three soldiers took aim and fired. The shouter instantly keeled over and collapsed into the spectators seated in front of him. The three soldiers who had fired kept their weapons leveled at the crowd, waiting for someone else to object. A whispered report circled the arena. Jack could sense the tension and fear. Parents clutched their children.

Randall continued as if nothing had happened. "Using state of the art retraining methods, our heroic citizens will find their calling within the Unity, and I for one am looking forward to seeing them come back to us as full productive members of our society, ready to give 100 percent for the greater good.

"Today is a day of soul searching here on Aetna. Today the citizens of Aetna must..."

Here Randall was forced to pause as someone on the podium started shouting, "No, this isn't right! You have to be stopped!" Randall turned to look.

Jack turned to see Bonnie standing up, her fist pumping into the air. Clearly she wanted the audience to join her. The soldiers didn't move. They remained eyes fixed on the crowd, but now all their weapons came up from the ground to the ready position.

The security guards on the stage had their guns drawn before she even finished shouting. She took one step toward Randall before a pink mist showed where the nannite-loaded fletch rounds hit her in the middle of the forehead. There was a moment in which Bonnie realized what was happening, a moment of awareness even as she died. Her eyes looked confused. They searched for something familiar, and then she was gone, body crumpling to the ground almost directly behind Randall.

Jack heard the 'thwap' of neural stunners begin in several parts of the building. The PA activated. "Citizens will remain in their seats until the end of the patriotic celebration."

The moment in which a true rebellion could have begun dwindled rapidly. It lasted for maybe a minute or a little more. Randall's security team made no move to clear the body but now came to stand between the seventy-five staff and Randall. Three of them also positioned themselves between Jack, Carla and Gunderson and the other guests on the dais. All the while, Randall stood at the podium still smiling. He waited, unperturbed, apparently without a care in the world. He might well have been listening to applause and not the sound of weapons fire. The ever observant Jack tried to count the shots fired. In the end, he estimated that twenty to thirty citizens fell to neural stunners. He wasn't sure if they had only been stunned, or if they were dead.

Once it was obvious which way it was going to go, Randall started talking again, even before the final shots were fired. "Today is to be a day of soul searching here on Aetna. Today must be a day in which each of us asks ourselves if we are suited to our roles. Do we serve the greater good, or are we selfish in our ends? Do we love our fellow citizens enough to give our all for the good of Mother Unity, or do we simply want more for ourselves? It is a day of repentance, a day of compassion, forgiveness, and a fresh start.

"If any of you in the stadium or watching elsewhere feel that you cannot serve Unity in your current position, I encourage you to talk to your supervisors. We can help you. I promise, we will find you a place where you can be content. Remember, Mother Unity loves her children, and we must be grateful for all that she does to clothe and feed us. I am so looking forward to the days to come. I promise you that we will accomplish great things."

With that, Randall turned to the flag and put his hand over his heart. As he did so, the soldiers surrounding the new recruits for reeducation began to herd them out of the stadium. Jack noticed Julia look back at him one more time. He couldn't look directly at her. His hand clenched at his side as a knot filled the pit of his stomach. "Will you

please stand and join me. I pledge allegiance to the flag..."
Jack, along with everyone else who remained conscious,
stood and pledged their allegiance to Mother Unity. The
great majority realized there was no freedom to do
anything else.

9
Collaborator

Randall's voice interrupted Jack's thoughts. "So what did you make of our little celebration today, Jack?"

Jack had been staring at the piece of red meat on his plate. He hadn't seen synthetic steak like this since he had come to Aetna. He had only eaten steak once as a boy.

That had been when his father had taken him to a business event at which fathers were required to bring their children. Jack only remembered a few things about the day. One of them was the beating his father had given him beforehand to make sure Jack would behave and another was the steak he had eaten that night. By the time he got home after the day at the office with his Dad, Jack had felt sick. He threw up the meat later that evening. His father beat him again for eating so much that he got sick, even though Jack had finished less than half the steak and his father had scolded him at the office for not eating enough.

"I'm not sure what to make of it, sir." Jack looked up from his plate. He was sitting to the right of Randall. Gunderson sat across from him, chowing down on his meal of red meat and green vegetables. On Jack's right, Carla ate a salad. "It's my first time to watch someone die." Jack had eaten only a few bites of his food.

Randall nodded and then cut another bite of his steak. The permanent smile momentarily disappeared from his face. "That was unfortunate. It didn't need to happen that way. I've seen..." He paused to count in his head for a second, "...twelve of these ceremonies in my years with the Unity. This is my third, no, fourth, as a team leader. I have only seen someone die on the platform twice, including today. That was unusual." Randall went back to eating.

"Your first time is never very pleasant." Carla's tone was consoling.

"Speak for yourself, Carla. I thoroughly enjoyed my first time," Gunderson added, through a mouthful of steak.

Randall laughed. Carla smiled and just rolled her eyes. Randall explained, "At Gunderson's first opening, we had a riot among the re-eds. That was a complete disaster. We ended up killing most of them and about 40 in the crowd before order was restored. What a mess."

"Yeah, but I ended up snapping the neck of the bastard who started it all. He was a wiry little dude." Gunderson sounded pleased with himself.

Jack forced himself to smile along with the others and cut a bite of the steak. It was too rich for his stomach. He felt his gut react as the first bite went down.

Jack didn't sleep well on the flight home, partly on account of his upset stomach, but mostly from the fact that he kept receiving angry glares from the other passengers.

Jack wondered if he should have asked for a security detail, but he liked even less the idea that someone would be watching his every move. However, Jack had reason to reevaluate his feelings when he got home. Arriving at the door to his quarters, he saw that someone had painted the word "murderer" on his door.

Jack entered his apartment, cautiously. He turned on every light and checked every corner before he got out a glass and a bottle of vodka. He filled the tumbler. Jack drank scotch for the savor. He drank vodka for the effect.

The electronic paper with Molly's information on Randall lay open on his desk. Jack picked it up and tried to read. He couldn't concentrate. All he could see was the pink mist erupting from Bonnie's forehead. He put the folder down again.

He could hear her voice. "This isn't right. You have to be stopped." The voice plagued him. Jack heard in her words the righteous indignation Bonnie had often leveled at him in staff meetings.

Jack took another large drink. Bonnie had always been an idiot. She never knew when to duck. Jack shook his head in disgust and poured another glass. Sometime later, he threw a quick message to maintenance and asked them to take care of his door before morning. Then he stumbled to the pharmacy in the bathroom, dispensed another REM pill, and fell into his bed.

Jack was gratified to see that by the time he left his quarters the next morning, the graffiti on his door had been painted over. A small piece of him had wondered if they would do it. Then again, he was part of Randall's team and that now made him someone to be feared. Jack felt sick to his stomach.

When he arrived at the office, Molly was not in her usual place as he crossed the lobby. Jack entered his office and saw the folded piece of hand-pressed paper on his desk. He put his bag down near the coat stand and sat down in his chair.

He opened the note. In Molly's hand, it contained one word, "goodbye." Jack folded the note and put it in a pocket in his slacks.

In the computer, Molly had given herself vacation time. She had a couple of weeks saved up. It would give her a pretty good head start before anyone noticed that she was missing. Jack noted that she had forged his thumbprint and DNA to get the approval. The plans were even back-dated. She had probably hacked the information off one of the papers he had signed the last time they were in the office together. Jack decided to give her the head start. She was scheduled for two weeks off. She would get it. Jack stood and headed out his office door to talk to what remained of his staff.

The next seventeen days passed with decidedly less drama than the previous three. But Jack found they wore on him. There were no more incidents of vandalism on Jack's door, although the anti-Unity graffiti around the station picked up.

Jack, Robert, and Joe covered for Molly. Molly was supposed to be back today, Monday. Of course, she didn't show. Jack was debating how long he could wait before he would have to tell Carla.

He was sitting at his desk after lunch figuring that he was going to have to tell her sometime that afternoon when Jack heard someone walking in the front door. He had set up the security cam to ping him on the big screen in his office. Jack looked up in time to see Robert walking across the lobby to his door. He knocked.

"Enter."

Robert entered his office and shut the door before he spoke. "Your packages have arrived on the dock."

Jack kept his face impassive. "Ok."

"Jack, are you going to hand them the makings of a bomb after what they did two weeks ago?"

"Do I have a choice?"

"Not really."

This was old ground for Jack and Robert. They had discussed it several times over the last couple of weeks. Jack was not happy to discuss it again, since their last discussions had proved to be largely fruitless.

"So what do you think they want with them?" asked Robert.

"I have no idea. There are just too many options. After what they pulled in the stadium, I wouldn't put anything past them."

"We could try to disable them somehow."

Jack leaned back in his chair. He had thought long and hard about this one in the last couple of weeks. Robert wanted to do something to stop the bombs from going off. There was a piece of Jack which wondered if he was right, but Jack hadn't been able to figure out any way to accomplish this without it leading right back to him.

"I would love to disable them, Robert. Any suggestions?" Jack said allowing a note of frustration to creep into his voice.

Robert thought for a moment, then shook his head. "None that we haven't discussed. We could at least try to warn people."

"And how do you propose to do that without getting killed?"

"There are worse things than dying, Jack."

"Really? Like what?"

"Like getting other people killed."

"So what would we tell them? And who would we tell? Do we just walk up to the man on the street and say, 'Hey, your new administrators have a bomb and they intend to use it but we don't know when or how'? It wouldn't work, Robert."

Robert looked at his toes for a moment. "I see your point." He looked up at Jack for a moment, wrinkled his face behind his beard, and took a breath like he was going to speak again, but the words never came. He exhaled and looking Jack in the eye, said sadly, "I guess there isn't anything we can do."

Jack looked down at his desk. "Not right now."

Jack took the afternoon shuttle down to the surface. The shuttle port on Aetna was too small to have a proper security checkpoint, so Jack had never needed to worry about contraband he brought down to the surface. Most often he had larger items stowed in the hold if he made the delivery run himself. But in this case, Jack felt better keeping the two briefcase-sized packages with him. He stowed them in the overhead as he boarded.

Jack tried to sleep, but he couldn't. The knot in his gut wouldn't let him. He closed his eyes again. Pink mist erupted from Bonnie's forehead. His eyes snapped open and he watched the fiery glow of atmospheric entry out his window. *There isn't any choice*, he thought as he parried with an invisible interlocutor. He closed his eyes again and saw the word 'murderer' painted on the door to his quarters. Jack's eyes came open, and he didn't try to sleep again.

Considering the cargo and the tension in the air after the patriotic celebration, Jack had been especially watchful as he had walked to the shuttle that afternoon. Jack wasn't looking forward to porting a bomb by himself through Utopia to the admin building. About halfway through the trip Jack threw Carla a message. It read, "Bringing supplies to surface. Would love a ride to admin." Jack figured that would be enough for Carla to understand but not enough to cause problems later.

When he stepped off the shuttle, there were two silent types in dark suits waiting for him. They escorted Jack to a black car outside the terminal. Jack stepped in and the car took off without either of the suits in the front asking for directions.

Ten minutes later, they banked into the parking garage located behind the main lobby of the admin building and Jack got out, entered the lobby, and waited at the bank of elevators. The two guards stayed in the garage by the vehicle.

The wait for the elevator seemed to take forever. Jack just wanted to be rid of the packages he carried. Finally, the doors opened, he stepped into the elevator, and voice commanded it to Carla Savage's office.

A few minutes later, Jack found himself tapping his foot on the nine by nine squares of the tile floor. The rounded back of the waiting room chair had never felt so uncomfortable. The five minute wait in Carla's lobby became ten.

Jack thought about just leaving the charges behind with the cute receptionist he had seen at the coliseum. He felt a bead of sweat run down his neck. He flexed his muscles ready to leave and looked up. The woman behind the desk smiled sweetly at him. Jack figured it was a trick of his nerves, but he could swear that she shook her head slightly. The impulse to flee evaporated. Jack stared at his feet.

Twenty minutes after he arrived, the door to Carla's office opened. A young man Jack recognized from Randall's staff exited. The top button of his white dress shirt was unbuttoned, and his tie was loose and slightly askew. Jack looked away but not quickly enough to avoid seeing Carla's hand brush his rump.

Jack felt himself flush with anger. Then immediately, he hated himself for it. He didn't want to know and he didn't want to care who Carla fucked. It was none of his business.

"I'll see you next week at the same time." Carla sounded authoritative. "Jack," she said warmly. "I'm so glad to see you!"

Jack looked up and saw her coming across the lobby to shake his hand, eyes gleaming. Jack stood slowly, making her wait half a beat before he shook her hand. She held it a second too long, as usual.

Jack turned and retrieved the two cases on the chair.

Carla turned to the desk. "Bea, I am in a meeting. Hold my calls."

"Yes, ma'am." The girl behind the desk responded perkily.

Carla turned and walked away.

Jack followed her into her office.

When she had closed the door behind him, Carla asked, "Jack, what brings you down today?"

"I sent you a message earlier. Didn't you get it?"

Carla smiled. "I was probably in a meeting. Sometimes Bea answers my messages."

Jack nodded and thought he understood why Bea had wanted him to stay to deliver the packages.

"I have the items you requested." Jack set the crates on the floor next to her desk. He just wanted to be done with them, to never see them again.

Carla smiled. "Great, Jack! That's great. Randall will be pleased."

Carla settled herself on the corner of her desk, neatly crossing her legs directly in front of him as he sat in a chair across from her.

"Also, I needed to let you know that Molly, my front office assistant, has not returned to her job after vacation."

Carla rolled her eyes and shook her straight blonde hair in a tsk-tsk manner. "Did she run, Jack?"

"Yeah, I think so."

"Typical. We always get a few of these right after the opening move." Carla thought for a moment. Then the corners of her mouth went up with a grin. "I have an idea which just might be to your liking. I have to talk to a couple of people, but I might be able to give you a replacement right away."

Jack had expected more drama about Molly leaving. He was cautious. "That sounds good. So you're not going to go after her?"

Carla smiled pleasantly. "Why would we, Jack? If she doesn't want to be here, then we don't want her here. Things work themselves out, and we aren't a vindictive group, Jack. Was there anything else on your mind?"

"No, that was all."

"Well then, I have some work to get done." Carla stood from her desk. Standing in front of Jack, she reached out a hand and helped him out of his chair. He was left standing very close to her. She reached out and played with the buttons on his jacket. "Why don't you and I catch dinner tonight? If things work out right, I might have a little treat for you. My place? I'll be done here in a couple of hours. What about 6:30?"

"All right." Jack's preservation instincts answered before he had even thought about the offer. He felt obligated to keep Carla happy.

"Great. It will be worth your time. I promise"

Jack turned and headed to the door. He had just opened it when Carla spoke up.

"By the way, Jack. Just an FYI. Cora Hanson's funeral is tomorrow."

Jack stopped. He didn't look back. "What happened?"

"Apparently, she slipped on the ice and hit her head. I told you these things have a way of working themselves out. See you for dinner tonight."

Jack felt sick. He shut the door without answering and walked away.

On the way down in the elevator, Jack made a decision. By the time he got out, he had the beginnings of a plan. A few minutes later, Jack climbed into a cab.

"Destination?"

Jack looked around. The fishing fleet warehouses were not hard to spot. Jack couldn't fly straight to them, or Team Randall would know exactly where he had gone.

Three minutes later, Jack landed outside the historical museum. He had picked it because it was somewhat closer to his destination, would be open late, and could also be a destination in itself. As the car descended, he got his bearings.

Jack walked into the vestibule. If Team Randall wanted to trace his whereabouts, they would now be able to see an image of him from the cameras mounted on the building. Jack hoped to change that shortly. Halfway down the left side of the building, he ducked inside. Working quickly, he took his wrist wallet and heads-up and stuffed them behind a camp stove inside a display case containing artifacts from the first settlers on Aetna. Then, he walked out the other side of the building. With a simple, short sprint across an open playground, Jack entered a camera-free residential complex. He took his time and circled back around to the other side of the museum and headed to his destination.

Jack was sweating in his parka when he finally arrived at the fishing warehouse. He waited, bundled against the cold. It didn't take long. About three minutes after arriving, a hovering forklift came out from the warehouse with a crate full of fish to be left outside to freeze. *Here's the real risk*, thought Jack. *If they want to find out where I went, then here is a person who will know. I wonder how many undercover HR officers there are on Aetna?*

Jogging, Jack crossed the distance between himself and the forklift, waving to the driver. He opened the heated cab. Jack looked up at him and yelled over the noise, "I need to get in to see Rick, but I don't want anyone to know I was here."

The driver thought about it for a moment, nodded, and signaled for him to wait. He turned, picked up an empty crate, and then took it inside. Another fifteen minutes went by. Jack was beginning to notice the cold when the driver came back. Before coming to Jack, he picked up a smaller crate with a lid and motioned for Jack to get inside.

As he climbed in and closed the lid, Jack laughed to himself. *Well, all my subterfuge is going to be useless. Carla will be able to tell just where I went by the smell.*

Jack huddled on the bottom of the carbon plastic crate and peeked out one of the holes as he was lifted from the ground and brought into the fishing warehouse. In all, it lasted for about five minutes until he felt himself being put down. Jack waited. He heard the hover vehicle leave. Nothing happened.

He was just about ready to open the lid of the crate when Rick opened it for him. He put his finger to his lips and signaled for him to follow. Jack climbed out of the crate and walked behind him. The crate was parked in a little-used part of the warehouse next to an older fishing submarine which was in the process of being scrapped for parts. Jack followed Rick inside.

Rick didn't speak until they were deep in the belly of the beast. Rusting metal pipes hung low on the ceilings everywhere. Here and there remnants of gray paint held out against the rust. A string of emergency lighting ran down the middle of the ship. Fiber sprouted from the walls like weeds in places where quantum chips and other components had been scavenged.

Rick turned to Jack. "Stand on the 'X'."

Jack looked at the floor. "Rick..."

"Stand on the 'X'." Rick had never used that tone with Jack before. Jack noticed Rick's hand in his pocket pointing something at him which looked distinctly like a firearm.

Jack stood on the 'X' marked in chalk on the floor. "Why is it that all my friends but me have a weapon on this moon? And why do they keep pointing them at me?" asked Jack to no one in particular.

Rick managed a short smile as he flipped a switch on the wall. Jack heard a hum as a green laser cross projected onto the top of his head. The laser came from a pristine white tool held at the end of a robotic arm hanging hidden on the ceiling. The arm dropped down and scanned every inch of his body. Finished, it flashed green, made a happy sounding 'ping', and then returned to its hidden lair.

Rick relaxed and let go of the weapon in his pocket. He even managed to smile. "Bet you didn't know I had that little machine, did you?"

Jack leaned back against an old control console behind him. "You're a man of many surprises, Rick. What the hell did that thing do?"

"It just scanned you for bugs. If you want to talk without being heard, this is about the only place on the moon in which you can be pretty well assured of privacy. "

"A month ago, I would have called you paranoid. Now I would just say you're smart."

Rick smiled. "I've seen things in my day. One can't be too careful, Jack. I mean, after all, you're a member of Randall's inner circle now, aren't you."

Jack rolled his eyes. "I didn't get a say in the matter. Randall sat me down and then showed me a very thorough accounting of everything I had done in the last five years. That kinda sucked and didn't leave me with any options."

Rick chuckled quietly. "That's usually the way of it. I heard from Musgrave you got tagged."

Jack paused. "Is my private life the talk of the town?" Jack kept his tone calm but raised an eyebrow to show his irritation. "That green laser claw didn't disable the bots, did it? I won't leave this sub if it did."

Rick smiled and shook his head. "No, Jack, it didn't do anything to your bots. You're still safely Randall's pet, and your problem isn't being broadcast all over Aetna." Rick shrugged his shoulders even as he crossed his arms. "Musgrave and I talk. We're the only ones who know. Not that your favor with Randall wasn't broadcast all over Aetna at the patriotic slaughter we had the other day. I can't imagine the average person on Aetna is too happy with you right now, but they're still too scared to do anything about it."

"Not all of them. There was a nasty greeting painted on my door when I got home that night." Jack paused and thought about what he wanted to say next. "Rick, I need a way out. Randall has me trapped. He's blocked all the exits. I need to get transferred somewhere else, or, if all else fails, go on the run. For some reason, I thought you might want to help me."

Rick was silent for a long moment. He looked hard at Jack. Jack understood he was being evaluated. Finally, Rick spoke. "I can help, but I don't think you're ready to pay the price."

"I'm not going to dicker with you. How much money does it take to get off someone's team?"

"Oh, it takes money, Jack. Probably more than you have, but it isn't the money I'm talking about. If *I* help you, you have to leave behind everything—your loyalties, your life, your identity, and your country. It means starting over completely. It means learning a new way to talk and a new way to think. It's like being born all over again."

Jack thought for a minute about what Rick had said. He had heard rumors about people smugglers in the past. They could supposedly get you out of Unity to a different country without exit papers. Rick must have a connection with them.

Jack's world shifted. He had thought that he had been the smuggler on Aetna. Here was Rick telling him that he smuggled people. Jack's ego threatened to cloud his judgment. He didn't like the fact that Rick had hidden from him something so vital for all these years. It did explain Rick's paranoia. Always pragmatic, Jack put his irritation aside almost as soon as it arose. Jack thought about a fresh start, somewhere in a new place, somewhere with a sane government.

As he was contemplating Rick's offer, out of nowhere he pictured Anna knocking on the door of his apartment on the station, a door he did not answer because he was not there. Jack hesitated.

He figured that he would have to start over, but he still wondered if he could live here quietly in some corner of Unity and not be bothered. He wasn't ready to give up everything, yet. What surprised Jack was that for the first time in his life, he hoped someone else would be there with him. The more he thought about it, the more Jack decided there had to be another way, a way which included Anna.

Jack shrugged his shoulders. "I'm not ready for that, yet."

Rick showed no surprise at Jack's answer. His usually jovial personality remained somber. He stood straight, and Jack assumed he was starting to leave. "If you change your mind, get to Musgrave's house. He'll know what to do." Without warning, he took the weapon from his pocket and fired on Jack. Jack felt himself sinking into unconsciousness. As his world went dark, Jack thought he heard Rick say, "If you change your mind Jack, you should know that we have room for two."

10
Clarity

Jack woke suddenly, his mind slow and dull. It was dark outside and cold, at least -60 C. He was shivering despite his insulated outerwear. He stood up from the ice and snow bank he lay in. As he got to his feet, Jack saw that he was clutching a folded piece of pressed paper. He was lying near a taxi call box just outside a vestibule that he did not recognize. He had never seen these buildings before.

He tried to think back. The last thing he remembered clearly was hopping in a cab that afternoon. The rest was just a blank, except for one thing. He could remember Rick telling him that if he wanted to get out he needed to get to Musgrave's house. Other than that, his memory was washed clean.

Jack looked at the paper and immediately recognized Rick's writing. *A taxi is on the way*, the note read. *Don't forget your meeting with Carla. You'll be fine by the time you get there. Sorry about the memory loss. See you soon.*

Jack took off one of his gloves and fumbled in the lining of his coat for a small laser cutter he kept there. As the taxi arrived overhead and came in for a landing, Jack burned the note from Rick. As soon as he was done, he sprinted for the safety of the cab.

Jack knocked on the door of Carla's apartment ten minutes late. He was still freezing, but for the moment had his shivers under control. He was cold, hypothermic. His brain still felt a little slow.

Carla answered the door. Her lips smiled and her voice purred, but her eyes showed only irritation. "Where have you been?"

Jack thought for a second and decided to play it cool. He answered honestly. "I don't remember."

Carla rolled her eyes. "OK, Jack." She stood there for a minute before saying harshly, "You look cold. Come in. Your stuff's on the table."

Jack entered Carla's apartment. It was decorated in an austere fashion similar to Musgrave's. Yet Jack felt a lack of warmth and style. Each item in Musgrave's apartment was chosen specifically for its effect—creating a unified aesthetic. In Carla's apartment, similar furnishings felt jarring and disjointed—as if they were chosen not for their aesthetic value, but merely because they were considered stylish.

Carla turned to face him, clearly furious. "Jack, I like you, but I can only cover for you once. If you do this again, I'll let Gunderson know you went off-grid and let him come and get you." Carla wandered to the kitchen. "You know you really shouldn't disappear like that. It isn't safe right now."

Jack felt a new wave of shivers begin as his body continued to warm up. He felt a bit sick, like he might throw up. He wasn't in a place to spar with Carla. He looked at Carla and said apologetically, "You're probably right. But you know something, I am cold, probably hypothermic, and I can't think straight right now." He looked at the table. Dinner settings were not yet laid out. "Would you mind if I took a hot shower before dinner? I need to warm up."

"Serves you right, Jack," said Carla with a callousness which showed she either didn't yet understand the fragility of human life on Aetna or didn't care. Basic politeness allowed a guest any means necessary to warm up. Most households had emergency heated blankets and anti-frostbite kits on hand, just for instances like this. "Shower's down the hall."

Four minutes later, Jack was standing in warm water. He let the spray run on his back as he continued to shiver. He heaved, empting his stomach into the drain on the floor. His head started to pound.

Not long after, there was a knock at the door. Without waiting for an answer, the door opened. Jack expected Carla. Instead, he got Bea, Carla's much younger adjunct.

"Hi, Jack. I'm going to be your new assistant. Carla suggested that this might be a good time to get to know each other." All the while she was speaking, her clothing was dropping to the floor.

Inwardly, Jack cringed. He was tired and sick. He hurriedly rinsed the last taste of his own bile out of his mouth as Beatrice climbed in the shower. As she wrapped herself around him, Jack felt her shaking. She kissed him. She didn't smile. Jack figured she was scared.

Jack thought about saying "no," but Bea equaled, if not surpassed, Carla in beauty. And while Carla was beginning to look broken-in, Bea still maintained the innocence of her youth. By the time he made his mind up to say something, Bea was already pressed against him and using her hands to get him ready. Jack fell into the rush.

Despite the headache, Jack managed to perform adequately, and ten minutes later Bea left the shower mentioning that she was looking forward to talking with him over dinner. The set of her shoulders and her refusal to look directly at him said something quite different. In a minute, Jack was left alone again, his head pounding harder then ever. Without understanding why, Jack found himself overwhelmed by a growing sense of despair.

In the two minutes in which Jack put his clothing back on, he tried to process his sense of emptiness. He was used to being in control of his sexual environment. Soon after he had discovered sex at the hands of an older teen, Jack had always been the one calling the shots. Jack no longer felt in control. He no longer felt safe, not since his first encounter with Carla. He didn't quite feel used, but he knew he didn't feel good.

Jack decided that over dinner he would get back in control—of himself and his situation. He went to the auto-pharmacy on the wall, and, typing in his personal ID, dispensed a pain patch specifically designed for him. By the time he sat down to dinner five minutes later, his headache was gone.

Both Bea and Carla were waiting for him. As he took his seat, Jack looked at Carla. "Thanks for the hot water."

Carla didn't smile. "No problem, Jack. What did you think of the entertainment?"

Jack looked at Bea. She smiled warmly but something in her body posture said that more rode on his answer than just her self-esteem. Taking a bite of his poorly-cooked fish, Jack looked Carla in the eye. "She was lovely, but you can't buy my loyalty with sex."

Carla nearly choked on her synthetic wine as she tried not to laugh until she swallowed. Then she let out howls of laughter. Bea sat silently, putting down her fork. She looked at Jack with a hint of surprise. Jack took it all in, keeping his face strictly neutral.

"Can't we, Jack?" Carla answered. "I think we already have. Except for your two little disappearing acts, you've done precisely what we asked of you, and if you're smart, you'll continue to do so."

"It's not the sex which keeps me in line. It's the threat of death which keeps me cooperating."

Carla rolled her eyes. "Yes, Jack. That's how it starts for most of us. The threats and tagging are effective. They bring you to heel. The sex is here to soften the blow, to make those things palatable. My job... our job is to help you become happy on the team."

Jack felt his anger rise. This time he let it creep into his voice. "So, what you're saying is that letting me screw you is just another part of the manipulation, another means of control."

Carla laughed again, then answered bitterly. "All sex is manipulation, Jack. Look me in the eye and tell me that any time you use a pick up line or buy a drink for some saggy, wrinkled traveler in that awful bar you haunt that you aren't manipulating her?" Carla's face turned red with anger as she spoke. She was almost yelling now.

Jack was pulled up short. He hadn't thought about it that way before, and perhaps his mind was slow from the hypothermia, but he didn't have a snappy comeback for Carla. In fact, he rather suspected she was right. Whatever he did to entice women definitely had an objective in mind. He was always looking for the right button to push to get the response he wanted. Even when he appeared to be a perfect gentleman, he was working toward a goal.

"All this love and intimacy stuff is just bullshit, Jack. All sex is manipulation. Your problem is that you have always been in control, and you don't like being the one on the receiving end of the manipulation. But I haven't met a man yet who won't manipulate me to get his rod in my crotch. I don't cry about it, Jack. It's just the way life is. The best I can do is to turn the tables on them. I climb over them and stay on top."

Jack sat there as the room filled with silence. He wasn't sure what he had done to bring on this kind of introspection from Carla, but what she said had a ring of authenticity to it unlike anything she had shared with him previously. The soggy fish on Jack's fork hanging halfway between his plate and his mouth gave up and succumbed to the overcooking. It fell back to his plate with a soft plop.

Carla stared at Jack, furious. She looked close to coming across the table at him and trying to rip his eyes out. Jack had the distinct impression that he was standing in for twenty years of resentment.

Slowly the left corner of Jack's mouth lifted. Unexpectedly, Carla's words created an unlooked for self-awareness. Jack found himself seeing his life in a new way, seeing new goals and possibilities. For the first time in many years, Jack knew exactly what he wanted. He also felt an unexpected empathy for Carla. In a certain way, he understood her, too.

When he spoke, he did so softly. He felt back in control. "Well, it's nice to finally understand you, Carla. We aren't so different, you and I. I should say, we weren't that different." He put his fork down. He spoke with a rare sincerity in his voice. "Thank you. You've helped me understand myself. I have been making a mistake and I only hope I have time to correct it."

He wiped his mouth with his napkin, and stood. "I am sure that Bea will be a great assistant in my office, and I am sure that we will have a very professional relationship." Taking his jacket from the coat rack, he opened the door. "Don't worry. I'm still on the team. Tell Randall I'll get him anything he needs, but from now on, I'll keep my hands to myself with you, Carla. I would appreciate it if you would do the same with me. By the way, you're a terrible cook." He stepped out into the cold.

During the trip home on the late shuttle, the explosions of understanding kept coming. Jack stared out the window making plans. Not all that he saw was good. Some of it he regretted, but those moments didn't matter to him now. Jack was never one to dwell on the past. By the time he arrived at the station, he was grinning. He left the shuttle with a light step.

As if called to him by his new sense of purpose, Anna was waiting for him as he disembarked. She wrapped her arms around him and, looking up at him, said, "You ought to check your messages. I've been trying to get a hold of you all day. If you weren't on this last shuttle, I was going to have to sleep on your doorstep."

Jack didn't answer her. He simply leaned down and filled her mouth with a kiss. He knew that he had started to communicate just a fraction of what he wanted to say to her when she melted into his embrace.

When they broke apart, she took in a small breath and brushed his lips with her index finger. "What's gotten into you, Jack?"

Jack just grinned at Anna. "Not here, Anna. It isn't safe. Come on. Let's get to my apartment. We have things to talk about."

A few minutes later, Jack led Anna in the door of his place. He went to the kitchen and got two glasses. He pulled out his most expensive bottle of simulated Islay scotch. It was one of his most prized possessions. Considering what he was proposing to do tomorrow, Jack decided that tonight was the night to try to finish the bottle.

He put down a glass in front of Anna and began to pour. "Anna, things have changed around here for me since you left. It started on our visit to I-MAM. Something changed for me that day. I don't understand it all, but that day made my relationship with you different."

Then Jack began to tell Anna about the arrival of Team Randall and all the changes which had taken place. He found himself talking with an earnestness and openness which he had never shown to any other human being. Anna just grinned as she sipped scotch from her glass.

Coming to his first meeting with Carla, Jack stumbled. He was just about to describe Carla waiting for him when he looked up. Anna gripped her glass. She tried to smile. Jack could see the pain. She knew.

"Come on now, Babydoll," Jack began. "We both know that you and I have never been committed to this monogamy thing."

Anna put her glass down on the table, but her grip tightened, and her fingers turned white. There were tears in her eyes. "Not in two years, Jack. I haven't slept with anyone else in two years. I had to stop. When I was with anyone but you, I regretted it."

Jack looked down at his hands wrapped around the glass. He spoke quietly, almost at a whisper. "Oh, I see."

"But I know, Jack. I know it's not the same for you. For you, relationships and sex don't go together easily. It's almost like you can't put them together, like you would rather keep them apart."

Jack kept looking down, but he spoke more firmly. "Before tonight Anna, you would have been right." He paused, looked up at Anna and then continued. "Before tonight, I didn't understand. But today I understand that I have had it all wrong, that I have made sex the goal and that I have manipulated you and many others toward that goal. That's what I'm trying to tell you. Tonight I understand, and I'm sorry." Jack looked up into Anna's eyes.

Anna's tears rolled. She tried not to sob but couldn't hold it in. Jack looked down at his glass. He hated emotions; most of all, he hated other people's emotions. They weren't safe. They threatened him. He just wanted Anna to stop. It made him hurt, and Jack didn't do hurt.

Jack pressed down hard against his natural instinct to become defensive, to push aside the damage he had done and declare it invalid. Instead, he tentatively reached out and took Anna's hand. He took it as a good sign that she didn't pull away.

In between the sobs, the words came as almost a whisper. "I forgive you, Jack."

Jack couldn't have said why or how, but at that moment, a dam which had held since he was fifteen years old and his dad beat him one last time broke. Tears flowed unbidden and unwanted. Jack sobbed.

And next thing he knew, Anna was there on his side of the table, arms around him. They stumbled to the couch, and she cradled him as they cried together. When he had himself together, Jack again tried to say, "I'm sorry."

Anna stopped him. "Jack your tears are a better sign of your sincerity than any words." She untangled herself, moved away from him and sat back on the other side of the couch pulling her knees up to her chest and wrapping her arms around them.

When she spoke again her voice had hardened and her vacant stare said she was far away from Jack thinking of other things. "The trouble is that sincerity doesn't really get you very far, Jack. It doesn't really matter when push comes to shove." Her eyes came back to the present and she looked directly at him, without softening her expression. "It's a start, but down the road, you'll have to find something stronger than sincerity if you want me."

"Like what?"

"Honesty, for starters. I always knew there was more to you than just a station bureaucrat, but you hid from me what you were doing and now I'm wrapped up in it."

Jack interrupted. He was beginning to feel defensive again. His tone was perhaps a note more dismissive than he would have liked. "Oh no, you're not. They don't have anything on you."

Anna raised her tone to match his. "Jack, I love you! That puts my heart right in the middle of what happens to you." She stopped, still staring at him, anger flushing her cheeks, willing him to understand.

And he did see it. He saw that his heart was entwined with Anna's whether he liked it or not and it almost threatened to undo him again. As he stared at the cheap red and white rug in front of his couch he saw all the plans which had been so clear on the shuttle shatter into a thousand pieces. "So if we are going to get a fresh start on the honesty thing, then there is more that I need to tell you." Without hope he finished his story, bringing Anna up to the present moment. He didn't have the courage any more to ask her outright to run away with him.

When he finished, Anna seemed scared, nervous. "What are you going to do, Jack?"

"Well, a lot of that depends upon you." Jack lifted he eyes so that he could see her expression.

For a couple of minutes, Anna remained quiet. Her brow furrowed as she thought over all that Jack had said.

"Do you trust Rick? Is he telling the truth? Can he get you out? I mean, after all, he wiped your memory. How do you know it isn't a trick?"

Jack breathed deeply and let it out slowly trying to calm his nerves. "I do trust Rick, Anna. He's the closest thing I have to a friend besides you. My guess is that when I went to him to discuss how to get out, I wasn't ready to go. After all, I didn't have you. I think he wiped my memory to protect himself."

Anna nodded, and was silent again. Looking down at her knees, she said, "I need you to ask me, Jack."

Jack knew what she wanted but pretended not to know. "What?"

She looked up at him, "If you want me to come with you I need you to ask me." Jack started to speak but she shook her head. "You have to understand Jack, if I come with you faithfulness and honesty are part of the deal. I won't do this any more. I won't live without integrity."

Jack was quiet and didn't respond right away. He thought over what she was asking and though he desperately wanted to say that he would be faithful, he was frightened, no longer sure he could commit to that. A parade of past erotic experiences danced through his mind.

His face must have shown what he was thinking, because Anna interrupted his thoughts. "I don't expect perfection Jack." He looked up at her but she avoided his gaze as she went on. "God knows I haven't earned the right to demand perfection." Now she looked at him, "But if we do this, it has to be a fresh start for both of us. No going back to the way things were before."

Jack made up his mind. "Anna Prindle, will you come with me?"

Speaking quietly she answered, "If you run, Jack, I'll come with you."

Jack moved across the couch and wrapped his arms more tightly around her. "I think we should go tomorrow evening. If I don't show up at work tomorrow, they'll get suspicious and be waiting for us at the terminal. But if we take the evening shuttle...."

An hour later, their plans were made, and Jack held Anna as they slept in his bed. It was the best night's sleep Jack had since Team Randall arrived on Aetna.

11
The Bomb

The next morning, Jack and Anna kissed their goodbyes with plans to catch the 5:30 down to Aetna. He got to work early so that he could prepare to show Bea the ropes. Bea arrived just after 8:00 AM, having taken the early shuttle. She looked fresh and ready to go. Jack introduced her to the team and then, after getting her assigned to an apartment near the office, he showed her the basics of Molly's responsibilities. Bea took to the work easily and was soon working her way through the HR training manual for the job.

It wasn't until mid-morning that Jack was finally able to sit down and think about checking his email. Then he remembered it didn't matter. Checking his mail was only keeping up appearances. He was just putting on his heads-up, getting ready to throw his mail up on the large screen across the room from him, when he heard a knock at the door. It was Joe. He looked worried.

Jack gestured for him to come in and take a seat.

Joe closed the door. "Check your mail," he said quietly, even before he had sat down. Jack was inclined to dismiss the note of fear in the younger Joe's voice. He didn't like drama.

Jack put on his heads-up and threw his inbox up on the large screen.

The first note from admin had arrived about 20 minutes prior. It stated: "A hydrogen leak has been discovered at processing plant number 4 located on the outskirts of Utopia. At this point in time workers are being evacuated from the area."

Joe stood up from the chair and turned to face the screen above his head. "There's another one," he said. "Came in about two minutes ago, from Bill Driscol."

As Jack scrolled through his box toward the present, he noticed a headline from Gloria Soren. "Will be in berth 6 in thirty minutes."

Jack kept scrolling until he came to the note marked "URGENT" which had arrived in Jack's inbox three minutes ago. It was marked to all staff and was from the Interim Head of H2 Production, William Driscol. Bill had been one of Bonnie's deputies. Jack liked the tall, blond beanpole Bill. He seemed to have a good head on his shoulders. The note read, "There is no leak at H2 plant number 4. It is a bomb! Suspect it was planted by Admin."

Jack stood up from his chair. His surge of adrenaline caused his feet to run cold and his fingertips to tingle.

With a picture in his mind, he cast the mail onto the screen behind his desk and threw a security cam feed of H2 plant number 4 up on the screen he and Joe were watching. Workers were flooding out of the plant, running, sprinting to save their lives. Within seconds there was a blinding flash, and the camera went dead.

Jack jumped, and Joe stifled a cry. Neither of them wanted Bea in the room right now, so they kept quiet.

Jack used his thoughts to ask for a feed further away. This view showed a plant shattered by a huge explosion and now burning off large amounts of excess hydrogen. Debris was still falling from the sky into the view of the camera which was at least a mile away.

Jack's mouth dropped. *How could they have been so stupid! Something must have gone wrong.* Jack doubted that inciting a riot was part of Team Randall's plan, and the deaths of so many experienced workers would not make Randall's task any easier. *I bet Bill or one of his men found the bomb when they weren't supposed to.*

Within seconds, the incoming message chime on his email became a near-constant hum. Jack had to think. He shut off both screens. Joe turned and looked at him.

"Have a seat," he said offhandedly as he continued to stand behind the desk. Joe had just put his butt in the chair before Jack came to a decision. "We're shutting the office. I need to get you and Bea out of harms way. I have no doubt the shit's going to hit the fan around here, and it may last for a while." Jack looked Joe in the eye for a second. "Goodbye, Joe. If I can, I'll get in touch."

Joe just nodded, and, without a word, he reached out and shook Jack's hand. Then, he turned and quietly left Jack's office, closing the door with barest of audible clicks.

Jack walked to his coat stand to pick up his bag, trying to formulate his next move. As he did so, the heads-up chimed in his ear. Across the display sitting scrolled the name "Robert."

He answered.

"Jack, tell me you've seen the news coming from the surface."

"I saw it, Robert."

"They'll be cutting the public channels of communication any time now to keep people from organizing. We have to discuss station security.

"Agreed. I will be with you in five minutes. I am just getting Joe and Bea out of harms way."

"Sounds good. Jack, whatever you do, don't go down to the docks. Let's meet at Chuck's instead. It's hot right now down there, and they want to take down anyone associated with Randall's team, and that means you."

Jack pressed his lips together. "I was afraid of that," he said to Robert.

"All right, I'll see you in five."

Jack stopped with his hand on the door handle to the office. Four weeks ago, those workers loved him. Four weeks ago, he was king of this little dung heap. He was the candy man—the one who made the world go round. Now they wanted to kill him. Jack sighed. *Well, at least that makes the path forward clear. I have to get to Musgrave's. There isn't anything left for me here now.*

Jack took the heads-up display off his head and folded it up in his hand. Then, taking a deep breath, he walked out his office door without looking back.

Jack walked hastily to the coat rack in the front office. Bea was sitting at her desk her face ashen. Obviously she had heard. Jack picked up her regulation sport coat and turned to walk back toward her. As he did so, he discretely dropped his heads-up into her pocket.

The heads-up was a liability. With its continuous connection to the cloud, Team Randall would know exactly where he was at all times. From now forward, he needed to disappear. Looking across the room, he said, "Bea, grab your things. We need to get out of here. This is going to get ugly. They're already rioting on the dock levels and will be heading this way. I want you to go home to your new apartment and keep the door closed until you hear from someone on Randall's team."

Since she seemed almost too stunned to move, Jack stepped behind the desk and helped her to her feet. That seemed to shake her loose, and she grabbed her coat from him, gathered her things, and followed him across the lobby to the door.

"I take it from your reaction that you've never seen anything like this before?"

"No. This wasn't part of the plan. Something has gone wrong."

The knot tightened in Jack's gut. He pressed his lips together as they walked out the door. He hit the palm lock, and, taking Bea by the arm, led her along the two-block walk to her apartment.

By the time Jack had her safely inside, the hairs on the back of his neck had started to tingle. He took off his wrist wallet and dropped it in the potted plant next to Bea's door. On this level, the residential corridors were too quiet. Jack wondered how many of the occupants inside these apartments wanted him dead.

He took off at a slow loping trot. He didn't want to draw attention to himself, but he needed speed. As he approached the main commercial corridor that ran around the outer part of the station, he slowed. Even from his position in the shadows, he could see that shops were hurriedly closing. Gendarmes weren't yet visible, but Jack didn't figure that would take long.

If Jack understood Robert's plan, he would wait for him outside Chuck's in full view of the cameras for a decent amount of time before taking off to meet him at their given rendezvous point.

The phrase "We have to discuss station security" was a code phrase which Robert, Molly, and Jack had set up early on when they established the smuggling ring on the station. It meant that everyone needed to go underground for a while. The plan was to meet up in one of the warehouses on the docks to discuss what they would do next. Almost all of the rest of what Robert said was a cover story to keep the security AIs and any listeners confused about their location.

However, Jack suspected that Robert wasn't kidding about the docks looking for his blood. It only made sense. He was the only piece of Team Randall they could get, and they were going to need blood, their own or others— probably both—before things returned to normal.

The public areas of the station had cameras everywhere, but there were other less public ways to get around which most people never frequented. Maintenance areas, back alleys, and freight elevators which were not watched.

From his vantage point in the shadows, Jack spent a minute or so watching a maintenance door which led into these off-grid areas. He took out the janitorial key card which he kept in the same pocket as his laser cutter.

That card, which Molly had made for him years before, still worked on the door across the way, disguising his tracks. It was the ID of a janitor who had long since quit and moved on to higher and better things, but Molly had left it open in the system and given each of them a card which would allow access to maintenance areas.

Jack used them on occasion, in order to avoid having to face merchants and other station personnel who wanted something from him, and they provided an easy way to smuggle items around the station without having a direct ID link to the smuggler.

Right now, Jack was trying to get to Anna in his apartment. He waited for about two minutes before taking his chance. He crept out and looked both directions.

There were few people left to be seen. Most everyone had either gone down to the docks or gone home. Jack made his break for it. He ducked low, trying to hide his face from any cameras and sprinted across the hall. He kept waiting for someone to shout at him or tell him to stop, but no one did. Those left on the commercial mall were much too busy trying to secure their government-owned stores to notice Jack.

Jack quickly keyed the lock and opened the door. He was careful to let it close quietly behind him so as not to make a racket. Once inside, he felt less exposed and breathed a little easier.

Making his way through heating pipes and miles of fiber, Jack walked briskly, following a path that led to a door almost directly across the corridor from his apartment. He was about ready to open it and sprint across the hall when he saw them come.

Six or eight gendarmes all in full riot gear arrived at his door. Jack, who had been watching the hall through the little window in the door, ducked to the ground. Sitting with his back against it, he heard their pounding as they demanded that he open his apartment. Jack heard them fry the lock, force the door, and shout as they entered. Anna screamed.

The raid on his apartment didn't surprise Jack. What surprised him was how quickly it was taking place. *They need a scapegoat*, he thought. *There isn't anyone better than me. They're looking for a quick execution in order to wash their hands of this.*

Jack put his head in his hands. If only he had seen Soren first; he didn't have a gun. He was helpless to stop them. He heard Anna screaming again. She was in pain. Anger rose in him as he heard Frank's high shrill voice. He couldn't bear the sound of Anna's continued cries, to know that she was in danger because of him. Impotent, Jack crawled away from the door, back down the passage from which he had come, and for the second time in twenty-seven years, Jack cried.

The Battle for Utopia

12
Baby Steps

The smell of smoke forced Jack to consider his surroundings again. He couldn't remember how he had arrived at the warehouse level of the station. It was as if a black hole had swallowed his memory when he had collapsed in the narrow maintenance corridor across the hall from his apartment. He wiped the last of the tears from his eyes and looked out the window in the closed door to the main passage on the warehouse level.

With fear, Jack noted a rolling black cloud drifting along the ceiling. Fires on space stations could be particularly deadly. They poisoned the air, removed oxygen, and overwhelmed the scrubbers. Thousands could die from just a small fire in the wrong place. He needed to get to Robert quickly, so they could make a plan to deal with the fire.

It took Jack a few seconds to recognize that the station was no longer his concern. It felt odd.

Jack flinched away from the window. He realized he had been too focused on the smoke to consider that someone might be looking back. Cautiously, Jack peeked down the corridor. He didn't see anyone.

He opened the door. His destination lay around the curve of the station about five hundred meters to his left. Glancing up, he noticed the smoke drifted toward him from the direction he wanted to go. Jack shivered. *There should be shouting and noise*. He wondered if the workers had all fled.

He jogged down the wide corridor, keeping as quiet as possible and hugging the wall. Against his will, Jack's mind relived the moment he heard Anna scream. While he pleaded with his conscience for the umpteenth time, telling it there was nothing he could have done, movement in front of him caught his attention.

Jack looked up to see a barricade erected across the corridor. Behind the barricade stood several hundred dock workers, all of them armed with makeshift weapons. Behind the rows of workers, Jack could see the source of the fire. The contents of one of the thirty-two, hangar-sized warehouses had been set ablaze. No one tried to stop it.

The front row of workers looked at him, surprised. However, they must have heard him coming because all eyes were on Jack by the time his mind recognized what lay in front of him. While Jack skidded to a halt, someone yelled, "It's Halloway! Get him!"

Jack glimpsed bodies beginning to climb over the barricades while he turned and started to run back the way he had come. He took off at a sprint.

Jack's height and his long, lanky stride made up somewhat for his poor conditioning. Even so, by the time he entered the maintenance corridor, he could hear the pounding of feet close behind him. He opened the door, slammed it shut, and kept running.

Before he had run more than ten steps, he heard pounding on the door. *Oh, shit!*, he thought. *Now they know where I've been hiding. How in the world am I going to get back upstairs?* Jack kept running but fully expected that the maintenance corridors would soon be crawling with workers looking for him. On the other hand, he appeared to be safe for now, and he had delayed those behind him. They wouldn't know exactly where he had gone. Deciding he would still meet Robert, Jack bee-lined it for a maintenance door on the other side of the circular station, behind the barricade the workers had erected. He hoped there wouldn't be any stragglers prowling around.

He gasped for air. Jack slowed his pace to a trot. It took him longer than he had hoped to cross through the heart of the huge warehouse level of the docks. Although the maintenance corridor provided a much straighter route to his destination, it was narrow, full of hanging cables, pipes, and detritus. These slowed him considerably. By the time he reached the other side, he figured he had saved just a few minutes over the time it would have taken him to use the wide, open corridors.

Jack burst out the door at a run, reasoning he had a better chance against anyone wanting to ambush him in the corridor if he had momentum on his side.

The metal door slammed open to his left. The blow followed from the right. Apparently some of the workers had anticipated him and simply back-tracked behind their barricade to the door where he came out. It would have been worse if Jack hadn't been running at full speed. The first blow intended for his gut caught him on the side and landed on his ribs, taking with it all the air out of his desperate lungs. The accompanying pop made him wonder if it would have been better to take the blow in the gut. He instantly felt light-headed. Jack's momentum propelled him until he stumbled and landed in a heap on the floor.

Jack instinctively curled into the fetal position. Lightning strikes of pain danced across his side. Desperately trying to inhale, he watched the ten or so workers who had been waiting for him. They all carried makeshift weapons of some sort. Jack caught a lucky break. Expecting little resistance, they moved more slowly than they should have to surround him.

Clarity arrived with the subtlety of a nuke. If he stayed on the floor, he would never get up again. Before he had managed to get his first breath, he forced himself back to his feet. His lack of air caused his accompanying scream to come out as a gurgle.

Jack didn't think about what came next. He simply let his street-kid survival instincts take over. He kicked out at the lead dock worker, a huge brute, somewhere well north of one hundred kilos. Expecting to find a paper-pushing desk jockey, the dock worker paid with a well-placed blow to his sternum. Jack felt rather than heard the crack and recognized he had given as good as he got. Even taken by surprise, the hulk managed to land another blow. The ragged sheet metal shank he carried effectively filleted Jack's thigh muscle. This time his scream came out full force.

His time on the streets as a teen had taught Jack how to fight and when to run. Jack used the momentary confusion he had created to make his escape. Fire erupted every time his wounded right thigh pushed off the ground. A warm, wet trail started to run down his leg. Broken ribs made full breaths impossible. Jack's mind screamed for air.

As he turned the corner, he heard the pursuit catching up to him. He wouldn't outlast them for long. Within a minute or so, Jack ducked into the warehouse he sought. He looked at the code pad next to the door. All he had to do was palm it and the doors would close, sealing his pursuers out but trapping him inside. It wasn't a solution. There might have been a better answer, but he didn't have time to work it out. He palmed the lock. The giant windowed doors slid shut just as his pursuers arrived on the other side. It would buy time but only a little. All it would take was a supervisor's key and an override code for the lock. To make matters worse, Jack had no doubt that the gendarmes now knew his exact location.

Seeing no other options, he got out of sight and started worming his way through the stacks of shipping containers toward the point where he and Robert had planned to meet. *Maybe Robert will have an idea on how to get out of this*, he thought as he limped forward, the long gash on his leg continuing to bleed.

Their rendezvous point lay in the corner of a large and little used area of the docks. They had picked this warehouse because it was stuffed with shipping containers, crates, and other items which had been abandoned and never claimed. Laid out like a labyrinth, there were plenty of places to get lost. Though—Jack noted ruefully—he left a nice, neat trail of liquid red breadcrumbs wherever he went.

When Jack reached the spot, Robert wasn't there. Worse, even through all the stacks of shipping containers, barrels, and crates, he could make out the sound of the door opening. Furious voices echoed from outside.

He had just turned to leave when he noticed the heads-up and paper note sitting on top of a yellow drum. He picked up the note. Jack recognized the handwriting. It didn't belong to Robert, but it was vaguely familiar. It read, "Put it on."

Jack hesitated. He stared at the heads-up. "Damn it!"

This was the last thing he wanted. With everyone out to kill him, he just wanted to see a friendly face. Despite running a smuggling ring, Jack hated cloak and dagger; he tried to avoid it. He found it much safer to bribe someone than sneak something past them. He routinely factored the costs of bribes into his prices.

Given no choice, he grabbed the heads-up and put it on. The screen which dropped down over his left eye scanned his retina, and the device pricked his ear as it sampled his DNA. *Identity confirmed* flashed momentarily across the screen.

An electronically distorted voice came through the headset. "It's about time, Jack. I was afraid you weren't going to make it."

Jack groaned. "Who is this? Robert?"

"You might not want to talk so loudly. There are two groups of workers already searching this warehouse. We have little time to keep you alive."

Jack repeated his question in a loud whisper. "Who is this?"

"Somebody who's trying to help you."

Jack wanted to scream, but instead he only let out a little hiss of exasperation because it had become too painful to get a deep breath. He heard someone knock a crate over somewhere in the warehouse, much closer than he would have liked. He wondered if he had permanently lost control of his own existence.

Recognizing that he had few options but to play along, Jack answered by using a thought to send a text message. *So, how do I get out of here?*

The voice responded audibly. "Good. I see you're still able to grasp the reality of your situation. Now move your ass."

A green path appeared on the heads-up display. As he started moving, Jack thought of demanding information on where the path led but a noise nearby kept him quiet. He suppressed his will to argue and took off through the maze of cargo, staying low and keeping as quiet as possible. The trail of blood he left behind him wouldn't be hard to follow.

The pathway ended outside the service airlock, right next to the huge doors which could be opened to the vacuum of space. The doors could be used to either depressurize the warehouse, or, most often, to connect it to the cargo bay of an incoming freighter. Dock workers used the service airlock when there was a problem getting a good seal between the freighter and the station.

Jack stopped.

"Get inside, Jack."

He didn't move, and his face purpled with silent rage. Jack hated heights, and he had no love for the perspective-bending, nausea-producing world of zero-g. Besides, stepping into an airlock on the advice of a modulated voice on a heads-up that he had picked up in a warehouse wasn't exactly his idea of safe.

Jack stepped over to the porthole and looked inside. The airlock appeared empty. He asked, *How do I know you won't space me?* As soon as he said it, a sinister idea appeared in his mind. Team Randall would want to make a spectacle of him. They wouldn't want him to get caught by the workers. They would probably want him alive, though it might be enough to simply show his decompressing body floating through the void. Jack's feet went cold. "Who is this?" he demanded again in a low, angry voice.

"Jack, this is an encrypted heads-up which doesn't use the cloud. It's some pretty high-end technology. That said, you don't get to know who this is, not yet. I hate to barge in on the slow grinding of your gears, but we have a problem. There's a small group of workers heading directly your way. They will be able to see you in about fifteen seconds. I need you to get in that airlock, right now."

He looked down at his leg and, seeing the continued bleeding, thought, *Damn, Jack,* and then quietly opened the heavy rubber gasket lined door and got in. He shut it behind him, without engaging the seals and locks. Over the porthole lay a piece of electronic paper which displayed a crisp three dimensional image of an empty airlock. Jack smiled at the simplicity of the trick. It had fooled him. From the outside, there would be no way to tell if the airlock was full or empty.

"Jack, for this trick to work you're going to need to seal the door. Otherwise, the perspective will be off. You've got about three seconds to decide." Jack really didn't like locking himself in. The airlock couldn't be opened to the vacuum of space unless the seals were engaged on the door to the station. He had thought that leaving them open would be his insurance policy. The thought of what might happen if he closed the lock terrified him.

"Jack, close the door now!" the voice on the other side of the line insisted.

Jack lunged and hit the button. The door sealed with a click so loud Jack felt sure someone must have heard it. The sudden movement caused his vision to turn red even as he winced at the sound of the door. Dizziness and nausea overcame him. With a crash, he stumbled into the door and slid down, causing a wave of pain to erupt from his damaged ribs.

"Are you still with me, Jack?"

Jack looked down at the blood running freely from his wounded thigh. "For now. Although I'm not sure for how much longer. I got cut up by the workers."

"Get in the pressure suit, Jack."

Jack turned around to see an EVA pressure suit and helmet laid out on the deck behind him.

Just at that moment, he heard someone brush against the door, then say, "It's empty."

Jack held his breath for a few seconds, staying absolutely still. "Maybe the blood is a trick."

A second voice joined the first. "He has to be close by. Let's keep looking."

Jack tiredness overwhelmed him. He sat there staring at the pressure suit across the floor, willing his body forward. It didn't cooperate. He gave up.

"Jack, stay with me now. You've trusted me this far and right now I could kill you by the push of an airlock button. I'm trying to help you. Put on the damn suit." The voice on the other end of the line adopted the tone of a drill sergeant with a wayward private.

Through his haze, it took a few seconds for Jack to reason out that he would feel safer in a pressure suit while in an airlock controlled by Randall, Gunderson, or anyone else. But since he was going to die anyway, it didn't seem to matter.

"Listen to me, Jack. You will get yourself into that suit and while you do it you *will* keep talking to me. Right now, that suit is the only thing which will save your life."

Why is someone helping me? In the Unity, where sticking your neck out inevitably meant having your head cut off, no one did anyone else any favors, especially if the favor could get the helper in trouble. It made him more suspect that his escape was simply a trick to ferret him away from the workers and capture him. He threw a thought at his mysterious interlocutor. *Why?*

"Do I really need to explain this? How else do you propose getting off the station? The whole place is looking for you. It isn't exactly like you can take the shuttle down to Utopia."

No. Why are you helping me?

"I have my reasons, Jack. You'll understand soon. For now, we both have the same objective. We both want to keep you alive."

For now, thought Jack. He couldn't see what the suit could do to help him, but he couldn't think of any other options. Even as he gingerly scooted across the floor, he kept asking questions. This time in a muted whisper. "How is stepping out of an airlock going to keep me alive?"

The voice remained silent, while Jack continued to wriggle painfully into the suit. He was about to speak again when the voice interrupted him. "Jack, I'm not in a position to answer your questions, and you're out of options. If you have a better plan, go for it, but I think we both know that you won't make it very far on that leg if you go back into the station."

Jack sighed. He wanted to take action, to lash out, and if he died so be it, but the voice was right and some small part of him knew that if he died, Anna would die with him. He had no doubt of that, not after the way he'd seen Team Randall treat people on Aetna. Right now the best insurance policy for Anna was to keep himself alive. Jack locked the helmet into place.

His heads-up flashed with alert messages telling Jack what he already knew. He was bleeding to death. Within seconds, the pressure suit tightened around his thigh, cutting off the flow of blood to his wound. Jack winced at the pain. At the same time, a message appeared on his heads-up. "Blood loss approaching dangerous levels. Right side ribs six and seven fractured. Right side rib eight possibly fractured. Tourniquet applied to right quadriceps. Initiating insertion of Emergency Medical Nanites."

The suit gave Jack a sharp poke in the back of his neck. *Medical nanites in a pressure suit?* From what Musgrave had said, they were still experimental in most Unity hospitals. "Ouch. What the hell is this thing? Is it military?"

"The answer to that question is above your pay grade, Jack. Let's just say the suit is doing what it needs to do."

Jack grunted to try to keep from passing out as he stood on his wounded leg. The pain of the tourniquet felt almost worse than the wound, but at least the bleeding would stop.

"All right, it's getting a little interesting on my end of things here. I should be able to stay with you for just a little while longer. We need to hurry, or I'm going to have to bug out. Let's get going. Have you clipped on yet?"

Jack looked down at the two carabiners and cords attached to his pressure suit. He clipped one onto the eye-ring next to the door and let out a deep breath. He managed to momentarily steam up the inside of the helmet. "I'm clipped on, and I am depressurizing the airlock."

Jack hesitated for a second before reaching above his head and cranking the valve open. He heard a loud hissing sound as the precious life giving air vented from the chamber. Jack took in a deep breath and worked to calm himself. When the pad next to the door turned green, Jack keyed the door open.

"Okay, this is going to be the tricky part. When you step out that door, you'll be stepping out of the station's gravity. I assume you know the procedure?"

"I've done free-fall three times, but I know what I'm doing," Jack texted to the voice. *...and I am tired of having anyone else tell me what to do*, he thought to himself.

Jack hated the mind-bending act of stepping out the door. Somehow, it messed with his head and his stomach. On the station, he had the comforting tug of manufactured gravity underneath him. Once he climbed outside, he would leave it behind. He would have to depend on his magnetic boots and clipped on-line to keep him from floating away into the unending void. On top of this, he would be walking perpendicular to his current orientation on the skin of the station. In essence, he would be walking across the other side of the wall in front of him. Jack's mind didn't like processing that change.

"Seriously? No sneaking out and floating around as a teen?"

"Did I mention that I managed to get sick in my helmet every time?" Jack's words came slowly, and he started to feel a little giddy. He guessed it was because of the blood loss.

Preparing to exit the station, Jack looked down at the floor below him. The steel grating had been cut so that from where he stood it appeared like he walked across the rungs of a ladder. The ladder continued out the door of the station, some eight feet. It ended in a catch-net for those who accidentally propelled themselves uncontrollably out of the manufactured gravity.

"Nice, Jack. Are you on your belly yet?"

Jack answered, "Almost." He finished lying down at the sill of the airlock, then said, "Okay. I'm there."

"Well, do yourself a favor today. Keep your eyes focused on the deck. Don't look up. It will help keep you from swimming in your own juices. Except now, of course. Now I need you to look up and clip yourself onto the catwalk outside the station."

Even while the voice talked, Jack reached up over his head and unclipped himself from the eye along the inside of the airlock. He gently moved forward and stretched his arms outside the gravity well of the station to clip himself to the railing of the catwalk which ran perpendicular to the open airlock along the shell of the station.

Without answering, Jack eased himself forward, crawling up the ladder on his hands and knees toward the void of space and the ladder extending above him. Jack never enjoyed the sensation of losing the predictable comfort of the manufactured gravity. He pushed forward. The sensation of floating increased as more of his body emerged from inside. Jack felt as if he were slowly pulling himself into a pool head first. Jack looked ever so carefully at the line he had attached to the railing, hoping it would hold. When his feet finally left the gravity well, his equilibrium told him that he was going to pitch head-over-heels. He started getting nauseated.

For a moment, he gripped the ladder tightly and then closed his eyes. He let his mind adjust to his new reality as he took a few breaths. To steady himself, Jack asked, "So where am I heading?" The voice didn't answer immediately. He opened his eyes and, looking beside him, took a careful step onto the walkway he needed to follow.

The satisfying "thunk" as his magnetic boots attached themselves to the station reassured Jack. Just as he stepped forward, the airlock doors behind him began to close on their own. He spoke up again. "Someone is closing the airlock." A long pause followed with no answer. "Hello? What do I do now?"

"Keep your shirt on, Jack. We're working on it." Jack could hear a distorted alarm going off in the background.

Another moment of silence. He waited.

When the mic kicked in again, the voice on the other end sounded tense. Jack thought he picked up other voices but couldn't make out what they said. "So, Jack, I have a bit of a situation here. I'm getting out of the way for a while. If you want to live follow the path." A green path clicked up on Jack's heads-up display. Without waiting for his answer, the mic went dead.

Jack stood there for a moment, then shook his head inside his helmet. *Great! Just great*, he thought. He briefly considered trying to reenter the airlock but realized that would create more problems than it solved. More than any time since his life had been turned upside down a few weeks ago, he felt alone.

He looked up. It was a mistake. The queasy sensation in his stomach increased, and the sudden movement almost caused him to pitch over backwards. Above him, Aetna hung in the void, blindingly white, reflecting the light from a distant sun. Behind it, the giant Catania erupted from its side, massive and impenetrable.

Jack shivered as he faced the tenuousness of his situation. Even with all the chaos of the last few weeks, just once had Jack thought his life might be on the line. Only when Gunderson had threatened him with the laser scalpel did he feel any personal danger, and that turned out to be an illusion.

Feeling the thin magnetic connection between his feet and the grating beneath him, Jack recognized how dependent he had become on others. He even had to rely upon his enemies at times. It left him cold to think that he had no one to help him at that moment in time. Whoever had been on the other end of the line had been his last link.

Paranoia threatened to engulf him, and he wondered again if this had been a trick to lure him out of the station into a trap. He decided that it very likely could have been and then pushed the worry back out of his consciousness. Nothing could be done about it. Jack took some tentative baby steps, grunting with each step. He shuffled forward along the catwalk, following the path laid out in front of him, dragging his safety line behind.

13
Prison Cell

When Jack finally found himself standing in front of the escape plan, he chuckled. How or why it had been stashed there Jack didn't know, but someone had strapped a Unity standard escape pod to the side of a solid waste processing unit in a location difficult to see from anywhere but straight above it. Even then, buried among the towers of exchangers and water purifiers, the dome of its heat shield would have appeared completely normal, like just another cooling tower. It would have been almost impossible to spot unless you walked right up to it. He would have ended up belly laughing if the pain in his side hadn't kept him from it.

The sixteen-foot capsule had been placed on the opposite side of the waste processing unit from the control panel and maintenance hatches. Getting to it hadn't been fun. It had required him to hop over the railing of the walkway and make his way untethered behind the unit. Jack had taken five minutes to find the courage to unhook his tether.

Standing at the foot of a capsule almost three times his height, Jack looked up and saw the ladder he would have to use to pull himself up hand over hand into the door which lay open on the narrow cylinder six feet above his head.

I guess I don't have any better options. Staring up, Jack put his gloved hands on the hips of his pressure suit. Thinking back, he realized that he had lost his ability to choose and plan the moment Randall and company set foot on Aetna. Jack reached for the lowest rung of the ladder and began to pull himself up. Jack wondered if he climbed toward his own prison cell.

He climbed without attaching his feet to the rungs. Since weight and gravity weren't a problem, it seemed more natural that way, and it did not require him to push off with his wounded leg. He reached the door without incident and clambered inside. The capsule was a cramped affair with barely enough room for eight passengers. In the zero-g environment, he spun himself gently into the command seat. He sat with his back to the engines and his legs pointing toward the void of space.

So what next? thought Jack.

Looking back, he realized that the hatch remained wide open. He painfully got out of his seat and, using a hand hold inside the capsule, gained the leverage he needed to shut the door. Once it closed, Jack noticed a pad next to it which blinked red. He palmed the pad, and the door sealed tight with a clunk, which he felt, rather than heard. At the same moment, the cabin began to pressurize.

In the midst of climbing back to the captain's chair, the ship startled him by recognizing his heads-up display and broadcasting information. *I thought this heads-up wasn't supposed to be part of the cloud. How could a Unity escape pod find it?* The screen above the command chair came to life and displayed similar information.

First, the ship sent him a set of critical alerts regarding the life support situation on board the vessel. An automated male voice spoke in Jack's ear. "Warning! Atmospheric pressure below safe levels. Maintain pressure suit integrity." A little bar appeared at the bottom of his heads-up, showing a slowly rising atmospheric pressure.

Once the ship had run through its list of critical failures, it brought up a countdown clock and stated, "Evacuation to extraction point Theta in fifteen seconds."

Jack heard a couple of pops outside the capsule as the straps which held it to the station fell away.

Give me a second!

Jack struggled to harness himself into the command seat. Twisting put him into spasms of pain from his fractured ribs. Gritting his teeth, he managed to strap in. *Medical nanites and tourniquets, but they couldn't do better with the anesthetics?* He closed his eyes for the last few seconds of the countdown. They passed achingly slowly. His imagination kept telling him that someone would show up at the window in the door to the capsule and shoot him before he could take off.

The pressure of lift-off forced Jack back into his seat, eliciting a grunt of pain. He opened his eyes. Out the small windows, just under the view screen, Jack watched the cooling towers recede. He gently turned to look behind him and saw the curve of the station appear. He relaxed, until he spotted a tiny squad of gendarmes in EVA suits looking up at his ship.

One of the three suited figures took a knee and pointed some kind of shoulder-fired weapon Jack's way. Jack closed his eyes for an eruption of destruction, and waited. *They're going to shoot me down*, thought Jack. *Fuck! They're going to shoot me down. I'm going to get spaced!*

After a good five seconds in which the end never came, he turned back to see a small speck put down weapon, while the squad continued to watch Jack's receding ship.

Why didn't they fire? Who stopped them? Where is this ship taking me? Jack imagined the escape pod landing right in the middle of Utopia's Penal and Reeducation Facility.

Jack's heart started to pound. From the evacuation simulations he used to supervise on the station, Jack knew something about how Unity escape pods were supposed to work. They had very little power, just enough to get them away from the station or ship. In the case of stations orbiting a habitable planet, they had enough juice to get them into the atmosphere. At that point, the computer used the heat shield and friction to fly the ship toward its targeted landing zone. Once it had entered far enough into the atmosphere, parachutes would deploy and carry it down to a gentle landing.

Jack spoke into his heads-up. "Computer, what is our destination?"

"That information is classified."

At this point, Jack didn't have it in him to either control his temper or yell. He found it difficult enough to stay conscious and form coherent thought. "Who classified the destination?"

"I am sorry. I am not allowed to reveal that information. Keep calm. Help is on the way."

Jack rolled his eyes. If possible, he had no intention of going where this ship wanted to take him. "Computer, alter course to bring me down fifty kilometers outside Utopia."

"I am sorry, but you do not have command authorization. Keep calm. Help is on the way."

Fear and adrenaline kept Jack at it for another ten minutes, but he was neither able to change the destination of the vessel or to find out any other useful information. Despite his worry, he lacked the energy to put up much of a fight. Although he couldn't find a way to alter its course, he did discover that under certain emergency conditions he might be able to control the ship. When he demanded that the ship land outside of Utopia because it was a medical emergency, the ship responded a little differently. "Altering target landing location is beyond the scope of emergency medical procedures allowed to occupant. Keep calm. Help is on the way."

In the end, his wounds and exhaustion won out, and Jack fell asleep. Some time later, the roar of atmospheric entry woke him. Flames shot past the windows as friction heated the frigid atmosphere of Aetna until it burned. Jack had no idea where he was, but entry seemed to go as planned. The engine package had jettisoned sometime before he regained consciousness, and on cue Jack's ship executed a series of turns to reduce its speed.

Everything seemed perfectly normal until a few seconds after the parachutes deployed. Jack came out of the clouds and realized they were approaching open water. He didn't like that at all but had little time to think about it because two military hovercraft buzzed close by the escape pod. Now Jack felt sure that the voice on the other end of the line had been Gunderson, or maybe Randall himself. It had all been a set-up. Jack decided he didn't want to go down without a fight. He didn't intend to be taken alive.

Up until this point he had paid little attention to the cabin itself. Now he scanned it for a weapon. He desperately wished he had gone to Soren and got the gun she owed him before all of this happened. He judged the large fire extinguisher near the door to be his best bet. Perhaps he could at least land a good blow before they captured him.

Jack strained to see as the two hovercraft disappeared below him. He tried to unstrap himself from the seat but found that the harness would not respond. The computer interrupted. "For safety reasons, your harness may not be removed during entry. Keep calm. Help is on the way."

Jack groaned and tried all the harder to unfasten his harness.

"Adjusting pitch of the vessel."

The ship tipped forward nose down to the oncoming ocean. Jack had never experienced that in any evacuation simulation, but this didn't surprise him. Unity corporate training had nothing to do with reality whatsoever.

He could now see that below him the two hovercraft had landed on the water. Squads of soldiers stood on their stubby wings, weapons aimed at his vessel. A few tens of feet above the water, a loud bang erupted from the vehicle as the parachutes cut away, taking some portion of the back of the escape pod with them. Jack twisted in his command seat trying to see what had happened when another bang at the front of the vessel announced the shearing away of much of the nose cone as well. Jack whipped around just in time to see the craft hit the water. Slammed against his harness, Jack's broken ribs let their displeasure be known. Jack would have sworn that someone had stuck a sword in his side. He screamed. Dull brownish liquid splashed up over the windows and the cabin went dark, only lit by the screen above him.

The craft shuddered underneath him. *It's going to sink!*

Jack desperately tried to get out of his restraints, now terrified that he would drown. Above him, the screen lit up, and the voice of the computer said in his heads-up, "One thousand, two hundred, and fifty-six kilometers to check point Theta. Underwater propulsion systems check out nominal. Proceeding to extraction point. Atmospheric pressure normal. You may now remove your harness and your helmet. Please remain in your pressure suit as it is necessary to stop the bleeding from your leg. Keep calm. Help is on the way."

Jack slumped back into his chair. *What the hell just happened?* He slowly unsnapped his harness, totally spent. Someone had sent soldiers to capture him, but somehow it hadn't happened. Clearly the military hadn't expected him to sink. That had not been part of their plan, or they would have known what to do. *Or maybe their job was just to make sure I stayed in the vessel?* On the other hand, it could have meant that it wasn't Randall, or someone working for him, on the line when he escaped the station after all. *Who, then?*

With effort, Jack reached up with both hands and unlatched the seal which kept the helmet attached and ran a gloved hand through his sweaty hair. He unbuckled his harness.

He hurt. His thigh throbbed as it remained locked in the grip of the tourniquet. His ribs made every breath a chore. Jack tried to fight but remained helpless as pain, exhaustion, and blood loss turned his vision red. Fatigue placed the escape pod and reality at the end of a long dark tunnel. The pin prick of vision blinked out. Coherent thoughts fled, and Jack thought he heard Anna's voice. The voice changed slightly and reminded him of a person he had almost forgotten. Jack's will gave in, and he let go.

14
Under Water

Jack's alcoholic mother never deeply cared for him. His birth had been an inconvenient accident in late menopause. From her, he had received food and shelter but little else. Jack never felt close to his mother.

Within a few months of her death, just before Jack's fifteenth birthday, his home life became so full of beatings and abuse that Jack went on the run. His first year on the streets had been hellish. He stole what he could but spent much of the time perpetually hungry. He was always cold—not the bracing cold of Aetna. His hometown had a much more temperate climate. Rather, Jack simply remembered his time on the streets as an absence of warmth wrapped in an eternal dampness.

His first break came one night in a club. He used to get in by climbing through a broken window in the alley because he was still underage. He had just scrambled through and carefully dropped to the floor when he turned around to face one of the staff dancers. Ginny wasn't much older than he was, probably minimum age or maybe nineteen. She wasn't exactly pretty, with bubblegum pink hair and dark black makeup, but she didn't yet look used up like so many in that hard place, and she had a sweet smile that had not yet lost its innocence and warmth. Jack had seen her before. They had talked a few times, and he thought he had caught her looking at him occasionally as she danced.

"You know that Moe would kill you if he found you doing that."

Jack tried to look cool. He brushed off his dirty jeans as if what he had done were perfectly natural. "Who's Moe?"

Ginny looked at him with the disdain only a teenage girl can muster, then put her hand on her bony hip, and said "The bouncer."

Rail thin, Jack put on his best street swagger. "Are you kidding me? I could take him. He's a pussycat."

Ginny raised her eyebrow; she didn't buy any of it.

Jack heard a loud squeal as the door at the end of the hall opened. From where he stood in the small alcove with the window, Jack couldn't see who was coming, but Ginny could.

Without saying a word to him, she stepped toward him and pushed him up against the wall of the corridor. She held her finger up to her lips and whispered in his ear. "I ought to make you prove that," but instead she kissed him. A second later, Moe walked by. He stopped and stared at them.

Ginny stopped kissing Jack. "What?" She gave Moe a murderous look.

Moe seemed startled, but then answered just as strongly, "Has he paid you?"

"Yes. He's paid me." Ginny reached into her tight leather pants and pulled out a credit chip. "And what the fuck business is it of yours?"

The bouncer shrugged, continued on his way, and then ducked into one of the doors farther along the hall.

Jack blushed as Ginny pulled back, all his swagger gone.

She leaned in. "We better at least pretend, or he'll know something's up." She began to pull Jack into a curtained alcove by the hand.

Jack blushed even harder and tugged her to a stop. "I don't have any money," he whispered.

Ginny lit up her face with her smile. "Don't worry. I'll take care of you."

It was the first time Jack had sex. It was also the first time he fell in love.

When they were done, Ginny stood up from the mattress on the floor and worked her way back into her *faux* leather pants. Overwhelmed by what had happened, Jack sat there staring at her disappearing flesh.

"You got a place to stay?" Ginny asked as she zipped up.

Jack shook his head.

Ginny grinned at his continued shyness. "Well, if you want, you can crash at my place."

Jack tried to appear low key. He shrugged. "That'd be all right."

Over the next three months, Ginny introduced Jack to a lot of different things. She continued his sexual education and taught him about a wide variety of drugs, legal and otherwise. She became mother, sister, and lover to Jack. He adored her, and Ginny seemed to enjoy his attention.

Years later, wisdom and hindsight would let Jack recognize the asymmetries in their relationship. At the time, he had been so naïve to the realities of the world that he hadn't really thought through the implications of the exchange between Ginny and the bouncer. Somewhere in his mind he knew that Ginny got paid for sex, but in his infatuation, he just assumed that it all came to an end when she invited him home. All he understood was that Ginny offered him a sense of safety he had never known before.

It happened one day when Jack walked in the door early from a delivery job he had picked up to help pay the rent. He had been a shy kid who stayed quiet, a habit which developed from growing up in a house with an abusive drunk for a Dad. They didn't hear him come in.

When she saw him standing in the door, she shoved their drug dealer off her and tried to talk to Jack. He didn't say a word. She tried to hold him by the wrist, but Jack balled his other fist. Seeing this, Ginny let him go, tears streaming down her face. Jack fled the apartment and never looked back.

Jack woke to a hard metallic tang in his mouth. He still felt exhausted, but the pain in his side seemed to have eased somewhat, and the pressure suit had relaxed its grip on his leg. He took that to be a good sign because if he were still bleeding, Jack doubted he would have ever reentered the world of the living. He didn't know how long he had been out but based on his mouth and how sore he felt, he guessed it must have been quite a while. Eyes still closed, he thought he noticed a bump in the so far smooth ride of the escape pod-turned-submarine. He opened his eyes to see a pale red light dancing and flashing across the dimmed ceiling of the pod. He sat up, careful not to aggravate his ribs.

"Oh," he whispered, as he absorbed the image coming out of the front window. Sending a message through his heads-up he thought, *Computer, can we hold this position?*

After a second or so, the computer responded audibly, "Negative."

Jack flipped up the eye piece of the heads-up. He decided to try something. This time he spoke in a commanding voice. "Computer, emergency medical hold. ten minutes." Jack thought he might be able to trick the AI into agreeing if he claimed he had a medical emergency, since it knew that he had injuries.

The computer chirped its compliance.

In front of the now slowing vessel, an innumerable number of red dots swam and scattered like snow. They flashed and swooshed as they got out of the way. In a surprisingly short space, the submersible came to a stop. Jack now sat inside an immense column of continuously dancing bits of light which were made up by an uncountable school of small, lean bait fish. These particular oily fish were known as lampheads for the red dot of bioluminescence on their widened forehead. They were one of the few fish on Aetna that had developed sight.

Little of the light from the star Sicily penetrated the icy crust of Aetna. Most of the diverse ocean life navigated or hunted using some kind of echo-location or electroreception. However, a select few had developed sight. A lamphead used its sight and bioluminescence to scoop up little bits of organic matter caught up in tall columns of warm water created by volcanism far below.

Despite his circumstances, Jack found himself overcome with wonder. He looked right and left as the lights darted and danced in the darkness that surrounded him. He watched the movement, thinking of little else, letting the patterns and swirls wash over him.

After a while, Jack noticed that certain small areas of the fish swirling around his vessel would suddenly go dark. In fact, he could trace these dark patches in a meandering path which traveled repeatedly through the swirling ball of fish.

Jack flipped down his heads-up. "Computer," he whispered, "place a real-time, sonar overlay on the heads-up, highest density, neutral magnification." Instantly, Jack saw in bright green a semi-transparent overlay which showed the outline of each of the thousands upon thousands of fish which surrounded him. He looked around through the roof and floor of the ship. Jack found himself engulfed in a swirling dance of life.

Jack shook his head at the wonder and beauty of it all. Then he turned toward one of the dark patches wandering through the great ball. He caught his breath. The lampheads were not alone. Hidden in the dark, sleek predators sliced through the moving mass, gorging themselves. Wherever they went, lights blinked off, and darkened lampheads dashed to the side, prompting other lights to go out, creating a trail of darkness that moved through the roiling ball.

For several minutes Jack watched the dance between predator and prey, entranced by its fluid motion and stung by its brutality. Beaten and trapped inside his escape pod, Jack found himself rooting for the prey.

The darkness came almost instantaneously. It rolled toward him from the direction of the bow as all the lights blinked out. The sonar showed Jack that the whole massive ball of fish had fled to the rear of his vessel, a few of them knocking themselves senseless on the windows in their blind flight.

Jack saw the monster coming from below on the sonar at least twenty seconds before it arrived.

"Computer, external lights to maximum."

Light flooded the water, even as the submersible gently backed away from the rising creature. A massive, toothless jaw swept a few short meters from the window. The mouth on that rounded, eyeless snout could have easily swallowed his entire vessel. It looked as if the nose cone of an ancient rocket had been sliced in half and opened on hinges. Behind the hinged mouth, segment after segment rose from the darkness. Its body swished back and forth as the sifter undulated through the water, pursuing the column of nutrients.

Sifters were the stuff of legend in the Utopia fishing community. Theoretically up to three hundred and fifty meters long and twenty-five meters in diameter, they lived by swallowing whole the nutrient and oxygen rich columns of rising sea water. Cilia and other mechanisms designed to filter out the particles of organic matter lined the whole length of their gut. When queried, the computer told Jack that the estimated length of the creature in question measured at least two hundred and ten meters.

Jack slumped in his chair. Very few living human beings had ever seen the creature he currently watched. *My God! It's amazing.* In the light of what he had just witnessed Jack appeared small in his own eyes, unimportant, and unnoticed. It bothered him. It felt like coming home and facing a truth long ignored.

There had been a time, when he was young and had first traveled into space, when he used to stare at the stars. He couldn't remember when he had last taken the time. Ever since humanity had gone to space, their insignificance in the universe was something they could no longer avoid. Most filled their lives with activity and technology, pushing the obvious behind a veil of noise and fury, but the obvious had a way of breaking through.

Long after the monster had disappeared from the view of the ship's lights, Jack continued to watch on the radar, fascinated. *I wish Anna could be with me to see that.* Jack recognized that Anna was probably suffering right then at the hands of her captors. For the briefest of moments, he grieved without fear. Perhaps it only came from his blood loss, but he found himself immersed in a strange, unnatural peace.

Finally the computer spoke. "Resuming normal speed and course. Arrival at extraction point Theta in approximately eight hours."

The words broke Jack's meditation. His thoughts returned to the metallic tang in his mouth.

"Computer," he said aloud. His voice had a sandpaper quality to it as he spoke through cracked and parched lips. "Give me my current medical status."

The computer chirped, then said, "Based on nanite information, your vital signs are stable, although your blood pressure remains below optimal levels. Without assistance, you could continue to feel lethargic for many days."

Jack had to agree. He would very much like to close his eyes again already. Just watching out the window had worn him out. He asked his next question. "Computer, how did you get data from the nanites?"

"Data has been retrieved continuously through your heads-up device."

Jack nodded. He suspected that the AI and the heads-up device worked together but wanted to make sure that the computer wasn't in control of his head directly. He had no intention of giving over his mind again to anyone, let alone a strange AI on a mysterious life pod. "What's the status of my injuries?"

"Right side ribs six and seven are seventy percent repaired. The hairline fracture in rib eight has been fully healed. Tissue damage to the right quadriceps has been thirty percent healed. All surface and internal bleeding has been stopped. Some nanites are being reassigned to work on various secondary bruises. They have found no other significant injuries."

"Can I move?"

"It is advisable to avoid significant use of your right leg for at least the next twenty-four hours. However, the pressure suit can provide temporary stabilization of your leg if necessary."

"I don't plan to go far," Jack answered sarcastically. "Do you need the helmet on to stabilize my leg?"

"That is not needed. The helmet only functions as a controller in the absence of a higher level AI."

Jack slowly pushed himself out of his seat. While shifting the right leg of his suit stiffened so that he could not move or bend his knee. It was like having a straight rod attached to his hip. He begrudged the computer's interference, even if it had prevented him from bleeding to death.

Right now he had two things on his mind. He wanted to eat and drink something, and then he wanted to find a place to sleep.

Jack stopped to take a look around. The oval shaped cabin looked like a Unity escape pod. Or rather it looked like a perfect model of a Unity escape pod. The ship had what amounted to one and a half decks' worth of space. In the center of the oval rear cabin sat a four-foot-high dais, with the captain's chair and its consoles. The captain's chair was raised up to take advantage of the short two-foot high, three hundred sixty-degree windows which surrounded the passenger compartment. The command screen for the ship lay above these narrow windows on the curving ceiling of the vessel.

Below the captain's chair, the pod had seats for seven, arranged along the curved walls facing each other. Jack gingerly let himself down off the dais. The side where he stood lacked one seat, replaced instead with the now sealed hatch.

Jack looked forward. Under the stubby bow of the ship lay four tightly packed bunks, as well as cupboards which held the ship's supplies. Unity protocols said that the ship needed to hold enough supplies to keep a crew of eight alive for three weeks.

Everything appeared just as it should, but something seemed off. *It's like a badly modified cynthy*, Jack thought. *It looks uncanny, almost too perfect.* The craft appeared to be in pristine condition, which in the Unity screamed anomaly. On a typical escape pod, someone would have taken pieces to fix some other more important machine for which parts were not available.

Jack worked his way forward and started opening cupboards to assess his situation. He could have probably asked the computer for a list of ship's stores, but he didn't want any assistance.

Some time later, Jack sat in the main cabin holding a steaming bowl of Ramen noodles. He ate, mostly out of habit. Jack emptied his bowl and stared at it.

He spent some time making up one of the four bunks buried with the supplies in the nose of the escape capsule.

It took him the better part of the next twenty-five minutes to worm his way out of his pressure suit. Not sure of what would happen next, he laid it out carefully on one of the passenger seats, in case he needed it. The computer complained at him about this, but Jack reassured it that he only intended to sleep.

He regretted leaving the damp but warm suit almost immediately. The cabin in the pod was cold, and his light cotton work clothes were soaked in old sweat and blood. His ripped pants had dried to his skin.

As he began to shiver he said, "Computer, please increase the cabin temperature by ten degrees." The computer chirped its compliance. He could have simply communicated with a thought through the heads-up, but he wanted to hear a voice, even if it was his own.

Jack used a pair of scissors he had retrieved from one of the first aid kits on board when rummaging for food. He shivered as he cut away as much as he could of the pants. The wound had almost fully closed at this point, the nanites having both sterilized it and facilitated its healing. Their work still seemed tentative, and Jack remained quite careful to avoid moving suddenly. He removed as much of his pants as he could and gently wandered the two steps to the head which sat curtained in a corner of the small bunk and storage room. He finished, putting on an ill-fitting jumpsuit he had also found in the cupboards and gently lay down on his bed. It seemed a sacrilege to put his filthy body in the clean jumpsuit and on the bed, but the escape pod had no shower, so Jack didn't have a choice.

Exhaustion crept over him. He was just drifting toward oblivion when he remembered Anna holding him the evening before. He casually wondered what was happening to her right then. As reality broke through the haze of sleep, Jack's body jerked awake. Needed rest fled miles away. For the next hour,

Jack found himself playing back the day's events in unwanted loops of recrimination and "what ifs." *I should have let Bea fend for herself. I should have been there at the apartment. I should never have left Anna alone.*

"But there's nothing I can do about that now," Jack complained aloud to his mind. "Shut up, all right?" He sat up in his bed.

"Computer, where's the auto-pharmacy?"

A chirp from the corner of the main cabin answered Jack's question. He kept his head low so as not to bang it on the ceiling of the storage and sleeping compartment. Without putting his pressure suit on, he gingerly ducked back out into the main lounge of the ship. He went toward the quiet chirp and found the auto-pharmacy mounted on a wall. It prescribed him a sleeping pill and an analgesic. Jack took both with a dispensed cup of water and returned to his bunk.

Lying down, Jack's thoughts prosecuted him until the medicines hit his bloodstream. *You shouldn't have left her, Jack.* He tossed and turned as he tried to push through his mental suffocation toward oblivion. *This is why you've always kept yourself free, Jack. Look at you. You're tied up in knots.* The prosecution started its attack again. Eventually, the pharmaceuticals won out, and he fell into a fitful sleep.

Sometime later, Jack's mind slit the veils of sleep and entered into the land of the living against his will. As soon as he became fully aware, the worry came back full force. It didn't take long for him to once again start beating himself up for his choices with Anna.

He didn't know just how long he had been under, but he still didn't feel rested. Jack tried to rub both the sleep and tension out of his eyes. He was pissed. First his mind told him that he should never have let himself get burned by a woman again, that he should have never gotten close to Anna. It doubted his choice to commit to her. Then it came along and berated him for not doing more to help her when she got in trouble. Jack found himself rubbing his forehead with growing force and speed as if the motion could somehow dissolve his fears about her safety and with it the double-bind.

Part of him wanted to bolt, to run from it all and make a new start, as he had that day in Ginny's apartment many years before. Instead, he lay trapped in a submersible tube without control and no certainty of what would come next. As Jack lay on his bed, the walls of the escape pod seemed cramped in a way they had not the moment before. Hopelessness engulfed him, as if he suffocated in a coffin of his own making.

At that moment, the clang of metal on metal brought Jack to the present. He reached blindly for his heads-up, looking toward the fire extinguisher in the main cabin. Without thinking, he stood up quickly, paying for it with stabbing pains from his thigh.

From the other cabin came a noise like someone banging on the door of his escape pod with a hammer. Someone wanted to talk.

15
Missing Pieces

Jack crouched at the door of the submersible, extinguisher at hand, ready to bash anyone who came through. He tried as best he could to keep weight off his damaged leg. It still throbbed. The computer kept putting little warning lights up in the corner of his heads-up, telling him to stand up and get the pressure off. He ignored them.

Again, someone banged on the door.

Jack opened the airlock. He brought the extinguisher up over his head and, as the door swung wide, had to stop himself from smashing Rick Carter in the head.

"About time you came fishing," Rick said as he entered. Then he saw the extinguisher. "Easy there, Jack." A momentary look of concern passed over his face.

"Rick? ...what the hell's going on?"

Rick started to laugh. "We were about to ask you the same thing. You're behind schedule and your medical report sucks. You okay?"

"I'm okay. The dock workers caught up with me on the station. I got cut up before I got away."

Rick grunted. "I'll say. You're as pale as a ghost. It looks like you nearly bled out."

"Yeah, it wasn't pretty, but I'm alive thanks to a nifty EVA suit that's also some kind of auto doc. You know anything about that?"

"A little." Rick gave Jack a mischievous smile as he spoke. "How 'bout we get you out of this bathtub and have a look see in our infirmary. Afterward, we'll get you a hot meal and a shower."

"That sounds good." Jack managed a weak smile. "But I'd rather have an explanation or two. Some things are starting to make sense, but I'm missing some pieces," Jack replied in a purposely casual tone.

"That you are. It's only one piece really, and it's about time we gave it to you." Rick laughed again. "Fair enough, a meal, a shower, and explanations coming up." He turned and walked back through the hatch.

Jack didn't like that Rick said "we." He liked Rick, trusted him, as much as Jack trusted anyone, and the thought that Rick had been working with other people behind his back and hadn't let him in made Jack a little suspicious. The momentary relaxation he felt at seeing Rick dissipated, and the knot in his gut returned to the place it had occupied for the last month. *Shit, I'm probably just being recruited for a different team.*

With resignation, Jack put the extinguisher down in the air lock before he entered Rick's sub.

"This way, Jack," said Rick, after they boarded his fishing sub, *The Flying Fish*. He gestured in a direction which Jack guessed led toward the bow, then set off at a brisk pace. Jack hobbled after him and quickly found that he couldn't keep up. His heart pounded in his chest and walking made him feel light headed. Noticing that he lagged, Rick finally stopped and asked if he needed help. Jack didn't have enough breath to answer and didn't resist as Rick put Jack's arm around his shoulder and helped him the rest of the way to the infirmary.

"Shit, Jack. They really did a number on you, didn't they?"

"I guess they did. I think I'm coming off a little of the adrenaline, too. It's nice to see a friendly face."

Rick smiled at Jack as he escorted him through the narrow door. "Welcome to the most state-of-the-art infirmary on any maritime vessel in Unity space."

Jack started to ask a question, but Rick interrupted.

"Don't bother to ask. It'll have to wait. We have to get you patched up first. I hope you don't mind if we flush Randall's bots along the way."

Jack momentarily panicked at that thought. He didn't want to do anything to upset Randall or his people. Then he remembered that Team Randall had worked to frame him for an explosion in Utopia. He relaxed, amazed at what a brain could forget in such a short time.

Rick assisted him to a bed in the center of the room as Jack's lightheadedness began to take hold. He gratefully lay down. Looking up, Jack vaguely recognized the device hanging from the ceiling. He couldn't remember what it did. Whatever it was, Jack didn't believe the white robotic arm had been manufactured in the Unity. "Weren't you pointing a gun at me last time I saw one of these things?" Jack asked on a whim. He had started to feel a little giddy again.

"Yeah, Jack, I was," answered Rick, the concern in his voice registering despite Jack's haze. "Why don't you just lay back and close your eyes for a while."

"That sounds good." Jack slurred the last word hearing the "d" in his head but not pronouncing it. He closed his eyes.

Semi-conscious, Jack remembered little of the next few minutes. He vaguely sensed the robotic arm insert an IV. He revived somewhat, when he had been blood typed and given a synthetic pint or two. He opened his eyes to see the scanning end of the arm irritatingly close to his face. He closed them again and heard a series of popping sounds as the claw methodically moved around his head, scanning every inch of his skull. A few minutes more and Jack heard the device retract back to the ceiling.

He opened his eyes and chuckled to himself as he recognized that he had finally obeyed his robotic overlord—he felt calm.

Jack heard Rick say, "How you feelin'?"

Still looking at the ceiling, Jack answered, "Better. Much better, actually."

Jack turned to look at the voice. Rick grinned at him from a chair in the corner of the tiny room. He lounged with his huge arms folded loosely across his chest. "Well, you were running a quart or two low. The synthetic blood we gave you should help—a lot. While you were out, the auto doc patched up your leg for you as well. You should be able to walk on it, but it will be sore for a while yet. The nanites should finish up the internal work on your muscles in another twelve hours or so. Overall, you're in good shape."

Rick paused, then, when Jack didn't answer immediately, went on. "You'll also be glad to know that we flushed all of Randall's nanites. That's what the auto doc was doing there at the end. The clicks were miniature directed EMP pulses. The weak spot for the nanites is always their circuitry. It isn't that hard to overload and fry a circuit that small. Your body should excrete all of them in the next few days."

"How do I know you didn't just put more of your own back in through the IV?" The question came out much stronger and more suspicious than Jack would have liked. Despite the blood, he remained exhausted.

Rick's smile faltered a little. "I guess I would probably be just as suspicious in your position, but where I come from, we don't use nanites without anyone's permission. It's considered an invasion of privacy. Jack, I'm your friend, and you're going to have to learn to trust someone, one of these days."

"Sorry, Rick."

The smile returned full force. "No sweat, Jack. Now how about we get you a shower?"

"That sounds good."

Jack's cabin turned out to be only a few feet down the corridor from the docking hatch. Unlike many, he had it to himself. It was about half as big as the sleeping compartment on the escape pod, with only enough room for a bed. He shared the shower and head with a separate compartment.

After nearly thirty-six hours stuck in the escape pod, Jack savored the hot water running over his back in the postage stamp-sized shower. He would have enjoyed it even more if he hadn't been so desperate for answers. A ping on the com system interrupted Jack's luxuriating. He waited but no message came. The com pinged again. This time Jack answered hesitantly, "Yes?"

"The captain would like to see you in his quarters as soon as possible. He says to tell you to just follow the corridor past the infirmary to the conn. His quarters are the first door on the right before you enter the control room. They're marked."

Jack took his cue and turned off the hot water. "Thank you."

He dressed himself in a clean, dark green jumpsuit with the name *Flying Fish* stenciled across his back. After tying the pair of polished black work boots that went with the uniform, Jack walked forward down the corridor.

Supposedly, *The Flying Fish* belonged to the Poseidon class of working submarines. Jack had never been on Rick's boat before. In fact, he had never been on any of the fishing subs housed in Utopia. However, fishing was an important part of Aetna's culture, so he knew something about it.

Ninety meters in length, Poseidon class submersibles had two decks and a crew of fifteen. The upper deck housed the control room, living quarters, mess hall, and other crew facilities. The lower deck contained a full fish processing plant which ideally ran 24/7. Although the fish processing plant lay a deck below where Jack stood, the smell permeated the whole of the boat, even the freshly laundered uniform Jack now wore. It smelled like he walked in the guts of a fish.

Despite the smell, as Jack walked along the main corridor heading to the conn, he had the same feeling which plagued him when he first boarded the escape pod. He had the impression he stood in a model of what a Unity fishing submarine should look like. There were tangles of wires hanging out here and there, and occasionally, a fixture was missing or a lighted panel was dark, but it all seemed wrong, unsettling. It took Jack almost the whole walk to figure out what bothered him. The surfaces on *The Flying Fish* were too shiny and neat. Everything was clean. Even the jumbles of wiring hanging out of exposed panels were organized and the missing lights appeared staged. Something bothered Jack about this. It didn't fit. The infirmary was proof enough of that.

Who are these people? Jack wondered. He nervously thought through options. Everything he came up with seemed too fantastic to be possible. The exercise seemed futile, and he gave up quickly. He didn't have enough information to make any decisions and that seemed to be the way people around him liked it.

Jack stopped in front of a door located just outside the control room. Looking past it, he could see three young sailors all manning different stations.

He knocked.

Rick answered, "Enter."

The captain's office was around three times as large as Jack's cabin. Jack noted the bunk folded up against the wall and recognized the room served as the captain's quarters as well.

"Welcome aboard, Jack." Rick smiled genuinely as he entered, although he didn't stand up from behind his small desk. Rick had a way of putting Jack at ease. He seemed genuine in whatever he did. Despite his current reservations, Jack found Rick's apparent authenticity hard to resist.

He took a seat in a chair with his back against the folded bunk and tried to remember that something didn't make sense about *The Flying Fish* and the escape pod. He also kept in mind that somehow other people were in on the joke as well.

Rick's large frame dominated the room. He looked completely out of place behind the undersized desk. Its working top had been designed to monitor ship functions. On one corner Jack could see a live vid stream from the fish processing plant on the second deck. Other sections told the current speed and depth and gave information on systems such as the fusion plant.

After a beat or two of silence, in which Rick seemed to size up Jack, he began, in a relaxed voice. "Jack, I've been hoping this day would come for a long time. But before I begin, I need to let you know the stakes. You'll have to make a choice. After you hear what we have to say, you can stay aboard or you can go away. If you choose to leave, I will wipe your memory of this whole event and put you on the ice somewhere where you can get other help, perhaps over in Nautica. They have no love for admin. You'll probably be able to hide out there…for a while."

Jack didn't know how to respond. On the one hand, Rick clearly wanted to let him in on the secret. On the other hand, Jack really didn't care that much anymore. He just wanted the nightmare to end. "I hope you can see that from my point of view it doesn't look like much of a choice." Now confident he was being recruited for a different political faction, he felt himself starting to warm. "Until a month ago, I was quite content. I made a living plus some, and nobody bothered me. I paid off any bureaucrats that came snooping around and went on my merry way. Then Randall showed up, and I've been mind-jacked, had weapons pointed at me several times, including by you—I believe. Although I can't be sure about that, Rick, because there's a great big hole in my memory which you helped create. The fact that you can wipe memories explains the hole, but it doesn't tell me what happened."Jack let his anger rise and continued, "Oh, what else? I had to listen to my girlfriend get beaten by Frank, and I couldn't do anything to stop it." Momentarily, it was as if he was sitting behind the door, hearing Anna scream. Jack rubbed his eyes. That story— which he had been telling himself over and over in the last couple of days—was getting tiresome, but Jack had to admit he enjoyed ranting a little to someone else. He shrugged, looking at the desktop, controlling his uncharacteristic outburst. "Tell me whatever it is you want from me. I'm listening. Just don't expect me to take kindly to another offer which makes me play more games." *I really need to get some sleep*, he thought to himself.

Rick surprised him when Jack glanced up and saw something akin to sympathy in Rick's eyes. He desperately wanted to relax, to trust him. "We think she's still alive, Jack. At least she was when Musgrave left the hospital."

Jack's hand involuntarily gripped the chair. "Anna? She's here on Aetna?"

Rick looked Jack in the eye but kept his voice dead calm. "They asked him to help make her look nice. They wanted him to do some skin repair work, and heal her bruises. It was the last thing he did before Admin shut down the hospital and turned it over to the military. He said the cynthy from HR didn't seem too happy with the way Frank handled her."

Jack furrowed his brow, looked down at the ground, and clenched his fists. His nails dug into his hands. Knowing that Carla now controlled Anna's care didn't comfort him in the least. Jack had no doubt of her ability to brutalize Anna if needed, but she was better than Gunderson or Frank. At least Carla wouldn't hurt Anna just for sport. Jack tried to sort through his thoughts and figure out which of the questions he wanted Rick to answer first.

Rick saved him the trouble by answering one on his own. "It's pretty obvious to me that they want to parade her around. They'll no doubt force a confession from her. She'll blame you."

"Did she say anything?"

"I don't know, Jack. Musgrave and I didn't have long to talk. He went off to try to open some kind of temporary field hospital where he could treat the wounded coming in from the riots."

Jack felt a tear roll down his cheek. He blinked hard. Rick stayed silent, looking uncharacteristically grave, giving him his moment of grief. Jack's shoulders heaved silently. He felt so ashamed and guilty. This wouldn't be happening to her if it hadn't been for him.

It took a few minutes for Jack to calm himself. When he did, Rick spoke quietly. "There have been many times when all of us have said that our efforts were for people like you—and Anna—people who want to just mind their own business and live their lives. What has happened to Aetna in the last month has only strengthened my resolve. When you work around people long enough, you get to care for them. I have to be honest, I'm worried. Aetna already lost some of its best people in the purge. I can't help but think about the Lutnear kids sometimes."

Jack grunted. "Teddy was a genius."

Rick continued. "The tyranny of the corporation must end, but I can see no possible way for it to end well for the people of Utopia. You're not alone, Jack. No one on Aetna will be the same. Relationships and families will be destroyed. People are getting hurt, and there is no going back. Everyone is going to lose someone." The room fell silent for a few seconds, each man lost in his own thoughts.

Rick rested his forearms on the desk, folded his hands, and leaned forward. "Jack, the Unity is a corrosive cancer to its own people. That much even its citizens can see if they have their eyes open. What most Unity citizens don't understand is that the Unity has a huge influence over the rest of the galaxy, as well. Other people... other leaders want to know what is going on in the Unity because what happens here will affect them, too."

Rick paused for a second, took a breath, and then continued. "What I tell you next could trigger an interstellar war if it got out. I'm here at the request of a foreign government."

"You're a spy?" Jack asked.

Without smiling, Rick nodded.

Jack started shaking his head. "Rick, you're pissing me off. I'm not in the mood for a joke."

Rick shrugged his shoulders. "Believe what you want. It's the truth."

Jack pressed forward, doing his best to stay calm but becoming even more suspicious of Rick and whatever it was that he wanted from him. "Rick, I'm not going to believe that. I just won't. Why would a spy set up in a little out of the way place like Aetna? It makes no sense. What kind of information can you gather in a place like this? A real spy would be better off on Sicily Four or one of the other major planets."

Rick answered in his rough fisherman's gravel, looking directly at Jack with blue eyes buried under bushy brown eyebrows, all hints of his usual jollity left aside. It was his ongoing demeanor, as much as anything he had to say, which caused Jack to consider the possibility that he might be telling the truth. "Would I, Jack? Would I be better off right in the thick of things where everyone is scanned and watched all the time, where the prying eyes of HR and the security apparatus never sleep? No, I like my life as much as you like yours. You'd be surprised what I can learn from our little observation post here. In fact, being out of the way makes it much easier to sort the signal from the noise, so to speak."

Jack had to agree about the security angle of things. There was no possible way he would have dared to set up a black market in any significant city. Life was rigidly controlled and the punishments severe. "For real?"

"Yes, Jack, for real."

"So, it was you who got me off the station."

"No. There are others."

Jack felt stupid for working in the midst of a bunch of spies for so long without picking up on it. "It has to be Musgrave. It makes sense of the way he treated me when I showed up at his home the other day, and you two always seem to know what the other has been up to."

Rick smiled, "I'm not going to say anything."

Jack went back in his mind over the last few days and gave Rick a look of disgust. This one hurt his pride. "I bet Robert's in on it. I bet he got me off the station."

Rick just continued to smile.

"It's pretty hard to swallow the idea that I could have been working next to you all these years and never noticed. I'm usually pretty good at that sort of thing. And I still don't see why you would set up shop here instead of some place more important. What can you really learn out here in the wilderness?"

"What better place to study the Unity and its people than at a fuel stop away from the prying eyes of big brother? Pretty much everything that comes and goes from this system makes a stop at your little station."

Jack sat there, letting his mind walk through the possibility. *Robert would have access to all the manifests.* The fact that almost all freighters stopped at their station on the way out of the system had been exactly why it had worked so well as a place to create a black market, a fact which Robert had showed Jack years ago.

"So how does Musgrave benefit? What's he study? The medical system?"

Rick just continued to smile and didn't say anything.

Then Jack hit upon what he supposed was the truth. "The cynthies. They're full of all the gossip. I bet he could learn quite a bit about who's in and who's out politically and even who might be bought off by a foreign government." In the past, Jack had occasionally gone after a cynthy in the bar but found that most of them were ever only interested in talking about their husbands and other gossip which bored Jack to tears. Usually he couldn't suffer through enough of it to get between their legs.

"You're smart, Jack. Too smart. I won't comment on anyone but myself. What they tell you is their business and frankly I don't know that much about it. It's better that way. I do know that my boss has given me permission to tell you this. My job is to find out about ordinary citizens in the Unity. I take their temperature and try to figure out what they believe about the outside world. More importantly, I try to find out whether or not they would support the central government if it were challenged by an outside power."

Rick's words made Jack stop for a second. Despite everything which happened to him, Jack was still a Unity citizen. He looked Rick in the eye and saw that Rick had used the words deliberately. It was a test. Where did his loyalties lie?

The decision was easier to make than Jack thought it ought to be. His experiences in the last month had showed him a cruel side to the Unity which he didn't really know existed before then, but in reality it was his visit to I-MAM which had changed his mind. It was coming face-to-face with the lies he had been told to keep him passive and in line which helped solidify his decision. The government of the Unity Corporation was corrupt to its very core. If someone from the outside decided to tip it over, whatever came next would have to be better.

Jack didn't answer Rick directly. Instead, he said, "You know your boat is a dead giveaway, don't you?"

Rick cocked his head to the side.

"It's too clean."

They both laughed a little, and the tension subsided for a moment.

Someone knocked at the door.

Rick said, "Enter."

A sailor in a cook's uniform came in with a tray of smoked fish sandwiches and a pot of coffee.

"Hungry?" Rick looked at Jack.

"Yeah, I'm hungry."

"Dig in."

Jack thought about the possibility of bots for a minute, before hunger won out. It had been two days since he had eaten something that wasn't rehydrated. He gratefully grabbed a sandwich and filled his mouth.

Rick followed suit.

The sandwich seemed to clear Jack's mind. He hadn't realized how ravenous he had been. He chewed slowly, as he thought the situation over. "So what do you want from me? Why tell me anything, and why stick your neck out like you did to help me off the station?"

"We want you to live, Jack. If you stay in the Unity, you are a marked man. We want to get you out—to have you work for us. My boss has talked to the higher-ups back home, and you're to be offered a job if we can get you out."

Jack was deeply suspicious now. He really wasn't interested in being manipulated by someone else. "Rick, I just helped get a bomb for some people that killed hundreds. That's where teamwork got me. Why would I ever want to go to work for another team, let alone another nation?"

Rick seemed pulled up short by the comment. He ran his hands through his hair. "I guess I haven't really given you much of a reason, have I." He puffed out his cheeks and thought for a moment. "Okay. I don't really have permission to tell you this part, but I'm going to do it anyway. You would find out soon enough. We work for the Empress, herself—in reality the Ministry of Information, but for the Empress, not some other state in the Pax. You wouldn't be beholden to anyone, and, in one sense, you would be above the fray. Plus, we don't treat people like they do in the Unity. No one hijacks minds or forces people to do their bidding. It's almost a paradise compared to the Unity. You won't believe it when you see the capital on Apollos."

"Right." Jack let the full force of his skepticism enter the word.

"Well, maybe I'm selling it too hard, but right now, I don't see other options, and I can promise you, no one is going to mind-jack you or blackmail you into doing stuff you don't want to do." Rick leaned toward him across the desk. "Jack, no one understands the patterns of how goods flow through the Unity like you do. No one knows how to smuggle things around like you. I believe that also means you'll be able to spot trends and give us the information we need to keep ahead of the game, and we also want to make sure someone tells the story of what happened on Aetna."

Jack purposefully remained silent for a time, thinking through what he had been told. A glimmer of hope entered his world, and he wanted to think it over before he acted on the impulse, so he asked about something different. "So what do you know about what happened with the bomb? Was I being set up from the beginning?"

"We don't *know* anything, really. Randall is a psychopath, and those around him aren't much better, so anything is possible. But, we're pretty sure that it wasn't part of the plan. In the past, some directors have used staged accidents to force Procurement's hand. He may not have been able to get a state of the art hydrogen plant on Aetna if he still had a working old plant. But if that one were to become disabled in some way, then Procurement would be forced to provide a new one."

Jack nodded his head at that thought. It fit with his experiences with Procurement. He and every manager in the Unity had done similar things, albeit on a smaller scale. The sheer hubris of blowing up a hydrogen plant to get a new one took Jack's breath away.

"Apparently, Bill Driscol had been warned in advance that he would be required to evacuate his people and that it wouldn't be a drill. He and one of his deputies went snooping around the plant. When they found the blasting cap, they sent out that message and then tried to dismantle it. From there we don't know exactly what happened; either they were unsuccessful, or someone set it off purposely at that point. Either way, this isn't what Team Randall wanted. They now have a full scale rebellion on their hands and not enough troops to contain it. This isn't Timothy Randall's finest hour."

"So what's it like in Utopia?"

"Grim… I've never seen anything like it. The people are done with the government, and they don't have any fear any longer. Right now they are fighting fierce street-to-street battles with Randall's forces, and frankly, they're winning."

Jack raised an eyebrow. "You mean there's a chance they might prevail?"

"I think there's a good chance for the moment, at least on the surface in Utopia. The villages are basically sitting this out because there isn't really any government out there, and the station—well, that is another matter. From what we can gather, the station itself is nothing more than a concentration camp at this point. They put those workers down hard—fletch rounds and even vented one of the warehouses they had set on fire without warning—spaced about thirty of them."

Rick continued. "But I doubt this will be the start of a major revolt in Unity. It can't go anywhere. The workers on the station managed to commandeer a couple of freighters. They wandered off to God knows where, but what are they going to do? If they go to a major system, they'll be gunned down before they get close. Even if they stick with the asteroids and marginal places, like Aetna, the best they could create is a quaint little peasants' uprising. If the Unity is going to be turned upside down by its own people, I doubt the revolt is going to start on Aetna or its orbital."

Jack couldn't quite let go of the hope that this could be the start of something. He raised his eyebrows at Rick and shrugged his shoulders. "You never know. Mao Tse-tung did pretty well with his peasants."

"Who?"

"Never mind."

Rick gave Jack a weak smile and humored him. "You're right, you never know. Whenever the real rebellion comes, we probably won't see it coming, will we? I guess I just think it more likely that the government forces regroup, bring in reinforcements, and kick ass. It's what we believe they've done in the past. Although, it's hard to say because there usually aren't many survivors afterward, and the ones left over don't willingly talk about it. "

Jack changed the topic. It was time to let his ray of hope have its say. "If I go with you, I want to take Anna with me."

Rick broke out into a grin which spilled over into a short laugh. "All these years of going it alone and now you fall in love? The timing is a little inconvenient, don't you think?"

Jack smiled for a moment, but then looked hard at Rick and said, "I don't think I'll leave without her. I have a really vague memory, something about you saying there would be room for two." The words were out of his mouth before Jack had really processed them. He wasn't sure himself if it were a bluff or not. Part of him deeply regretted saying it. He lost a chance to escape and make a clean start again without any strings.

Rick's brow puckered, and a frown formed on his lips. "Jack, things are different now. She's in the hands of the gendarme, HR, or the Army. It's going to be hard enough to get you out."

Rick drifted into silence for a minute as he thought it through. "Even if there were a way to liberate her—and there won't be—to do so would put our whole mission in jeopardy. It would reveal us and require the evacuation of all our personnel. That isn't something we can allow to happen."

Jack's heart skipped a beat when he realized that he hadn't told Rick about his welcoming party when he arrived on Aetna. "Rick, your cover may already be blown."

"What do you mean?"

"When I parachuted into open water here on Aetna, there was a greeting party all dressed in fatigues, circling in two hovercraft. They saw the escape pod break apart, hit the water, and sink. It won't take them much to figure out that it swam away."

Rick's bearded face lost its usual ruddy complexion. "That's bad, Jack. That's really bad."

Rick altered his screen even before he had finished speaking. He flipped down his heads-up eyepiece. "Larry, stop deploying the gear. Get the nets back on board, and get your ass in my office."

Before getting a reply, Rick punched a button on the screen in front of him. "Jake, get The White Knight, Rook, and Queen on the line, priority alpha."

Rick again changed channels and announced over the com. "Now hear this. Now hear this. This is not a drill. General quarters. General quarters." Within a second, the lighting changed, tinged red, and a klaxon sounded momentarily.

Shortly thereafter, there came a quick knock on the door. Without waiting for an answer, a dark-haired man Jack recognized from the submarine docks entered the room. Larry Flynn was thin and young, with a nondescript narrow face, and a clean cut chin. Jack knew Larry as a no-nonsense kind of guy. He looked both surprised and concerned. The adrenaline was running high.

Rick motioned Larry over to the vid screen desk and simultaneously brought up the feeds from Jack's heads-up and the submersible's own external cameras. Jack watched the landing again.

"Marines," said Larry. "Regulars, with little or no arctic gear or training. It looks like the same outfit that's been holed up at the airport. Could they have tracked the submersible after it entered the water?"

"I doubt it. They certainly weren't armed for water combat, or Jack wouldn't be sitting here right now."

Jack spoke up. "Don't be so sure, Rick. The gendarmes had an opportunity to shoot me down when I launched off the orbital, but they didn't do it. I assume that must have been on Randall's orders."

Rick shook his head. "They might have been able to track you for a few kilometers in the open water, but by the time two hours had passed, you were buried under a several kilometers of ice. It's unlikely even their best amphibious craft could track you from the air through that. At best, they know the direction you went, but little else."

Rick continued to stare at the looping replay of Jack's landing on the monitor as he spoke, but his thoughts were elsewhere. "I'm more concerned with what Randall's staff will be able to put together from this little mishap. I'm not sure what he or his security team will make of it. They will likely think another political faction recruited you out from under their nose, or maybe they'll worry that you ran a successful black market because you already were part of someone else's network. That thought will scare the shit out of them, because you're in a position to finger them for the bomb at the plant."

Rick looked up. "If you weren't before, your escape will make you priority number one for Randall and that poses a problem for all of us. Once you disappeared under the ice, you had to pop up somewhere sooner or later. That means Randall will be spending a lot of resources trying to find out how you got back to the surface and where. He will definitely be searching every sub he can get his hands on. For now, I think we have to assume our cover is blown. Larry, I want the boat kept on heightened readiness. From this point forward, we're now a military boat, at least until we know otherwise."

"I agree, sir. Should we dump the gear?"

"Not yet. It's not really my call. Our fearless leader will have to make that decision. This is where it gets ballsy. If they don't put the pieces together, we may yet still be able to keep our place. But for now, it's drills and combat training all the way. You hear me? Get this boat ready for whatever is coming."

"Aye, sir." Larry turned and left the room.

"Don't underestimate him, Rick. Randall's pretty smart, and he won't rest until he finds out what's actually taking place. He had my whole black market operation worked out before he even arrived."

Rick nodded as a message appeared on his desk. He put his palm flat on the desk allowing the AI to verify his identity. Jack watched the heads-up scrape a bit of skin off his ear for the DNA. He assumed the device had also scanned his retina.

Soon after, three images appeared on Rick's desktop. Two-dimensional images lifted off the table and projected themselves in a semicircle. Jack assumed Rick had used a thought command through his heads-up. They looked like individual vid screens tipped on edge. To Jack, they appeared blank with a bright red "Classified" written across them, but they must have made sense to Rick because he started talking to them. "Jack was seen on the way down to the surface."

Rick listened to the reply, but Jack couldn't hear it. "I don't know, Queen. I'm a little worried about all of this. Randall has been on top of it from the beginning. He apparently had Jack's black market activity pegged before he even arrived. I am beginning to think that there may be more than we want to believe in his appearance here."

Jack spoke up. "Tell them that Robert needs to get out as soon as possible. If Randall suspects something, Robert and Molly will be top on his list."

Rick smirked. "They can hear you, Jack. You just can't hear or see them."

Jack continued, "I told Rick just before this that the gendarmes had a chance to shoot me down but stopped. I would guess that was on Randall's orders. He must have assumed he could just track me to the planet and send troops to pick me up. He'll be royally pissed that I got away. The fact that I got away through some kind of souped-up escape pod will make him want to know everything about the pod and anyone who might have helped me. He'll put some time and effort into it. I'll bet there will be enough bread crumbs to lead him to the truth, or at least something close to it. I think your cover is blown already or will be shortly, which means that Robert better get out of the way."

One of the images flashed for a second and an image of Robert appeared on the screen. It was hard to tell, but he appeared to be somewhere on the station. It certainly wasn't his quarters. "Hi, Jack. I figured it was a good bet they'd want to question me, especially after they grabbed your girl. I got to a safe place I had prepared right after things went sideways on the dock. Just wanted you to know I was safe." The transmission clicked off again and went back to the word "Classified."

Jack sat and watched intently for a bit while the other four discussed something without him. At first, Rick didn't say anything but listened intently. Eventually, he weighed in. "It's a risk whenever we let him in. At least right now if he doesn't agree, we can clean things up and drop him off somewhere."

Jack raised an eyebrow. "Listen, I don't have many choices right now. What I've appreciated so far is that no one has forced me into anything. That's a point in your corner. You've also stuck your neck out for me. I think you at least owe me a chance to say thank you."

Rick face brightened and he chuckled. He was obviously responding to something someone else said. "Fair enough."

With that, all three screens changed, and Jack saw Robert, Tony Musgrave, and, to his surprise, Gloria Soren on the other end of the line. Soren spoke. "Hey, Jack. You gave me quite a scare on the station. I wasn't sure you were going to make it. I'm glad you're feeling better."

"Thanks." It was all he could think to say at first. It surprised him to learn who led the team. Then he quickly added, "You still owe me a gun."

"Yes, I do, but I'm glad I didn't get it to you on the station. If I had, you'd be dead by now. It's good to see you alive. Jack, we're going to trust you right now, and I think we all consider you a friend, but I need you to understand something. If you decide you don't like it, and try to make a break for it, we will take measures to stop you. We can't risk exposure. Too many lives are at stake."

"I understand."

"Good. Now, Tony, what were you saying?"

Musgrave paused briefly before going on. "I think that we're really close to putting some of the pieces together on my end. I'm pretty sure that I have the evidence we're looking for. First, the girl I saw yesterday had clearly been tortured. That crime has been damned hard to prove in the Unity, though we all know it happens. I was able to get some data while treating her. I also have some other suspicions as well. We had two fighters turn on their fellow troops yesterday—got this glazed look in their eyes and just started attacking them—teeth, shanks, weapons, anything. They showed signs of hysterical strength as well. The two of them killed six more before they were finally gunned down."

Musgrave gestured to the hazmat suit he wore. "I was just suiting up to do an autopsy when your call came through. Both of them had been sent to inspect an artillery rocket of some sort which had apparently been a dud. I have reason to suspect zombie gas." Jack noticed Rick sit up a little higher at the name. "If we cut and run too quickly, we could miss out on the evidence that we have wanted. I think we can really nail the central administration here."

Soren nodded. "Well, I believe I have some good news on the question of why the military seems so interested in this system. The lead we had about construction ships dropping into Catania's outer ring paid off. Despite our abrupt exit—rather, because everyone scrambled to get undocked at about the same time—we were finally able to track a couple of those construction vessels as we left the system. Jones did an amazing job sorting through the interference put up by the rings. Sure enough, they dropped right into Bronte's orbit and followed the cleared path through the rings. We were able to track them to within two hundred and fifty klicks of the surface, but by then, the angle on our sensor packages was all wrong, and we lost them. However, it's a good bet that we finally have a lead on whatever is going on military-wise at Catania. We dropped off a couple of remote sensor packages on our way outbound. After we pick up Jack, we should be able to grab them on the way out. For now, we can say for sure that mother Unity is building something at Catania."

Some time in the distant past, two of Catania's outer moons had collided. For all intents and purposes both were destroyed, leaving in their wake a small ring of dust, meteoroids, small asteroids, and a few larger proto-moons, like Bronte. Everyone on Aetna knew that Unity Mining had surveyed the debris and found it to be a ready source of metals for construction. However, bureaucratic inefficiency had supposedly kept them from ever capitalizing on the resource.

"I bet it's a fleet," said Jack. "It would explain why Randall needs to increase H2 production on Aetna."

Rick spoke up. "I think Jack is right. That puts all the pieces..."

At that moment several things happened simultaneously. A voice interrupted Rick mid-sentence on the com system in his office. "Conn! Sensors! High-speed contacts at approximately a hundred ten thousand meters, bearing three hundred fifty-six degrees. They are closing, fast!"

At the same moment, Robert grabbed a neural stunner from beside him and disappeared from his video pick-up. A blinding flash followed, as someone apparently used precision explosives to blow open a hole in the steel wall behind where he had been sitting the moment before. Musgrave cocked his head and appeared to listen to something which Jack didn't hear and then dropped the hood on his hazmat suit down and began frantically sealing it. Soren looked surprised by it all.

Jack just had time to see heavily armored gendarmes start pouring though the hole in Robert's wall when Soren yelled, "Cover blown! Link corrupted! Abort plan Beta!"

The transmission ended abruptly. Rick stood and bolted out the door.

16
A Change of Plans

Even before Jack could follow, Rick was on the com. "Cover has been blown. We're now under attack. We have two AI inbound. Mission abort is scheduled for sixty-eight hours from now. Just do the jobs you've trained to do, and we'll get home safe and sound."

Jack exited the compartment and took three steps into the very busy control center of the submarine. He sensed the tension as soon as he stepped in the door. In the center of the room, Rick and Larry stood over a larger version of the table in Rick's office. Both of them wore heads-up displays and hunched as they looked at ever-changing data. Rick wore his usual grin. He seemed unperturbed. On the other hand, Larry concentrated hard on the data in front of him, furrowing his brow. Around the periphery of the room, young men and women manipulated data and gave commands on three dimensional displays.

"Benitez, what are we looking at?" Rick kept a calm demeanor as he looked across the room to a young woman who appeared to be all of eighteen.

Benitez wore a full intraspace cap and sweated profusely. Her eyes were covered with darkened heads-up goggles. Jack wondered if she could even hear her captain with the intraspace cap on. Apparently she could because she spoke. "They look to be older models. Based on their chatter, I would say they're mark fifty-fours."

"Fifty-fours top out at thirteen hundred and twenty KPH, so we have about a ten minute run-time from launch," said Rick. He looked at Larry. "Do we have an impact time?"

"We have impact in seven minutes and fifty-six seconds. Optimal time for nuclear detonation is somewhere around seven minutes and twenty seconds."

Rick smiled at Larry. "If they melt us to glass, there won't be evidence to parade around."

Larry shrugged, keeping his grim expression. "It doesn't seem prudent to assume otherwise."

Rick nodded. "All right, Benitez. Let's go fry us up some AI brains. Get those countermeasures going. Remember, our cover may be blown but we want this to look like a petty squabble between two political factions, okay? We still don't want this to point to anything outside the Unity, so nothing too fancy."

Jack adrenaline pulsed. The cramped conn of the boat seemed entirely too small. In fact, to Jack's heightened senses the whole boat seemed to be caving in. He wanted off, and he wanted off now. Jack heard the whine and felt the boat lurch slightly as multiple countermeasures launched from the vehicle.

Rick glanced up and noticed Jack in the corner. Without a word, the tactical display for the boat appeared on Jack's heads-up.

He watched as three little points of light raced toward the incoming missiles. As they went, they spewed data back to their handlers. Jack noted another set of three waiting in the water near the submarine.

As they approached, the incoming missiles attempted to outwit the countermeasures. They split wide, forcing the three friendlies to make a decision on which they were to follow. The leading countermeasure went to port, and the next went to starboard. The third turned and backtracked, giving itself room to make a run if the first two were unsuccessful.

Unity missiles used a combination of flexible skins and retractable fins, along with highly pressurized jets of air, to gyrate and turn in an apparently random pattern that seemed impossible in water. They hoped to gain an edge which would allow them to break past their oncoming opponents.

The countermeasures exquisitely measured, analyzed, and neutralized each jink and turn by the incoming missiles. What looked to Jack as if it were a nearly straight line trajectory toward incoming death by the imperial countermeasures actually played out a complex game of bluffs and counter-bluffs, at speeds beyond human thought. Once in range, the countermeasures detonated their charges, destroying themselves and their opponents. The four remaining countermeasures returned to the submarine, ready to be retrieved and refueled in case they were needed in the future.

Rick spoke to a relaxed conning tower. "All right folks, we aren't out of the woods yet. Let's get down low. Keep on that forty degree down bubble, Chip. Take us down to a comfortable eighteen hundred meters. That gives us about a kilometer of cushion if we need to go deeper."

He stopped for moment and looked at Larry. "Do you see any reason to avoid using mass reduction?"

Larry put his hands on his hips and pinched his lips together as he thought before he answered. "No, not really. The most it gives away is that we aren't the run-of-the-mill Unity fishing sub, but we just sent that calling card with our countermeasures. The jig is up, so there isn't any good reason to hold back at this point. Unity military boats use reduced mass acceleration, so we shouldn't be telling them that we aren't from around these parts."

Rick nodded. "Yeah, those were my thoughts. I don't want to scream foreign intelligence if we can still manage to convincingly say different political faction."

Then speaking to the room he said, "Right now whoever just tried to smoke us out knows exactly where we are, but they don't know exactly what we can do. From this point forward, we are rigging for silent running. We need to get home, pick up Musgrave, and get out as quickly as possible. Propulsion, you are authorized for redline plus ten percent on your speed but keep full and flank in reserve for the most dire of situations. Mass engineer, mass reduction is authorized to fifty percent capacity. That should match Unity military technology." Rick looked toward a pair of young sailors sitting in one corner of the conn. "What I do want, Chan and White, is for the two of you to make sure that we are optimizing our mass reduction and speed for silent running. The best thing we can do right now is make like a hole in the water, so keep on it. Any thermals or changes in pressure outside, and I want you adjusting double quick. You got that?"

Both Chan and White answered, "Aye, Sir."

Rick began walking toward Jack and out of the conn. He motioned for Jack to follow. In the narrow corridor outside, Rick spoke. "Get some sleep. We'll be in port in about ten hours time. You'll want to get your rest now. Things will get interesting then, and you might want to take a sleeping pill, 'cause mass reduction can make you feel a little queasy until you're used to it."

Jack smirked and considered his dislike of zero-g. He decided Rick was right about the sleeping pill, but he doubted he could sleep. "Yeah, I could use some sleep, if I could get some. Someone just tried to kill us, Rick."

"No, they didn't, Jack. If they really wanted to kill us, it would have been way more than two older missiles. Whoever attacked us just wanted to know our location and confirm their suspicions that we weren't simply the fishing vessel we claimed to be. They also learned just the kinds of things we would do if they attacked us in earnest. They got all the information they wanted about us. The question is why they didn't try to kill us, and I would guess you're the answer to that question."

"What about Robert?"

Jack saw a momentary look of concern pass through Rick's eyes. "Robert is one of canniest men I know. He'll have a plan. No matter what, they won't catch him alive. We'll sort it all out in the next few hours. For now there really isn't anything we can do."

Jack returned to his bunk expecting to find sleep difficult. He took a pill from the auto-doc and, unable to physically sustain all his worries, fell asleep.

A few short hours later Jack woke to the sound of a knock on his cabin door. "Come in."

He sat up as Rick opened the hatch and stepped inside. "Sorry to wake you, Jack. There's something we need you to see."

Rick threw a video from his heads-up to the monitor embedded in the wall of Jack's cabin. Musgrave appeared on the screen there. He still wore a full hazmat suit with his hood tipped back. "Hello, Jack. I need to show you something. You won't like it. When we're done, we'll have something to say about it."

An image of Anna appeared on the screen. Tears streaked down her cheeks as she looked at the camera. "I helped Deputy Director Jack Halloway plant the bomb at the hydrogen plant in Utopia. We had been recruited by a network of international spies working for the Kingdom of Athena. Our job was to turn the people of the Unity against their Administrators."

At this point, Anna began to sob. It took some time before she could look at the camera again. Her voice pleaded with the audience as she continued. "I feel so ashamed for helping kill so many innocent men and women, not to mention children. I deserve the death sentence I've been given."

The sleep must have done Jack some good, because although he balled his fists he managed to keep from punching the bed. Watching Anna didn't overwhelm him like it would have hours before. It also helped to know that some part of him wanted to get her back. Trapped on Rick's sub with nowhere to go, he felt like a caged predator, conserving his energy and watching, just waiting for a chance to escape.

When the video ended, Rick held up his hands in a gesture which asked for patience from Jack, expecting a rising tide of impotent fury which never came. "I know, Jack. I know how much this must frustrate you. What we want you to know is we think there may be a chance we can help her."

The dozing predator in Jack pricked up its ears.

Musgrave cut in. "Clearly she is being forced to confess, but I am almost positive she has had her memory altered. There are certain tells, especially around the eyes, which indicate she has been attacked by bots. She's likely been mind-jacked more than once."

Both Rick and Musgrave seemed to want Jack to react, to say something. Jack remained silent.

Musgrave continued. "Significantly altering a person's memory is considered a crime in most states. Mind-jacking and beatings to force a confession are considered crimes against humanity in the Pax Imperium. It's a known secret that it happens in the Unity but little direct evidence has been presented in the Empire. If we can get her out, it will force other states to grapple with what is taking place in the Unity."

Jack looked at Rick for second before speaking. "I thought you didn't want to do anything which screamed foreign agents."

Rick shrugged. "That won't be a problem, Jack. Another political faction might want to get their hands on Anna, as well. If they could prove that Randall mind-jacked a confession out of someone, it would be the end of him politically. This is a plum which anyone would want. Randall is in a bad way after the explosion to even try this."

"If that's true then as soon as you grab her the gloves are going to come off for Randall. He'll want to wipe away any evidence as soon as possible." As he finished, the implications of what he just said sank in. "If she's that dangerous to him, then she's already dead, isn't she?"

Rick answered. "They'll keep her for a little longer yet. They'll want to use her to implicate you. As far as they know you still have the defense bots, so your mind won't be so easy to crack. Besides, I doubt that you intend to give them another shot."

"I'd rather die first."

"That's the conclusion we've all reached."

Musgrave interrupted, "Noble sentiments aside, Jack, I need to tell you to replace your own defense bots before you land in Utopia. My autopsy confirmed the use of zombie gas. They've hacked a few minds around here. You best get yourself some protection."

Jack just nodded at Musgrave. He didn't want to have anyone putting things in his head, but quickly decided that he would rather have Musgrave doing it than Randall.

"You said something about helping Anna?"

Rick nodded once before answering. "Things have been going really well in Utopia…"

"Too well…" Musgrave interrupted.

"Maybe so," Rick acknowledged. "For now, Randall's staff, the few civilians who support him, and the military are confined to the administrative tower and the shuttle pad. Everything seems to show they are preparing to retreat from the surface to the station. Last night they shipped out a small group of prisoners. Today, equipment has been leaving the surface."

Musgrave spoke up. "It has to be just a strategic retreat until reinforcements come. There really is no way that the rebels should have been able to do this so quickly."

"I tend to agree with you. What do Mike and Andy think?"

"I don't know. One moment they seem to sober up and see it that way, the next moment they're so high from their latest victory that they are determined to believe they are actually defeating the central administration of the Unity."

Jack decided to draw the conversation back to his concerns. "So what does this have to do with Anna?"

Rick answered, "Sorry, Jack."

Musgrave spoke up, "Right now the concern here on the ground is to make sure that the military doesn't ship any more prisoners off the planet. The rebels have been taking territory, but in the last couple of days the marines seem to have adopted a strategy which tries to take as many prisoners as possible. They're using neural overload weapons like at the rally and keeping them on stun, not kill. Then they're grabbing bodies before they retreat. They've grabbed a lot of fighters that way, and yesterday it looks like they began to ship them off the planet. The prisoners are being held somewhere in the admin building, which is where we believe Anna is also being held."

Rick picked up the thread. "The rebels would like to attack Admin before they have a chance to ship out more prisoners, but they have a little problem, which we think you could help solve."

Jack was wary now. "Oh?"

Rick continued. "We need your security codes, Jack."

"Those won't help you at all. They will have surely changed them by now."

Musgrave looked grim. "Not those codes, Jack, the other codes."

"How do you know about those?" Then Jack thought it through. "Never mind, it was Robert who suggested that I get them, and Soren helped set them up. How long have I been working for you and just didn't know it?"

Rick chuckled.

Musgrave answered. "Jack, it's time for you to pay your bill. We aren't doing you any favors for free. You could just be glad that an opportunity has come about where it makes sense for us to try to help you and Anna out. We could just keep our noses clean. Do remember that our cover got blown because we tried to help you in the first place. "

"They won't do much. You only get ten minutes."

Musgrave answered again. "Well, let's hope that ten minutes will be enough."

Four hours later, Jack found himself wishing he were somewhere else, while sitting in Rick's office in the sub hangar. He and Musgrave talked about the situation on the ground in Utopia. Outside, one of the young sailors from *The Flying Fish* stood guard with a side arm. There were other guards posted at the only remaining entrance to the warehouse. The rest had been sealed with giant metal plates ripped from old submarines and other pieces of debris in the sub hangar.

Jack saw their guests clear the makeshift security checkpoint at the entrance. His stomach clenched a little. He had no idea what would happen.

Mike Fisher and Andy Sherwood made an unlikely pair to lead the workers revolt in Utopia. Mike was in his middle fifties, healthy and strong, with some graying hair, and a short cropped silver beard. He didn't particularly strike Jack as the militant type. Jack thought of him as a book nerd. In the past, Fisher had approached Jack several times to see if he could get copies of old books for him. Jack had been able to produce a couple, and Fisher had paid handsomely. On the other hand, Musgrave seemed to think quite highly of him. Somewhere in the past he had military experience which he had used to great effect as he formed a ragtag band of rioters into the beginnings of a rebel army.

Jack didn't really have much knowledge of Andy, other than that he worked in IT when Lewis had been in charge. He was taller than Fisher, with dark curly hair and a lanky frame.

The office door opened. Fisher looked shocked to see jack. "You!" he said, as his face purpled.

"I'm gonna kill you!" Andy's anger equaled Mike's.

Musgrave stood and spoke firmly. "Mike, do you trust me?"

Mike looked at Musgrave but didn't say a word. After a heartbeat, he nodded ever so slightly.

"Then have a seat and hear what we have to say."

Mike dropped into one of the synthetic leather chairs arranged around the small coffee table in Rick's office. He refused to look at Jack. Andy refused to sit down. He remained three steps away from the table with his hands on his hips. Musgrave looked at him directly and said in a voice with all of the calm of the eye of a hurricane, "Have a seat, Andy. I didn't leave behind my work reopening the hospital just to have you muck things up. I have better things to do than to waste my time. It isn't like you haven't provided me with enough people to treat." Andy sat down.

Mike spoke up. "When you said you had a way to defeat the security codes, I wouldn't have even showed up if you had told me that he was part of the plan."

Musgrave remained standing. "I know that, which is why I didn't tell you that he is the plan."

"But he planted the bomb! He killed hundreds of people!"

Jack's anger rose, but he managed to keep it in check as he spoke. "I didn't plant the bomb."

Rick chimed in, "Why do you believe anything Randall has to say at this point?"

Andy spoke as if the answers were obvious. "He was on the stage when they took away Lewis. Everyone knew that he's wanted Lewis' job for years, prancing around here as if he were the prince of us all but never good enough to actually associate with any of us."

Jack considered what he wanted to say. "Andy, I don't care what you think of me. You don't know me well enough to know what motivates me and why I do what I do, but I can tell you that I wasn't given any choice about participating in that rally or helping Randall."

"Yes, you were. Everyone always has a choice. You just say 'no.' But you don't have a habit of saying 'no', do you, Jack? How many times did you say 'no' when that cynthy bitch from HR asked to get in your pants?"

Andy's perceptiveness caught Jack off guard. *How did anyone know about that?* It wasn't any of his business.

Musgrave interrupted immediately. "If we go down this road, this isn't going to be a very productive discussion. We don't all have to like each other or sing kumbaya together, but Jack may be the key to getting our friends and relatives back. Now are you going to listen to what we have to say or is this conversation at an end?"

Mike reached over and grabbed Andy by the wrist. "We'll listen, but I can't promise anything else."

Musgrave kept his eyes on Mike and nodded. "Good. Jack, why don't you explain what you have to offer?"

Keeping in mind that he desperately wanted to get Anna back, Jack refused the proffered bait, controlled his anger, and began. "I have a deactivated level three back door spider in the Aetna mainframe, just waiting to be activated."

Andy obviously understood just what Jack had said because he suddenly relaxed. Mike clearly didn't understand. Ironically, Jack probably understood just about as much as Mike.

Andy asked the first question. "How long's the spike?"

"Say again?"

Andy sized up Jack's ignorance in about a millisecond. His eyes narrowed. "You don't know what the hell I just said, do you? For that matter, you don't really know what you put in the system. I asked, how long will it disable the security codes?"

"I was told it would be good for ten minutes."

Andy continued to glare. "And how do you know that the person who sold it to you wasn't just bullshitting you?"

Rick spoke up. "I know that person well. He or she is as good as their word."

Mike looked somewhat skeptical, but Andy's interest seemed to have convinced him to listen more carefully. He looked at Musgrave and asked, "So, what you're saying is that he can disable the security codes for ten minutes? Is that all of them or just in the admin building?"

Jack answered, "It's designed to blow out the security codes for the building I am currently in, or the station, if I was there. The truth is, I put them in the system so long ago that I had almost forgotten they existed until Rick explained your situation." Jack remembered the fake ID card Molly had made that he used on the station. "And on the station, I had other ways of getting around."

Mike continued to ask questions. "Why would you need it? What good would ten minutes do you?"

Jack recognized Mike's attempt to check out his story. "When I was bringing things into Aetna illegally, I always had to worry about my future. I wasn't ever worried about admin or the gendarmes. Until Randall showed up, I had never met a company man you couldn't bribe or corrupt in some way, and I figured that if I did run into some hard ass, then there really wouldn't be much that I could do. Well, that proved to be the case, mostly, didn't it?"

Jack paused and waited for a response. Mike just continued to look at him. Jack went on, "What concerned me most was an unhappy customer. I worried that someone might decide they wanted to take their disappointment out on my hide, or worse, try to kill me. So I had a separate set of access codes built into the Aetna computing core as an escape plan. The fly in the ointment was always that I couldn't keep them activated and ready to go on a moment's notice or the Unity security AI would have taken note and just swept them away when they came through to clean up our systems. In order to be useful, I would have had to put them in ready mode no more than a day or two before I used them. Then I could activate the codes with the use of any palm reader or keypad to simultaneously disable all the locks in the station. Hopefully ten minutes would be enough for me to make a quick getaway."

Mike shrugged his shoulders, refusing to dignify Jack's story with a response. He looked at Musgrave. "How do you know this isn't all a double-cross, that we aren't being set up right now?"

"Mike, on that you're going to have to trust me. Let's just say Jack owes me and my friends his life, more than once. I can tell you that he's clean, no zombie bots or anything else, so he's telling you the truth."

Jack interrupted, "Look, I understand your concern. It only makes sense, and I would be suspicious in your position as well. But you have to understand, the day Randall arrived he sat me down in his office and showed me a list of almost every item I helped smuggle into this godforsaken place. By my count, twelve items were worthy of death sentences. Then he looked me in the eye and said that I could stay alive if I started helping him get what he needed to run the H2 operations on Aetna. I wasn't really given a choice. I didn't understand what that meant until the rally. I've been trying to find a way out since then."

"Did you get him the blasting cap?" For the first time since sitting down, Mike looked him in the eye.

Jack refused to flinch or look away "I did. It was the first and only thing I was asked to provide. When I was asked, I demanded to know what they were going to do with it. Carla, the head of HR, refused to tell me."

Mike looked at Jack for a moment, sizing him up. Then he turned to Musgrave, who still stood. "I don't suppose you can think of a way for Andy to verify the code is still there before we risk our lives for this."

"Not really. All the access to the core has been restricted to the admin building. There really isn't any way to access it except to get in there and see. Besides, Mike, you were going to try to do something before you even heard about this. If we get in there and the code is gone or it gets defeated, we just go back to your old plans."

Mike thought for a minute, reached a decision, and looked again at Jack. "You understand that I am not in charge of any of the other workers, right? It's not like we're a disciplined army. We're just a bunch of people singing a song of angry men. I may understand why you did what you did, but I wouldn't expect any of them to understand. If you want to come out alive tonight, then stay close by me and your friends..." Mike gestured at Rick and Tony. "...and keep your head down."

17
The Battle For Utopia

In the few hours after his meeting with the rebel leaders, Jack had found himself shuttled from person to person, each one tasked to prepare Jack for combat in some way. He received a new set of defensive bots from Musgrave, who was also handing out doses to all the rebel fighters willing to take them. Few resisted. They had all at least heard about what had happened when the zombie gas attack took place. Jack was also outfitted for the cold and given instructions on using a flechette rifle. The training was done in intraspace because, according to Rick, intraspace was shown to help students learn subjects faster and retain the memory longer. Normally, this would have bothered Jack, however, he didn't care because he was finally taking action to rescue Anna.

Late in the next dark cycle, Jack found himself crouching as he ran from building to building. He and the sixty or so rebels in their group crept behind deserted homes and trotted through empty vestibules, some of which showed the decidedly obvious scars of recent fighting. A city of children at play and neighbors talking to neighbors had been replaced by an empty, hollow, fearful thing. There were six other bands of similar size doing the same around the city, each approaching the center of town from different directions.

The crew of *The Fish* outfitted Jack for the dark and cold. He laughed to himself as he thought of Mike's warning that not everyone would take kindly to having him come with the rebels. *I'm covered head-to-toe in insulated gear. No one is ever going to recognize me.*

Jack used the heads-up he had from Soren to track the other members of *The Flying Fish*. The fifteen members of the crew who also wore heads-up gear had a bright green X above their heads along with their names. Once the battle began in earnest, the team would use these to keep track of each other and act as a unit. Jack tried to pick out Mike and Andy, as well, but after a while hiking and jostling in the dark, he lost track of both them. He tried to stay near the front of the pack with the other members of *The Flying Fish.*

The padded outdoor gear protected Jack from two different dangers. It was an unusually cold dark cycle in Utopia. The last move had forced the city farther away from the equator than usual. The temperatures were nearing minus eighty Celcius. In places, a light snow of carbon dioxide fell as it froze from the atmosphere. The design of Jack's cold suit trapped every ounce of heat possible. His suit also contained a small heat exchanger designed to take the warm air he breathed out and transfer as much of its heat as possible to the cold air coming in. While this kept his lungs from freezing, the cold air still stung with every breath.

The insulation of his gear also kept the outer layer of his clothing to within a few tenths of a degree of the atmosphere itself. This allowed him to remain almost invisible to the heat sensitive cameras and observation drones. The exchanger created the only real chink in the armor. In the extreme cold, the breath coming out of the exchanger stood out like a street lamp in the dark. Rebels learned to keep their heads down, and the exchanger pointed at the ground as they moved. This lessened the chance that it would become visible to any observers located above.

However, looking down couldn't provide perfect concealment. The attack came without warning just about halfway through their journey. Somewhere above Jack, he heard a loud "thwop" as the fighter next to him collapsed. After the stadium rally, Jack instantly recognized the sound of a neural stunner being fired.

Jack did as he had been instructed before they left the sub dock. He froze in place and looked down at the ground, keeping his heat signature hidden from the airborne robotic predator. To his right, Rick exchanged a series of hand signals with one of the other members of *The Flying Fish.* The crewman carefully crept behind an abandoned play structure and hid herself in a way in which she could look up without being seen. Spotting the small drone hovering above, she signaled back to Rick. Further signals were exchanged and ever so carefully, she took out her rifle and slowly pointed it skyward.

Drones were always a touch-and-go thing on Aetna. The cold air frequently damaged them. Combined with the loose watch kept on the population, they had never been the ubiquitous symbols of Unity control that they were in any of the major cities.

The nearly silent shot from the magnetic coil flechette rifle came before Jack expected it. The gunner had the weapon positioned for only a second before she fired. The needle shaped rounds ran true and the drone soon crashed to the ground, landing on the ice not far from where the group of fighters still sat.

When wounded but not down for the count, drones could continue to pose a danger, so even as it fell, Jack watched a dozen or so members of his group bolt toward the spot where it crashed and begin to beat on it with the makeshift weapons they had at hand. He and the members of *The Flying Fish* carried flechette rifles. A few others carried neural stunners captured from the enemy. Over half of Jack's group still had no weapons of their own.

The drone tried to swivel its gun toward the now exposed fighters but couldn't, due to the angle at which it had buried itself in the ground. The workers soon had it dismantled and removed the stunner from the device. The group stood and got moving as soon as they recovered the stunner. The victorious worker who removed the stunner dropped the metal bar on the ground, and Jack guessed the weapon would be powered and working as an improvised hand weapon by the time they reached the battle in earnest.

The rest of their journey remained relatively quiet. There were two holds as drones passed nearby, but each time the group successfully hid their heat, and the drones passed on. As they approached the center of the city, Jack noted those around him kept a little lower and made more effort to stay out of sight. He imitated their behavior. Within a few blocks of their rendezvous point, Jack's group went underground through a natural fissure into the relative warmth of the sea ice below them. Jack shuffled in the dark, blindly following the footsteps in front of him. After what seemed like an hour, but was only several blocks, the group stopped.

Those at the front began to climb through a narrow crevice in the ice. When Jack's turn came, he removed the backpack he wore and his rifle. He made sure the gun's safety was securely on, raised them over his head with one hand and began to climb as he had seen others do.

With men on top of him and right below him, Jack was incredibly grateful that he didn't have any claustrophobia. Once inside the narrow opening, Jack found the one-handed climbing difficult. His lack of conditioning hampered him, and he soon gasped for air, terrified that he would lose his grip on the spikes and other debris pounded into the ice to make an improvised ladder. He tightened his grasp as he imagined himself tumbling down on the people below. He kept pushing. Near the top, someone grabbed his weapon and his bag and helped him out of the hole. Then they shoved his gear back into his hands and motioned for him to follow the others who had climbed out before him.

Jack looked up into the low-hanging plumbing and sprayed-on insulation which made up the underbelly of the financial services building. The floor of the building lay only a few inches above his head. He stood in a narrow alley between treads on the mobile building. He and the other rebel fighters hurried to enter on a thin carbon staircase which lowered to the ground from the first floor. As Jack ran forward, he tried to throw his backpack on again. He found it difficult when padded up in the warm suit.

As soon as Jack entered the building, Rick approached him. "This way." Jack followed Rick and most of the other members of *The Flying Fish* up the stairs to the third floor of the building. They'd left Musgrave on the ground floor with a few of the other medical staff. Jack had seen them busily setting up a makeshift triage point. The newly reopened hospital had been quietly put on standby with all the doctors and nurses called in. Ambulances were ready to race to the scene as soon as it appeared safe to get them there.

Andy from IT also joined Rick and his team. Jack could tell where he was located by the lack of an ID above him on the heads-up. Rick had asked Andy to join them because of his innate knowledge of the Admin IT system. For the moment, they crouched in the hall outside the offices which faced the admin building. One of the team crept into their chosen office and attached explosives to the windows in front of them.

Jack checked the time on his heads-up. Ten minutes until go-time. The wait was interminable. *I'm going to get Anna back.* Jack breathed hard into his heat exchanger, trying to calm his nerves.

At six minutes and twenty-three seconds, Jack again checked the time when a text-based message came in from Rick. "Remember to hold back until I get the sensor packages deployed in front of us. We want to know what's coming—"

All hell broke loose. A bright flash and a strong concussion knocked Jack and the other fighters with him to the ground. Ceiling panels, wiring, and other debris rained down. Other concussions followed rapidly, some closer, some farther away. The building shuddered under each. Jack shook his head, trying to get his hearing back.

Within a few seconds of the first blast, Jack felt the power plant of the building light up below him. They were going early. The building started to rumble forward in an awkward motion. At about the same instant another huge blast knocked Jack flat again. This time, Jack lost consciousness for a moment.

As Jack came to, a voice which he recognized but couldn't place rang over the continued concussions of rocket fire all around them. "Get your fucking heads-up devices off now!"

Larry's voice followed. "Marquette and Johnson, you get White downstairs to the medics on the first floor."

Someone began pounding on Jack's shoulder. He opened his eyes and shook his head. "Get that heads-up off, Jack!" This time he knew the voice belonged to Rick. Not quite able to remember why it was important, Jack turned off his heads-up.

Before he thought he could move, Rick dragged him to his feet. "Move Jack. They've cracked our communications. Keep moving! We've got to get out of the way, or I'm going to be picking pieces of you up off the fucking wall."

Jack stumbled forward, leaning on Rick. The ringing in his ears began to subside.

The plan had been to load up the financial services building with fighters and then ram the six-story siege tower into the larger admin building. Fighters would then break out the windows on the façade of the admin building and fight their way, hand-to-hand, to the makeshift prison located on level eight. Some four hundred rebel fighters were hidden on the top floor for this purpose. Ugly hand-to-hand close quarters combat made the best use of the workers numerical advantage and had determined the strategy used in this raid. At the same moment, a contingent of some three hundred fighters would also attack the shuttle port. They intended to keep the marines busy so they couldn't come to the aid of those in the administrative complex.

Jack and his team were supposed to find access to the mainframe in IT on level three, so he could override all the security features of the building for ten minutes and allow the prisoners to escape. That was the plan. The plan hadn't included being pounded with artillery all the way across the street.

Jack now waited helplessly on the floor alongside the other crew from *The Flying Fish* as blast after blast rocked the building, raining debris upon his head. Above the continued rumble of the rockets, Jack felt the initial contact between the two buildings more than he heard it. The vestibules of the two huge buildings ground into each other with a loud screeching whine. The vibration of the financial building's power plant cranked up, accompanied by the tearing sounds of metal on metal. Jack could feel the financial building begin to tip forward as the gap between it and the admin building suddenly closed. For a moment, Jack worried that the building would tip over. Instead, a rending crash announced that the façades of the two buildings had come in contact. The sounds of shattering glass soon followed. The building seemed to straighten somewhat and all motion stopped.

Jack watched as one of the crew from *The Flying Fish* punched a detonator. Nothing happened. A sudden encompassing silence fell as the firing from the admin building and its drones ceased. As soon as the noise stopped, Jack surprised himself by springing into a crouch, ready to sprint through the adjoining office into the admin building. *Anything to get out of this hell*, he thought.

"Get up," Rick hissed to the others in the sudden silence. "Stay off the com system. Hand signals only when we move forward. Keep your heads-ups powered down." Rick tugged members of his crew to their feet. As he did so, he dropped several remote cameras which scurried forward on their own legs. He took a pocket sized data pad out of one of the zippered pockets on his thermal pants, and with a couple of taps on the screen, watched their progress.

He held his team back with a series of hand gestures. Standing close-by, Jack looked over one of his shoulders. To Jack, the hallway where he stood seemed like it had been badly rocked by the blasts from the rockets and other weapons aimed at their building. The walls had buckled and cracked. But the office on the other side of the door where they now crouched lay in ruins. Apparently the first blast had been a direct hit on the adjoining space. The outer wall no longer existed. It had fallen away, along with a large portion of the floor. The buildings were clearly not touching in a straight manner either. A large gap stood between the two. The admin building appeared vertical, but the financial building appeared to be tipped forward into it.

Metal support beams seemed dangerously bent. Jack had the image of a badly beaten prize boxer slumped into his competitor, trying to find the support needed to continue standing.

As Rick recon'ed the situation in the office, the darkness came alive with the sounds of explosions. The cracks and pops of small arms fire echoed down to them from above.

Rick trained one of the rolling cameras on the office in the admin building on the other side. Jack couldn't see much in the visible spectrum through the smoke and haze. Rick tried the heat cameras, but the camera showed that the glass on the other side remained intact, blocking efforts to see through it.

Rick made a series of hand gestures to his team, and they began to move forward through the damaged office. As they approached the gap between the two buildings, the lead commando lifted his rifle and fired at the window across the way. Jack didn't hear a crack but the heat efficient glass on the other side crumpled into thousands of small pieces and fell away.

As soon as the glass dropped out of the way, Jack began to hear high pitched smacks landing all around him. Then he heard the quiet pop of flechette rifles, followed by the audible "thwop" from a neural stunner.

Rick grabbed Jack and threw him to the ground. "Everyone down!" he yelled as others on the team tried to find cover. Jack crouched behind a flimsy metal chair as fletch rounds dug in all around him.

He still couldn't see their attackers, but the commandos began to return fire. *They* at least had some idea of where they wanted to shoot.

Someone on Jack's right began to scream while Rick frantically conferred with someone on his left. Jack couldn't hear anything they said, but Rick's voice rose above the cacophony. "Flash!" he bellowed as the person next to him quickly stood for just an instant and threw something. Rick reached over with his giant hand and smashed Jack's head into the deck.

For a second, the world turned whiter than any sun Jack had ever seen. Even through his closed eyelids, he felt blinded. A high pitched bang followed, which sounded like it came from the office across the way. Rick released the pressure on Jack's head.

Rick stood, looking down at Jack and the figure who had thrown the flash grenade, and said, "Follow me."

As they were standing, the dark suited figure on the other side of Rick spoke to Jack. "Don't think, Jack. Just do." Jack recognized the voice as that of Larry, Rick's second in command.

Rick yelled, "Covering fire."

The crack of weapons erupted around Jack even as he stood in the center of the room. Suddenly Rick started running toward the gap between the two buildings and Jack understood what Rick expected him to do. Jack didn't think; he ran and he jumped. He didn't consider the consequences of failure until he had already launched himself into the air. By then it was too late.

Jack landed hard, taking the sill of the broken window in the chest. He couldn't get a breath but that was the least of his worries. He desperately looked for something to hold as he slipped backward toward the thirty-foot drop below his dangling legs. In the end, Jack grabbed the metal window frame and fought to lift himself into the building. All the while, he gasped for air.

Rick and Larry both did better than Jack, landing on their feet. Rick fell heavily into a roll and then took cover behind a metal desk which he quickly turned over to provide better protection in the new office.

Larry turned and helped Jack get in the window. In the meantime, whoever or whatever opposed them in the admin building started to recover from the flash grenade. Once again, audible shots rang out from behind the counter on the other side of the large office filled with portable work spaces and desks. As Larry and Jack gathered with Rick in the cover behind the desk, Larry looked at Rick and said, "Far left corner of the office. I count three AI and at least one controller. I don't think they're mobile."

Rick grunted his agreement and didn't waste any time. He twisted the dial on the grenade in his hand before reaching up over the desk and letting go. The grenade shocked Jack by zipping off on its own. Unity grenades still had to be thrown. Rick crouched behind the desk, curled into a fetal position, and covered his head. Jack imitated him. The grenade went off without the concussion Jack anticipated. Instead of a thump, the world tipped over, and he quickly began to slide along the floor. He heard the sounds of things crashing together all over the office. For nearly a second or more Jack slid toward the far corner of the room. Then as quickly as it started, it let go. Jack now lay some fifteen feet further into the office than when he started. All around him furnishings and cubicle walls had been pulled inward toward the corner where Rick had aimed his weapon.

Rick stood up and yelled back across the now silent gap behind them. "Go!"

Jack saw dark shapes begin to stand and run toward the gap. Even as they did so the sounds of firing from a level above them could be heard. Flechette rifles and stunners poured fire from above. A few at a time, men and women jumped into the void. Jack saw one young person cut down in mid-jump. Hit with a stunner, she simply went limp and slipped into the gap between the buildings. Rick grabbed his rifle off his shoulder. He scooted toward the gap, laying brazenly on his back as he aimed into the air and fired as the last team members made the leap.

Once the remainder of his team had safely jumped, Rick came back. Some members were already working to secure the door into the corridor beyond.

Jack couldn't help but look into the corner of the room where the gravity grenade had gone off. Twisted metal desks, chairs, and even a broken countertop all lay compacted into a single massive ball. The wall behind had buckled inward as well. Jack noticed that not all of the pile was office furniture and debris. There were at least two people, or what had been people, buried there as well. The sight horrified a distant part of Jack. Noticing that one of the Marine's eyes still seemed to recognize the world around him, Jack looked away.

Andy was busy talking with Larry and Rick. "We need to get out into this hallway and go three or four doors down. We came in a couple of offices further up the hallway than we intended. It's been a while since I've had to come to Admin for training, but I'm almost sure this is the front office for the clerical pool, which is a few doors up from where we want to be."

Rick turned to one of the other soldiers, who crouched by the door looking at a data pad. Apparently, they had already sent cameras down the hall to investigate. "You get that, Jones?"

"Already on it. It looks clear so far. I don't think we're going to have any trouble getting to the door."

"All right, everyone, get a move on. They know we're down here, and they ought to have a good guess where we want to go. I wouldn't expect this to last. Those shots were coming down on us from five so it won't take them long to get down here to three."

Both assessments turned out to be correct. They got to the central computing mainframe with little trouble. Larry, Rick, Andy, and Jack entered. The four of them took off their head gear. Shortly thereafter, a loud bang followed by the pop of small arms outside announced the return of hostilities. With a flick of his head, Rick sent Larry back out in the corridor to assess the situation.

Andy approached a terminal in the corner and started typing for a minute on the screen. "Jack, you can access the system from this terminal." Jack came up behind Andy and saw a terminal already logged in waiting for input. Even while he spoke, Andy looked around the room for a moment, eyeing the cabling. He stopped and retraced the wires a couple of times back and forth. "This is where I tap into the security system for the building." He grabbed a tool out of his pocket and started to cut the wires.

"Jack, activate your back door." Rick's voice no longer carried the friendly tone Jack knew. Rick had entered a kind of full command mode Jack had never seen from him, hand on his hips, jaw set. Realizing that he had been watching Andy, Jack turned his attention to the monitor in front of him.

Before they had left the sub hangar, Jack had tried to remember exactly how to activate his back door on the Aetna security system. No matter how hard he tried, he hadn't been able to remember the passcode. Reluctantly, Jack had let Rick use a memory assistance AI to walk him through the associated thoughts. The AI used an intraspace cap to pick away at the old memories until it got to the information they needed. Or at least that was what Rick told him would happen. To Jack, it felt as if he randomly started remembering a whole bunch of useless and disparate information which didn't make sense. The whole thing had been quite disconcerting. Without warning, the numerical code for the shuttle port locker that he used for his belongings while on the streets popped into his head. Several other memories flashed by before they found the one they wanted. Lacking all context or introduction, Jack walked into a living memory. He was back setting up the hack with Robert looking over his shoulder.

Now in IT, Jack hurriedly typed "A!! women R whores" into the prompt. Years ago, they had set it up after a particularly disastrous night at Chuck's Place. He cringed as he thought of Anna, the reason he currently risked his life. The screen changed and flashed in bright red letters, *Security override ready. Activation will occur on your next security access.* Jack looked up at Rick and noticed the fighting outside seemed to be intensifying. Rick pointed across the room to a palm scanner. Jack ran to the device and let it scan him. Nothing appeared to happen. "Did that work?" Jack asked Rick.

"I don't know." He turned to the IT tech. "Did it work, Andy?"

Andy grabbed a tool from his mouth as he concentrated on his work. "I'll be able to tell you in a second. I'm almost tapped in to the security feeds from the building. Mike could have done this better and faster, you know."

"Get a move on, Andy. We only have ten minutes, and it sounds like we're pinned down in the hall."

"One last item," Andy answered, as he clipped some kind of device Jack didn't understand to the wires behind a rack of servers. "Done. Let's see what we have, shall we?" Andy stood away from his work and grabbed his data pad from the table next to them.

Before Andy could tell them anything, Jack heard a change in the sounds of fighting above them. At first Jack thought it sounded like horrible screaming but then he recognized what he believed to be cheering. With the security override, the prisoners were supposed to have been let out of their cells. They would be joining the fight. They could hear their cheers even three floors down.

Rick looked up. "I'll take that to mean it's working." He clapped Jack on his back. For a moment, a wide smile broke across his face. It didn't last. "Andy, now it's your turn to keep your end of the bargain. Where's Anna? We need to find her."

"The facial recognition software is already on it." Staring at the data pad, Andy walked over to where Rick and Jack waited. Images flashed by at impossible speed. Suddenly the image stopped, focusing on a woman in a prison cell. She sat on the edge of her bunk, hands folded, looking down. The door to her cell remained closed. The image came from one of the upper corners of the cell, which made a positive identification impossible for the recognition software.

"That's her!" Jack felt sure.

Rick spoke quietly, keeping an exaggeratedly calm demeanor. "Where is she, Andy?"

"Level eight. Room forty-six." He looked up at Rick. "She's on the prison level!"

Rick only nodded and turned toward the door. He opened it carefully.

For his efforts, Rick nearly took an eye full of flechette shot. He ducked back just in time. "Well, that doesn't look so good." He looked a little bit like he could be sick. "Jack, I need you to help me cover them. We're getting the shit pounded out of us by a couple of armored bots. I don't think they have more than four of them on the planet, and we have two in the hall in front of us. Our team has got to get some better cover. There's another stairway behind us. It will slow them down. The fighting is coming from our front. So the plan will be to tuck our tail and make a break for the back stairs. But the two of us need to create a little diversion for a moment, while the others get out of harm's way. You ready for that?"

Jack wasn't sure, but he nodded.

"Andy, I need you to get the rest of those still on their feet moving in the right direction. Get them headed to the back staircase and wait for us at the door." Rick pointed his finger in Andy's face. "And get our wounded. We leave no one. You hear me?"

"Right." Andy's face projected a mixture of grim determination and terror.

Rick turned back to Jack. "About ten feet in front of us there's another couple of doorways into the main IT offices. They're deeper set than this one. We need to make a break forward for that. It's going to put us really close to the enemy. That's what the cutter on the end of the gun is for. Use it if you have to." Rick took his weapon off his shoulder, pressing a button near the trigger. A spring-loaded laser cutter attached near the muzzle of the device popped out. It instantly lit up, turning both sides of the barrel into an effective cutting torch. It had proven a useful weapon for close quarters combat against both metal AI and "flesh and bone" people. Jack shuddered internally but wasn't given any time to think.

Rick flicked the device off. "Make sure you turn that thing off when you're done, or you'll cut yourself to hell on accident. Besides, there's only enough juice for about twenty minutes, so don't turn it on until you need it. Keep low and move forward while firing at the end of the hallway. There are a bunch of Marines down there." Rick didn't give either Jack or Andy time to answer or think. He simply moved to the door, opened it, tossed his grenade, and yelled something inaudible to his team. Then he let the door close and crouched as he waited. Even buried in IT, Jack's chest seemed to cave in at the thump from the grenade. Dust rose from the racks of servers behind him, hanging in the air.

As soon as the explosion went off, Rick threw open the door and screamed at the rest of his team, "Move out! Back the way we came!" even as he himself advanced into the teeth of the firefight. Jack followed him, finding himself screaming at the enemy as he fired. In front of Jack, two tread mounted AI lay on their sides. One looked like it was out of commission, but the one on his side of the corridor was already trying to right itself and swivel its gun at him. Farther down, he spotted several combat helmets peeking out of doorways. He couldn't tell how many there were at the other end of the hall, but the air seemed thick with munitions and the sounds of weapons being discharged. Jack fired in their direction, trying to keep them at bay as he and Rick advanced. He felt almost invincible when he got to the doorway without being hit.

He ducked into the alcove only five feet from where one of the treaded and armored AI had almost righted itself. Knowing he would die the moment it could aim at him, Jack flipped on his cutting tool and jumped forward, slashing as he went. Sparks flew off the wounded bot. He managed to slice off one of its weapons which swung dangerously in his direction. Then he wildly slashed at the protruding arm it was using to sit up, knocking it back down on the ground. Finally, he aimed the barrel of his weapon at the "eyes" of the beast— the sensor package located down low in a heavily armored area. Jack fired over and over again.

"Jack, get cover." Rick's panic penetrated Jack's instinctual rage. He dived backward to the protection of the doorway as something nicked his chest. Looking down, Jack saw he had a long rip torn across his cold suit. *Shit. I almost bought it*, he thought.

As he ducked back into the doorway, time seemed to slow down and several things happened all at once. Pressed against the wall, he faced backward for the moment and saw the small group of commandos who remained on their feet, dragging away the dead and wounded, Larry among them. Jack also remembered that they were trying to get to Anna, who was somewhere in the building, and he recognized that his time to do so without all the doors working against him was running short.

At that moment, without the formalities of thought or reason, something clicked in Jack. It was as if coming this close to death, it no longer appeared to be the enemy he had thought it to be. For a moment, he lost all his fear. *If I don't stop them, the rest of our team will get mowed down.* Even as fragments of broken tile sprayed around him from shots aimed at his head, he brazenly stepped out from the door and raised his weapon. He took careful aim at one of the marines who appeared in a doorway, pulled the trigger, and watched his head shoot backwards. He moved forward, firing over and over again, every time someone appeared in a doorway, more often than not watching his shots hit their targets. Jack welcomed the thought of death, anything to be done with the horror around him, the horror he had helped create. Without pausing for cover behind the disabled AIs, he kept moving forward. Only after he had shot two marines in the back as the group retreated away from him did he discover that he had been screaming.

Someone tapped him on the shoulder from behind. Jack turned, flicking on his cutter in one smooth motion. He almost gutted Rick, who had the presence of mind to step back.

"They're gone, Jack. There's no one left to fight."

Jack released his rifle, allowing it to drop to the floor. The cutter screeched, and the weapon skittered wildly on the tile before it turned itself off.

Rick flinched. Obviously concerned, he stepped forward and picked up the rifle. "All right, buddy. Let's go. This way." He spoke quietly to Jack. They returned to find that only six of their team remained unwounded. In the eerie quiet, Rick assessed their situation. Four were dead outright, and three others had wounds which might kill them soon enough. "Sherwood, how much time do we have left on those doors?"

"Six minutes."

"Shit." Rick grimaced. "Johnson, stay with the wounded. I'll have help on the way shortly." He turned to Jack. "I think you better stay here. We'll get Anna and bring her to you."

Jack processed the concerned look on Rick's face. He had no intention of letting Rick leave him behind. He removed his grimace and called his thoughts back to the present, from the dark place they currently resided. "I'm fine, Rick."

"Like hell you are." Rick's scowl softened, and his face broke into the hint of a grin. "I've never... you are one crazy son-of-a-bitch, Jack Halloway." He handed back his rifle. "You are definitely not okay." Glancing at his dead, the smile disappeared as if it never had existed. His scowl returned.

Without another word, he turned and led his remaining team members up the flight of stairs at a run. He pulled his heads-up out of his pocket. "I guess we'll have to risk it. It's not like they don't know where we are." He pinged Musgrave who was in the middle of triaging a flood of wounded fighters. Musgrave got a team with stretchers headed their direction. Rick turned off the device and stuck it back in his pocket.

18
Finding Anna

What had sounded like a celebration five floors below became something ugly as Jack and the others neared the top floor. His legs were on fire, but he refused to notice. Time was running short. By the time they reached the landing, Jack estimated that they only had about a minute left to get into the prison before it locked itself down. The melee in the atrium of the Department of Law and Order appeared to be utter madness, the worst of what humanity could do. The room stank of bile, blood, and wasted human lives, while the anguish of the wounded and dying filled the air.

With no time to think on such matters, Jack and the others from *The Flying Fish* waded in, trying to cross the room as quickly as possible. Jack found himself stumbling over the bodies of friend and foe alike as he sought to avoid getting caught in the melee. He and the other team members had almost made it to the far side of the room before one of the rebels recognized him. He charged toward Jack with some kind of homemade club. Jack, who had left his head gear back in IT, saw him coming in time to raise his weapon at him and shout, "I'm on your side! I didn't plant the bomb and I don't work for Randall!"

Jack saw the fear of death momentarily pass through the worker's eyes as the cutting torch lit up the barrel of Jack's gun. Jack knew that he would defend himself if necessary but really had no interest in killing someone who should be on his side.

Rick, who had been a few steps ahead of Jack, came back and leveled his weapon at the few workers who were gathering behind the first. "Keith, he's telling the truth! We're both fighting the same people. Now back off."

Keith looked puzzled for a moment as comprehension dawned on him, but it appeared that Rick's word seemed enough for him. He backed away mumbling, "Sorry. I didn't know." All the while, he continued to stare at the barrel of Jack's gun. A twitchy Jack refused to lower it. Rick finally took hold of the gun behind the cutting torch and pushed the barrel toward the ground. Jack let the torch go off with a pop.

The lobby of the jail was quiet compared to the cries of the atrium. As they entered, Jack heard an ominous set of clicks as his computer hack on the security system ran its course. He would have panicked if it weren't for the bodies stacked in the door. It appeared that there had been a crush as people tried to push their way out. Both the door into the lobby and the door from the holding area into the cell block were held open by dead bodies.

There were others here as well, wounded and a few who tended them. They shrank back at the sight of the team's weapons. In the corner, a child began to cry.

Rick and the others took little notice as they proceeded on into the cell block, stepping over the dead as best they could. The horror continued in the two-story jail. It was clear that when the cell doors opened the prisoners had made a break for it. Some had fallen and been trampled. Others had been shot in the back. Here and there the wounded lay on the ground.

A single man dressed in the purple of the gendarmes tended to them the best he could. He had a slight build, a small paunch, and a combover. Jack couldn't remember his name but recognized him as one of the easygoing guys on Frank's team, someone who Jack guessed had joined more so he could meet people and be seen as important, rather than someone with an axe to grind.

Rick raised his weapon at him and approached. "You, stand up! Who are you?"

The man jumped at the shout and, seeing the weapons of the team aimed at him, began to shake. A tear rolled down his cheek. "I didn't kill anybody. I didn't do it. When I was told to shoot, I refused to fire. I promise. I didn't kill anyone. I have a family in Utopia. I don't want any part of this." His voice begged for understanding.

"Stand up." Rick took a commanding tone.

The gendarme complied.

"Put your gun on the ground, slowly."

The gendarme reached into his holster, put down the flechette pistol, and backed away from his weapon. Jack stepped forward and collected it. He tucked it into his belt.

"Can you get us into cell number forty-six?"

The gendarme looked surprised. He relaxed a bit, knowing he wasn't going to be shot on the spot. "That's where they're holding the girl who planted the bomb." He stood up straighter. "I can't do that." Looking at Jack, recognition dawned.

"We didn't plant the bomb. Someone on Randall's team planted it. We're just supposed to take the blame which rightfully belongs to him."

A puzzled expression followed Jack's outburst. Then he looked at the ground and shrugged his shoulders. "I don't know who to believe anymore." He started slowly walking toward the far end of the cell block. "If the admin can behave this way… if Mother Unity doesn't care for her little children, what do we do?"

Rick's voice cut like a knife as he kept his weapon trained on the gendarme. "Stop working for her."

At the far end of the cell block, the gendarme scanned in to a smaller set of cells. Here the door remained closed, and Rick held it open. He assigned one of his remaining crew to stand watch and make sure the door didn't shut. The door led to a second single hallway lined with a few cells on each side. They were numbered, starting with forty-one. None of them were open.

Fearing a booby-trap, Rick and his team approached Anna's cell slowly. Jack got there first and looked inside. Anna sat on her bunk. He knocked on the door. Anna looked up. The gendarme stepped up and opened the cell. Seeing the people with weapons entering, Anna shrank away from the door. Jack stepped inside. "Anna. It's me, Jack."

Recognition, followed by fear, crossed Anna's face. "What are you doing here? I don't want to see you. Why are they bringing you to me? You made me do awful things." Anna shrank into the corner, still wearing her thin hospital gown.

"Anna, I didn't make you do anything. I won't make you do anything. They've changed your memories." He reached out a hand. Anna refused to take it. "Anna, you know they're going to kill you, right?"

Anna nodded and then began to cry. "I deserve to die. I killed all those children and babies. I want to die."

Jack deflated, suddenly helpless. He turned to Rick.

Rick answered him calmly. "We've got to get her to Musgrave. We'll see what he can do to get her memories back. Sometimes it turns out fine, and sometimes there's nothing to be done. But we have to get her out of here. Jack, why don't you step out and let us handle this. Give me your backpack."

Without another word to Anna, Jack took the pack off his back and walked out the door.

"Benitez, I need you to get her dressed in that cold suit. We have to get her out of here. It won't be long before they come looking for her."

"Yes, sir." The last standing female member of Rick's team stepped forward. "All right, honey. I promise, I'm not going to hurt you."

"Johnson step out with Jack. Let's give her some space."

Anna didn't want to leave her cell. In the end, Rick had to threaten her to get her to comply. Benitez played the good cop and tried to coax her forward. Jack flinched when he heard Rick raise his voice with Anna. He stepped away from the door. Part of him knew it was necessary, but he hated hearing it. He felt so guilty about her treatment at the hands of Carla and the other members of the team.

Jack looked up and caught a glimpse of a little girl barely peeking out of the window of another cell. She had to be standing on something, probably the bed. Surprised, Jack called to the gendarme who sulked at the end of the cell block. "Hey, are there other people still in here?"

"Yes. I mean, I think so."

"How come the doors didn't open when we overrode the security?"

The gendarme pointed down at one of the doors. "The maximum security cells have a physical backup to make sure that no one gets out if a lock fails."

Jack raised his weapon and jabbed it toward the gendarme. "Open the doors." When the gendarme didn't move fast enough, Jack screamed. "Now!"

The gendarme flinched and quickly began to open the doors to the cell block. The first three cells were empty. In the fourth, Jack looked in and found a bruised and barely conscious Robert. He stepped back to the cell in which Benitez had Anna almost dressed. "Rick, I found Robert."

Rick looked up. "What?"

"He looks like he's had the shit knocked out of him, but I think he's alive."

"Fuck." Rick hurried to the next cell, pointing at Jack. "Get the rest of them open, now."

Jack nodded. "Already on it." All but one of the last few cells were empty. Jack stood behind the gendarme hoping beyond hope that he was right about the face he had seen in the window. When the door opened, the little girl shrank back in the corner.

"Mommy? Where's my Mommy?" The girl sounded frightened.

Jack had been right. He got down on his knees. "Jo. It's okay. You're safe now. It's Uncle Jack."

At the sound of a voice she recognized, little Jo Lutnear ran forward and hugged Jack. She started to sob. Other than a dirty jumper and a black eye, she didn't look too bad. At least she had been fed.

Jack turned on the gendarme. "Did you know they had a little girl back here?"

"No. I didn't. I swear. Recently we haven't been allowed back here; only those who came with the new people were allowed in."

Jack could see that he was lying. He stood up from Jo and took a step toward the gendarme. "Jo, have you ever seen this man before?"

Jo began to cry. She could sense Jack's anger.

Jack cocked back the butt of his gun, ready to beat out of the gendarme whatever other lies he may have told. "What's your name?"

"Gordon. My name is Gordon." The slight man backed up against the wall of the cell, trying to get as far away from Jack as possible.

"Jo, I need you to tell me if you've ever seen this man before."

Jo just nodded. She cried louder.

The gendarme flinched. He slid down the wall in the corner. "Listen, I was scared. I sometimes come back here. I have seen her before. I hated that they brought her here."

"What did you do to her? Did you ever hurt her?"

"No. I didn't hurt her. I never touched her. I'm not like that. You have to listen to me."

"Has this man ever hurt you, Jo?" Jack turned back to Gordon. "You're a liar. You know that?"

"I'm just scared. This isn't what I signed up for."

"Well, I think the butt of my gun might help you lose a little bit of your fear, because you're going to tell me exactly how this little girl got back here." Jack raised his gun ready to pound the man in the chest.

Gordon curled up into a ball. "I just did what I was told. I didn't do anything. I did what I was supposed to do. Just like you did."

Jack flinched as he remembered the knot in the pit of his stomach as Gunderson pushed him forward into a waving crowd where he shook hands with children no older than Jo. He remembered refusing to come to the Lutnears' defense as they were dragged away into this hell hole.

The butt of Jack's gun dropped back to his side. The man continued to whimper, huddled in a ball in the corner of the cell. Jo quieted her crying, and came and patted the man on his shoulder. "Uncle Jack, He was the nice one. He brought me my dinner."

Jack sat back on the cot, crushed. Gordon continued to cry.

With only a glance at the weeping man in the corner, Rick appeared in the door a minute or two later. "I think we're ready out here. What's going on?"

Jack stood up. "I found Jo Lutnear locked in this cell. Gordon and I were having a little chat about her treatment and whether or not he had anything to do with her black eye."

Rick raised an eyebrow. "And did he?"

"No." Jack walked over to the corner and extended a hand to Gordon, pulling him up. "You're right. I was scared, just like you. I'm not so scared anymore."

Rick asked the gendarme, "Do you know where Lewis and her mother are? How about her brothers?"

Gordon looked grim and glanced at the little girl.

Jack picked up little Jo in his arms and stepped out of the cell, allowing Rick to talk privately with Gordon.

Robert leaned unsteadily on his cell door. Anna sat against a wall with her knees pulled up to her chest. Jack started to walk toward Anna. He wanted to talk with her, but she flinched at the sight of him and began to cry again. Jack's gut tied itself in a knot. *Easy Jack. There will be time enough later. Just get her out of this alive.* Jack gave her the space she needed and instead turned to Robert.

"You look like hell, Robert."

"I feel like it."

"Are you okay?"

"No." Robert shook his head. "I'm not okay, but I will be if we can get out of here." He managed a weak smile. After setting Jo down on her feet next to him, Jack took the gendarme's gun out of his belt and passed it along to Robert. "Let's hope you don't need to use it, but it's a real mess in the atrium."

Gordon and Rick walked out of the cell together. Rick looked grim. He leaned in and whispered to Jack, "We might find Mom or Teddy, but they shot her when the prisoners bolted."

Jack nodded. "The others?"

Rick shook his head. Turning, he said, "All right, let's get moving. Anna, please keep quiet. I wouldn't want to have to make you stay quiet." Rick did his best to look threatening. To Jack it wasn't much, but in her fragile state, it overwhelmed Anna. She nodded and bit back tears, shrinking away from Rick. Benitez held her firmly by the arm.

Jack picked up little Jo again and followed.

The silence in the cell block made it feel like a mausoleum. Most of the wounded had been moved out. Here and there, smears of blood remained on the floor, but no one had yet bothered with the dead. Jack looked at Jo and saw a glazed look of fear come over her eyes. "Close your eyes, honey," Jack said. When she didn't respond, Jack stopped for a moment, swung his rifle back on his shoulder and closed them with his now free hand. Jo responded by burying her head on his shoulder. The group walked quickly together out of the cell block.

The transformation a few minutes had created in the lobby of the jail surprised Jack. Most of the wounded had been removed, and the door to the atrium stood open wide. Only those who seemed unable to move themselves had been left behind. The sounds of the deadly scrum were no longer to be heard on the other side of the door. Rick took Robert's arm off his shoulder and put him in a chair in the corner of the room. He slumped down and appeared to lose consciousness. Rick motioned Anna into the chair next to him and crept forward to look out the door. A quick glance and his shoulders relaxed. He turned around with a grim expression, "It's over. We won. I don't think there will be a victory celebration. The workers paid a price."

"We need to get help up here for our wounded." Rick pulled out the heads-up. "I think I can risk this again."

The communication channel appeared to kick in, and Rick looked suddenly alert. "Understood," was all he said. He took off the heads-up and turned it off. "We've got a little mop-up to be done down on the first floor of the financial building. There's a small group of Marines trying to take out the wounded. Musgrave needs our help. Benitez, Jordan, and Chan, you're with me." Rick glanced at the little girl in Jack's arms. "Jack, I want you to stay here and keep everyone safe. We'll be back with help as soon as we can. Radio if there's trouble." Jack started to protest and then looked down at the blond curls buried on his shoulder. He stepped to the side as Jordan, who had been behind him, passed by. Jack sat down in a chair surrounded by the dead and dying.

Once Rick had left, the room became eerily quiet, except for the raspy breathing of a wounded woman slumped in the chair next to him. Jack didn't bother to try to speak to Anna. He smiled at her, but she didn't respond. She appeared catatonic, simply existing until her nightmare ended.

"Jack? Is that you, or am I dreaming?" The voice sounded familiar.

"Mommy?" Jo lifted her head.

Jack turned to see Julia Lutnear in the chair next to him. Blood stained the thin prison blanket which covered her. Her face looked white as a sheet. Although only half open, her eyes were alert. She looked like she hadn't eaten well in the few weeks since Jack had seen her.

Jo scrambled off Jack's lap and wrapped her arms around her mother. She instinctively tried to climb up on her mother's lap. Julia winced. Jack stood and put Jo back on the floor.

"Mommy can't have you on her lap right now," said Julia. "But I love you, honey." Julia put a dirty hand on Jo's head. Even those simple words required a great effort.

Jo snuggled as close as she could to her mother and put her head on one of her breasts.

Julia looked at Jack. "You have to listen to me, Jack. I want you to take Jo with you."

"What?"

"Wherever you're going, I want you to take Jo with you."

Jack shook his head. "You're not going to die, Julia. Rick Carter just went to get the medics. He'll be back any moment."

Julia tried to sit up a little, and she stared hard at Jack, forcing her eyes to focus. "No. For once you will listen to me, Jack. You have to get Jo out of here. I may or may not make it. It doesn't matter. You know what comes next. There will be more troops, and they won't play nice. There isn't any life left for her here, and I am sure you're trying to escape. You are my only hope for my child. You have to take her with you. Please, Jack."

"What makes you think I have any better plan to get out of here than you do?"

Julia slumped back in her chair, "Because you do, Jack. I know you. You always find a way to escape from trouble. Now you're going to take the dying wish of a mother and make Josephine part of your plan." Julia took Jo's hand and put it in Jack's.

Jo started to cry.

Jack wanted to tell her how impossible it would be for him to take care of a child, how he hadn't had a plan to get away, and how he had lucked into one, but it didn't really seem to matter. What mattered was whether or not he was going to honor Julia Lutnear's dying wish.

"If you see my Teddy, tell him that I love him." Julia's eyes seemed to focus on something behind Jack. He felt the cold metal of a weapon pressed against the back of his skull.

"Well, this is touching." The voice belonged to Carla. "Stay still, Jack."

Little Josephine began to cry in earnest.

Jack even heard a small whimper from Anna in the corner. He tried to look her direction without moving his head.

"How convenient that you're all together. You don't realize how you're going to save my ass, especially you, Jack." Carla's voice sounded tense, but Jack thought he heard a note of fear in it, as well.

"You know, it isn't very smart of you to be wandering around here alone. There are wounded in this room. My friends will be coming back any minute."

"The workers didn't give me much of a choice, Jack. There aren't many of us left in the admin building, and Randall couldn't spare any to protect little old me." Her words carried the tang of bitterness. "But I think it will take at least a few more minutes for your terrorist friends to come back. They're tied up helping rescue your wounded from a squad of marines that Gunderson sent their way. When I tell Randall that I have you and Anna, my people will get here first." The room remained silent for a second. The gun pressed harder into the back of Jack's head. "They're on their way." Jack could hear the smile in Carla's voice. "Randall wants you bad, Jack. I've never seen him so concerned. You're his 'get out of jail' card, and Randall doesn't do jail." Out of the corner of his eye, Jack saw Carla look around the room. "You're such an idiot, Jack. You have no idea what a shitty hole you've dug yourself."

"I dug myself? I don't remember being given any choices, and I wasn't the one who screwed up with the bomb." The gun in Carla's hand begin to shake. Her behavior hinted of desperation. Jack wasn't exactly sure what she would do. Despite his pounding heart and fear that Carla would blow his brains out, he asked, "Did you screw that up, Carla?"

"No, it wasn't my screw up. The plant was huge, and where I put the bomb there was no way anyone could have found it so easily. Someone had to tip off the manager. There's no other way." Carla laughed loudly, almost maniacally, but without mirth. The sound sent a chill down Jack's spine. "But their plan all went to hell when the plant manager crossed the wrong wires while trying to disarm it and 'boom' went the city."

Jack heard an intake of breath from the corner where Anna sat. *That's right, you and I never planted the bomb.*

Carla must have heard it, too, because she viciously smashed the weapon into the back of Jack's head. "You shut up!" Carla kept the gun pointed at Jack but turned on Anna. "So you want to know the truth, you little whiny bitch? All that crap we told you about how evil you were, all those memories we gave you, it was all bullshit, but we got what we needed—a nice little confession. And in the end, it doesn't really matter, because you're going to die just the same."

Jack winced from the pain of the blow to his head but refused to cry out. He slowly turned around and faced Carla.

She pressed the flechette to his forehead. Carla's precisely manufactured beauty sagged under the weight of her fear. She had lost her manicured air of confidence, and Jack sensed that she was all the more dangerous without it. Stripped of all her swagger, he was finally seeing the real Carla. It wasn't a pretty sight. He guessed that she felt trapped and wanted a way out. Jack had little hope that she would be brave enough to take it. He guessed that Carla wanted to talk, and he thought it was a good idea. She might have despised him, but without Jack around, there was really no one to trust. He asked a question. "Who?"

"How stupid can one person be, Jack? It had to be Gunderson. He gave me the location and time for the bomb to go off. I did exactly what he recommended. What you don't seem to realize is that he was after you, as well. If the bomb had been disarmed, there still would have been huge problems for both of us, but mostly for you. I would have looked bad in the eyes of Randall, but you would have taken the fall."

"So Gunderson was trying to undermine you and I was going to end up taking the blame?" Jack asked.

"Shit rolls downhill, as they say. Glad to see you can keep up. One thing's for sure, I have no intention of taking the blame myself. You're the easiest target. You're the local sympathizer with the motive to tip off the plant managers."

"But why would Gunderson try to undermine you?"

"Jack, you are so fucking naive. Does he need a reason? It's just politics. He technically reports to me. He's a gendarme, part of HR. Not that he ever does anything I tell him to do, but that doesn't matter. With me gone, there isn't anyone between him and Randall. He'll be Randall's right hand man. Its a power game. One of us would take the other out eventually. Men like Randall and Gunderson play power games, Jack. Small men—men like you—hear their thunder and tremble before your gods."

After contemplating what to say next, Jack doubted that his idea would fly, but he couldn't think of anything better to say, so he went with it. "You're not in a very good position here, Carla. You have to know that. You took care of me, and now it's my turn to return the favor. Come with us. We can help you escape." He tried to use his charm. The words were part invitation, part sincerity, and all bluff.

The look of derision on Carla's face could have melted steel. "A weak hand? No, Jack. I have you. I have a very strong hand, and you don't think I actually cared about you, do you? You were just another project to manage, part of my job. One I gladly handed off to my assistant. You don't interest me, Jack. You're just as simpering as the next man."

From the corner, Robert spoke up. "Jack is a better person than you will ever know." He had the flechette pistol out of his pocket and pointed at Carla. He slowly stood out of his chair.

"You put that down, or I'll kill him." Carla's voice crackled. Desperation shone though. Jack's heart pounded faster.

"Ms. Savage, you have no intention of killing Jack or any of us. You want to deliver Jack to Randall and your ass out of a sling. Jack might even be right. If you put the pistol down, you might be able to come with us."

"I don't think so, Mr. Logan, I think we can wait right here for the marines to show up."

"Carla, I will shoot you. Putting the gun down is the only way you get to see if the marines show up."

Carla let out an animal-like grunt, her face twisted with fury, but she slowly put her weapon on the floor and held her hands in the air. Within a minute or two, boots could be heard crossing the atrium outside. Robert kept his weapon trained on Carla, who looked triumphant. Jack swung his rifle off his shoulder and pointed it at the door.

"State who you are, or I will shoot you on sight!" Jack yelled to the approaching group.

"It's me." Jack relaxed when Rick stepped inside. "They backed off as soon as we arrived. Several shuttles just left the roof. I think they all retreated to the airport."

Seeing him, Carla deflated. She looked at the ground, shaking her head, tears of frustration appeared in the corners of her eyes. "Those fucking bastards."

"Sounds like your strong position isn't so strong any more, Carla." Jack tried his best to hide his growing contempt. "You don't have many choices left. Why don't you think about coming with us?"

"Fuck you, Jack! You don't understand, you all fucked this up. Those shuttles were your last ticket out of town. Randall wanted to save all of these people. Now you've killed them, and you've killed me. The prisoners were to be transfered off the planet where they would be safe, and now they're dead. What do you think is going to happen here? They're coming back to this moon. You know that, don't you? Now everyone here is going to die."

In the second of silence which followed this pronouncement, Carla looked directly at Robert, stepped forward, and leaned down to pick up her gun lying on the floor. It was an act of suicide, and she knew it. Even as Jack raised his rifle, Robert didn't hesitate. He hit her square in the chest. Carla stumbled ungracefully into a chair. Anna screamed briefly, horrified, but unable to turn away. Carla breathed only for a few seconds more. Her eyes lost their focus and rolled into her head.

Robert sat down heavily and lowered his gun.

On cue, Carla's heads-up began to bleat. Curiosity forced Jack to see who wanted to contact Carla so much. As Jack suspected, the readout said Randall. *He probably knows she's dead. He probably killed her.* Jack debated the merits of talking with him. In the end, he decided that if Randall wanted to talk, he wouldn't give him the pleasure. Before turning back to little Josephine who desperately tried to quiet her whimpers, Jack dropped the device on the floor and smashed it under his heel.

Josephine clung to the bloody blanket that covered her mother. Julia's hand still rested on her head, but Julia was no longer there. Josephine took it and began to rub it against her cheek. Jack bent down, not exactly sure what to say. "Jo, I think it's time that we let your Mommy sleep for a while. We need to get you out of here."

Josephine turned to Jack and looked at him with her wondrous blue eyes. "Mommy isn't sleeping, Uncle Jack. I'm just saying goodbye. Are you going to take care of me now, or am I all alone?"

Jack blinked hard. He nodded as his heart made a promise that he wasn't sure his mind and body could keep. He wanted to bolt, but he couldn't say anything else. "Yes, Josephine, I'm going to take care of you now."

Jack turned as he heard the bustling sounds of people entering the room. Medics rushed to the remaining wounded. They moved Jack aside as they attended to Julia. He found himself standing near Anna, holding Josephine as she once again buried her face in his shoulder. She refused to watch as they took her mother away, covered in a sheet.

Jack managed to give a thin smile to Anna. He imagined the effort appeared quite pitiful. She still looked at him tentatively, but she didn't flinch. *Progress*, he thought.

19
The Fish Takes Flight

Jack sat with his back to the wall across from the hospital room in which Dr. Musgrave treated Anna. Musgrave had arrived about forty-five minutes beforehand. Josephine lay curled up beside him. She absolutely refused to leave his side, even when a doctor wanted to examine her, and since she didn't appear to have life threatening injuries, no one objected in the chaos after the battle. Twice she had woken up screaming for her mother, lashing out at Jack with her fists until recognition and remembrance brought reality crashing in. Then she clung to Jack, and all he could do was put his arms around her and stroke her hair.

It frightened him to no end to have her so dependent upon him. Ironically, he found some confidence in thinking that he wanted to give everything to her that he had never had from his parents. He realized that if he just did the opposite of anything his parents had done, he was probably on the right track to do something good for the little girl. Jack reached down and stroked little Jo's curls as she became restless again in her sleep. It seemed to settle her down.

He looked up to see her older brother Teddy limping down the hall toward them with Mike Fisher. Seeing his little sister in Jack's arms, Teddy started to trot.

"Rick Carter said we would find the two of you here." Mike smiled at Jack, but the smile couldn't disguise the worry underneath it all. He looked noticeably more careworn than when Jack met him the day before.

Jack started to stand and then, remembering the little girl in his lap, hesitated. Seeing the problem, Teddy sat down and leaned his little sister onto his shoulder. She opened her eyes for a second and just smiled. Then her lids fluttered closed again, and she snuggled into her brother. Jack felt a momentary pang of regret. In a better universe, a twelve-year-old boy wouldn't have to take on the duties of a father. Life could be cruel.

Jack stood and decided to try to break the ice with Mike. "I'm glad you made it through, Mike. You're a good leader."

Mike rubbed his hand through mostly silver hair. "I don't know about that, but I just wanted to say thank you. None of this would have been possible without you. Families have been reunited and that is good." He reached out to shake Jack's hand.

Jack returned the handshake. "You're welcome." Jack could tell that Mike wanted to say something more, so he waited.

"I guess I also wanted to tell you that, for my part, I don't hold any grudge against you. I would have done the same thing in your place."

"Thanks. I appreciate that. I don't think I understood how good I had it, until it all got destroyed." A few seconds of silence passed between them. Mike didn't strike Jack as the most talkative of people. Finally, Jack asked, "What will you do now that you're in control of Utopia?"

"The only thing we can do. Sue for peace, and beg for mercy." Mike's brow furrowed. "There really isn't anything else we can do. Mother Unity can't let this stand. She's going to come down on us hard, unless we stop right now. Randall and his ilk are rogues that have no place in the system. He crossed the line when he killed all of our people. I have to believe that the board of directors won't let that stand."

Jack nodded. "So now you go from warrior to diplomat."

Mike chuckled at the thought. "Something like that. We have a couple of feelers out to other parts of the political spectrum in the board room. Hopefully, someone will understand why we did what we did." Mike paused before continuing. "Rick told me a little bit about your plans for escape. I hope that you can get someone outside Unity to pay attention to our situation."

Jack didn't know what story Rick had told Mike, so he just nodded and didn't say anything.

"The Unity won't be able to do anything stupid here if the rest of the galaxy is watching. At least, that's my hope."

"You're a good man, Mike."

Mike put his hands on his pockets and laughed, "Nah. Just someone who's incapable of sitting back when there's something that needs doing. I need to get back to my workers." Jack and Mike shook hands again, and Mike headed off down the corridor.

Still holding the sleeping girl in his arms, Teddy looked up at Jack. "I guess we're on our own now."

"Not on your own."

Jack's answer clearly surprised Teddy.

"Your mother said to tell you that she loved you." Jack saw the sobs start to rise in the boy in front of him, but Teddy would not let them come. Jack gave him a moment's peace. When he thought it was safe, he spoke. "Has Rick talked to you about our offer?"

Teddy nodded.

"Good. So what do you think?"

"I'm going to come with you. I don't want to stay here."

"Good man, Teddy. Your sister will need you."

At that moment, the door to Anna's room opened, and Musgrave walked out. He was dirty, his copper-threaded scrubs covered in blood. Jack knew he hadn't stopped since the attack began eight hours prior. Only the imminent departure of *The Flying Fish* had forced him to examine Anna's non-life-threatening injuries. Taking off a pair of examination gloves, he said, "You can go in if you like."

Motioning to the door, Jack asked, "How is she?"

Musgrave gave Jack a frank look. "Physically, she's healthy. The nanites did their job. They will have a little work to do for the next day or so. She has some deep bruises on her back where she was beaten. She will certainly be stiff and sore, but she will be ready to go with you back to *The Flying Fish.*"

Musgrave continued. "Mentally, she's not well. She's been through some serious trauma in the last few days. All of it on top of having her memories jacked around and manipulated. It won't all heal overnight, and with the hospital just reopening, I don't have all my tools at my disposal."

"But, were you able to put her memories back? Will she remember me? I mean, will she remember what really happened before they grabbed her?"

Musgrave gave Jack a short exhausted grin. "The brain is a remarkable thing, Jack. Everything it remembers is embedded in a web of experiences and other connections which are associated with even more memories. Mind jacking—even terrifying and serious mind jacking, like the kind Anna just experienced—can't touch the interconnected holistic method in which the brain stores and processes experiences. It's impossible to mimic perfectly. Implanted memories, like those given to her by Randall, ring hollow. They don't fit, and for all that they can do, they seem wrong in some way. In the short term, this disorientation works to the advantage of the interrogator. The confusion about what is real makes it easier to get a person to cooperate. Over time, Anna's brain will learn to distinguish between her authentic memories which still exist and those she's been told to accept."

Musgrave put his hand on Jack's shoulder. "She'll be fine, but it will take time. Just take care of her, Jack." He took a step back, and looking down at the kids sitting on the floor, said, "But it looks like she won't be the only one you have to take care of." He smiled. "You did good today, Jack, in more ways than one."

He stared into his heads-up for a second and a look of concern crossed his face. "I really have to keep going. I have patients whose lives hang in the balance, and I walked away from them to take care of this." Without another word, Musgrave turned and hurried down the hall.

Leaving Teddy to watch his sister, Jack opened the door to Anna's room with caution. Her bed lay in the center of the cramped space, surrounded by instruments. Anna opened her eyes.

"Hey, champ. How're you feeling?"

Anna looked pensive. She hesitated before she spoke, and when she did, she sounded like she addressed a stranger. "You're asking the wrong question. It should be, '*who* are you feeling?', because I don't really know who I am right now."

Jack didn't know what to say. Anna had a way of pulling him up short and taking away all his words. He felt like a salesperson holding his hat in his hand, desperately trying not to beg to be let in the door. He simply nodded.

"Nothing to say?" Her tone was caustic.

"'I'm sorry' doesn't seem to cut it."

"Would it hurt too much to try?"

Jack sat down in the chair next to Anna's bed, feeling the iciness flowing from her. "I'm so sorry." For once, Jack didn't calculate all the angles before he spoke. He simply meant it. "I was so worried about you. I'm just glad you're alive."

Anna's expression didn't change a bit. "You're right. It doesn't cut it."

The room descended into an awkward silence. Jack took Anna's hand. The gesture was so natural that he reached over the railing before he realized what he was doing. He almost took his hand back but decided that would be worse. He felt the warm skin of her fingers as they lay on the covers of her bed. Jack flinched, expecting Anna's rejection to follow. It didn't happen. Instead, she wrapped her fingers around his, held his hand, and started to cry.

Jack tentatively stood up, reached over the bed, and embraced her while she sobbed. Anna squeezed his hand, and putting her other hand around his back, pulled him tightly to her. Jack let it all go and sobbed with her. In the last few days, he had cried more than in all the years since he left home, and he had experienced terror and worry on a level that he didn't know existed. This time, crying felt cathartic, healing, but it still completely unmanned him.

After a moment, she loosened her grip, and Jack, who had pressed his head into her shoulder, looked into her glistening eyes. "I love you."

"I know you do. Dr. Musgrave told me about all you went through to get me back. Thank you."

"I had to listen as Frank grabbed you from…"

Anna's body stiffened. "Don't, Jack. I can't think about that, yet."

Jack pulled back a little giving her some space. "I'm sorry. I'm an idiot. I just wanted to say that it was the worst moment of my life."

"Mine, too." She went cold in his arms. Fear appeared in her eyes as suddenly as the setting of the wan Aetna sun.

Jack felt his embarrassment force the blood rise to his cheeks. "What am I saying? I can't seem to get this right. Here I am talking about my suffering, and I'm not really the one who suffered."

Anna shrugged her shoulders a little, acknowledging the truth in what Jack said. "I think you're just trying to say you love me. But for this moment, I need a little space, Jack." She avoided looking him in the eye.

Jack backed off, sitting in the chair again. "All right. Whatever you need." He let go of her hand.

"No, Jack. Put your hand back. I need to know I am not alone."

Jack reached back over the bed. Anna griped his fingers tightly. After a moment's pause, he said, "You're not alone, Anna. I'm right here with you. We'll go through it together."

"It terrifies me that I don't know what's real any more. Did you come and visit me on Sicily four?"

"No. I never visited you. I should have come to visit long ago, but I didn't. I was too much of a chicken. The only times we met were when you came to me on the station."

Anna furrowed her brow. "Maybe it's because I wished that you would come to visit me on Sicily that I have such a strong pull toward that one. It seems so real."

"That might explain it." Jack had no idea whether or not that made sense. He was just happy to have Anna speaking to him, and being agreeable seemed the best way to keep that moving forward.

Rick knocked on the door and then entered. "We've got about ten minutes to go before our convoy is ready to move out. I'll need the four of you at the south doors by then." He looked exhausted. There were purple circles under his sagging eyelids, and he frowned. He refused to make eye contact as he spoke.

Jack asked, "How many died?"

"On my team or total?"

"Either."

"I lost a total of six so far, including Larry. Johnson's in bad shape, so it might end up at seven. We'll be transporting four, plus Johnson, back to the sub on stretchers. They should be okay if we can get them to the auto-doc in our infirmary. Overall, the rebels put their dead at thirty-two and one hundred and fifty total injured, but that's bullshit put out by Mike to keep from scaring everyone. There were many more than that."

Anna let go of Jack's hand, gripped her blankets, and looked down. "I feel so ashamed. Why did you do this for me?"

Rick looked at Anna. "Losing people is part of the job. You need to understand, for years we've been trying to prove that some factions in the Unity use mind-jacking and the like for their own ends. It's the only time that a team from another state has been on scene while it goes down. Your existence is proof that the Unity lies."

Rick didn't really want to talk, and Jack wondered whether he believed what he had just said about losing people. Rick opened the door without waiting for a reply. "I need to get some things together. I'll see you in seven minutes at the south entrance."

A few minutes later, Jack found himself loading Anna into the front of a taxi and shepherding Teddy and a sleepy little Jo into the back. Jack crawled into the back with them, shutting the door behind him. He stuffed his rifle down at their feet. A tense-looking Rick crawled into the driver's side capsule. He handed his rifle to Anna, who held it as if it were a live snake. In the hours after the attack on the admin building, the civilian transport network had been hacked by Andy and a team from IT. Now for the first time since the rebellion began, the automated taxis and work vans were controlled by the rebels. Rick had only begrudgingly agreed to use them when it was pointed out that it would be almost impossible to keep his wounded warm enough during the long hike back to the sub hangar.

Few people in the Unity knew how to pilot a vehicle. The automated taxi and public transportation systems were all they had known. Even in large cities, personal vehicles were a privilege of the politically connected, and these were still piloted automatically by AI. Jack watched out the back window as Musgrave supervised the loading of the last of the wounded into one of two delivery trucks that made up part of their five vehicle caravan. The other truck carried seven stretchers covered in sheets. Johnson hadn't made it. Jack tried to break the tension. "Where did you learn to drive, Rick?"

"Where I come from, we all know how to drive."

"Why? Don't you have an automated traffic system?"

"Sure we do, but just about everyone still learns to drive. I suppose we learn in case there is a problem with the system, but really, it's mostly that we like to make our own decisions, I guess. There are people who hardly ever use the automated system, except when on the skyways, which require it as a safety measure."

"Will I get to learn to drive?" Teddy sounded excited.

Rick checked the mirror as he answered. "Sure, Teddy. You'll learn to drive when you're old enough."

Jack looked behind them out the back window and saw Musgrave give the convoy the high sign, then climb into the back of the truck with the wounded.

"All right, Teddy, I am going to need you and Jo to keep quiet for a few minutes." Rick launched the idling taxi into the air at a speed which left Jack's stomach on the ice below him, banking hard as he did so. He pointed the nose of the vehicle directly at the submarine hangar visible on the far side of town, then accelerated to a speed which Jack didn't know the taxi could do. A still tender Anna whimpered in the front seat and gripped the handle of the door as hard as she could.

Jack was reaching forward to put his hand on her shoulder when he noticed the missile exhaust plumes coming from the airport far off to his right. "Rick!" There were probably seven or eight of them already in the air, with more appearing all the time.

"I see them! I see them!" Rick yelled. He pointed their vehicle at the ground and dove steeply.

Jack looked behind to see the other vehicles doing the same.

"Get your heads-up out, Jack."

Jack fumbled in the pockets of his bulky cold suit, finally landing on the device. He got ready to put it on, but Rick interrupted.

"Not you, Jack! Put it on me!"

Jack leaned into the front seat and shoved the heads-up device onto Rick while Rick concentrated on keeping his vehicle traveling at breakneck speeds low to the ground through a maze of homes and commercial buildings. Jack flipped the eyepiece down and then sat back in his seat, now gripping the door handle himself.

"Good girl!" Rick yelled as he concentrated hard on the task at hand. "She saw them coming and launched countermeasures automatically." A sudden look of panic crossed his face. "It's going to be close. This could get ugly."

Rick banked hard onto a wide street which divided the industrial part of town from a residential neighborhood. Jack could see that many of the homes here were scorched and blackened. They had to be passing near hydrogen plant number four, the one which exploded. Rick nearly bottomed the car out on the ice below them, a move which would been fatal, as it was likely to send the vehicle tumbling down the icy street. Above their heads, Jack saw a set of missiles pass above them. They moved so fast that Jack barely had time to register their arrival. Milliseconds later, the explosions in the sky began as the countermeasures met their attackers overhead.

The concussions felt like they stopped Jack's heart. Little Josephine screamed. Anna crouched in the front seat, covering her head. Even Rick let out a long "Shiiit!" as he made every effort to keep their vehicle from plowing into the ground. Fragments of destroyed missiles rained down among the vehicles.

Jack looked over at Josephine and her brother Teddy. His eyes appeared as big as saucers. Jack reached around the fearful Jo and put his hand on Teddy's shoulder, putting his arm on both of them. The children moved closer to him.

In front of Rick, the ice erupted with the flames of an explosion. Bashed by the concussion, Rick almost lost control of the vehicle. He instinctively banked into the twisted ravine of the nearby neighborhood. "Where did those come from?"

Jack strained to look up out the back window. "I don't know. I can't see anything. Wait! There's a hovercraft behind and above the caravan."

Rick pulled up hard. "If they found us, there's no use hiding anymore." Rising above the rim of the buildings surrounding them, the caravan was greeted by three more hovercraft between them and the sub hangar, which was tantalizingly close.

"Damn it! This is just what I was afraid would happen." Rick tried to make a break for it but was cut off. He ignored the vehicle standing in his way and was greeted with some kind of large caliber shell from one of the hovercraft. The shell exploded dangerously close to the front of the taxi. The threat was clear. Rick banked away from the hangar, forced back. They were quickly surrounded. The only way of escape left open led right toward the airport. "Damn. It's like a fox hunt. We're just being herded right to the hunters. Well, they aren't paying attention to the fact that this fox has teeth."

Rick ripped off the heads-up and threw it at Jack. "Put that on!"

Jack picked up the device which had landed on the floor of the vehicle. *Why don't they just try to kill us?* Jack answered his own question. *They're still trying to take us alive. That's why they launched missiles at the sub and not us.* Jack put the heads-up on. "Got it!" he told Rick even as the screen showed him some kind of menu of options, which Jack guessed came from the systems of *The Flying Fish.*

"Jack, you send *The Fish* the commands I tell you to. You hear me?" Even as he talked, Rick attempted to force his way again through the cordon which blocked his path. Another warning. This one close enough to rock the taxi in the air. A terrified little Jo let out a small scream and hid her face in her brother's lap.

"I got it."

"Start by getting into the threat window and then choose 'visual targeting.'"

Jack followed Rick's instructions and found that the display on the heads-up turned into a crosshair "Got it. Which vehicle?"

"The one just in front of us right now and off to the left a little. Tell the heads-up to acquire the target. Your job is to keep staring at that target no matter which direction I bank or turn. You got that? I will try to keep it visible for you, but if I can't, you just stare where you think it is located. The missile will do the rest once it's out of the hangar."

The heads-up told Jack that it had acquired the the target, and the crosshair flashed green. "Got it!"

"Get ready to fire, when I tell you. Once the crosshairs turn red, just move on to the next one and do the same thing. Try to take out the ones which seem to be in the best position to threaten us."

"Just tell me when to fire."

"Fire now!"

"Missile launch confirmed."

Rick waited a couple of beats, then brought the vehicle into a hard turn. He ran it directly at the hovercraft blocking their path to the hangar. Jack hoped the rest of the caravan had fallen in behind. For a couple of seconds, nothing seemed to happen. Then the heads-up declared target locked and flashed red again. At the same instant, the hovercraft started to veer wildly and fire some kind of rail gun at their vehicle, even as countermeasures erupted from the back.

The wild shots zipped uncomfortably close for Jack, but he didn't wait to see the results of his handiwork. He turned to look at the hovercraft on the right and told *The Flying Fish* to fire on it as well. Even as he did so, he was rewarded with a flash and a thump from the left side of the taxi, which was now flying at the only sub hangar door that hadn't been welded shut.

"You got it!" shouted Teddy. "It's going down!"

The second hovercraft began to veer wildly as the missile acquired.

Rick yelled much louder than necessary, considering the small space. "Hang on, everybody!"

Jack was still trying to find the third and fourth hovercraft as they entered the building, flying at near top speed. Rick slammed on the brakes as they bolted down the long hangar. He brought his vehicle to a stop right at the feet of *The Flying Fish.*

"Did we get the second one?"

"No, I don't think we did," Rick answered, as he threw his door open and started barking orders to the remainder of his crew. He was already putting on his own heads-up. The targeting crosshair disappeared from Jack's device. "Take care of these three. I'll get the hatch open for them!"

Jack looked at the two kids and Anna. They all looked terrified. Josephine was completely overwhelmed, and Anna seemed nearly there herself. Jack went to Anna and leaned down to put his face on her level. "Anna, listen to me. You get the kids onto that boat." Jack pointed at *The Flying Fish* as he kept his eyes on Anna. "Climb those stairs up there. The hatch on the far side will be open. You'll have to climb down a ladder. Can you do that?"

Anna nodded at him. She didn't speak. Jack didn't like that.

"I'm going to help Rick with the wounded and the others."

Jack shepherded Teddy and Jo into Anna's care. The three of them headed off across the ice toward the ramp. Anna scooped up Jo as they went. Jack ran to help get the stretchers out of the medical truck. He was just approaching the open doors of the truck when he looked back to check on Anna's progress and saw something which made his blood run cold. Above the boat, the roof of the hangar had been torn to shreds by the missile fire and the countermeasures launched against the initial salvo from the airport. Already, one person dressed in black stood on top of the *The Flying Fish's* conning tower and another seemed to be falling silently through one of the holes in the roof of the building. The one falling was laid out on his belly like he was in free fall, except he moved too slowly. At the last moment, he put his feet down and landed at regular speed on the lower deck of the boat. He immediately attempted to open a nearby deck hatch. Even before he had landed, a third jumper appeared in the hole in the roof. Jack watched as the first soldier on the conning tower raised a weapon and pointed it at Anna and the kids. Anna had seen him, too, and was now sprinting back toward the taxi.

"NO!" Jack's scream brought those standing nearby to a halt. They all looked in the direction Jack faced. He watched in horror as one by one Anna, Josephine, and Teddy were all brought down. The pop of a neural stunner was audible above the noise of the warehouse. Jack took his gun off his shoulder and started firing wildly. He wasted most of his ammunition before he was able to do any good. He managed to knock down the commando on the main deck of the boat who was out in the open while he was opening the hatch. In the meantime, Jack positioned himself between Anna and the boat. The commandos would have to come through him to get to her.

Someone tackled Jack from behind and yelled in his ear, "Get some cover, you idiot, before they kill you. It's you they want the most!" Jack recognized Musgrave's voice. Crouching, they ran forward to a small metal walkway that offered some protection from the fire now raining down from above. There wasn't much they could do but huddle there as neural stunner rounds landed all around them. One round hit Jack low on his right leg. He winced from the momentary pain and curled up in the fetal position. Then he screamed. Although he didn't lose consciousness, his leg went numb and lifeless.

Without warning, the power plant on *The Flying Fish* erupted above the noise of the battle. This close, the sound of the anti-gravity generators deafened Jack. He turned and saw Musgrave grab the only pair of ear protectors hanging on the railing above them and throw them on. Jack stuffed his hands into his ears, trying to block out the noise. The effort was futile. His bones vibrated, and his head felt like it was splitting open. Jack looked back at the vehicles they had arrived in. He saw several of the remaining crew huddled behind one of the work vans, all with heads-up devices on, concentrating. Without disconnecting the ramp or any of its umbilicals, the boat lifted from its berth. There was a grinding noise as the warehouse's steel docking ramp tore away from the walkway along the wall, going with the now-rising sub. Once free, the sub accelerated upwards through the damaged roof. Jack and Musgrave huddled as close as they could to the walkway as chunks of roof and steel frame fell around them. All Jack could do was worry about Anna.

With a tearing smack, the depth-hardened sub slammed into the lightweight hovercraft which had been unloading commandos above them. The hovercraft sank heavily onto the much larger submarine's deck. Jack watched through the gaping hole in the roof as far above him as *The Flying Fish* tipped steeply to the right, allowing the wounded hovercraft to slide off its deck. He barely heard the explosion as it hit the ground behind the warehouse. The boat accelerated away, launching missiles as it went.

Once Jack's brain could process something other than the teeth grinding noise, he turned to see if Anna and the kids had been buried by the debris falling from the damaged roof. He couldn't make anything out, except that they were still lying in a heap where they had fallen. None of them were moving. Jack tried to put weight on his dead leg and found that it erupted in a pins and needles feeling, much more akin to being stabbed by a thousand knives than to having your leg fall asleep from sitting in one position too long. He took it as a good sign that it hurt, but he let out another scream. This one sounded as if it were buried in cotton in his right ear, and in his left ear, he heard nothing at all. He collapsed onto the walkway behind him and tried to rub the pain out.

Musgrave made it to Anna and the children before Jack finished rubbing his leg back to life. He tried to say something to Jack, but Jack couldn't make it out. He reached up to rub his ears, and his left hand came away bloody. Jack tapped his ear showing Musgrave that he couldn't hear. Musgrave nodded at Jack, pointed at Anna and the kids, and gave Jack a thumbs up.

Jack gave Musgrave a weary thumbs up in response and leaned into the railing of the walkway they had sheltered behind. For the moment, he felt too exhausted to do anything more. Somewhere in the distance Jack thought he heard the sounds of a rail gun firing, but it sounded either far away or buried underground. He couldn't worry about it anymore. Instead, he sat there on the grating, staring at the ice in front of him, listening to the ringing nothing of his broken ears. His left ear continued to bleed, but it no longer mattered. There might have been a battle raging right around him for all he knew. It was good not to feel. It seemed so simple to turn off all his desires and emotions that Jack wondered why he hadn't done this long before.

After a time, Jack didn't know how long, someone stepped into his space. He looked up and saw one of the crew gesturing for him to follow. Jack stood and followed apathetically. He barely registered the line of stretchers laid out in a row near the one hundred-meter-long hole cut in the ice, which allowed submarines to enter and exit the world below. Jack sat down at the end of the stretcher line.

Eventually, someone daubed at the blood on his ear and put a pair of ear coverings on him. Jack noticed that everyone else also wore ear protection. He idly wondered if Anna was wearing any and looked around for her and the kids. Looking up, he saw her standing next to him. She smiled, still holding the bloody gauze with which she had daubed his ear. He reached out, took her hand, and stood. She put her arms around him, and he held her close. Her lips moved, but Jack couldn't understand what she said.

A slight rumble in the ground announced the return of their boat. He watched as *The Flying Fish* slid into the hangar from the door at the far end. Jack couldn't hear a thing, but he could feel the growl of her anti-grav generators in the ice below him. As soon as the sub positioned itself above the hole in the ice, the remaining crew scrambled to load the wounded and the dead. They entered the sub through its rear-facing fishing bay, the hatch of which opened wide enough for two stretchers to enter at the same time.

Anna guided the two children and Jack into the fish processing plant, sitting with them in a corner. Rick seemed to be holding everyone up here. Jack wasn't sure why, but he let that be someone else's problem. He leaned his head down on Anna's shoulder and closed his eyes.

20
The Fish in Orbit

Jack woke to the humming of the boat. Without opening his eyes, he moved the covers up a little and rolled over on the pillow.

"Are you awake? Can you hear me?" The voice behind him belonged to Anna.

Jack blinked and found that he now lay facing the wall. He rolled back the other direction. Anna sat in a chair next to his bed dressed in a jumpsuit which looked at least a size too big. She had showered, and she smiled. Jack thought she looked wonderful.

"Yes, I can hear you. Why?"

"What do you remember?"

Several images flashed through Jack's head. He sat up on one elbow. "Hearing anything is a good thing, isn't it?" He rubbed his eyes. "I can't think of anything I would rather hear again than the sound of your voice."

Anna laughed gently.

Jack continued, "But I still don't remember much after we got on the boat. How long ago was that?"

"I don't know for sure, but something like ten hours, I think."

"How did my ears get fixed?"

"The doctor gave you an IV full of stuff, nanites and a sedative—or something like that. You were pretty out of it when I got you on board—some kind of shell shock. He said that when you woke up you'd be able to hear pretty well again."

Jack sat up. For a moment his stomach turned over, and the room spun. "I'm dizzy."

Anna reached over and held his arm to steady him.

The look of concern on her face did as much or more to reassure him that she still cared for him than anything she could have said. He reached over and touched Anna's cheek. She rubbed the side of her face against his hand, and then, gently turned and kissed it. "I'm okay," said Jack. Anna placed Jack's hand on her side, leaned forward, and pressed her soft lips against his.

After a minute or so Anna slipped their lips apart and moved back to look at him. "Thank you, Jack. Thank you for everything you risked and for your courage."

Anna's affection floored him. At that moment he knew that he would have done anything she asked of him.

Anna crawled on top of Jack's covers and laid herself down next to him. She put her head on his bare chest. Jack brushed his hand over the top of her head.

After a moment or two, Anna brought her head up near Jack's and laid her leg over him. She kissed him again. Jack let his hands begin to roam and reached with his lips for the softness of her neck. Anna pressed his head into her tender skin.

He started to undo the zipper at the top of her jumpsuit, ready to explore her breasts and feel her flesh pressed against his. Even before she pulled away, Jack felt the change. She grabbed the hand Jack had placed on her zipper and moved it. Then she rolled off him and started to shake as she silently wept.

Anna's words sounded full of failure. "I can't do this. I want to...but I can't" She faced away from Jack, turning toward the wall in the narrow bunk.

Anna's sudden change of demeanor confused Jack. "Can't do what, Anna?" Anna didn't answer, instead her body heaved all the harder as she wept. Jack didn't know what to do. He wasn't sure how anything he did would be perceived. Part of him was a little frustrated. Anna's comments and affection had gone a long way toward getting him turned on. Jack put those feelings aside. He would take care of them later. "Anna, talk to me. Don't cry by yourself. Tell me what happened. Turn around." Anna didn't respond. Jack reached out, tentatively put his hand on Anna's shoulder, and gently pulled her toward him.

His touch seemed to do something for Anna. As soon as he put his hand on her shoulder she melted. In a few seconds more she rolled back over and put her head back on his chest, still overcome.

"It's all right, Anna. Whatever it is, it will be okay. I didn't go through all of that just to give up on you now. I'm here."

For a long while Anna didn't say anything but just continued to cry. Inside Jack began to squirm. He was feeling a bit of whiplash from the sudden change of emotion. After a time Anna finally regained her composure. When she spoke her voice was gravelly. "Jack, some really bad things happened to me while they had me. They did things to me. They hurt me, and they made me see things I wish I had never seen. They took over my mind, and made me feel things I didn't want to feel."

While this information didn't surprise Jack, it made him very uncomfortable to hear it from Anna's mouth. He asked the first question which came to mind. "If you weren't ready, why did you kiss me?" Jack asked the question mostly from his confusion, but he instantly regretted that he heard a tinge of frustration as well.

Anna seemed to deflate on his chest. "I don't know. It's all confusing. I'm scared, Jack. I'm sorry."

Jack shrugged. "It happens. You don't have anything to be sorry about" Jack was grateful that this time he was able to keep the frustration out of his voice. He let the silence sit between them for a while. When he broke it he tried to put as much gentleness into his tone as he could possibly muster. "What are you scared of, Anna?"

Anna seemed uncomfortable with the question. She shifted and took her time responding. When she spoke, her voice sounded thick, and there were tears in the corners of her eyes. "I have a lot to sort through, right now, and I don't know how long it will take, Jack. Our relationship, Jack ... well it's been... we've spent most of our time in bed. I'm afraid I'm going to lose you, while I figure things out."

"No… Look… Anna, it's exactly the opposite. I finally feel like I'm understanding the value of being together outside of sex. Anna, when I lost you I hurt more than I have ever hurt in my life, but I chose not to run from it. I let myself hurt, and I did something about it. I finally realized that there was no other way forward for me. Even if I didn't get you back, I couldn't have lived with it if I had just run away. Anna, I want to be with you, I really do, and I want to be your lover, *but* I want to be your friend, as well."

Anna didn't relent. "I hear you, and I know exactly what you're talking about. For the last two years, I've been growing to see it the same way. I just don't think I've ever heard a guy talk like that before. It's not the way I'd expect you of all people to respond."

Jack laughed a little. "Yeah, well, it's not what I'd expect myself to say either, so just go with it, before I change my mind. But I bet there are lots of guys out there who think this way. Julia and Lewis seemed to get along swimmingly, and I doubt that it was all about the sex for them."

"Who?"

"Jo's mom and dad, but never mind."

"Jack, most guys are all balls and prick with a tiny brain in between. They will play at relationship as long as they're getting laid. As soon as the sex is gone, they're done"

Jack laughed again. It helped melt the tension between them. "Does that include me?"

Anna hesitated, a little embarrassed. "No… Well, sort of…I'm not sure. I guess that's what scares me."

Jack found himself simultaneously amused at Anna's thoughts about guys and a little irritated that she didn't yet trust him. *But,* Jack thought, *that's probably a fair summary of my thinking, until very recently.* "Anna, I don't think your judgment about men is as objective as you think it is."

Anna raised an eyebrow. "And why's that?"

"Because you've spent most of your time trying to understand how men tick while in a bar wearing a black mini-dress. It won't give you an objective point of view."

Anna laughed. "Touché. But I will point out, the little dress caught you, didn't it?"

"Yeah, I guess it did." Jack reached down again to stroke the top of Anna's head. "Some part of me thinks we've just been lucky. It's as if through no fault of our own, over the last three years we've both been figuring stuff out. It feels like we've been accidentally stumbling forward ever since we met."

Anna lifted her head and Jack kissed her again. Anna kissed him back. This time Jack pulled back. "I need to stop now. If you're not ready for more, then we're going to have to be careful or both of us are going to spend much of our time frustrated." Jack moved out from under Anna and left the bunk. "I'm going to get a shower." Anna just smiled and nodded.

After a shower he came back in the room. Anna lay with her eyes closed but when he entered she opened them and sat up. Jack got dressed in a fresh jumpsuit, and when he turned again Anna sat huddled on the bunk, arms wrapped around her knees. Jack finished tying his laces and scooted his chair over to Anna. He wanted to look her in the eye. He took both of her hands in his own. "Anna, I don't know why it's this way, but we're good for each other. When we're together, things seem to straighten themselves out in the end. I promise I'm not going anywhere. I want to stumble forward with *you*. You're my friend, and I was scared out of my mind when you were gone. I have no intention of ever letting you go again."

It became silent in the cabin for a few seconds. They just looked at each other. Jack watched as Anna's neck got blotchy and red. She suddenly broke Jack's gaze. "Yeah. If we're going to find a steadier footing until I'm in a better place, then we better set some ground rules."

Before Jack could respond, a knock on the cabin door broke the moment. Jack cursed under his breath. His adrenaline had started running again, and he had just started to enjoy the heady brew. "Uncle Jack? Uncle Jack, are you in there with that woman?"

"Uncle?" Anna's eyes twinkled with silent laughter as she covered her mouth with her hand.

Jack just shook his head.

Another voice came through the all-too-thin door. Jack wondered who else had been hearing their conversation. "Josephine. Stop that!"

"You're not the boss of me, Teddy! Uncle Jack takes care of me now." Josephine pounded on the door again. The sounds of a scuffle erupted in the hall, and Jo could be heard screaming, "You let me go Teddy! Let me go!"

Jack opened the door and found Teddy leaning backwards as he lifted his sister off the ground by her waist. Jo flailed madly, trying to hit him. "Hey, Teddy. There's no need for that. It's okay. You can put her down."

Teddy, who strained to keep Jo from bashing him in the face with a stray fist, put his sister down, none too gently. Josephine quickly moved out of his grasp, coming forward to stand nearer Jack's protection.

"Uncle Jack, Captain Rick said that we needed to leave the bridge and come find you."

"He did, did he? Well, it looks like you found me, Jo. What can I do for you?"

"We're hungry."

"Well, then go get yourself something to eat. The kitchen is down that way." Jack pointed down the corridor.

Jo scrunched up her face. Jack had obviously missed something. "I don't know how to make something to eat. My… my… Mommy made things to eat for me. I don't want to have to make my own food now." Jo melted into a puddle of tears on the floor at Jack's feet.

Teddy moved forward to pick her up.

"Oh, you're going to be a real pro at this, I can tell." Anna's sarcasm didn't help as Jack gaped at the puddle of despair on the floor in front of him.

Teddy lifted his sister to her feet. He cooed at her. "I'm right here, Jo. Uncle Jack is busy right now. I'll make you some food. Maybe we'll come back when we're done."

Josephine wiped tears from her puffy red cheeks and tried to stop her sobs.

Jack finally caught up to the situation and interrupted. "Actually, I'm kind of hungry. How about you, Anna? Do you think we could go with these two young sailors and find ourselves some fish sandwiches?"

Anna gave him a wry look, and mouthed *better*, before standing up and taking his hand.

"Jo, how about one of my famous vinegar and plancho supremes? Does that sound good?"

Jo nodded and took Jack's other hand.

As he walked down the corridor behind Teddy, Jack shook his head. With Jo and Anna on each arm, the image of a family wasn't lost on him, or Anna, either. Every time he looked at her, she chuckled under her breath. *How did it come to this? How did I end up here?* Jack's pulse sped up a little. He figured this must be the same feeling a stallion feels when someone puts a bit and bridle in its mouth and then rides it down the road for the first time. *This stallion just got broken, and I didn't even really have a say in the matter.* A small knot began to grow in Jack's gut. He took a deep breath to calm his nerves. Anna burst out laughing.

After getting some food, Jack and Anna spent the next few hours helping prepare *The Flying Fish* to leave Aetna's atmosphere, in order to rendezvous with Soren in low orbit. Having lost seven of its crew, *The Fish* needed all the help she could find. Rick assigned them to lighten the load by dumping fishing gear overboard. Even Teddy and little Jo helped. The process included repeatedly filling one of the two fish retrieval compartments and then flooding it as if it were being used to deploy nets. The boat's computer used the *Fish's* over-sized ballast tanks to keep the boat balanced through the whole procedure. Once the black water washed out the abandoned gear, Jack sealed and drained the compartment. Then, they repeated the whole process.

The Fish had consumed almost all of its defensive weaponry when stopping the missiles from the airport. Any serious attack could have become deadly. Even as he worked, Jack's unease grew. He couldn't believe that Randall would give up so easily.

As the hours ticked by without an attack, the tension mounted. A couple of times, Jack found himself jumping at shadows as he hefted fishing gear and other detritus into the fish retrieval compartment.

Besides packing for orbit, Musgrave had his hands full with the wounded. It took him almost three quarters of a day to get the gravely wounded through the auto-doc. Even afterwards, three of them were still in need of careful observation. Once he finished, he spent more hours on the nicks and bruises, and then packing. When Rick found him sitting against a wall in the main corridor fast asleep, he threatened to confine him to quarters unless he got some rest. That didn't sit well with Musgrave, but he went.

Now six hours later, one final task remained in order to prepare for their rendezvous with Soren. Anna, Jack, and the remaining crew outfitted themselves in pressure suits. When *The Flying Fish* left the atmosphere, it would be slowly depressurized. Standard practice on all military vessels, and some freighters as well, kept pressurized areas to a minimum. This helped prevent fires and also prevented a stray meteor or weapon from causing explosive decompression, which had a tendency to suck unprepared crewmen into space.

With the low number of remaining crew, finding enough suits for Jack and Anna hadn't been a problem. Teddy and Josephine were the fly in the ointment. Nothing on board would fit them adequately. After discussing the problem with Jack, Musgrave and Rick decided that they would be placed together in the only remaining pressurized gurney. The gurney would keep them safe, at least until something more permanent could be arranged on *The Clarion*.

Jack sat holding Josephine's hand as a sedative from the auto doc helped her relax. Jo stared at him, inspecting his face. Her gaze made him uncomfortable. Jack wanted to do right by the little girl who was in his care. He tried to remember what it was like to be that young and failed. Time and his ugly childhood had pretty much wiped away all of his memories, except those traumatic enough to survive the years in between. Instead, Jack decided he would simply do for Jo what he thought he might like in her situation. He patted the top of her blond curls and tried to smile.

"Your eyes look sad, but underneath, you're a nice man."

Jack was taken aback by the matter-of-fact observation. "Yours look sad, too."

"I miss my mom."

Jack nodded but kept silent.

Jo gave him a look which said he hadn't played the game correctly. "What makes you so sad?" Her eyes went out of focus, and she yawned as the sedative hit her blood stream. Without waiting for Jack's answer, she closed her eyes.

Jack whispered in the sleeping girl's ear. "I miss your mom and dad, too."

He helped Musgrave place Jo into the gurney alongside her brother. He had worried they would feel cramped, but they were both slight children, and there turned out to be plenty of room. Musgrave attached the arm patches which would monitor their vital signs and administer another sedative when necessary.

He and Jack had just sealed the gurney when the monitor, near where Anna sat watching, chirped at them. Jack stood beside her, as Musgrave pressed the button on the monitor and answered the ping.

A grim-looking Robert appeared on the other end of the line. Since Larry had been killed in the firefight in Utopia, Robert had been acting as Rick's second. He had mostly recovered from the beatings he had received at the hands of Randall's troops, but Jack could tell that the pressure suit was still keeping his left arm bent at an awkward angle, while the bots repaired his collar bone. "The captain would like you and Jack to come to his office." Seeing Musgrave look around at the four sealed gurneys, he added, "It's urgent, and it won't take long." Something about his demeanor and the way he said the last few words made the hairs on the back of Jack's neck stand up.

"What's the countdown? I need to be back here before we lift off. I want to be in the infirmary while the ship is vented."

"We've got nineteen minutes until lift off. You'll be back in time."

"All right. We're on our way." Musgrave shut off the monitor, grabbed a data pad, and started for the door.

Jack looked at Anna. She smiled. "I'll be all right, Jack. Go. The quiet moment will be good for my brain. It gets tired with all the activity right now." Jack trotted after Musgrave.

Before the door to his office had closed, Rick announced, "Something horrific just happened in Utopia. We've got seismic signals going off around the globe and pressure wave detection equipment as far south as the equator has registered something big." Rick brought up the data for Jack and Musgrave to see.

"Is it volcanic?" asked Musgrave.

Robert, who stood behind Rick with his arms crossed, answered, "No. At least it doesn't look like any volcanic event I've ever seen. For those, the signal always starts on the sea floor. There's an earthquake, an audio signal, or something. For this event, it started with the pressure sensors and then moved to the seismic stuff, first on the ice and then later on the sea floor. We have readings coming in from all over the planet now. There's sea ice breaking up at least two hundred and fifty kilometers from the source and growing. It's a giant tsunami, and it's moving fast. We won't really know how bad until it reaches this point, but that'll be hours from now."

"They nuked it from space." Musgrave spoke in a matter-of-fact tone, like he was diagnosing a patient, although he frowned.

"Maybe, but we haven't picked up any radioactivity at all, not on the sensors in town before they quit and nothing outside of town," said Robert. "Besides, the tsunami is too big for a nuke. We're going to see something which goes almost around the globe. Nautica might be spared the worst of it, but that's about all."

Rick's face turned an ashen gray. "We killed them, Tony." He paused. "If we hadn't freed those prisoners, they'd be safe on the station by now, and we've killed them."

"*I* didn't kill anyone, Rick. We did the best we thought we could under the circumstances. *The Unity* killed them, or more precisely, Randall killed them. Remember, if we hadn't done what we did, Robert here might be dead, as well."

Rick grimaced. "Of course, you're right. It doesn't make me feel any better."

Something clicked while Jack stared at the growing pattern of data flooding into the monitor in Rick's desktop. He saw himself standing in front of a sign in the Imperial Museum of Modern Art. "It was an asteroid. They chucked an asteroid at Utopia."

After a moment of silence, Robert nodded his agreement. "It's the explanation that makes the most sense to me."

Rick shook his head. "How could they do that? They don't have any ships that large. They were banned three hundred years ago at the end of the last war. Besides, they couldn't have gotten one here so fast. It used to take months, if not years, to alter the course of an asteroid. If it was an asteroid, then it was just a damn unfortunate accident, and I don't buy that. It has to be a nuke. Some new kind of weapon which doesn't leave behind any radiation."

Robert shrugged. "There's been no electromagnetic signature. You can't split or fuse atoms without some kind of electromagnetic storm."

Musgrave chimed in. "It's not a nuke, Rick. They may not have redirected an asteroid in the last three hundred years, but it looks like the Unity has done so now."

"But it's so fast. How could they do that?"

"Well, for starters, I think now we know what they've been building out near Bronte." Musgrave continued to frown and look down at the table. "Three hundred years ago, we didn't have mass bending technology. Now that we can effectively reduce the mass of an object, it would be much easier to move large asteroids and then simply restore their mass once they are in position to target the city, planet, or moon the Unity wants to hit."

Rick checked the time on the countdown clock. There were fourteen minutes left until the launch window opened.

The PA system interrupted their conversation. "Captain, this is communications."

"Go ahead."

"We have an encrypted, tight-beam laser message from *The Clarion* aimed at our orbital recon buoy."

"Send it through."

A wavy picture of Soren appeared on Rick's desk. She skipped any pleasantries. Her voice radiated concern. "I need you to go now. Get off the ground. Some very bad shit just went down on Aetna. I have no time to explain, but this is all related to what we found out about why Aetna matters to the Unity. There are at least four Unity warships in orbit, including one giant S.O.B. that just lobbed an asteroid at Utopia. Observed the whole thing. We've got the data to report. The Ministry will have to listen to us this time."

Rick started to speak, but Soren held up her hand to keep him quiet. "We don't have time to talk about it right now. A Lincoln class destroyer just dropped out of formation and into an orbit which is on a direct intercept with you. How the hell do they know where you are?"

This time, she let Rick answer. "I'm not sure. We had some trouble getting out of town and had to fight off some troops when we left. It took most of our firepower to do so. At one point, some commandos tried to board us. Maybe they put some sort of tracking device on our hull somewhere."

Soren pinched her lips together. "We have also been told to be prepared for boarding. I have no intention of letting that happen, so I am starting to make a run for it. They have no idea what *The Clarion* can really do, so I don't believe they will catch me. Rick, I need you to slave your AI to mine so that nothing goes haywire at the pick-up. It's going to be a serious game of AI chess for a little while up here. I have the advantage though, since I'm in a lower orbit than the fleet. You, on the other hand, are going to be in the thick of it until we can get to you. They're going to be right on top of you when you break the atmosphere. We're getting settled into the bridge. I suggest you do the same. Strap down, it's going to be a rough ride. We may decompress you a little quickly, as well, so helmets on gentlemen. I'll see you aboard *The Clarion*."

Soren's transmission ended as abruptly as it began. Rick was on the PA as soon as Soren got done, sounding both general quarters and prepare for launch. Musgrave and Jack headed back at a sprint to their precious cargo in the infirmary.

Musgrave entered the infirmary several steps ahead of Jack. He died quickly. The killing blows came from behind. First came a kick to the knee to lower his head followed by a quick jerk of the neck to break it. By the time Jack entered, it was already too late, and the assailant was turning around and drawing his flechette pistol. He didn't bother pointing it at Jack. He pointed it at Anna, who sat in a chair in the corner, helmet in place, her mouth sealed closed with medical tape.

"Aw, Jack, was he your friend? Such a waste. I was supposed to let him heroically fight back before I killed him, wasn't I?" Gunderson smiled through the helmet of the stolen pressure suit. Seeing that one eye was covered by a heads-up device, Jack understood how the fleet knew exactly where they were located. As Musgrave gurgled his last breath on the floor beneath him, Gunderson's face turned cold. "Well, I didn't have time for that." His voice sounded tinny on the external speaker. "Jack, I told you that if you tried to mess with us, there'd be hell to pay. I've already raped your girl once. I figure you should watch the next time. Put your helmet on, unless you want your blood to boil." Without moving the gun away from Anna, Gunderson reached down and tossed Jack his helmet.

Jack caught it, but refused to put it on. "Fuck you, Gunderson."

"Temper, temper, Jack. We already have her taped confession. She really isn't much use to us. I might just kill her for the fun of it."

Tears streamed freely down Anna's face inside her helmet. If not for the medical tape, she would have been wailing from fright.

Jack slowly put on the head gear and sealed it.

Gunderson walked over to Anna, grabbed her by the arm, and stood her up, pointing his gun at the side of her head. "I believe your quarters are located quite close to the docking hatch. You will take us there quietly. No extraneous noise and no sudden moves, or I blow her brains out. Are we clear? Oh, and I have my heads-up managing communications between our three suits, so feel free to give me some more lip, because no one will hear you, and I just love the sight of brains floating around in the fishbowl of a helmet."

Jack hesitated. He worried that complying with anything that Gunderson wanted would only make matters worse.

"I *will* kill her, Jack. Don't test me. This is your last warning."

Every fiber of Jack's being wanted to take action, to lash out. Gunderson was a cancer, a disease that brought misery wherever he went. Jack's rage coalesced around the thought of stopping whatever plans Gunderson had in mind. Looking down at Musgrave's lifeless body, he decided he would rather die with Anna than become Randall's tool again. Still, he hesitated. The small part of Jack's mind not consumed by impotent rage argued for patience. *Not yet*, it told him. *Wait for the right moment and maybe you can at least take him with you.* Jack decided to play for time.

Then he remembered Teddy and little Jo. He took a surreptitious glance around the room. Nothing seemed to be disturbed, but Jack decided getting Gunderson out of the infirmary sat high on his priority list. When they exited, help lay only a few feet away, hidden by one small jog in the corridor. But Jack held little hope that someone would wander down the passage from the conn. The understaffed crew would have their hands full just keeping the boat on course. For a moment, he felt a swooping sensation as *The Flying Fish* launched itself, but that quickly subsided as someone in the conn adjusted the internal gravity to compensate for their acceleration. He led them quietly down the hall to his quarters, even as the growl of the anti-grav engines grew louder.

Jack entered his quarters and then turned to face Gunderson, who still held Anna with a firm grip on her arm. Jack was grateful to see that Anna seemed much more in control of herself. She made eye contact with him as they faced each other. A brief look told him that she had mastered her fear and, like Jack, now looked for both vengeance and an opportunity to escape.

"Sit." Gunderson waved his gun at the only chair in the room.

Having no choices, Jack complied. Gunderson pulled out a roll of medical tape he had stolen from the infirmary and walked toward Jack. Jack thought his opportunity might come while Gunderson taped him to the chair. Halfway through taping down his first arm, Gunderson must have sensed Jack's intentions. Letting go of the tape, he pressed the gun up against the helmet of Anna's suit again and said, "Try it, Jack. Please." Jack relaxed and made sure to hold still while Gunderson strapped him down.

Shortly after Gunderson finished, Jack heard the sounds of the atmosphere being vented from the ship. He spoke into the pickup mike in his helmet. "Now what?"

Gunderson smirked. He sat in an almost relaxed fashion on the edge of Jack's bed. He still pointed his weapon at Anna. "Shut up, Halloway. What do you think I am, some kind of mustache twirling villain? I'm not going to tell you my plans. You'll know when they happen."

He made Anna stand next to Jack. After a silent minute or two, the ship shuddered slightly as Jack felt what he thought were two rocket launches. If he guessed correctly, they were the last two rockets on board the ship.

Gunderson sneered, "Is that all you've got left? Oh, this is going to be a cakewalk." Waving his gun at Jack, he said, "Your friends are going to end up as tiny bits of frozen meat."

Almost on cue, Rick sounded a collision alarm on the PA. Jack's pulse began to race and he gripped the arm of his chair tightly. Anna sat down against the wall and covered her head with her hands. Shortly thereafter, the ship shuddered violently, and the vibrations from the anti-grav engines changed slightly. The lights in Jack's compartment went out briefly, then flickered back to life. Anna reached up and took Jack's hand. He looked down at her expecting to see fear, but he was instead greeted with grim determination.

The collision alarm wailed again, but didn't stop this time. For the next few minutes, *The Flying Fish* rocked and swayed violently. The dampeners helped soften the blows, but they couldn't cover all the angles, and, at times, it created an extremely rough ride. The vibration of the engines changed intensity and direction continuously as the ship adjusted course and speed to avoid its attackers. The silence of it all shocked Jack and made it hard to take their danger seriously. The ship bucked and shuddered, but in the near vacuum of the vessel, the sound was almost non-existent, vibrations carried through the floor rather than through the air. Danger was much more felt than heard.

At one point, when the ship pitched violently, Jack almost fell over. This time, he also sensed something different, something other than the concussion of impact. Jack guessed that at least one shell had finally penetrated the armor of the depth-hardened submarine. Jack started to sweat and surprised himself by worrying about Teddy and Jo in the infirmary again. More weaponry found its mark, and Jack thought that behind the facade of stability created by the inertial dampeners, he could just perceive that *The Flying Fish* now tumbled out of control. Jack saw one of the bolts on the bulkhead in his quarters shear as another rocket or shell caused two pieces of the vessel to fight against each other.

After twenty eternal minutes of terror, Gunderson, who had sat calmly through it all, laughed. "The two of you look scared shitless. This is nothing, just a little hunting and pecking for weaknesses."

As if on cue, a rending crash vibrated through the ship, dust rose from all the surfaces, the lights went out, and stayed out. Battery-operated emergency lighting blinked on, bathing the cabin in a dim red glow.

"Now that was trying to kill you," Gunderson said with an apparently cheerful grin. "Relax, Jack. I was just kidding, but it is my cue." Gunderson stood, still pointing the gun at Anna, and took a laser cutter out of his pocket with his free hand. He flicked it on and spoke as if he were pronouncing judgment. "Jack Halloway," he began, "you are accused of aiding foreign powers who seek the destruction of the Unity." He stepped forward, holding the laser cutter above Jack's hand.

"Did you or did you not aid foreign powers in planting the bomb at the hydrogen plant in Utopia?" Jack tried to move away from the laser cutter, but couldn't.

Anna stood up and started to step forward toward Gunderson. He turned on her, brandishing the laser cutter in the small space between them. "Step back, bitch, or so help me, I *will* kill you!"

Anna stepped back but kept her fists balled. She looked like she was screaming bloody murder behind the tape.

"Jack, did you help the terrorists who bombed the plant? Yes or no?" Gunderson placed the laser cutter right above Jack's hand again.

"Stop it!" Jack screamed. "Stop it! I'll say whatever you want me to say. Just stop!" Gunderson didn't move the cutter. Jack again tried to wrench his hands free but the tape held fast. Gunderson just glared at him. "I did it, all right? I did it. Just don't cut my hand off! I'll say anything that you want."

"Good boy, Jack," Gunderson crooned. "See how easy that was? When it comes time for your real confession, you'll do fine. Now hold still, or you might get hurt." Gunderson deftly cut the medical tape holding Jack's hand to the chair. He stepped back from Jack, flicked off the cutter, and said, "Get yourself out of the chair, and don't do anything stupid. You hear me?"

Jack worked with his free hand to get the tape off the other. It was nearly impossible in the gloves of the pressure suit, but somehow he managed it. Then he went to work on his ankles. Gunderson stepped to the door and, keeping his gun pointed at the two of them, looked out. "Damn, it's a mess out there. Looks like someone did a bit of a number on this ship. I wonder who that could have been?" Gunderson smiled. "All right, let's get to the docking hatch. Our ride should be here any moment. You first, Jack."

Jack stepped out into the corridor of a decimated ship which continued to get pounded by enemy shells and missiles. Tucked in their small cabin, he hadn't understood how badly the enemy weapons had damaged *The Fish*. Wires hung loosely in the hall, panels hung off hinges. Here and there, walls warped into the hallway. At one point, Jack saw a baseball-sized hole in a wall which appeared to lead through to the void beyond. He was surprised the gravity generators were still working, and even more surprised to feel the anti-grav engines still throbbing away, if perhaps with a little more growl to their vibrations than otherwise.

Jack walked the few feet of corridor to the airlock and docking collar, through which he had entered *The Flying Fish* from an escape pod, not so many days ago. "Now what?" he asked Gunderson.

"Get inside."

Jack and Anna stepped in. Gunderson entered last.

The shallow bubble of glass which made up the docking airlock on the side of *The Flying Fish* gave the only physical view outside the vessel. The bubble functioned to allow the docking collar operator to extend the collar while in close proximity to another vessel. Considering the beating that *The Flying Fish* had taken, the airlock remained miraculously intact. There were a couple of small holes punched into the vacuum of space, but it remained together.

Gunderson shut the airlock behind them while Jack and Anna stood looking out into the void. Anna reached over and took Jack's hand. Jack's imagination had gotten the better of him while strapped to the chair. *The Flying Fish* appeared to remain on a stable trajectory. Below them, the moon Aetna shone white, its cloud tops hanging placidly in its sky, but they were much farther away than Jack would have guessed for the twenty-five minutes or so since they had left the surface. *The Flying Fish* was definitely attempting to escape from Aetna. From this distance, Jack found it hard to believe that the moon which he had called home for so many years had just been decimated by an asteroid. It looked so peaceful.

The ship shuddered even as he noticed the bright flash toward the rear of the vessel. He hadn't seen the shell coming. Apparently the armor on *The Flying Fish* had held up better than Jack had thought because, although Jack saw chunks of the back of the vessel peel away, it appeared that the shell didn't penetrate. Another shell further forward immediately followed the first. This one sent debris flying at the airlock.

Even Gunderson ducked, but the spinning piece of debris just bounced off. Jack tried to see where the artillery came from. He looked above them and saw a vessel at least twice the length of the sub bearing down. Jack was no expert at fleet identification, but the station had seen its share of military hardware over the years. Jack instantly recognized the smooth lines of a Lincoln class destroyer. It seemed to be having little trouble catching up to *The Flying Fish*. Jack also noted that the damage seemed much worse toward the back end of the boat. He guessed that the destroyer aimed to knock out their engines.

"That's right, Jack. It's our ride knocking on the door. Are you ready to go home?"

Jack didn't answer, but he began to wonder if he had been mistaken to cooperate at all with Gunderson. It would be better to die trying to do something than to end up back in the hands of Randall and the Unity where no rescue would come.

Anna gently squeezed Jack's hand. Jack carefully looked over at her, trying to move his helmet as little as possible. Anna glanced down at the pad which controlled the door on the airlock. She squeezed his hand a little harder.

While it was good to know that he and Anna were in agreement about not letting themselves get captured again, Jack wondered, *has it really come to that? Are we really at the point where the best we can do is die together?* Jack looked up again at the approaching destroyer. It had come significantly closer than it had been the last time. *The Flying Fish* was losing its battle to keep from being boarded. Unless they did something now, they would be back in Unity custody in a few short minutes. Jack nodded his head ever so slightly.

At that point, several things happened at once. Anna reached down and pressed the button to release the airlock door. As soon as that happed, a noticeable shudder ran through the ship as the lock let go. Jack hurriedly started to open the door, and at the same moment, Gunderson lunged at Anna, trying to keep her from moving forward.

"Like hell you do!" he yelled.

At the same instant, another shell hit *The Flying Fish*. This one hit the vessel up high and much farther forward than any Jack had yet seen. The airlock shook violently with the concussion of impact, and Gunderson stumbled. Even as he crashed to the floor, he managed to get an arm around Anna's waist and pull her back toward him. However, his other hand lost control of his weapon, and it skittered across the floor toward the now open airlock door. Jack, who was just trying to hang on and make sure he didn't end up falling out without Anna, watched helplessly as the weapon floated just beyond his reach into the void.

As she lost her grip on Jack's hand, Anna screamed. Jack turned and threw himself into the fray. He managed to get Anna free of Gunderson's grasp, but Gunderson, the experienced commando, fought like a madman. He now stood behind Jack, blocking the exit. Jack managed to get turned around and barreled forward into him, trying to knock both of them out the door. Gunderson anticipated him and dodged to the side, then grabbed Jack's leg as he went by. Jack stumbled to the ground, his helmet and shoulders hanging into the void. Gunderson started to twist his knee, trying to break it. Jack screamed and rolled over on his back in order to straighten his knee. He kicked at Gunderson with his free leg, and by chance, his kick caught Gunderson just above one of his ankles and knocked him off balance.

At the same moment, Anna charged Gunderson. With two hands, she swung a fire extinguisher at Gunderson's head. It looked suspiciously like the one Jack had left in the airlock days before. The extinguisher hit Gunderson square in the helmet, knocking his head sideways. Gunderson's grip on Jack's leg loosened. However, Anna hadn't finished yet. She charged Gunderson, slamming the extinguisher into his stomach. The much slighter Anna might not have made much of an impact if Gunderson hadn't already been off balance from Jack's lucky blow and the fire extinguisher to the head. Gunderson lost hold of Jack's leg completely as Anna's blow propelled him forward through the airlock and short docking collar into the void beyond, followed closely by the fire extinguisher. For just an instant, Jack saw a look of irritation cross Gunderson's face as he desperately groped for anything to hold on to. Anna landed on top of Jack in a heap. He now lay on his back and quickly wrapped his arms around her to make sure that she didn't slide after Gunderson.

Gunderson's tone sounded as calm and as cold as usual when he finally spoke on the radio. "Fuck you, Jack Halloway." The transmission from Gunderson's radio faded to static. By the time he spoke, he tumbled in the void kilometers behind *The Fish* which continued to try to accelerate away from its pursuers.

Exhausted, Jack relaxed and looked into the face plate pressed into his. Behind the medical tape, Jack could see that Anna smiled.

Another nearby shell brought back the reality of their situation. From his position on his back, Jack could see that the destroyer had almost caught them. Flying less than a kilometer above them, its bow had already overtaken their engines. They had only a couple of minutes before they would be boarded.

"Anna, get up! We have to find out what's going on in the ship."

Anna and Jack scrambled to get up, even as the destroyer opened up on *The Fish's* engines with its close range rail guns.

Inside, Jack could see just how badly the the destroyer had pounded *The Fish* in the few minutes they had been in the airlock. Bulkheads were warped and in places the structure had collapsed. Here and there, gaping holes opened into space. Jack hadn't been paying attention, but the gravity also seemed weaker, and he wondered if this explained why it had been so easy for Anna to knock Gunderson out the docking collar. They even found a place where the boat seemed to only be held together by the walkway they ran along. Jack worried about little Jo as the made their way toward the infirmary.

"Rick, can you hear me?" Jack waited for an answer as they worked their way through the debris. "Can anybody hear me?"

No one answered Jack.

As they came in sight of the infirmary, Jack felt relieved to see that the crew was already getting the undamaged gurneys out of the room. Jack and Anna started to run forward but stopped dead in their tracks when one of the crew leveled a rifle their direction. Jack immediately put his hands high in the air, and Anna did the same. He worried that perhaps there had been other saboteurs on board and maybe these weren't the crew after all. A significantly larger person stepped out of the infirmary. Jack guessed that it was Rick. He too pointed his weapon at them and approached cautiously. Finally, he came close enough to see into their helmets. He looked relieved. Immediately, the rifles were pointed at the ground.

Jack could see that Rick was talking up a storm in his helmet, but Jack couldn't hear a thing. Jack tapped the side of his visor, and Rick nodded. He pointed at both of them and then gestured for them to follow. By this time, the rest of the remaining crew had come up behind. Rick physically guided Jack and Anna to the middle of the group and then took the lead as they marched quickly toward the aft end of the sub. Jack hadn't been given any time to check on little Jo and Teddy, but he felt grateful that there were four gurneys traveling with them. Apparently, the infirmary had held together. Much to Rick's obvious frustration, they moved slowly at points as the hovering gurneys had to be wormed through some tight spaces created by the collapsing boat. Most disturbing to Jack, the shakes and shudders of weapons fire from the nearing destroyer ceased. As they made their way down into the relatively unscathed and empty fish processing area, the boat took a decided bump sideways. Jack had the image in his head of the destroyer coming along side and nudging into *The Fish* as they prepared to board it.

Rick's head jerked up at the bump, and he gestured everyone forward. The crew passed into the processing plant and the rear gear retrieval hatch. Robert now entered first with Rick supervising on the side. Robert opened the hatch into space. Jack suddenly had an idea of what they were about to do. His toes ran cold. Anna, who stood behind him, grabbed his hand and squeezed it. Jack squeezed back but kept his eyes on Robert. He reached down on his pressure suit and extended a short retractable line. The crewman next in line turned inward as well, and Robert hooked himself to the back of the sailor in front of him. He then did the same, and so on down the line, each person in turn hooking themselves to the next person until Rick satisfied himself that all his crew were hooked together. Somewhere near the middle, the gurneys were stacked together and attached to the line of sailors. Then sailors attached themselves to either end of these living coffins. Once Rick felt confident that everyone was secure, he took his place at the end of the line. He would be the last to leave the boat.

Jack guessed that Rick must have given the boat a command with the heads-up, because the gravity suddenly disappeared. He unintentionally bounced off what had been the floor of the compartment, floating toward the ceiling. Jack's errant flight quickly solved itself when the line in his suit retracted, bringing him tight against Anna who was now in front of him as he faced inward. He also felt the sailor behind him tuck tight against his back. For a moment, Jack had a funny picture of a fifteen person tandem parachute jump, except in this case there were four long boxes tied in the middle of the jumpers.

Rick seemed to be the only one not tucked in line. He jumped up off the floor and grabbed two handles in the ceiling. "Life Raft" was stenciled in bright red letters next to the two handles. Rick put his feet in braces on the wall which Jack had not noticed. He steadied himself and twisted. A significant portion of the ceiling started to turn and then gave way. Rick must have had some kind of magnetic boots on as he walked himself down the wall and then positioned himself back in the front of the line.

Jack felt himself tugged forward a little, and then the pressure suit forced him into the fetal position. He could see little else than Anna's back, and he could no longer feel the wall he had been holding or the floor underneath him. For a second, he hung there watching the walls of the boat out of his peripheral vision. He was pulled backward. Without even a second passing by, *The Flying Fish* simply disappeared. Jack floated freely in the void. It took only a minute or so for the suit to relax and allow him freedom of movement, but by that time, *The Flying Fish* and the destroyer near it were already small and far away. They continued to shrink at an incredible rate of speed. Jack realized that the stubborn *Fish* had fought to accelerate, even as the destroyer held it in its grasp. This allowed the crew to escape by stepping backward out of the protection of its inertial dampeners. The boat simply accelerated away from them. Jack watched in silence as the boats shrank, until within a minute more, neither of them were visible any longer, except for an occasional flash of reflected sunlight.

Without any say from Jack, his visor went black. He could no longer see anything around him. He had just wondered to himself whether this was an accident when the flash arrived. Even through the visor it blinded him. For a few seconds, Jack could see Anna's bones through her pressure suit, and then the light slowly subsided into an expanding, blue, glowing ball, hundreds of times brighter than the distant star Sicily.

After their visors returned to something resembling transparent, Rick deployed the life raft. Black pliable material erupted into a giant geodesic sphere. There were no visible markings on the outside, and it reflected little to no sunlight, making it incredibly difficult to see in the black void. Light seemed to bend to go around it. Even just a few feet away from it, Jack had a hard time seeing where it ended and where the space behind it began.

Rick, who had been tethered to the life-raft, now climbed inside. He then gently turned around, braced himself on the stirrups built into the bottom of the shelter, and one by one pulled the other sailors-turned-astronauts and the gurneys into their shelter. Once all were inside, Robert turned and pressed a small button on one side of the door. The ball contracted a little as its seam closed together, sealing as if it had never existed at all.

While unhooking himself from Anna, Jack drifted a little. He guessed that the bubble had started to pressurize. He waited, holding Anna gently to his chest as they floated randomly around the bubble, going wherever the currents might take them. After a few minutes, Rick gingerly removed his helmet. Several others of his team did as well. Anna didn't hesitate. Jack decided to join her.

While they worked to remove their helmets, Jack watched Rick deftly push off the wall of the shelter and spin his way toward him and Anna. When he got close, he grabbed onto a couple of the many soft fabric loops on the wall of the dome, then waited for them to get their helmets off. A look of frustration and pain crossed his face. "What happened in the infirmary?"

While Anna tried to gently remove the tape from her mouth with a still gloved hand, Jack answered Rick. "I don't know everything. We'll have to ask Anna. Gunderson ambushed Tony as we came in the door. He didn't stand a chance. He took out a leg and then snapped his neck before he even knew what hit him. It was quick."

Rick nodded grimly but something in his eyes told Jack that he was taking this all too personally.

Jack thought about saying something but decided that this wasn't the time or place. They were all going to need some time to heal.

Anna, who had finally accomplished her nearly impossible task, spoke up. "He came in just after Dr. Musgrave and Jack left to go to your office. As far as I know, he didn't do anything other than tape my mouth so that I couldn't speak and force me to put on my helmet. Oh, and he did something to them so that we couldn't communicate with anyone but him."

Rick looked a little worried at this and quickly turned Jack around to inspect the inside of his helmet, which now hung limply behind him on the cord to his oxygen and scrubbing system. After a minute, he relaxed. "He just set your suit to a Unity standard communications channel." Rick quickly switched both helmets back to their original encrypted frequencies.

"How long until Soren arrives?"

Rick gave a tired grin. "Assuming she can pick up our homing beacon, somewhere around an hour." After hearing the rest of the story, Rick moved on to check on the rest of his crew.

Jack pulled Anna to him, in the process putting both of them into a bit of a spin as they drifted helplessly away from the wall. Anna laughed a little and smiled wearily at Jack. He was so grateful to have her alive, and he wasn't sure how long it would last. With a gloved hand, Jack brushed Anna's hair out of her face. Anna leaned into his glove. "Jack, I'm so tired. I feel like I'm going to need a whole year of vacation to recover."

"Several years is more like it. It's going to take time." Jack and Anna drifted into silence as they floated together in the dim light. There didn't seem anything else to say.

Twenty minutes later, a shadow covered the sunlight drifting in through one side of the dome.

"Helmets on! Weapons at the ready! Soren's not expected for another forty minutes. It's possible someone tracked us down."

Jack and Anna scrambled to get their helmets back in place. Jack didn't have a weapon any longer, having left his behind in the infirmary of *The Fish*. They held hands, and the dome darkened. Jack guessed they were being loaded on board someone's ship. Soon a gentle gravity took hold, and they all slowly sank to the floor of the sphere which now resembled a dome.

As the side of the dome unsealed itself, the comforting voice of Gloria Soren announced, "Welcome to *The Clarion*. It's time to go home."

21
Beginnings

Jack examined himself in the bathroom mirror of his apartment as he shaved. He tried to stand a little straighter. Recently, he had noticed that his shoulders had begun to adopt the same rounded posture he associated with his father. It made him feel distinctly middle-aged, although technically that was still a few years off. He sucked in his gut and resigned himself to the work ahead, but at least it was going in the right direction. The first year after he and Anna had arrived in Apollos, they both had trouble adjusting to their new dietary options. Anna seemed to have figured things out and lost what she had gained. Jack was still figuring things out. Even now, two years after their arrival, a simple trip into intraspace in order to purchase groceries could be overwhelming. An attempt to leave the safety of his transition room and enter a virtual market brought an assault of AI vendors shoving various foodstuffs at him, demanding that he try a bite. The experience still unnerved Jack. He missed the quiet of stepping into a commissary on the station orbiting Aetna and picking up some dried fish and a package of artificial bread.

Food and dietary options weren't the only places where Jack's choices overwhelmed him. Unity housing was normally assigned by the corporation. The Unity Housing Bureau claimed the practice allowed the corporation to make sure its workers lived near their places of employment. It was supposed to promote efficiency. It was really done to cover up the housing shortage, and once again everyone knew that if you had influence you could find places to live in gated communities with options not available to the average citizen. Here on Apollos, housing had to be chosen. Jack remembered the first time he and Anna went out with a real estate agent to rent an apartment. She walked them in the door and started talking about the modern efficiencies of the Apollonarian kitchen, and she kept asking what they liked and didn't like. Jack's stomach ended in his toes. Unsure of what they would do with all of the space they were being shown, he and Anna simply said they liked it all. Jo and Teddy, who had come with them stood silently in the corner, afraid to even step on the wooden floor in case they might damage it. It took their agent only another few seconds to figure out that her normal process wasn't going to work. Her warm smile turned suddenly plastic. She said, "I think I have the perfect thing for you."

Without another word, she escorted them to a different building in an older part of town. Among the stately taupe and gray façades, its pink marble could be seen a mile away. Jack liked it immediately. With a cringe that she tried to hide behind overly white teeth, their agent palmed the salesperson's lock and escorted them into an apartment in which the walls were painted a sunny orange and red. The furnishings followed suit. Anna's eyes lit up from the moment they entered. Jack couldn't believe their luck when he saw the stainless steel bar in the kitchen and neon yellow bar stools which went with it. He could tell that their agent watched their every move as he and Anna each took a bar stool and looked around. The kids were already up the metal spiral staircase and poking their noses into all the corners. Sitting on the stools, Jack caught Anna's eye. "Can I buy you a drink?" he asked. They both snickered and then started to laugh. Their agent looked mortified. When he could control himself, Jack said, "We'll take it," much to their agent's relief. She tried hard not to look like she was going to throwup.

Jack would discover later that his apartment was considered inadequately small by most citizens, and it was supposed to be located in a not so nice part of town. That was okay by Jack. He still felt lost in all the space at times. He had a whole room just dedicated to a desk for him to work. No other furnishings at all, just the desk and a chair or two to go with it. To Jack, an office at home seemed like an almost obscene excess. Besides, the rent on his apartment had only taken about two-thirds of his monthly housing allowance. Technically, Jack was supposed to have given any extra back to the government, but instead, he decided to stash the rest away in case he and Anna ever needed it. He had felt better knowing that he had something in reserve.

From the start, Jack loved his neighbors. In his building alone there were people from at least eleven different nations. Jack and Anna even discovered a few refugees from the Unity like themselves, or at least they guessed they were from Unity. No one ever said so, as it was a touchy subject for the Kingdom of Apollos to take in political refugees from anywhere. The Pax charter declared it to be the strictly neutral home of the emperor. The central administration of the Unity (and every other nation) took a very dim view of the practice, but around Apollos it was a known secret that political refugees lived in the capital on Apollo. Jack and Anna soon learned to recognize their own without asking. Relationships were often friendly, but the fear of spies from home also made an open conversation feel dangerous and quite rare. Jack remembered gratefully that soon after they moved in, one of these neighbors introduced him to a physical store catering to immigrants. In the back corner, they always stocked a couple of tins of smoked fish. While it didn't taste nearly as good as what he and Anna were used to, it was far better than nothing.

As he buttoned his ridiculously frilly white shirt in the mirror, and tucked it into his new high-waisted and brocaded, black-on-black pants, he recognized that this apartment, the smoked fish, and the neighbors had probably saved his relationship with Anna, and possibly his sanity as well. The first six months after their arrival had been a nightmare. He hadn't expected to be greeted as a hero or anything, but he had expected to be treated with respect. Instead, the Ministry of Immigration behaved like he was a spy. At least three days a week for the first six months, he and Anna spent eight to twelve hours being questioned over and over again by the same three or four bureaucrats. The whole process infuriated Jack. It made no sense. They could have easily looked at his memories and found out that he told the truth. But for some reason, which they never explained, they would hook him up each day to a machine which supposedly could tell if he lied, and they would question him all day. Just three weeks into the process, Anna was apoplectic. She retreated into herself. It certainly didn't help her healing when she stopped eating and quit talking to Jack. Nothing he could do would bring her out of her shell. When they did talk, they fought. Without saying a word, Anna made it clear that she regretted her choice to come with Jack.

Jack lost the shreds of his remaining patience with the process when they tried to get Teddy into the act, questioning him four times in the first few weeks. Jack's gray-suited case worker wore her hair pulled up in a bun, with prim little glasses with which she attempted to intimidate Jack. She made sure to look skeptical at everything he said. After they had left Teddy in tears the day before, Jack lit into her when she entered the room, refusing to answer any of her questions and demanding that they never talk to Teddy again. Needless to say, he hadn't particularly enjoyed that day, but it seemed to have the necessary effect. They left Teddy alone.

The only one they didn't question was little Jo. Although, in some ways, Jack believed she had suffered the most of all four of them. She never talked about home, her parents, or her brothers. She spent long days at the neighbor's, whom Jack paid to watch her. The government social worker assigned to their family told him that she was supposed to start school, but Jack couldn't bring himself to do that to her yet. Without anyone her age to talk to, she took to sitting in the corner, staring at the wall. Looking back, he recognized that he couldn't have been much of a caregiver at that point. He and Anna were irritable all the time and hardly spoke. Teddy was busy just trying to figure out life, so he wasn't available much either.

At some point every night, Jo would wake up screaming for her mother. For the first couple of weeks, Jack would wake up from the adrenaline and then get angry. When he didn't respond to Jo's cries right away, Anna would huff on her side of the bed, throw back the covers, and comfort the little girl. She finally came back to bed one night and said, "I didn't sign up to be a parent. You better figure this out, or I'm gone." Jack didn't answer her but made sure to get up the next night and take care of little Jo.

Things eventually got better. Neighbors rallied. One of them confessed that he had been through the same when he arrived. Sometimes when Jack and Anna were at their worst and yelling, a knock on their door would precede a plate of cookies. Mrs. Beacock, their neighbor on the left, would smile at Jack and simply say she understood how tough it could be to adjust. Then she would escort Anna out the door and help them cool off. At first Jack resented Mrs. B's interference, but he quickly realized that Anna felt safe with her, and he started feeling quite grateful when she would show up at the door. Anna started to improve once she began talking to Mrs. B. At home in the Unity, such an interference in someone else's affairs would never have occurred. When Jack opaquely mentioned this, Mrs. B. just said, "Well, we aren't at home any more, Jack, and here the immigrant community looks out for its own."

A huge change happened one morning when Miss Tight Bun unexpectedly announced that they had been given refugee status and that the Ministry of Information wanted to offer Jack a position as an analyst, if he paid back the money he had been stealing from his housing allowance. Jack hesitated, until he heard the salary. They had offered him almost ten times the amount they had been given for housing and food. He figured that someone had gone to bat for him somewhere, but since arriving on Apollos, they had never been allowed to see any of the crew who came back with them.

If he had known then what he knew now, Jack wouldn't have been so eager to take the job at the Ministry of Information. Contrary to Soren's predictions that someone would now have to listen to her at the Ministry, no one wanted to hear that the Unity had built at least one ship which could throw asteroids. Even fewer wanted to pay attention to Jack's reports that he suspected they had built several more. If it were true, the threat to the Pax would require a response, and that would mean war. Even after three hundred years, the horrors of the last war brought terror to a galaxy steeped in three centuries of peace. Jack thought this was especially true for the spoiled wealthy on Apollos.

Those who couldn't stomach the thought of war worked hard to discredit anyone who said anything which might destabilize the status quo. After providing direct evidence of the attack on Aetna, Soren had been quickly reassigned to the field, and Jack had been tucked away as a low-level analyst. No one took him seriously. To be fair, that wasn't quite the case. There were a few like him who saw the threat, but they were outnumbered by those who refused to listen. Until recently, the refusal to listen had started with the Minister herself, a woman determined to have peace at all costs. She wasn't exactly a fan of Jack's work. She found him hawkish and brash. Jack had wondered how long it would take before she found a way to get rid of him.

However, just this week she had been suddenly replaced by a former general. All the news feeds were abuzz with the change, and even a couple of Jack's buddies at work had gotten all excited by the news. Jack had been burned enough by governments of all stripes that he didn't trust anything they told him. He decided to take a wait-and-see kind of attitude.

Jack didn't think he could have lasted as long as he had at the ministry without the support of Robert and Rick, both of whom no longer worked there. When he had first arrived, during his interrogation, Jack had demanded to see Robert and Rick at least once a week, but at the time he had simply been told that they were also being debriefed. "When the process is done, you may be able to see them," Tight Bun would say.

The first thing he asked when told that he had been given refugee status was when he could see Rick. Tight Bun looked a little grim. "Mr. Carter has been ill since his return. He has been suffering from what we call combat fatigue. He's shut down and has been unable to look after himself for some time."

Jack raised his voice a little. "What did you do to him?"

"I assure you we did nothing."

"So you're telling me that with all your technology and medical science, you can't make him better? I'm not going to buy that, because even back home when someone suffered, Health Services would just institutionalize them, give them the drugs they need, and get them on their way."

Tight Bun listened with a patience she hadn't had the day before. "Oh, we could make him better. It isn't a matter of technology, Jack. It's a matter of philosophy. As you know too well, your former home also tortures people. It murders its own citizens. After what we have put you through for the last few months, it may be hard to believe, but here in Apollos, we have a high regard for our people, and we try to interfere with their choices as little as possible. Simply put, Rick has refused all treatment, and so he has not gotten better."

Jack didn't know what to say to that, so he went on. "What about Robert Logan? Can I see him?"

Tight Bun smiled. "He's waiting outside the door. You're free to go, Mr. Halloway."

Robert greeted Jack with a huge smile and a hug. Jack pushed him back to look at him. He wore long black robes, a peculiar hat, and a red sash. Somewhere in the last few months, Robert had taken vows and become an Apollonarian Catholic priest.

"What is this, a costume contest?"

Robert just smiled and shook his head. "No, Jack. It's no joke."

Robert took Jack to visit Rick that afternoon. Months later, Rick told him that the visit had made a profound impact on him. Since he had arrived back on Apollos, he had become so consumed with the memory of the dead that he had forgotten about the living. Seeing Jack helped change his focus and gave him the courage to seek the treatment he needed.

Jack mumbled to the mirror in his bathroom, "So today you get married, Rick." He tried for the third time to create the necktie knot favored by the royal house on Apollos. He failed miserably. Jack untied it and started over again.

"What did you say?" Anna wandered into the bathroom to finish getting dressed.

"Nothing."

"I *thought* I heard you mumbling again about Rick getting married."

"Well, it still makes me uncomfortable. It's so soon."

Anna put her arms around Jack and squeezed him. "Well, not everyone chooses to wait a century before they get married, and be honest."

"All right. It still creeps me out that he's marrying one of his nurses. There, I said it."

Anna smiled up at him and didn't let go. "Nice try. Out with it."

"She's royalty. It just feels wrong somehow."

Anna snorted with laughter. "Hardly. She's like a fifth cousin four times removed, or something like that. They played a game at her shower in which we had to guess how close she was to becoming the Empress. You know what her number is?"

Jack rolled his eyes. "What?"

"Five hundred and two. I completely embarrassed myself by guessing something below one hundred. Most of the guests thought I was trying to flatter the girl. Only a few of them knew I was just being a complete idiot."

Now Jack had his turn to laugh. "It's just all so pompous and idiotic to let your birth determine your rank in a society. It makes no sense, and Rick makes such a big deal out of it, calling her 'princess' and all, and they're having their wedding at the palace."

"Well, she seems rather sensible and sweet, and she understands something of what we all went through. She respects Rick for it. Thinks he's a hero. She seems a person driven by compassion, and that, I think, has been a major factor in Rick's recovery. If it weren't for her, you might not have a friend to see married." Anna let Jack think about that for a moment and then went on. "Will you zip me up?"

She turned around, causing the flare of her robins egg blue dress to twist out a little. Jack still had trouble adjusting to the highly decorative style of clothing on Apollos. Anna's dress was heavily embroidered with lemon yellow flowers and light pink leaves, but when she turned, Jack had to admit that she was still delightful to see. He enjoyed the long curve of her spine and the color of her olive skin against the dress. "Besides, Marcie told me that it wasn't her call to have the wedding at the palace. It was her mother's decision."

"You see, that's exactly what I'm talking about, privilege and all that. If she's so far away from the throne, why are they letting her get married there?" As he spoke, he reached his hands inside her dress, rubbed the skin on her belly, and pulled her close. Anna still seemed worried about the weight she had gained since coming to Apollos, and Jack knew that perusing her stomach with his hands made her feel particularly safe and cared for.

"Well, Marcie is as baffled as you are. She says she didn't think the palace still knew they existed. Except for the annual Christmas card, this is the only communication she's had with the royal family since her christening." Anna's mouth twitched a little, but she doggedly pretended to work on her makeup.

Jack kissed her neck while continuing to let his hands roam. He whispered in Anna's ear, "You are, of course, right as usual. It's probably a good thing for Rick."

Anna sunk into his embrace. "One day you'll just accept that I am always right, and we'll finally quit fighting."

Jack laughed again, and Anna giggled as she shrugged the dress off her shoulders so that she could turn and kiss him. Jack took a deep breath, inhaling her smell. He forced his mind and body to relax and then let go of Anna.

"Aw, that's not fair!" Anna protested with mock frustration. "Don't we have a few minutes for something quick?" she complained.

"Cool your jets there, fly-girl. I wasn't the one who started shedding clothing. Besides, the car from the palace is due in twenty minutes. I promise, it will be worth the wait."

With a false pout, Anna put the dress back on her shoulders and shrugged it back on. Before Jack had even had time to zip her up, there came a knock at the door. "Anna? Anna? Are you in there?"

Jack answered. "Jo, you're supposed to knock on our *bedroom* door when it's closed."

Without waiting to be invited, little Jo marched into the bathroom dressed in silver satin and an ornate golden sash. "I did, but no one answered. I need some help with my dress, and Anna said that she would do my hair."

Jack zipped Anna up.

She touched a finger to Jack's lips. "All right, tonight then, but get ready because I will have had several glasses of champagne, and I am already feeling a little stratospheric." She turned to Jo. "And how can I help you today, little miss flower girl?" She smiled as she said it.

Anna and Jo had just stepped out when Teddy came in. Jack wondered to himself how their bathroom had become the hub of family activity. He turned to Teddy with a touch of irritation in his voice. "Can I help you?"

Fourteen-year-old Teddy had grown at least six inches in the last two years. Keeping him fed and clothed had become a major undertaking. Looking Jack nearly in the eye, his voice cracked as he asked, while holding the ends of his tie, "I was wondering whether you could help me figure out how—oh, never mind."

On Apollos, social events like wedding receptions were a particular hell for Jack. Even on Aetna, he had always avoided these kind of parties whenever possible. Anna seemed to be able to blend in and mingle without getting asked all sorts of awkward questions about her accent and background. Jack just couldn't seem to manage it. Inevitably, his interlocutor would ask about his work, and this always brought trouble because of his classified position at the Ministry. If the Unity government found out that the Empress had hired an asylum seeker to work in the Ministry of Information, at best it would be a major diplomatic incident, at worst it might mean the end of the Pax. Besides, as far as the Unity knew, he and the other crew members had died in an act of suicide when their ship went nuke. Jack liked it that way. So in its wisdom, The Ministry had given Jack a cover story. When someone asked what he did for a living, he told them that he coded AIs for a private company. More often than not, it led to questions Jack couldn't answer and puzzled looks from his questioners.

Today he felt happy to fill his plate from the buffet and sit in a corner away from all the frivolity and small talk. Anna followed her usual routine and circulated some but then came back to Jack when she needed a break. Rick was in his glory, hanging on the arm of his new bride. He looked like a giant puppy. Jack watched the happy couple talking with Robert who had received a special dispensation to attend the event. Jack smiled. It was good to see the two of them together. Yet, the absurdity of seeing Robert in robes and Rick hanging on the arm of a socialite left Jack feeling more than a bit disoriented. It felt as if he knew the actors but the characters were all wrong.

Then again, he thought as he picked up his glass of champagne, there were days where he didn't recognize himself, either. For one, he never thought he would end up with kids to manage, and at times he still found it completely overwhelming, but as he sat in his chair watching Jo skip around the room, he felt an affection which more than made up for any grief she caused. The old Jack would never have understood that affection or even thought it valuable.

Every once in a while he wondered what would happen if his former secretary Molly happened to bump into him. He didn't know if she would even recognize him. Molly had always disliked Anna. She saw Anna as a destabilizing force who made her boss moody. She preferred Jack predictable and even-keeled. If that meant that Jack lived an almost completely isolated life, numb to the world around him, then so be it.

There were certainly moments when Jack regretted his choice to follow Anna. Even now, a part of him still wondered if he had made the right decision. When he fought with Anna or when little Jo acted up, he still looked back and envied his previous lack of responsibility to others.

Habits die hard. Right now, he could see at least three different women in the room that he thought he could bed if he tried. Their vulnerability and availability remained palpable to

Jack. He smiled as he watched a young man ply a particularly voluptuous maiden with another glass of champagne. Jack had seen him personally hand her at least four glasses. She was pretty much ready to go. If the young paramour knew what to do, Jack assumed they would be making their exit shortly. There were always fine lines between drunk, too drunk, and passed out.

Still watching the alcohol-fueled mating rituals across the room, Jack's thoughts wandered through his past. When he came back to reality, he caught Anna staring at him. She smiled, rolled her eyes at the public display of foreplay, and walked his way, fresh glass of champagne in her hand. "Do you miss it, playboy?" she asked.

One of the things Jack had always respected about Anna was her ability to listen to the truth without taking it personally. "Sometimes. I miss the sense of conquest and adventure the most. The means to the end were always a little different. It was a fun puzzle, trying to figure them out."

Anna nodded and sat down in the chair next to him. "I miss the hot young sailors buying me drinks. It was always gratifying to feel like I was attractive."

Jack looked at her. "Was? I think objectively you're the most beautiful woman in this room."

Anna shook her head, snorted and said, "You flatter like a politician."

As Jack watched the young couple tipsily stand and prepare to leave, he said, "Apparently four glasses of champagne will get you laid with little miss curvy." He sat up and replaced his empty glass with a full one from the waiter who wandered by.

"You know what I don't miss, Jack?"

"What's that?"

"I don't miss having to perform. I don't miss feeling like a piece of merchandise, constantly looking for a new buyer."

Jack nodded. "I can see that. I don't miss the loneliness and the self-absorption. Besides, familiarity and intimacy have their charms as well, as long as you can stay friends." Jack shrugged his shoulders. "In the end, life is a series of trade-offs." He took a drink as he watched the young couple disappear out the door. Turning to Anna, he put his arm around her and placed his forehead against hers. "...and I think I got the better end of the deal."

"Damn straight you did, and don't you forget it." Anna brought her hand up to Jack's jaw and rubbed it over his cheek. Then she kissed him.

A Letter to Fans

Hey Fans,

I hope you enjoyed *Aetna Adrift*. I discovered that I needed to write this book when I started my forthcoming three-book series *The Fall of Athena*. After writing about thirty-three thousand words, I ran into characters from the Unity and realized I needed to figure out how my bad guys operated. *Aetna Adrift* arose from that thought experiment.

The Fall of Athena will carry forward from close to where we left off at the end of *Aetna Adrift,* although from a different perspective. (Chapter 1 follows in a few pages.) Discovering that some of my characters will come with me into the next series has been one of the joys of writing this book. I know now that both Jack Halloway and Timothy Randall will have significant roles to play. For those of you waiting for Randall's comeuppance, I beg your patience. A good author can't kill off Moriarty when he is first introduced. Who knows? Like a good Moriarty, he might even escape. For reasons which will become apparent, I suspect that Teddy and Josephine will also have larger roles than I would have intended. We shall see how it all shakes out.

In the meantime, your support makes a huge difference in helping me make sure that I can continue to write full-time. The most important thing you could do is to personally recommend my book to a friend. It has always been true that the best way to sell books has been word of mouth. That is ever more the case now that the e-publishing revolution has allowed writers of all sorts to take their work directly to the fans without interference from publishers and (unfortunately) editors as well. If you enjoyed *Aetna Adrift*, please tell someone. (If you're feeling really enthusiastic, there is a whole list of other things you can do to help out on the next page.)

Some of you may have received this book for free. I am happy to let you try the product before you buy it, or just have it for free if that is what you want. However, I do hope to make a living from my work. You can find a Pay Pal button in the upper right corner of my website at erikwecks.com. If *Aetna Adrift* or any of my other writing has entertained you, would you make a donation toward the cause?

Again, thank you so much for all of your support. I love to hear from my fans. Feel free to email me your thoughts or comments at erikwecks@gmail.com. You can also follow me on twitter @erikwecks.

Sincerely,
Erik Wecks
July 3rd, 2013

On the Next Few Pages You Can:
Find list of things you can do to spread the word about *Aetna Rising*
Read the first chapter of *The Fall of the House of Athena*
Find links to other fiction by Erik Wecks
Get a copy of Erik's bestselling book on everyday personal finance
Read Erik's Bio

How to Help Support Aetna Adrift

Tell someone else
Write an Amazon review
Press the "like" button on Amazon
Purchase copies for others
Write a review on Goodreads
Write a review on your own blog or website
Tell other websites to review Aetna Adrift
Talk about Aetna Adrift on social media sites
Facebook
Twitter
Reddit
Pinterest
G+
Any other social sites you use
Host a book club and read Aetna Adrift
Make a donation at erikwecks.com
Link to the book's page at erikwecks.com

The Humiliation of Athena

Listen up all you word-nerds, grammar Nazis, and sticklers for consistency. First, thank you. Many of you make me look good. I respect your place in the universe. However, this is a roughish draft. Names, places, and plot may change without notice, and it certainly isn't error free. The author takes no responsibility for broken Kindles, strained vocal cords, or self-immolation due to errors in grammar, spelling, or content. Read at your own risk. — The Author

1
Afternoon

"Jonas? Son, where are you?"

Some small part of Jonas' brain recognized the warm, deep tones of his father's voice. That same part of his fourteen-year-old mind also instantly recognized that the tone his father used was neither concerned nor corrective, so Jonas continued to squat on the ground in the sunshine, without acknowledging him. Instead, he adjusted the dial on his monocle style microscope and observed the whooping ant in front of him, as it held in its fingertips the fragment of sandwich Jonas had been eating for lunch. The two centimeter long "ant" pulled the offered food toward its front mouth with its forward facing hands. Since he had started his studies of ecology with his tutor at the age of five, the whooping ant had always fascinated Jonas. The individual ant in question seemed particularly adept with its use of the thumb. It was able to grasp the edge of the offered ham and cheese sandwich, and with a twisting motion, pull the food toward its mouth. Thumbs were what made the whooping ant so interesting to Jonas. The ant had the smallest opposable thumb in the known galaxy.

Jonas' father squatted down beside him. "What have you found?"

"A whooping ant."

Jonas' father fished in several pockets on his hiking shirt before he found an identical microscope and put it in his eye. "Wow, Jonas. It's a fine specimen. What is its technical name?"

"The microscope said it was Athenian, extra-small scavenger 32k.45 or 46, but that depended upon whether or not it consumed animal protein. Apparently it's 46 because it's eating the ham."

"Hmmm." Jonas' father squatted down next to his son and silently watched the whooping ant.

"Dmitri is always going on and on about the fact that on the ancient world, ant didn't mean the same thing as it does today. It never made sense to me. Ant means extra small scavenger, doesn't it?"

"Well, it's been a long time since I studied historical ecology, but I remember learning something about that when I was your age," said Jonas' father as he stood up. He stretched out his back and rubbed his fingers on the side of his temple before looking back down at Jonas and saying, "If memory serves me, ants on the ancient world were a group of small scavengers. They weren't the only ones, but they were so common that when the ancient empire expanded, humans used the word 'ant' as a stand in for every extra-small scavenger on any planet they colonized."

Jonas took the monocle out of his eye and stood up beside his father. He put his hands on his hips and surveyed the scene before him. He could see the royal shuttle and its companion shuttle parked nearby. Their crews were leaning against the common shuttle in a relaxed fashion, talking with each other. In front of the ships stood thirty pairs of fathers and sons. Jonas watched a group of boys huddled together, talking with each other. Suddenly, they laughed. Jonas experienced the reoccurring longing to be with them. As a prince, he had little experience with other children and no friends other than his older brother. Jonas sighed and instinctively took a step closer to his father. Even from this distance, he could tell from the body language of the group that lunch was over, and they were politely waiting for the King and his son to return. "We better get going, Dad. The bishop is starting to sigh."

The King looked down at his son and chuckled. "Bishop Dominic is an impatient man. Occasionally, it does him good to make him wait." Removing his hands from his hips, he started walking and said, "However, it *is* time that we get back. After all, we want to finish our hike just at sunset. That is the whole point, and it wouldn't do any good for the second prince and his father to wreck it for the others."

Jonas fell in behind the King and looked down at the sixty or so people standing below them. Nearly all of them looked back at him or his dad. Most took quick glances and looked away when they realized the prince was watching them. Jonas, used to this response, stared back brazenly and wished he could have done this without them. As much as he was lonely, he wanted to be alone with his father, but if he had spoken his wish aloud, he knew that his father would have said that being alone would have wrecked the point. His father would have said that the tradition of the Pilgrimage of the Sun had always been done as a group on Athena on Midsummer's day. Jonas knew this because they had discussed the matter several times prior to the pilgrimage, and his father had said those words or something similar each time, but it didn't mean Jonas wanted time alone with his father any less.

The religious rite of the Pilgrimage of the Sun had been practiced on planets and moons across the galaxy by fourteen-year-old boys and their father's for nearly a thousand years. The rite intended to teach each boy humility by showing him how small he was compared to the vastness of space. However, as with most religion, it had become something different for the majority of Athenians—in this case, a simple excuse for male play. The rite consisted of a pilgrimage hike laid out in advance by the local priest or bishop in each parish. Over the course of several hours, the pilgrims traced out a scale model of the local star system. The hike was meant to take some time and end at sunset. Traditionally on Athena, a large bonfire was lit at the end of the hike. The fire became a thing of play for boys, and most often sons and dads consumed some small quantity of alcohol, just enough to make the sons feel like men but not enough to cause trouble. Then the fathers and sons slept out under the stars.

However, for Bishop Dominic, religion remained serious business. The bishop for the royal parish was from a sect of the new ascetics, a group which took its religion seriously enough to once again renew the practice of celibacy among its priests. A portly man, the bishop was a weak counselor at court, but a man who had the ear of the King in matters of faith. He had hand picked the parishioners who would be privileged to accompany the king as he hiked the pilgrimage with his second and last son. Most of them were important parishioners who had done favors for the sect, a few were charitable cases. On the whole, they were an austere group, and Jonas found himself both attracted to the boys but simultaneously repelled by their coldness.

As Jonas and his father joined the back of the group, a nod from the King sent the fat man into full priestly mode. Using a deep voice which Jonas knew he reserved only for the pulpit, the man lifted up his arms and intoned from memory, "In his deepest mind the fool says there is not God...." Jonas' thoughts wandered. When he again picked up the thread of the priest's speech, he was holding up what looked like a large ball on a stick. The ball was approximately a meter in diameter. "All right, boys," he said in his normal high effeminate voice. "This will be our sun...."

Jonas looked at the blue colored ball on the stick and wrinkled up his face in a puzzled expression. He had twice experienced the vast size of the sun when he had traveled with his family to other star systems. Interstellar ships sometimes passed near the blue giant which lay at the center of the Athenian system on their way to the Hadris gates. Twice in his fourteen years, Jonas stood on the command deck of his father's ship while the vast bulk of the star Athena grew until it filled all vision.

Jonas leaned over to his father and, looking up, whispered, "I thought this hike was supposed to take all afternoon?" His father looked down and nodded. "But with the sun so small we are going to be done in no time. I mean, it only takes us three days to reach the Hadris gate."

His father smiled and with a hand on his son's back, leaned down and whispered. "You have no idea how fast we were traveling. Mass bending technology does incredible things for our acceleration curves." The priest gently shook the ball loose from the top of the pole and watched as it rose approximately twenty feet in the air and began to hover. Soon after, the hike began.

Jonas was to remember that afternoon for the rest of his life. All of the boys and many of the fathers found themselves in a perpetual state of awe as they walked. Balls no larger than a fist stood in for gas giants and nearly disappeared as they floated up into the air, and the three inhabited planets of the Athenian system fit together in the palm of the priest's hand. But it was the vast distances between the sixteen planets which left an impression on Jonas. Hundreds of paces divided the inner planets, and whole kilometers passed by between the outer ones.

The hike, which had seemed to Jonas like it would be over quickly, went on for nearly eight hours, and Jonas was forever grateful for the time. It wasn't until years later that he found out that through the priest, the King had given the other participants strict instructions to leave them alone. That day would become one of the rare instances in Jonas' life where he had his father to himself. For a few hours, he was simply a boy who finally had the full attention of a busy dad.

By the time Jonas and his father finished, the hike had covered nearly thirty kilometers, and the deep, violet blue sky of Athena moved on to hues of fluorescent orange and purple. For the last couple of kilometers, the hike had been tough, even for the adults. It ended with a five hundred meter climb up a steep trail to a bluff which had a commanding view of the surrounding country. Here the priest placed the last marker in the sky above the bluff. The Hadris space gate was represented by a tiny prick of light. It was as if the priest had let go of a faerie or a firefly. As the point of light sparked above his head, the priest explained to the boys what they already knew. The gate and its twin represented Athena's only connections with other star systems and the empire. It also marked the end of the Athenian system and the beginning of interstellar space.

After placing the last object in the sky, the sweaty, hot boys and their fathers took some time to enjoy the view. Placed in between rolling hills and occasional fields, small lakes dominated the surrounding countryside below them. Herds of slowly moving trees gathered in the remaining patches of sunlight in order to photosynthesize the last possible drops of energy before night set in. Jonas watched as they turned their many, long limbs to the sunset. Soon the quiet of the hilltop was broken by the cries of boys at play. Jonas and his father sat apart, hardly noticing the noise around them.

Not to be outdone by noisy boys, the priest raised his voice above the crowd and called attention to the point of land below them where the hike had begun. There, Jonas noticed a prick of light begin to glow in the falling darkness. The orb, placed in the sky as the sun, lit itself from within, showing how far they had come that day. At this distance, its light looked no greater than that of a bright star. Soon after, a bright flash lit up the sky from the first planet followed by flashes in order from each of the fifteen other orbs placed in the sky. Although the priest said that they were all glowing as brightly as their scale model star, only a few of them were visible to the naked eye unless they flashed, which they all continued to do at regular intervals. Using his priestly voice, the cleric sung, "All the stars and galaxies tell of God's beauty and power. Skies declare his artistry....."

Jonas didn't bother to listen. Instead, he looked down on the tiny points of light which represented Athena's planets and tried to pick out Athena Six where he stood right now. Then he looked above him at the tiny prick of light that stood in for the Hadris gate which, with its twin, represented their only connection to the Empire. Suddenly, he felt the weight of the vast emptiness which surrounded him. A deep loneliness overwhelmed him. There was so much space between each point of light. Worse yet, he was just a single person on a very large planet with five major continents and billions of people. Jonas felt like the hill was beginning to pitch forward and tip him into the abyss in front of him. He reached back to steady himself.

"Father?"

"Yes?"

"Do you believe we were made by God?"

Sitting next to him with his arms wrapped around his knees, the King's lips hinted at a smile. Looking at his son, he said "Yes, I do. What makes you ask, Jonas?"

"I don't know. It just seems so impossible to believe in God when there is so much space out there. I mean, we only walked out the Athena system today. Our Kingdom has nearly seventy stars, forty-eight inhabited planets, and over four hundred planets in all, and we only walked out one star system. *And* we are only one kingdom in the empire. The empire has over three hundred members, and they all have star systems with planets and vast distances between them. That doesn't consider the fact that there are uncountable kilometers between each and every star. I mean, even the light from Athena takes four and a half years to reach Padran, our closest neighbor star. The light we see from Apollos is nearly three hundred years old when it gets here. I guess, it just seems impossible to think that in all of this vast space a God could even exist. It seems even more ridiculous to pray to such a God, or think that he... or she, or it, had anything to do with my creation. It's like a whooping ant praying to me or worshiping me. If God exists, it has no idea I exist and has little or nothing to do with my life." Jonas looked again at the void in front of him, now almost completely black, and paused for a few seconds before he went on. "I mean, it just seems so impossible with all of that space. We are so small and insignificant. Think of the history, Dad. Think about it. We have been exploring other star systems for a thousand years. Dad, there have been literally trillions of human beings who have lived in this universe. How could God care about any of us or even know us? It just doesn't make any sense."

Jonas' father laughed quietly as the bishop continued to sing. "And that, Jonas, is why we do this. The bishop would be proud." He reached into his shirt pocket and produced a small crystal flask. "Here, Jonas," he said. "Have a swallow. It will relax your mind."

Other Fiction by Erik Wecks

Brody: Hope Unconquered

Brody: Hope Unconquered takes place in the Pax Universe approximately fifteen years after the events in *Aetna Adrift.* If you're a stickler for spoilers, be careful! This story will let you know the broad strokes of what will happen in The Pax. However, if you want more of the Pax, this is the only game in town for now.

What does it take to stick together in tough times? Roger and Helena are about to find out.

Roger Gillian and Helena Porter are a happily married professional couple living in the aftermath of an interstellar war. They never intend to leave home. All that changes when Roger's military past catches up to them. Desperate, they agree to a relativistic journey which will bring them home 47 years in the future. Things go sideways when Helena becomes unexpectedly pregnant. With no means to shorten their journey, and supplies only for two, they find themselves scrambling to preserve their resources and find new ones in order to make it back alive. But it isn't only physical resources they must find. Finding the inner strength to go forward requires taking action in spite of their desperate situation. Surprisingly, they experience hope where none should exist.

The Device

At first, shutting off your pain at-will sounds like the means to a perfectly content life—a leap forward for human evolution. Then evolution has its revenge. As a man retires from a university, he gives a speech looking back on the effects which the Dopamine Enhancement Device has had in his life and in society at large. (3500 words)

How to Mangage Your Money When You Don't Have Any

Praise for the Amazon Best Seller in Kindle Personal Finance and Kindle Budgeting

"We'd argue that Mr Wecks' book is the definitive guide to a better life with your finances—especially if you're currently battling with debt."— Payday Angels.co.uk

"I've watched pledge-drive specials on PBS, where financial gurus offer "sure-fire" steps promising to take me from the depths of debt to the lap of luxury.... Wecks offers more practical advice than those specials, with a more plausible goal: avoiding the traps laid by a system and culture that seems to accept debt as a simple part of everyday existence."— T. Weber (brightdreamer.com)

I bought this book today. I started reading and I did not close this book until I finished it. It took me 10 hrs. I normally don't like books and I hate to read but this one is an exception. This is an amazing book and I would recommend to all my friends.
—Riza, Amazon Review

Mr. Wecks eloquently lays a very practical plan on how to spend your money no matter how much you bring in each month, but the real genius of Mr. Wecks book is his advice on how we need to reset our values when it comes to spending our money. —Tim, Amazon Review

Unlike many personal finance books, How to Manage Your Money When You Don't Have Any was specifically written for Americans of all income levels who struggle to make it on a monthly basis. It provides both a respectful, no-nonsense look at the difficult realities of life after the Great Recession and a hope-filled, easy to follow path toward better financial stability for even the most financially strapped households. Created by a financial expert who hasn't struck it rich, How to Manage Your Money When You Don't Have Any offers a first hand story of financial survival in the face of rough times. Rather than emphasizing wealth creation, How to Manage Your Money When You Don't Have Any teaches readers to do the best they can with their income no matter it size. Content rich, personal, and jargon free, the book is opinionated and at times humorous. Full of current everyday references, it is meant to be a quick read which will appeal to the average reader just struggling to make ends meet.

Authors Biography

I am a full time writer and blogger living in Vancouver, Washington. I am the author of both non-fiction and fiction, as well as a contributor to the GeekDad.com and LitReactor.com. I enjoy writing on a wide range of topics. When not waxing poetic on various aspects of fiscal responsibility, I tend toward the geeky.

When not poised over the keyboard, I love to spend time with his family. I am married to an angel, Jaylene, who has taught me more than anyone else about true mercy and compassion. We are the parents of three wonderful girls. As a group we like swimming at the local pool, gardening, reading aloud, playing piano, and beating each other soundly at whatever table top game is handy.

Made in the USA
Charleston, SC
22 July 2013